PRAISE FOR THE
MERLIN SPIRAL

"A sweeping, deeply detailed fantasy that reimagines the adventures of Arthurian legend ... The author skillfully crafts intense action scenes and vivid settings."

— *Publishers Weekly*

"Trekillard has achieved one of the most difficult feats to master in high fantasy epics like this — weaving together a handful of storylines into a cohesive, expertly paced narrative."

— **Crosswalk.com**

"A fresh approach to an ancient genre ... an absolute must-read."

— **Award-winning author Douglas Bond**

"*Merlin's Blade* is a masterful story, well told ... a must read for fans of the Arthurian legend and for fantasy fans of all stripes ... The book easily spans the gap between twelve and adult."

— **Fantasy and sci-fi reviewer Rebecca Luella Miller**

"A fabulous reimagining of the legends."

— **Fantasy author Scott Appleton**

"Turn the pages, and you can almost feel the fog rolling in off the moors, smell the low heather, and catch a glint off a blade."

— **Bestselling author Wayne Thomas Batson**

"Treskillard builds a real person in Merlin ... whose belief in honor and family make him a figure to cheer for."

— **Christy Award-winning author Jill Williamson**

Other books by Robert Treskillard:

Merlin's Blade

MERLIN'S SHADOW

Book Two in the
Merlin's Spiral series

ROBERT TRESKILLARD

BLINK

Merlin's Shadow
Copyright © 2013 by Robert Treskillard

This title is also available as a Blink ebook. Visit www.zondervan.com/ebooks.

Requests for information should be addressed to:

Blink, 5300 Patterson Avenue, Grand Rapids, Michigan 49530

Library of Congress Cataloging-in-Publication Data

Treskillard, Robert.
     Merlin's shadow / Robert Treskillard.
          pages cm. — (Merlin's spiral series ; book 2)
     Summary: Relentlessly pursued by his old nemesis Vortigern, Merlin must
sail to the lands of eternal darkness and once again cleanse the world from an
ancient and powerful evil.
     ISBN 978-0-310-73508-3
     1. Merlin (Legendary character)—Juvenile fiction. 2. Arthur, King—Juvenile fic-
tion. [1. Merlin (Legendary character)—Fiction. 2. Arthur, King—Fiction. 3. Druids
and druidism—Fiction. 4. Fantasy.] I. Title.
     PZ7.T73175Me 2013
     [Fic]—dc23   2013028068

Cover design: brandnavigation.com
Cover photography: Dreamstime/Fotolia/iStockphoto.com
Interior design: Ben Fetterley and Greg Johnson/Textbook Perfect

Printed in the United States of America

---

13 14 15 16 17 18 19 /DCI/ 20 19 18 17 16 15 14 13 12 11 10 9 8 7 6 5 4 3 2

For Robin

Psalm 33:20–22

BRITAIN, 477 A.D.

Picti

Tavchen
Twilloch
Dinpelder
Dineidean
Gvotodin

Luguvalium
Rheged
Dinas
Crag
Elmekow

Inis Môn
Bregantow
Gwyneth
Oswistor
Eltavor!
Ekenia
Powys
Dobunni
Dyfed
Silures
Glevum
Lundnisow
Baegowhyr
Bolgi
Kentow
Difnonia
Dintaga
Bosventor
Kernow

20 Leagues

THE MAPS OF
MERLIN'S SHADOW

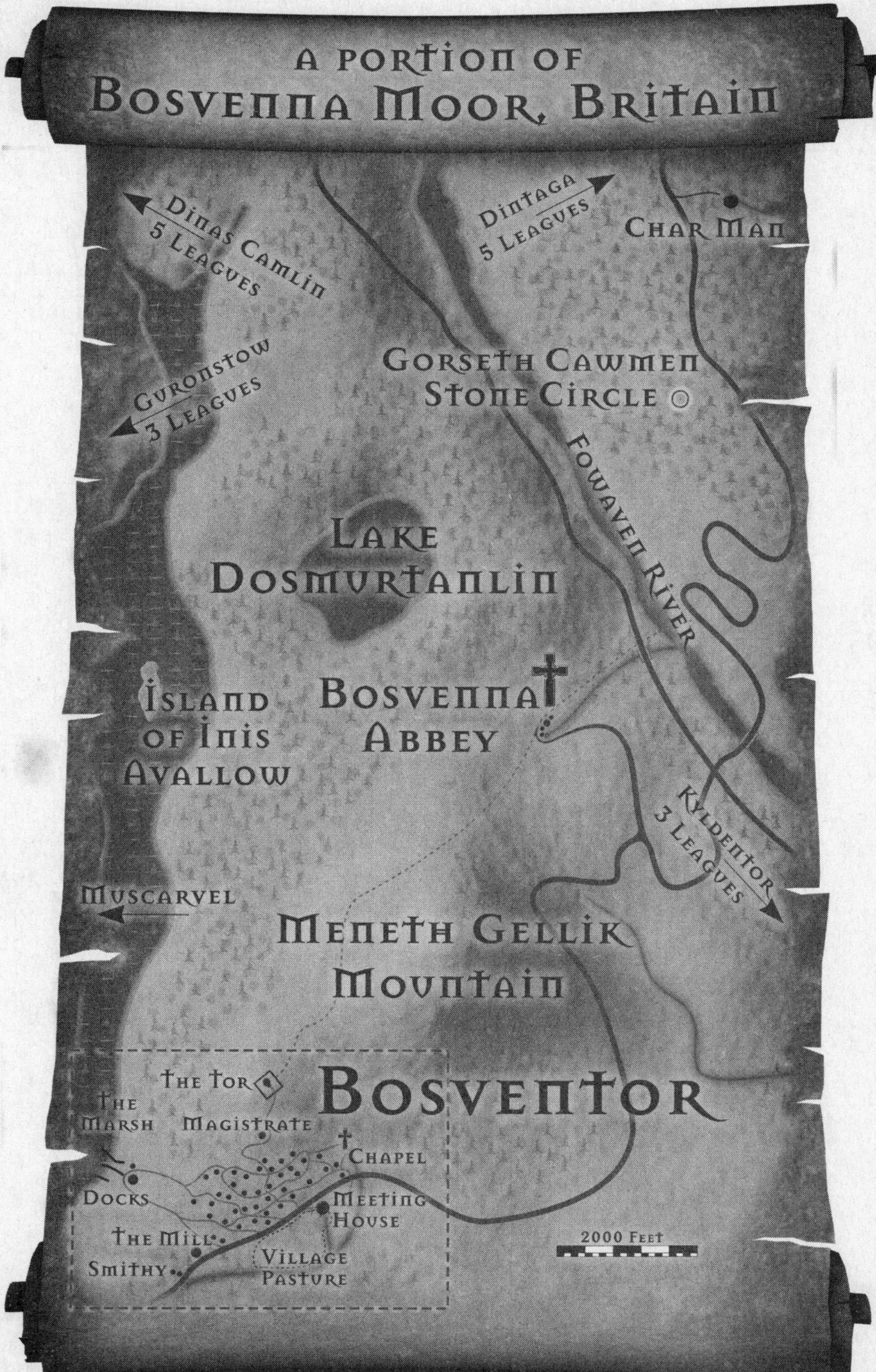

A PORTION OF
BOSVENNA MOOR, BRITAIN

Dinas Camlin
5 Leagues

Dintaga
5 Leagues

Char Man

Guronstow
3 Leagues

GORSETH CAWMEN
STONE CIRCLE ◎

LAKE
DOSMURTANLIN

Fowaven River

ISLAND
OF INIS
AVALLOW

BOSVENNA
ABBEY

Kyldentor
3 Leagues

MUSCARVEL

MENETH GELLIK
MOUNTAIN

THE TOR

BOSVENTOR

THE
MARSH

MAGISTRATE

CHAPEL

DOCKS

MEETING
HOUSE

THE MILL

SMITHY

VILLAGE
PASTURE

2000 FEET

THE VILLAGE OF BOSVENTOR,
BAEGOWER, AND THE FORTRESS OF DINTAGA

THE TOR

MAGISTER

WEAVERS

CHAPEL †

DOCKS

MEETING
HOUSE

THE MILL

VILLAGE
PASTURE

SMITHY
(BURNED DOWN)

1000 FEET

THE TOMB IN
THE GORGE

GORLAS'S
ISLAND
FORTRESS OF
DINTAGA

STEEP
STAIRS

ANFRI'S
HOUSE †

THE VILLAGE
OF BAEGOWER

1500 FEET

THE CAUSEWAY

THE BEACH

500 FEET

KEMBRY SEA

KEMBRY SEA

THE STORY SO FAR...

The Stone — In 407 A.D., a meteorite crashes to Britain, depositing a black stone in a crater, which fills with water to become a mysterious lake. In 463, Merlin's mother supposedly drowns in the lake, and her body is never found.

Mórganthu — The arch druid finds the Stone in 477. With it he can enchant the Britons, and intends to restore the power of the druids — starting in Merlin's village.

Merlin — The swordsmith's son. Half-blinded by wolves seven years ago, he is protected from the Stone's enchantment because he can't see it. Despite his weakness, he begins to fight against Mórganthu and the Stone.

Natalenya — The seventeen-year-old daughter of the Magister, and Merlin's love interest. She must see beyond Merlin's scars to his courageous leadership and join with him to fight the Stone.

Ganieda — Merlin's nine-year-old half-sister; she seems to have an affinity for wolves.

Garth — A friend of Merlin who is an orphan and a rascal. He lives at the abbey and despises the abbot's discipline. He is the first to be enchanted, motivating Merlin to fight against the Stone.

Owain — Merlin's father, and a swordsmith, who deserted the High King's warband many years ago. He also becomes enchanted by the Stone.

The Blade — Made by Merlin's father, who gives it to the newly arrived High King Uther to appease his wrath. When the king is not satisfied, Owain gives Merlin to him as a servant.

Uther — The proud High King and father to Arthur. When the druids prevent the villagers from swearing fealty, he cuts off the head of Mórganthu's son. Mórganthu swears revenge.

Colvarth — The king's bard, a former druid and now a Christian, who agrees to mentor Merlin. In his new role, Merlin advises the king to destroy the Stone.

Vortigern — A battle chief. He is enchanted and betrays Uther and Arthur to the druids.

Arthur — The young son of King Uther. Garth sees Mórganthu's cruelty, and his plan to murder the royal family, and saves Arthur's life.

Dybris — A monk who works with Merlin and Owain to take the Stone and destroy it before a key druid ritual could increase its power. He discovers the other monks were caught by Mórganthu and will be burned to death during the ritual. While trying to free his fellow monks and remove the Stone, Dybris and Owain are captured, leaving Merlin to try and save everyone on his own. In the end, Merlin conspires with a sympathetic druid named Caygek.

Connek — A thief hired by Mórganthu to kill Merlin, and by Vortigern to kill Natalenya after she refuses to marry his son. When Natalenya visits the mill to borrow a mule to haul the Stone away, Connek hides there and tries to kill Natalenya, but he dies when the millstone falls on him.

The Murder — During the druid ritual, Uther and Owain are to be sacrificed to the Stone, and the monks to be burned. Vortigern hides his men and arrives to make sure Uther is dead. When he finds the High King alive, he intends to kill him, and after a brief skirmish with Merlin, he succeeds. The druids, cheated of their sacrifice, attack. Vortigern calls his men to fight.

The Escape — The monks are freed by Caygek's friends, and Owain is freed by Caygek himself. Merlin, Owain, and Dybris escape with the Stone, but are chased by both the druids and Vortigern's warriors. Natalenya rescues them, and they haul the Stone to the smithy, barricading the doors.

The Fight — Owain can't destroy the Stone. While trying, Vortigern's men try to break in, and Garth sets fire to the fortress where their horses are kept. The warriors run off, and the druids break into the smithy alone. Mórganthu enters with the dead king's new blade. Dybris and Owain are injured, but Merlin cuts off Mórganthu's hand and reclaims the blade.

The Hammering — Natalenya is trapped by flames erupting from the Stone, and Merlin must save her. He tries to hammer the blade into the Stone, and burns his hands in the process. Natalenya steadies him, and they are both given a vision.

The Vision — is of Natalenya being taken to a red dragon and a white dragon so they can eat her. Merlin fights the dragons, chops off a fang from one, and stabs the other in the eye.

The Victory — The vision ends. Merlin and Natalenya hammer the blade into the Stone, which causes an explosion, knocking out the druids.

The Aftermath — An angel heals Merlin of his blindness, and he, along with Natalenya, Colvarth, and Garth, take Arthur away to save the boy from Vortigern. Before leaving, Merlin visits the lake where his mother supposedly drowned and finds her alive — a water creature freed from serving the Stone, but forever confined to the lake. Vortigern rallies his men in pursuit, setting the stage for book two, *Merlin's Shadow*.

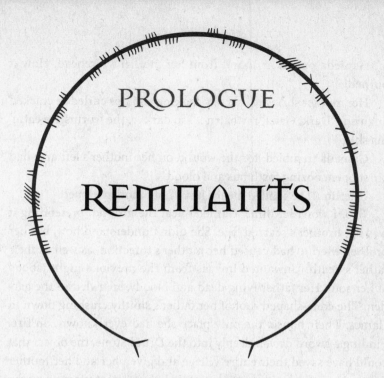

PROLOGUE

REMNANTS

In the half-light of a dying day, Ganieda wept in her mother's embrace. She felt again the burning of her mother's forehead.

Ashen birds silenced their squawking and watched the two with hungry eyes. Dark clouds gathered overhead, and farther up the tree-lined ravine, a spring gurgled out brown water that trickled past them in dirge-like procession toward the marsh.

Ganieda had been hungry in the morning — so hungry — but now fear had soured her stomach. As the day had worn on, her mother began to rave, refusing to drink and scratching her puffed, infected arm. Now screeching cries filled the gaps between her mother's words.

Ganieda pulled her hand from her mother's forehead. How it burned!

Her mother shrieked, her jaw shaking and lips curled in cracked anguish. "Dark, Gana, my bairn ... so dark ... the worms are eatin' ma skin."

Ganieda trembled, for the wound on her mother's left arm had burst open, oozing forth pus and blood.

"Merlin ... he's killed me, ya hear?" her mother rasped.

"No. I won't let him." Ganieda beat the ground, pretending it was her brother's scarred face. She didn't understand how, but her brother, Merlin, had caused her mother's infection, as well as their father's death. Unwanted images from the previous night jabbed at her soul: Her father lying dead and bloody, sprawled in the garden. The cone-shaped roof of her father's smithy crashing down in flames. Their house, the only place she had ever known, on fire. Finding a sword driven deeply into the Druid Stone, the object that could have saved their entire village and given her and her mother power. Now the druidow were scattered, the stone stagnant, and the world turned asunder.

Ganieda cursed Merlin's name.

Her mother cried out again, gurgling and choking. Her eyes rolled back, and she groped the horrid dirt. Breath fled from her lungs like grain spilling from a torn bag — and she moved no more.

Ganieda lifted herself from the ground and ran, leaving her mother's body to lay forever dead beside the woodland ferns. She screamed and pulled at her hair, twisting and ripping it out. And with every step, she cursed her brother's name.

Hours later the moon rose and called to Ganieda, laughing. Its gleaming robe of darkness drew her forth like a friend, and she followed it — cold, and alone — until she found herself again on the edge of her family's property. Her hand searched vainly for even a crumb of food in the bag that hung from her belt.

Through tear-blurred eyes, she climbed over the rock wall and beheld her home standing just as she had remembered. The conical roof reached up to the stars in thatched splendor. The low stone walls lay stout and strong. And there stood her father, Owain, with a hoe in one hand — waving to her. Ganieda smiled as Mônda, her mother, stepped over to him and placed an arm around his waist, her black hair tossed in the breeze, her smile a delight, and her cheeks full of youthful color. She knelt and beckoned.

Come!

Ganieda ran, arms outstretched. *Mammu.* And as Ganieda was about to fall happily into that loving embrace, her mother vanished. Ganieda fell upon a pile of stones — a cairn. The wicked edges of the rocks cut her fingers. She cried out, looking everywhere for her mother, her father, her house.

They were all gone, and nothing existed but the burnt timbers of the roof perched over the broken walls, like a great black spider sucking the life juice from its prey. The smithy beside it was worse. Even the timbers had fallen, broken amidst the firestorm of the previous night. The fire that Merlin had started. *He* was responsible. *He* destroyed it all. *He* caused her mother to die by destroying all she loved.

The blood from her hands dripped down upon the rocks of the cairn. The cairn? There had been no cairn here — this was their garden. The cabbages lay smashed and broken — kicked, forgotten, and weed-strangled. What was a cairn doing here? Her father. His precious body lay under it, eternally cut off from her. Entombed.

Never again would she hold on to his belt. Hear him sweetly call her name. Feel his rough hands combing her hair. Swing from his arms. Look into his eyes. They were sad eyes, and she never knew why. And the cruel rocks whispered at her, raising their voice for justice. Calling out for the blood of her brother. It would never be sated. She screamed. *She* would never be sated.

A dog barked from over near the smithy.

But it wasn't a dog — it was a wolf. Was it her wolf? "Tellyk?" she shouted.

The wolf whined in answer.

She pulled her hands from the jagged grasp of the stones, ran to the smithy, and Tellyk stood before its charred and fallen wall. *Her* special wolf among the many wolves she had befriended, creatures who in turn became her protectors.

He raised his snout, closed his green eyes, and licked the blood from her left hand as she pet his soft, furry head with her right. But Tellyk pushed his head against her firmly. Almost too firmly. "Stop it, Tellyk. What do you want?"

The wolf pushed her farther now, toward the broken door of the smithy. He padded before her into the gray ash of the interior.

She followed, her feet warmed by the thick layer of ashes, and stepped warily through broken, heaped timbers that still smoked and hissed like black snakes waiting to strike.

The wolf led her to the forge, its sides intact despite the furious blaze of the previous night. In the center of the forge lay a large black stone, from which protruded a long blade — the blade she had seen her father crafting these many weeks. It stood shining and perfect — strangely unmarred by the fire. The red triple spiral inlaid in the hilt sparkled in the moonlight.

Ganieda's eyes opened wide, and she reached out to grasp it — but the wolf growled and shoved her back. She fell amidst the ashes and burned her hand on a live ember. Standing up again, she sucked her fingers and was surprised to see Tellyk digging at the base of the black stone — *the* Stone — the Druid Stone! The special Stone of Mórganthu, the arch druid, her grandfather.

And the blade had killed it. Merlin had done it. Ganieda and her mother had seen through the doorway as he thrust the sword into the Stone. Everything he touched, he destroyed.

But the wolf had found something, and whimpered at her with mournful eyes.

She leaned forward, and there in the bottom of the forge, amid a black and sticky liquid, lay a luminous orb slightly larger than a chicken egg. She snatched it up and pulled it to her chest, the liquid staining her fingers and dripping onto her dress.

She felt the entire surface of the orb. One side was smooth, almost glasslike, while the other felt rough. From the rough side trailed out broken fibers, like a horse's tail or a plant's cut roots.

She studied the shiny side — and then yelped. The orb almost slipped from her fingers and fell, but she held on to it. Inside flashed purple fire, and then the image changed to glimmering stars and wheeled around until she beheld the scarred face of her brother standing in the dark next to a tree. The faint sound of crickets could be heard, and the rustle of leaves.

She sobbed. "If only I had a dagger, I'd hurt you! Really hurt you ..."

Tellyk whimpered again.

She pulled her gaze away from the orb and saw his paws scratching into the forge once more. Underneath his snuffing nose there lay a curved, sharp spike coated in the dark liquid. Some old nail, she mused, dropped by her father into the forge. She reached out a trembling left hand and picked it up by two fingers, sliming them. She wiped it clean on her skirt — and the spike shone a pale ivory in the moonlight.

This wasn't iron, and it wasn't copper. It looked like one of Tellyk's fangs, only much longer, maybe half a foot, and much sharper. The curve felt good in her hand, and as she held it, a thrill tingled in her fingers. It fled up her arm like a bat caught in her sleeve.

A voice rasped from behind her, "What? What have you found there?"

Tellyk growled and Ganieda whirled around, her heart pulsing up into her throat.

An old man hobbled forward through the gaping hole where the front doors had been. His left arm leaned upon a long staff, and his right arm protruded from his sleeve, ending at a stub bound in a bloody rag.

His long sweat-streaked hair lay gray and black upon his green robe, and his face —

"Grandpa," she cried, and ran to him.

PART ONE

FOOL'S
CHOICE

Fast as the fox, the hider hiding;
Wild as the wolf, the hunter hunting;
Hard as the horse, the burden bearing;
High as the hawk, the searcher spying;
Prison by sea, fear the red sunrise.

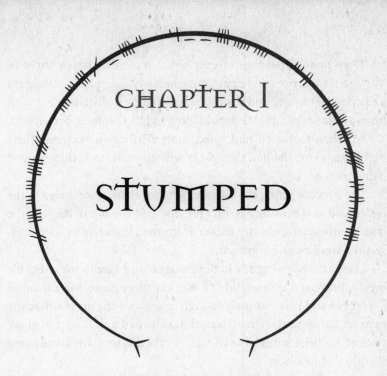

CHAPTER I

STUMPED

**THE WILDS OF KERNOW
IN THE YEAR OF OUR LORD 477**

The sun had long ago sunk below the granite-boned horizon, and Merlin crept up the mound hoping to catch the stranger asleep. Halfway to the top he drew his sword — gashing his arm on a blackthorn bush. He bit his tongue and continued to climb through the shadowed grass, once again thankful he could now see, and see clearly. Unfortunately, the miracle that had restored his sight had not made him a perfect scout.

Whoever this man was who had camped so close to them, Merlin and Garth had to find out. Hopefully Garth would quietly scale the other side of the hill and not disturb the man's horse they had heard. If the stranger was alerted to their presence, and if he was one of Vortigern's men, Merlin might need to capture — or kill him.

They had all been wary ever since yesterday, when three of Vortigern's warriors rode past their hasty hiding place. Natalenya had cried afterward, and the orphaned Arthur had studied her with his gray-blue eyes, his little fists holding tight to her long, brown hair.

So when Colvarth had spied some flitting smoke near their nighttime camp, he had thought it wise to make sure they weren't being tracked.

The beeches lining the hillside twitched their ovate leaves in the light wind as if sensing Merlin's presence. At the top of the hill, the trunks reflected a ghostly flicker from the man's fire as the mold-scented smoke curled upward.

Leaves crunched lightly in the distance, and Merlin sucked in his breath, praying Garth wouldn't make any more noise. Merlin found a foothold and lifted himself enough to see over the grass where the man sat stiffly near a fire. His back was turned and his green cloak covered his head to keep the chill off. In the distance, his horse stood silently tied to a tree.

Setting his sword on the ground in front of him, Merlin pulled himself up and crouched behind a towering oak. The man didn't stir and must have fallen asleep before the fire, which would make it easier for Merlin to sneak up and see if he was one of Vortigern's soldiers — as long as Garth could keep his big toes off the branches.

Merlin picked up his sword and stole quietly through the trees. At the outer ring of the campsite he paused, spotting Garth behind a pine on the opposite side.

The boy waved to him, eyes bulging.

Merlin signaled for him to be quiet, and began circling left toward the hunched man. If he could glimpse the man's cloak pin, he would know what type of man he faced. For all of the warriors — those who now served the traitor Vortigern — had their cloaks pinned with a golden boar, a symbol of the recently murdered High King Uther. If this man had such a pin, then Merlin and Garth could slip away. They would then break camp and travel through the night … despite their aching weariness.

But if the man awoke ... Merlin tensed his sword arm for action.

Garth walked out, gesticulating and pointing at Merlin. His head shook wildly. The only thing he didn't do was ruin their ambush by throwing a rock at the man.

Merlin made a face back at Garth and stepped farther sideways to peek at the dozing man's cloak — only to have someone grab his hair tightly from behind and slide a blade across his shoulder very close to his neck.

"Toss your sword or you're dead," the man said.

The metal edge bit into Merlin's skin as he felt his blood pulsing through the nearest vein.

He stiffened and dropped his blade.

"Good. Now tell your foolish friend to toss his knife in that pile of brush."

Garth snarled at Merlin and tossed his dirk away. "Why didn't you listen to me signals? I tried to tell you he was sneakin' up behind."

"Why'd you just wave your arms then?" Merlin said, looking sideways at the blade on his shoulder. It was of good quality — sharp and lethal.

Garth pointed at the hunched man. "I didn't want to wake this guy up."

"Lot of good that did us."

"Enough," the second stranger said. "Why were you sneaking up on me?"

"You mean you and your sleeping friend."

"Only me."

The stranger, pushing Merlin forward, approached the hooded man hunched near the fire and kicked him. He cracked and fell over, exposing a rotten, mushroom-spattered stump. A balled-up saddle blanket had sufficed for the head.

Garth snorted. "How'n did you know we were comin'?"

"Those that are quietest ask the questions. Tell me your names."

Merlin felt suddenly cold with the blade at his neck. "I'm called

Merlin . . . mab Owain . . . sworn servant of Uther." If the warrior was loyal to the High King—and he wasn't purely Vortigern's man— maybe that would save their lives. Possibly even allow them to clear their names and tell the truth about Vortigern, who had slain Arthur's father two days ago to usurp the High Kingship. Merlin, Garth, and Natalenya had been living as vagabonds, along with Uther's ancient bard, Colvarth, in an attempt to save their lives and that of Uther's young son and the future king, Arthur.

"Either you're lying or you're a fool. The High King is dead."

The fire flared up for a moment, and Garth dropped his hood back and peered closer at the man standing in the dark behind Merlin. "Caygek . . . is that you?"

The blade shuddered as it pulled away from Merlin's neck. The man let go of his hair. "By Crom's mound," the stranger said, "Garth . . . Garthwys? What are you—?"

Merlin spun, the blade now pointing straight at his chest. The man wore a blue tunic over brown breeches, and stood a little shorter than Merlin. His arms and face bore the spidery blue scars of a druid—meaning this was likely the same man who had helped Merlin save his father and the monks at the Druid Stone. Though not much older than Merlin's eighteen winters, Caygek had a blond, curly beard that hung thick to the middle of his chest, and a head of long hair to match. But his eyes were what caught Merlin's interest. They were red and the skin around was puffy—almost as if he'd been sick. Perhaps weeping.

Merlin backed up, almost stumbling over the rotten log and into the crackling fire. "If you mean us no harm . . . then you have nothing to fear from Garth or me. We thought you were following us— that you were one of Vortigern's men."

Caygek squinted his eyes. "I don't follow anyone. Not anymore."

Distant sounds of crashing, cracking, and rustling from the woods to the east made the three freeze. Soon they heard the clopping of hoofs. Merlin lunged to grab his and Garth's blades. "The fire," he realized. "Vortigern's seen the smoke!"

Caygek scanned the eastern darkness, alarmed.

Merlin yanked Garth by the cloak. "Let's go."

Garth refused to budge. "What about Caygek?"

"He's a druid."

"Take him with us ... He'll be caught, an' he knows about us."

Caygek ran to his horse and cut the reins knotted to the tree. He hastily tried to mount the horse, but it bucked, reared, and sent him sprawling to the ground.

"There's no time." Merlin pulled Garth toward the hillside.

The approaching horses pounded closer.

Caygek held on to the reins as his horse wheeled around him, nearly trampling his face. He finally let go, and the horse ran off toward the south.

The shouts of approaching warriors were close.

Caygek scuttled down the hill and caught up to them, clutching his saddlebag and cloak. "I'm coming."

Merlin called back, "Go away."

"You've no choice," Caygek said, running with them.

Merlin ran, leading the way back, and hoping they'd have time before Vortigern found their trail. Breaking through the pines to their hidden camp, Merlin stopped in time to avoid the point of Natalenya's dirk finding its way through his tunic.

"Who are you?" she said, peering into the darkness.

"Natalenya! It's me, Merlin ... Merlin."

She dropped the blade and wrapped her arms around him. Garth crashed through the branches and into Merlin's back. The three of them fell.

"Very careful woodsmen the lot of you are," Caygek said, breathing hard. "Now why's Vortigern chasing you?"

Merlin was about to explain that Vortigern wanted to kill Arthur, who was just a child, when Colvarth stepped from the dark trees holding the very boy and a small dagger. "Who is this you have brought, Merlin? This is unex — " But his words stopped short as he and Caygek faced each other.

Merlin rolled Garth off his legs, and stood. "This is Caygek — "

The druid bowed. "Colvarth ... or should I say Bledri mab Cadfan? We have not met, but I have heard much of you."

"Are you mad to bring a follower of Mórganthu into our midst?"

"He came without my permission, and I — "

Garth stepped into the center. "I can explain ..."

In the distance, the sounds of horses could still be heard.

Merlin took hold of Colvarth's shoulders. "Vortigern! We have to leave *now*."

Natalenya had already mounted, and thankfully the horses they'd taken from Vortigern two days before had been equipped with four-horn military saddles, which allowed her to ride fairly safe in a sidesaddle position. She rode up with Colvarth's black horse.

After glancing quickly at Caygek, Colvarth shook his aged head at Merlin. He handed Arthur up to Natalenya, braced his staff, and clambered onto his horse. Within five breaths the rest of them were mounted, Caygek riding with Garth. They followed Colvarth into the darkness and away from Vortigern's men.

Rain began to fall, and the already sodden paths became slippery. Merlin had hoped this would slow their foes as well — but they could still hear the crashing of Vortigern's reckless men.

Merlin stirred his mount next to Colvarth, who was hunched over, scrutinizing the path ahead. While wise, Colvarth was advanced in years, and they didn't have time to wait for him to weigh out a decision.

"May I lead?" Merlin asked.

Colvarth sat up, and his leather-wrapped harp jangled on his back. "We must find the main road eastward ... or we will be lost."

"That's what they expect us to do, and that's where most of Vortigern's men are. They're trying to flush us out."

"Where then do we go? Northward and westward is only trackless woods ... and then the coast ... we cannot swim away."

"King Gorlas," Merlin whispered. "Dintaga, his fortress, is on the coast."

Colvarth's eyes were dark slits in the gloom. "Gorlas is no friend. Uther was going to him out of necessity ... to raise more warriors for battle, but there ... was no love between them. Only after Uther had scoured Kembry, and there were still not enough warriors to fully repel the Saxenow ... did he consider going to Gorlas."

"Then we use that to our advantage. We remind him that Vortigern is Uther's man."

Colvarth coughed. "Do not speak such of that ... traitor. *I am* Uther's man — his bard."

Merlin trotted his mount in front of Colvarth. "Then persuade Gorlas to protect us."

"That is madness, I cannot — "

Arthur began crying, and the sound echoed through the woods. Natalenya desperately tried to comfort the boy, but he would not quiet.

The sound of the pursuing horses grew louder and clearer.

Ganieda ran to Mórganthu, who knelt to catch her. "Grandpa, oh *Tasgwyn*." Her tears fell freely upon his cheek, and she squeezed him tightly — all the while holding the two strange objects she had fetched from beneath the Stone in her father's forge.

"My daughter's daughter," he said. His voice was like a warm bath driving off the chill that blew through the burned-out smithy. And its lilt was like her mother's, with that wonderful Eirish accent that she loved to imitate. Grandpa held her close, though after kissing her cheek he pushed her to arm's length with his one hand. "What have you discovered? What are these?"

Ganieda looked into his face and saw not just curiosity, but hunger. His eyes, dark and shrunken, searched desperately at the oddities hidden in her hands.

What *were* these things? she wondered. In her left she felt the curved smoothness of the long fang. As she thought about its sharpness, a spark of warmth filled her arm.

In the other hand she held the cold, somewhat firm ball, through which she'd seen an image of her brother. *Curse him.*. Stringy tendrils hung out through her fingers.

Grandfather tried to pry open those fingers.

She lashed out at him without even thinking. The fang scratched his hand. No — she had fully gashed it, and a thrill climbed up her arm. She suddenly felt taller, stronger.

Grandpa yelled and flailed his only hand backward.

She slid the orb into her bag and hid the fang under her shift. "No, Grandpa, don't touch them again." She had flung the language of Kernow aside and now she spoke in the druidow tongue her mother had taught her. Ah, but he would understand. He spoke it too. He was the leader of all the druidow. *The most respected o' men in all the world, ya hear?*, her mother had told her during the past many years. And her grandpa had come to them but two weeks ago, bringing his Stone, now ruined, and all his druidow.

Sucking his wound, Grandpa nodded. The blood covered his teeth and dripped down onto his beard.

"Where, then," he rasped, "is your mother? Where is my daughter?"

Ganieda's tongue caught in her throat. She turned away and shook her head.

"What? What are you saying? Did her little infection from that armband get so bad that — ?" He clucked his tongue, and took two deep, deep breaths. "Oh, to think that my lineage has come down to this," he cried, "and in such a little time."

Ganieda looked at him, and he was crying.

"And all because of that Merlin, that scourge upon my house, has this happened. And so you, little vengeful girl, you are all that I have left in the world. Come, then," he said. "Come ... come back to my tent in the woods. Remember the dried strawberries and smoked meat? You — you are hungry, yes?"

Her stomach was burning. The strength she felt from the fang didn't fill *that* emptiness. She would go with him. Tellyk padded over to her, and she stroked his fur, climbing onto his broad back.

Grandfather's smoldering gaze flitted to her bag — which hung from her belt over the side of the wolf — but he said nothing.

He led the way, first picking his way through the smoking debris of the smithy and then out onto the clouded and thundering moor.

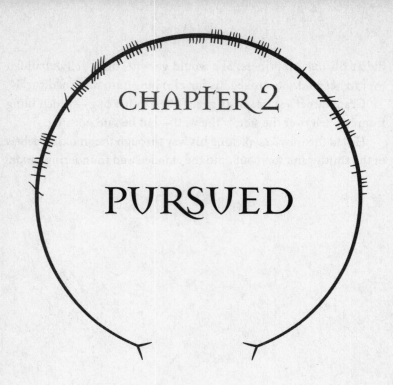

CHAPTER 2

PURSUED

Merlin's chest tightened as Arthur's cries grew louder. Colvarth listened to the oncoming sounds of their pursuers and looked at Merlin anxiously. "I will follow you to Gorlas," Colvarth relented. "But we have come too far east. Keep the moon left of your back, so that we'll head toward the coast. Hopefully to Dintaga."

Merlin turned them away from the direction of the moon — as well as the road where Vortigern's men lay in wait — and led them down into a valley. Arthur ceased his bawling and sucked on an oatcake.

Onward Merlin led them, through the dark fastness of the trees and toward the northern coast, but he was tired and his body ached from the jolting horse. Even when the sound of their pursuers had completely faded, Merlin kept looking backward, and Natalenya always met his gaze, urging him onward. But she leaned upon her mount like a wilted flower, clutching the mane with her free hand and holding Arthur with the other. How much longer could they go?

When the path broadened somewhat, Colvarth rode up beside Merlin. "The coast is not far," he said. "So we must talk now of what is to come."

"I've been there before," Merlin said, "even if I couldn't see it."

"But have you been to Dintaga itself? Gorlas's fortress is not like Bosventor's. It lies on an island out in the sea, and there is only a narrow, treacherous causeway that leads to it."

"So we'll leave the horses behind. We'll make it." Merlin spurred his mount forward, but Colvarth reached out and clutched his sleeve.

"You are a like a bull," he whispered, "who knows not where he is rushing. Long ago Gorlas was in love with Uther's wife, but she spurned him. You may regret entering his fortress with Uther's child."

"But Uther brought Arthur along. It appears he was going to do that."

"No, he was not," Colvarth said. "He would never have entered there without his men — and never to stay."

Merlin ducked under a looming pine branch. "Is Gorlas so dangerous?"

Colvarth chewed on this question before answering. "No, Gorlas is not a traitor ... he has answered Uther's call for men before. But Uther would not have brought his wife and children *into* Dintaga. Of that I am certain."

"Isn't Arthur the child of Igerna as well? Isn't that in our favor?"

Colvarth shook his head. "I do not think so. It has been many years since I have seen Gorlas, but I fear his anger has not abated. He will take the news hard that Igerna has died."

"Then we tell him the truth, that Vortigern, her own brother, had her killed."

Colvarth shrugged his shoulders, pulled his hood up, and let his horse fall back into line.

Garth trotted up, his mount breathing heavily under the extra strain of carrying Caygek.

Despite Merlin's anger that the druid had joined them, he was relieved they had an extra blade in case of trouble. But what went on

31

inside Caygek's head? Why would he put himself in danger? He'd lost his own mount, but wouldn't he be safer to slip off alone?

Garth yawned. "Don't mind me sayin', but where're we goin'?"

"To Dintaga. We're going to ask Gorlas for refuge from Vortigern."

Garth woke up suddenly and his eyes widened. "Dintaga?"

"Shaa ... lower your voice."

Garth gulped. "Sorry. But I didn't know we were headed to the Kembry Sea. It's been so long — this just fills my sail right up."

Merlin leaned over and mussed Garth's hair. "Well, then, keep your sail tied down — "

"Knotted. You knot down a sail."

"Fine, but we're only going to the fortress." He wished he could have a private talk about Caygek, but with the steely eyed druid sitting right there, it would have to wait.

Or so Merlin thought, until Caygek spoke up.

"Garth's explained to me what's happening, and I wanted you to know that despite the danger I plan on sticking with him ... and so with you."

So this druid thought he could decide by himself? Merlin's tunic suddenly felt hot, even in the drizzle. As much as Caygek didn't seem a bad sort like most of the other druidow, Merlin didn't want him spending time with Garth. The boy had just escaped the clutches of the druidow, and Merlin didn't want him becoming involved again. "Why?" Merlin asked. "Haven't had enough punishment yet for using your Druid Stone to enchant everyone?"

Caygek blinked twice, but his expression didn't change. "So I'm responsible for what Mórganthu does — is that it? You and your kind are all alike."

"Look, I didn't invite you to join us. I appreciate your help in saving my father and the monks back in Bosventor, but you're welcome to leave."

"And why should I? These woods aren't yours, and as I understand it, neither is the horse I'm sitting on."

Merlin whipped out his blade and held it at Caygek's shoulder — only to have it flipped out of his hand by Caygek's own sword.

The sword fell into a bush, and Merlin was forced to dismount to retrieve it.

"Those that are fastest make the decisions," Caygek said. "And for your knowledge, I did more to oppose Mórganthu than simply help you out on the night of Beltayne."

Garth, who'd ducked when the swords came out, found his voice. "It's true, Merlin. Caygek actually led the group that tried to stop Mórganthu. I saw it when I was ... stayin' with the druidow."

"A lot of good you did, then, Caygek." Merlin retrieved his sword, sheathed it, and climbed back onto his mount. "My father's dead."

Caygek held his sword ready. "I saw Vortigern knock you out, so you probably don't even know that I personally untied your father at the Stone. And my filidow freed the monks as well. If it hadn't been for us, you would have all died and never escaped to destroy the Stone."

Merlin shut his mouth. Was this true? Having been blind at the time *and* incapacitated by Vortigern, he truly hadn't seen any of this. And things had happened so fast that he'd never had time to ask his father what had occurred. Their time together was gone — like a raindrop slipping through his hand into a creek and away. He would never see his father again, because Mórganthu had killed him in the smithy during a fit of rage.

He looked to Garth for confirmation of Caygek's story, but the boy only shrugged his shoulders.

Merlin kicked his mount forward and left them behind. All this talk was slowing them down, and he didn't want to think about his father's death.

They continued on for a few hours, and the trees slowly changed from oak and beech to pine. The whole time Merlin did his best to keep the moon at his back left — until Colvarth called to him.

"Hold the moon more to your left now. Soon we will come to the Camel River. As it must be swollen with all this rain, we will need to find the bridge. From there we still have a long trot to Dintaga."

Merlin's legs and back ached. "That far?"

"Yes, and the trees will thin. If Vortigern has suspected our direction, he may head us off by taking the road — pray, Merlin, that the bridge is clear.

"Is there no other ford?"

Colvarth tilted his head and thought. "Into the hills, to the east … how far, I don't know, but out of our way, and Vortigern would get to Dintaga first. The best way is by the bridge and its road."

A wolf howled somewhere off to their right.

Merlin turned and called to the group. "We must move faster." He motioned them forward, and they clipped through the pines as fast as the horses could pick their way. Soon the ground sloped downward and they could hear the rushing of a stream. Upon coming to the water, Merlin halted the party, and surveyed the swiftness of the current. "Colvarth is right," he called. "We have to find the bridge."

Behind them, a wolf howled again, closer.

Merlin's horse tensed, ready to bolt.

Eight wolves stalked from the cover of the pines.

Merlin had his sword halfway from its sheath when his horse plunged headlong into the stream. It was all he could do to hold on as the horse struggled against the current, diving and rearing. Behind him, Natalenya screamed. Merlin's horse turned with the current now, and he was nearly thrown off into the churning water. From the corner of his eye, he saw Natalenya's horse vault into the water. She held on past midstream, where the horse lost its footing. Down she went with Arthur into the water and disappeared.

Merlin gasped. Having grown up mostly blind, he barely knew how to swim.

Natalenya fought and kicked up to the surface, holding a gasping Arthur. She swirled toward Merlin, and the current pulled them under again.

Merlin panicked. He couldn't lose her! They'd just become engaged two days before and had received the blessing of Natalenya's mother.

The flexible branch of a nearby plane tree extended over the stream, and Merlin reached up and grabbed it, dove into the water, and with his free hand grabbed Natalenya's tunic.

She spluttered to the air, and he held on tightly as the current pulled at their legs.

The thicker part of the branch cracked — and broke off the tree.

Merlin dragged the wood closer, and Natalenya gripped it, her chin shaking and her tresses soaked.

The river swept all three downstream, and finally, in a wide and calmer spot, Merlin kicked them over to the other side and they scrambled ashore. Not far downstream, their two riderless horses ascended the bank.

Natalenya sat on a rock and looked at Arthur. "He's not breathing!"

Merlin took the child from her. He was pale, with his eyes closed. Merlin held him upside down, and water trickled, then gushed out. The child choked — and cried.

Natalenya pulled him close, warming him.

"That's one way to learn how to swim," Merlin said, but it wasn't funny. He went to get the horses, wondering what had become of Colvarth, Garth, and Caygek. The horses seemed glad to be on land, and he led them back. After helping Natalenya mount her horse, they tracked upstream to where they had plunged in — but there was no sign of the others.

"We're alone," he said. "Not even the wolves."

She shivered in the cold early morning air. "What'll we do?"

"They must have stayed on the other bank and tried to outrun the wolves. They'll make for the bridge, and we'd better too."

Downstream, they traveled as fast as they could through a tangle of trees and vines. Farther on they located a game trail that seemed to follow the stream.

By the time the sun had risen behind the storm clouds to their left, they came across the rutted, muddy road — and their companions, riding fast.

"Put on your wings!" Colvarth yelled as they rode past. His horse's right flank was streaked with blood.

Merlin spurred Natalenya forward and then kicked his own horse to action.

"Are the wolves behind us?" he called to Caygek, who seemed intent on not falling off behind Garth.

"A different wolf," the druid shouted. "Vortigern."

And sure enough, Merlin saw in the far distance, beyond a small bridge over the Camel River, men on horseback chasing them.

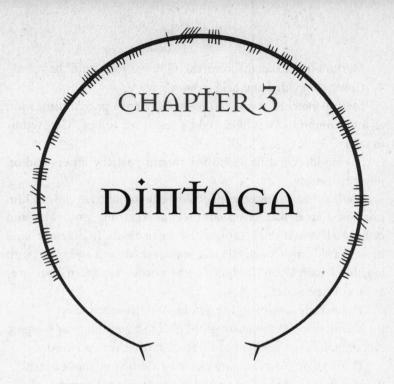

CHAPTER 3

DINTAGA

Merlin's horse flew as fast as the wind, smooth galloping upon hooves of necessity. He had never ridden thus during his days of blindness, and yet now he wished their lives did not depend upon speed.

The trees thinned as they rode, lightning splitting the sky and deep thunder rolling over and over their heads. They came to a plain filled with yellow broom and followed the road until it rose over a hill. Merlin slowed and beheld — just beyond a small stream and a distant sleepy village with some dilapidated stables — the island fortress of Dintaga. Out in the Kembry Sea it sat, and he trusted that Colvarth was right about the causeway, because he could not see the path to the island from the hill.

Turning back, he was surprised to see that one lone rider had left the others far behind. Merlin kicked his horse's sides and picked up speed.

The man would catch them before they made it to the fortress.

Merlin raced to catch Colvarth. "Give me your staff," he yelled.
Colvarth nodded and held it out.

Merlin snatched it and fell back. Natalenya passed him, wind flying through her wet hair, and he called out to her, "Get Arthur to safety."

She nodded and hastened her mount past the others and on toward Dintaga.

Merlin's heart almost stopped as the man pulled even with him just past a crossroad. His mount was dark, strong, and swift, and he bore a leathern shield, oval with bronze bands. In his right hand he held a shining sword. His face was clean-shaven and grim, with long black hair. Upon his shoulders he wore a deep green cloak over a shirt of iron scales.

The sword came swinging out, but the stroke fell short.

Merlin gripped the staff tightly, glad to have a familiar weapon. Not only that, but one that could reach farther than a sword.

The man pulled his mount closer to Merlin and made a stab.

Merlin rushed forward and narrowly avoided the blade.

Lightning tore through the sky just above them, and the roar sent a shock through the air.

Merlin thrust out Colvarth's staff and rammed the rider hard in the chest.

He and Merlin's eyes met, and he gave Merlin a strange look. Was it because of the scars on Merlin's face? Did the man recognize him ... or was he just confused by Merlin's choice of attack?

The warrior fell from his horse.

On Merlin rode, and sent up a prayer of thanks for God's protection.

Ahead of him, the others dismounted near a stable, seemingly at the edge of the world with the endless sea beyond. He joined them and slipped from his horse, handing back Colvarth's staff.

He looked down, stepped backward, and took a breath. The stairs, cut unevenly from the rock, wended downward, steep and wet. One slip and any of them might plunge to break their neck, or fall into the sea to be swept away. From the bottom of the stairs the path led to the island across a crooked finger of land.

It was their only hope of escape from Vortigern.

But the island itself rose up before Merlin like the crown of a skull wedged amongst the crashing waves. And like a war hammer smote upon the crumpled right side of this rocky head lay the high and unbroken walls of Dintaga. From its few and narrow windows, no light shone.

The last remnants of storm blew past, and a single stray lightning bolt leapt from the sky and struck the island's summit. An old and crooked bush smoked and lit on fire. The blaze began at the roots and quickly spread until every branch was aflame. Eerie light danced over the walls of the fortress.

"Merlin, come," Natalenya called. She and the others had already gone two flights down before he realized his delay. Caygek and Garth steadied her as she carried Arthur.

Behind him, Vortigern's horsemen had reached the crossroad.

Taking a deep breath, Merlin dropped his feet to the first step and climbed down, fingers throttling every ledge and hold he could find, legs trembling at every movement.

Halfway, Merlin looked to the right, and there jutting out into the sea lay a shelf of rock, scarred and barren. It reached out to the island as if it, too, had once touched it and been a path, but was now sheared off. Merlin wondered if the stairs beneath his own feet might give way and fall into the sea.

Finally at the bottom, the wheeling gulls seemed to call, "Go back, go back," but *back* didn't exist. Forward he rushed even as Vortigern's men reached the top of the stairs and began the long descent toward them.

Ahead of him the others ran, Colvarth leading with his black hood flying, harp in one hand and staff in the other. Garth and Caygek ran together, with Natalenya close behind.

She slipped and fell, turning her body to protect Arthur from the rocks.

Merlin caught up with her and helped her just as an arrow whizzed overhead.

She sucked in air, her right elbow scraped and bleeding.

A swell of water rose up and churned over the rocks, almost knocking Merlin's feet from under him.

"The tide," Natalenya yelled over the salty spray.

He held on to her tightly. If the water swept her away, he was going with her — but the waves fell back and they slipped forward to higher ground just as more arrows fell and shattered on the rocks behind them.

Above loomed another stair, but less severe. Upward they climbed, right and then left — dodging arrows and hiding when possible — until they came to an open portcullis through a high wall. This cut off the island from the causeway and the rest of the mainland beyond.

"Come through, come through," Colvarth said as an arrow struck the wood of the door.

Vortigern's men had now reached the bottom of the opposite stair, but were wise not to brave the foaming water rushing over the rocks.

Garth pulled Merlin and Natalenya through the opening, while Colvarth released the chains holding the portcullis, which slid down with a crash.

"No one guards the gate?" Merlin asked.

"There is always a sentinel on duty at Dintaga, watching," Colvarth said. "If we had come with a large host or had looked unfriendly, he would have come and shut the gate before we had got here. It is good we were not barred."

And there Dintaga stood — the fortress of Gorlas, king of the people of Kernow. Merlin had heard a few whispered stories of this man, but little was truly known. Although his warriors collected taxes, few could attest to having seen the king himself. A customer of Merlin's father had been judged once by Gorlas for starting a brawl that ended in someone's death. It was a severe judgment — if one could count the ragged scars upon the man's back.

A mist, which had been rising from the sea, reached the island and began to cover it.

Upward they climbed as the light of the burning shrub mingled with the shrouded sunrise. To the left, far out in the sea, Merlin spied two peaks rising from the water like teeth, sharp and dark. They were there for an instant and then the mist veiled them ... and all that was left in the world was the door of Dintaga, the "strangled fortress" rising above him.

Bedwir opened his eyes and took a deep breath as the jolt of being knocked from his horse wore off. His back felt bent, and his ribs hurt. Nearby, his horse roamed amongst the heather and broom, finally coming near enough that Bedwir grabbed the reins and pulled himself to a sitting position. Now his head hurt too, and just as he was trying to think.

Who had knocked him from his horse? It had been the man with the scarred face. And where had Bedwir seen him before? Ahh, it had been in Uther's tent. Merlin, he remembered now, had given advice to Uther. Hadn't Colvarth been there as well?

Bedwir rubbed his temples. Colvarth ... now *there* was a mystery. Hadn't Colvarth and Vortigern both served together for many years under Uther? And when Vortigern had told the warriors how the druidow had slain Uther, all of the warriors assumed the old man was dead as well — killed with the High King's family. But Bedwir had just seen Colvarth riding on ahead of Merlin. How had he survived? Why would Colvarth run from Vortigern?

Oh ... but there was another side to the riddle. Bedwir had spied two of them riding tandem — and the man in back had blue designs upon his arms that displayed the telltale sign of a druid. Were Merlin and Colvarth in league with the druidow? He'd heard tales that Colvarth was a former druid. Had the bard betrayed Uther? This was something Bedwir would have to puzzle over.

Three warriors rode up and surrounded him, the sweat running down their horse's legs. "You fool — get off your rear," Vortigern called, "before the worms eat your flesh."

Bedwir stood, with some pain, and brushed the dirt off his breeches. "I'm sorry for not stopping them, I — "

Vortigern vaulted down, grabbed Bedwir and yanked him close. "Did you see who it was? Did they have Arthur?" His eyes were wild, and a strange hatred filled them.

Bedwir paused.

"Did you?"

"Only a druid, and ... and some woman carrying Arthur."

The warrior next to Vortigern spoke, and it was the battle chief's son, Vortipor. "The girl — did she have long, dark hair?"

"Yes, I think so — "

"Was it Natalenya?"

The man seemed so concerned that it surprised Bedwir. Maybe the rumors of Vortipor's planned engagement to Natalenya were true. But Bedwir had to answer truthfully. "I don't know who it was."

Vortigern growled and lifted Bedwir up so only his toes touched. "I saw four, maybe five. Who were the others?"

Bedwir couldn't breathe with Vortigern's fists shoving his tunic into his throat. And one of the man's rings pressed sharply into his cheek. "I hit my head when I fell ..." he blurted out.

"What a waste of a warrior you are." Vortigern threw him back, and Bedwir slipped on some horse manure and fell to the grass. Vortipor and the other warrior laughed.

Another man rode up. "What do we do, my lord?" he asked. "The tide has come in and we can't get to the fortress."

"We wait. And when the water is gone, Gorlas will let me in."

"Are you sure, my lord? If he is harboring the fugitives — "

Vortigern snorted. "Eh ... Gorlas will let *me* in, you'll see. And he doesn't keep boats, so there's no escape."

Ganieda held on tightly to her wolf's fur as Grandfather led them through the sloping, sticky pine branches. Tellyk bore her easily, his snout always sniffing the air, but Grandfather stumbled twice. Tired, she guessed. He rarely looked at her, and when he did, it was a strange glance such as a poor beggar might give.

Ahead of them, shining in the morning sun that perched over the trees, circled carrion birds. They arrived at the circle of stones — where Grandfather halted. All around the field lay the bodies of dead druidow, bloody and surrounded by the fresh hoof prints of the tall warriors who murdered them.

And southeast stood a new cairn. "Who's buried there, G'andpa?" she asked.

He turned and studied her with a light in his eye. "Do you not remember? The High King, a pestilence upon his house. Judged, yes judged he was upon the Stone in revenge for your uncle's ... your uncle's murder." The gleam faded, and his head drooped.

"What'll you do for the sleeping ones? I thought Belornos would take them home ... won't Belornos take mother home?" Mammu had always said the druid god would care for them.

"Soon, soon, our remnant shall come and care for them. Ten ... twen ... forty at most, and half of those — the foolish filidow — have left. Our numbers are few ... so few. They are camped beyond these pines, and must rest before undertaking this task." Grandpa straightened his back, and his lips quivered. "They will dig an Honor Pit, and line it with holly leaves, and rowan ... and pine branches, and put the bodies within."

"And bury them? Should we bury mother?"

"No, no — they are left to behold the Wheel of the Sun, and the Horns of the Moon. Môndargana will be happy where you have left her. And I have not the strength" — here he gasped, clutching his chest — "to see her sleeping thus ... the second and last of my children to die in the breadth of a single week. *May I witness* the entrails of Merlin, my enemy, spilled and knotted upon the ground one day!"

Ganieda screwed up her nose. "Won't an'mals and birds eat Mammu — and these dead ones?" For even now the crows began to descend in their black-feathered tunics to pluck and rend the bodies.

"Has your druid mother not taught you this? She had no fear of such, and none of these did either," he said, pinching Ganieda's chin. "It is given that their souls will pass into the animals and joyous birds, and thus they will live again, forever serving the druidow."

They walked through a final stand of trees and found the druidow's camp. There sat two dozen or so of their number — all that was left of the hundred who had breathed freely of the wind of Ogmios the day before, hoping the Stone would restore them to power in the land. They sat before fires, along with their wives and a few children Ganieda recognized, and there they smeared smoking charcoal on their bodies to appease the multitude of the gods.

None spoke, yet they looked to their leader, Mórganthu, with gaunt faces and twisted, frowning lips. Grandfather ignored them, but Ganieda saw a tear escape his eye as she rode Tellyk beside him.

Half of the tents had been ransacked and ripped but the other half were strangely untouched, including Grandfather's tent, which sat in a private clump of thick pines at the far end. Entering within, Ganieda looked up and beheld again the bones hanging from the ceiling, and once again they made that wonderful tinking, clinking sound as the wind caressed the tent. Ganieda felt safe here, as her mother had before getting sick.

He gave her some smoked venison, and she lay upon an animal fur and devoured the meat.

Grandfather did not eat anything. He sat and watched her, and when she was halfway through, he inched closer and whispered to her. "Darling daughter of my offspring, do you love your grandfather?"

"Yes, Grandpa." The meat was cold, but it lined her empty stomach, and the grease upon her fingers was sweet.

"Then, oh, then, may your grandfather see what you have hidden in your bag?"

Ganieda flared her nostrils at him, and sat up.

"I will not touch, I promise, I promise. Only a look …"

She finished the deer meat, and he gave her some more.

Grandpa tilted his head, and his eyebrows softened. "Your mother, you know, would want you to share with me these secrets."

Ganieda looked at him, at his long nose and wrinkled eyes. How old he looked and how sad. His soft, black beard had grown more gray over these few weeks, and Ganieda felt sorry for him. "I have *two* things, you know …" she said.

"Two, yes, but what mysteries? How thoughtful of you to save them!"

She smacked her lips, feeling sleepy. "… But I will only show you one."

She reached into her bag and touched the fang's sharp tip, almost pricking her finger. No, she would keep that hidden — in case Grandfather tried to take the orb. Reaching deeper, she found the orb, slipped it out, and held it before Grandfather.

In the morning light, the inside of it seemed dark, with a tinge of red worming its way throughout. Ganieda looked deeper inside, and suddenly it lit up with a pale purple flame.

Grandfather snapped his head back as if his eyebrows had caught fire. He circled around, keeping his hand obviously behind his back, until he sat next to Ganieda on her left and pressed his furry cheek up to hers. "What is this, my daughter's daughter? What remnant of the Stone have you found? Surely its power — "

His voice stopped abruptly as the flame faded, and an image appeared in the orb. It was a bush, burning brightly, yet surrounded by a ghostly mist. And below the bush, five people climbed a stairway cut into the rock. They came to a door in a high wall, and beat upon it with their fists.

These five waited for a long while, shivering in the dark, until finally a porter opened the door, his lantern falling upon their faces.

Grandfather hissed, for the scarred face of Ganieda's brother was revealed, and that of another man, white of beard and with a harp.

These two entered, and as they passed by the porter, three others were revealed: a druid whom Ganieda did not know, a girl holding a child, and a young boy whom she had seen with her brother and then later with the druidow.

"The child!" her grandfather bellowed. "It is Arthur, the High King's son, and he *yet lives* when mine was cruelly treated and slain. My Eirish warriors told me the boy had died. They lied to me … lied *and* failed me."

Ganieda did not know who this Arthur was, but she knew her brother and she hated him for ruining her life. And if Grandfather hated this Arthur, then she would hate him too. She would hate them all.

Ganieda hugged Grandfather's shaking shoulder. "It's all right, G'andpa. We will hurt them. We can hurt them."

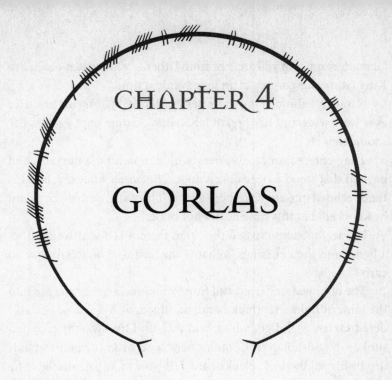

CHAPTER 4

GORLAS

Merlin ducked under an arch as the porter led them into the rock-walled fortress of Dintaga and through passages choked with debris and mud.

Colvarth stopped, lifted a filthy boot, and studied it intently. "Your lord Gorlas," he called loudly, "needs his warriors to become his muckers."

The porter turned, and with his right eyebrow raised below his black, puffy hat, said, "These are but the lower passages, and his warriors have finer things to attend to."

Indeed, Merlin was taken aback at what these "finer" things entailed as they entered the feasting hall. All around the men slept, some in their kidneyed mead and some in their bile-soaked supper. The place stank, and the tables were filled with animal bones and rotting fruit amongst broken jars of foreign pottery — perhaps from the seat of the now-crumbled empire.

The porter sniffed as he took them up a broad and winding stair.

"It matters not that you are sent from Uther — you must apologize to King Gorlas for coming at an inconvenient time."

Natalenya climbed the stairs beside Merlin, holding his belt. Her eyes were wide and her breath labored as Arthur slept against her shoulder.

They entered an alcove, nearly hidden behind a curtain, and beyond that stood a large oaken door. The porter knocked, and his thuds echoed into the chamber beyond. There was no answer. Again he knocked, but this time he did not cease.

Inside, footsteps crossed the floor, there was a scuffling sound, a bang, and then cursing. "What is the meaning of waking me so early?"

The door was unbarred and flung wide, and a man emerged into the lantern light. His thick hands fumbled with a yellow embroidered tartan of indigo, white, and teal, and his swarthy face had sunken, bloodshot eyes. Upon his neck lay a silver torc, almost hidden by his wildly thick, black beard. His wide mouth grimaced as he yelled again. "A curse on you, Sulain ... I'll cut your seven spleens out for this — " He stopped speaking when the porter lifted his lantern so the whole party could be seen.

Colvarth stepped forward. "King Gorlas, we have come bearing news of great import concerning the High King. May we enter, and rest our tired legs?"

Gorlas scowled and blinked at them. "Yes, yes," he said, but his expression said *no*.

He studied each of them in turn, pausing on Natalenya and Arthur. Lastly his eyes met Merlin's, and his frown twisted as he traced unkempt fingernails along his own face — over the same path as Merlin's gouges. He did this for his other cheek as well.

"My lord," the porter interrupted, "may I return to my duties?"

Gorlas looked at his porter as if for the first time. "No, no," he said, but then nodded in affirmation, and the porter left them.

The pale light of dawn misted through a few high windows, but the room behind Gorlas slept in gloom. He turned from them without a word, entered, and walked around an open hearth near a broad table. At the back wall he sat upon a chair with his face hidden in shadow. "What is it?" he said. "Has that pig sent you to torment me again?"

Colvarth entered first, and the others followed. Merlin brought up the rear and closed the door, but did not bar it.

Colvarth cleared his throat and stuck out his scruffy white beard. "The Boar of Britain is no pig, young Gorlas, and you will speak in kinder terms of the dead."

"The *dead*?" Gorlas said. His legs snapped as if to stand up, but the rest of him remained leaning against the back of the chair.

Natalenya blew on a half-burnt twig from the hearth and lit some candles set in a silver pedestal set upon a tablecloth.

The light began filling the room.

Merlin stepped back, for the glow revealed a woman sitting to the left of Gorlas, and a man to his right. The man's thin face scowled down as if he were about to raise the thick blade laying in his lap — and smite off Merlin's head.

But the two were only flat tapestries, cleverly stitched so as to appear alive.

The man, bald and wearing a battle-red cloak under bright mail, sat upon a wide throne. At his throat lay a golden torc, and upon his head rested a crown of laurel. Above him, amongst the woven storm-clouds, were embroidered some words. Merlin's eyes had trouble making these out, having not read anything during the prior seven years of blindness. After puzzling a bit, he determined its meaning: "Vitalinus, High King of the Britons."

Merlin pulled his gaze away and studied the tapestry of the woman, also lifelike. Her hair was flaxen-red and her face lovely. Her dress, with pearls and silver thread, bore the same plaid as Gorlas's wrinkled tartan. Upon her throat rested a braided silver torc, and she held a slim yet deadly blade. Above her head had been embroidered the words, "Igerna, Beloved Queen of the people of Kernow."

Queen? Kernow had no queen. As far as rumor told, Gorlas, the king, had never married. Merlin blanched. This image was of *Uther's* wife. The rivalry for her love was deeper than Colvarth had let on. Maybe deeper than Colvarth knew.

Gorlas put a hand over one of his eyes to block the sudden intrusion of candlelight. "Uther is dead, you say? That swindler is dead?" He jumped up and danced, growling like some animal. He nearly ran into Garth, who bounded backward.

Prancing around to Merlin, Gorlas jerked to a stop and pulled at the curls of his beard. "The crook is dead! He, he stole her away … By dressing up like me he *tricked* her, but no more, do you hear? She's *my* love, and she'll come back."

Colvarth thunked his staff onto Gorlas's foot. "Cease. Igerna is dead as well. They were both murdered by the traitor Vortigern. We have brought her son, Arthur, here for your protection, for Vortigern stands outside your walls ready to … ready to claim the throne of the High King by killing Uther's heir."

Gorlas blinked at Colvarth and nodded as if in agreement, but said, "No … no. Igerna is alive. She'll never, never die …"

A door creaked from the left, and a woman stepped forth holding a stubby candle. Behind her lay a room with a wide and rumpled bed. She pulled a robe tightly around her shoulders and looked at all of them in surprise. "What is it, my love? What has wakened you?"

Her tousled hair was red with a tinge of brown, and Merlin thought she resembled the Igerna of the tapestry a little too much.

Gorlas looked at her, and his eyes brightened. "She is here … Igerna is here, you see? She has come back. She always and only loves *me*."

The woman stepped next to Natalenya and peered at the sleeping Arthur. "I am Ewenna, from a fishing village down the coast," she whispered, "but he often forgets when we are together." She touched Arthur's soft head and smiled.

Gorlas glared at Arthur, and then turned on Ewenna. "How could you carry *his* child," he said, gnashing his teeth and biting his lip bloody. "Why did you betray me?" And he slapped her in the face and then turned on Natalenya, trapping her against the table and a large chair. Arthur awoke and cried out.

Gorlas raised his fist to strike the child.

Merlin ran. Grabbing the back of Gorlas's neck, he thumped him face-first down upon the wood table. The candles fell over onto the tablecloth, and Natalenya rushed away.

Gorlas roared, broke free, and lashed his hand out.

Merlin ducked, and after leaping back put his fingers on the hilt of his sword. "We have come for your protection."

"The bastard child of Uther shall not stay in my house!" Gorlas darted to the door, banged it open, and was gone.

The spilled wax from the candles spread out on the tablecloth, and it caught fire.

Merlin fetched a goblet and threw the contents on the fire, but it was strong drink, and the fire leapt even higher.

Garth yanked the cloth down to the stone floor. Colvarth slung off his wet cloak and smothered the flames.

Ewenna sobbed, her cheek red with the handprint of Gorlas. After Natalenya had quieted Arthur some, she went and touched Ewenna's shoulder.

"He usually treats me better," Ewenna said through her tears. "But he's all that I have. No one else will take me now." She smiled at Arthur again through her tears and held his hand while the child studied her shaking candle with his soft, brown eyes.

The tramping of feet could be heard beyond the open door, and soon a bevy of warriors entered the room with spears, swords, and bows leveled at the group.

Merlin stepped forward and spoke to them, hands out. "Do not hurt us, simply let us leave."

The warriors marched them out of the fortress, and set them

free out the door they had come — but with Vortigern guarding the causeway, there was no escape.

Above them and through the mist, Gorlas yelled, his smiling face leaning out from a ledge. "*Igerna is mine*, and her bastard is thrown to the cowering rocks where he belongs!" He laughed — a howling, barking laugh that sent a chill down Merlin's back. "When the tide goes out I shall go and parley with Vortigern — the faithful brother of my love — and together we will decide your fate."

Merlin wandered aimlessly across the island, climbing boulders and crossing fissures until he found himself on the summit where the pale sunlight had begun to burn the mist away. The others probably followed, but he hoped they would stay away.

He had failed them by bringing them here. Every disaster Colvarth had warned him about had come, and what could he do now? Vortigern guarded the causeway, the sea surrounded them, and the only boat in sight was so far away that the sailors would never hear their shouts, or see them wave.

Colvarth, breathing hard, finally caught up with Merlin and leaned on his staff. "I told you we might regret coming here."

"It's my fault."

"I am not here to bring blame."

Merlin turned away from him. "Yes, you are. I've failed you. Failed Arthur."

Pointing toward the coast, Colvarth said, "They would have caught us in the forest or on the road. Vortigern has too many warriors."

"And I have what — a boy, a druid, a girl, and an old man?" Merlin regretted these words, but they were out. He looked back, and saw Colvarth's expression droop.

"The child Arthur is not your burden," Colvarth said, pulling up his hood against the whistling wind. "He is the burden of this decrepit old man — but I have something Vortigern does not have."

"What do you have?" Merlin asked. "Can your harp turn into a magic boat?"

"What I have is you." Colvarth tugged Merlin's sleeve and made him look eye to eye. "You are the wise one through whom our Creator has spoken. You are the brave one who overcame the Druid Stone. You are the blind one who has been healed. We may yet find a way, if —"

"Leave me alone."

"The tide will not tarry —"

"Leave me *alone*." Merlin pulled away and ran off, leaving Colvarth's empty words to echo on the summit.

Down the hill he went and hid in a scrubby hollow, where a small pool had been caught. A foul-looking gull came and brushed its bill in the rainwater. The reflection of the bird lay upon the surface, and Merlin realized it was like a mirror. He shooed the bird away, and leaned over the water to see his own face for the first time in seven years.

He cringed.

The scars were worse than he'd imagined. Though they had aged, and faded some, they were ugly. Bulges of flesh had grown on his eyelids, and scratches had dug deep into his nose, cheeks, and forehead. At best, he looked like a bird of prey, evil and outcast — at worst, a monster. Long ago, it seemed, he had felt the scars with his fingers in the darkness of his wounded eyesight. But now, in the full light of day, he saw them for what they were. Only now did he fully understand why he had been a pariah in Bosventor. Why people whispered around him. Why children ran away at his coming.

So how could Natalenya love him? She was so beautiful, with her dark hair and darker eyes. He had never dreamed someone could care for him. And now he knew the truth: No one could. Ever. Sure, her heart seemed steadfast, but she was just trying to get away from Vortipor, leaving with Merlin only because it was better than having to marry that scoundrel. Someday soon she would meet a handsome, unscarred someone — and they would fall in love. She would forget about foolish, ugly Merlin, and the bond that had grown between them in these difficult days would wither away.

He loved her and cared for her so deeply, and his heart ached to marry her, but now that he could see his own repulsiveness he could also see the future, and it hurt.

He wanted to weep, but held back the tears, and he was angry at God for not taking his scars away along with his blindness. And because of that, he would have to protect himself. Harden his heart like a sword from his father's smithy. She would be snipped from his life like everyone else had been — cut off by a chisel on an anvil of pain. He had to face it. He was a wanderer now, forsaken, lost — and now trapped. The best he could do was to protect Natalenya, Arthur, and the others. Maybe by some miracle get them off the island … and then set her free.

And if he died here, then it didn't matter. None of it mattered.

Ganieda rested upon a white bull's furred hide, and soon her hatred of Merlin faded from memory. She slept, a great, drowsy, tumbling sleep. There in a dream, in a dark cove near the sea, her mother visited her. She lay down upon the rocks; her infected arm wept from its wound, and she called to Ganieda, screaming for vengeance. The sea crashed over them and swept her mother off.

Ganieda awoke, startled — but still the pained visage of her mother's face swam before her eyes. And then was gone. She became aware of Grandfather sitting upon his carved chair, watching her. His eyes reflected the coals of the fire, and he breathed in its herbed smoke deeply through his nostrils. "You have slept only a little, and the remnant of the druidow have come to me and gone, and the Honor Pit is being dug."

Ganieda sat up, confused. Next to her lay a bowl of fresh water, and a pot of porridge smelling of honey.

Grandpa leaned over. "Tell me … tell me what dreams you have walked within. For you have slept upon the Sacred Hide of Visions."

Scooping some porridge into her fingers, she slipped it into her mouth, twirled it across her tongue, and found the mixure was still warm. "I have seen Mammu."

"And what does she require?"

"She's in pain, and she suffers. She will always suffer."

"The gangrene of this *Christus* has taken her ..." Grandfather scoffed.

"She wants us to hurt them. She told me." Indeed, her mother *had* told her. But there was another voice, besides her mother's, which rumbled in her deepest sleep. It spoke to her too, but she did not fully understand it. If her mother had told her *what* to do, then the other voice told her *how* to do it.

"Hurt your brother, yes, yes ... but how, dear one? Using the druid magic of your orb, I have beheld him — but how can we hurt him?"

"We must see them first." And she pulled out the orb and held it up.

Grandfather fell to his knees next to her and looked within.

The purple fire leapt up inside, and Ganieda almost dropped it for fear of being burned, but it felt almost cold to the touch. Shifting, the image cleared and showed her brother sitting next to a girl. Ganieda recognized her from the village but could not remember her name. A small pool of water lay before them and a wall of rock behind them. The girl's hands held out the child Arthur and placed him in the arms of Ganieda's brother. He looked awkward holding the child, and said as much, his words strangely emanating from the orb.

"Disease for disease," Mórganthu said. "Can you do this? Can you take vengeance upon Merlin for the stolen life of my daughter — thy mother?"

Ganieda reached into her bag and touched the fang. A ripple of power swept up her arm, a thrill, a tingle of sweet strength. Pulling the fang from the bag, she held it out before Grandfather, and green fire curled around its surface. Ganieda called out loudly in the tongue of the druidow, but the words she heard were not her own. "A *curse* on the one bearing the child, a sickness of suffering, a scourge upon the flesh!"

The sickly flames soared up from the fang. Ganieda held her breath as they spiraled toward the orb. But before they touched it, Ganieda's brother hastily handed the child *back* to the girl. The flames struck the orb. For a moment, the orb blinked like an eye and the image narrowed, sucking in the green fire.

The girl within the orb shrieked as if injured — the sound echoing through Mórganthu's tent. Her image faded. The orb and fang became hot, and smoke rose from Ganieda's hands. A burning wormed through her arms and met in her chest as a white-hot pain. From there, it spread to her entire body.

Ganieda tried to scream, but couldn't breathe in or out. She fell to her side and wanted to throw the orb and fang away — but then Grandfather might take them. She held on tightly, and soon the pain subsided to a dull ache in her bones.

"You failed," her grandfather hissed. "You hurt the girl instead!"

"I didn't mean to ..."

"Do it again. Do it again to *Merlin*!" he said. "He must bleed for his crimes." Grandfather waved the stump of his right forearm, and its bloody cloth almost fell off.

Ganieda sat up, shaken. "Hurting her hurt *me*. I won't do it ..." she said, quickly putting the orb and fang into her bag so she could wipe the tears from her eyes.

Her grandfather stepped back and studied her as if something was wrong.

Ganieda pulled herself to her feet and stared, confused, at her grandfather. She felt different — strange.

"What, what has happened to you, my daughter's daughter?"

"G'andpa, you've shrunk." In the past her eyes had barely reached his belt, but now she looked clearly at the tunic buttons below his chest.

"No, no," he said. "You have grown!"

Ganieda looked down, and it was true. She had always been small and thin, but now she had grown taller and her arms and legs felt stronger.

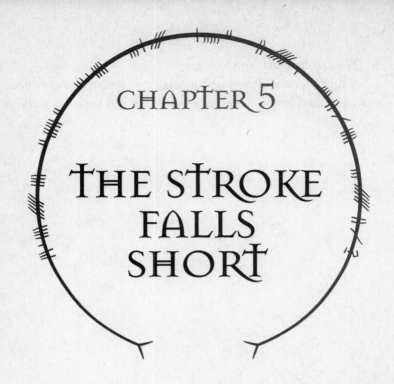

CHAPTER 5

THE STROKE FALLS SHORT

Merlin held on to Natalenya's hand and then arm while she screamed in pain.

Her face contorted, and her back arched, but then it quickly passed and she breathed again. Her tears streamed down her cheeks, and Arthur cried too. She tried to comfort him as best as she could, but her eyes were closed and her teeth clenched.

Merlin did not understand what had happened. One moment she was fine — receiving Arthur from his hands — and the next it was as if a hundred hornets had burst from some crack in the stones and stung her. He looked behind her but saw nothing.

"What happened?" he asked.

She shook her head and slumped against him. "The pain's gone … but … I don't know what happened."

"We're all exhausted. I'm exhausted," he said. "Just rest." But even as he was about to put his arm around her, his heart curled up and he pulled his hand away. It felt like death to not hug her, but he had to protect himself for when … for the time when she would reject him. He wanted to lean forward again and look at his ugly visage in the water, but he felt awkward in front of her.

Above him, beyond the hollow, Garth's bagpipe began skirling. It was loud, it went on and on, and it irritated Merlin. How could Garth think of playing a song while Gorlas brought Vortigern onto the island? What? Should Colvarth get out his harp, Merlin his, and they all play together while death slithered through the gate?

Merlin rose, startling Natalenya. He climbed out of the hollow and stood upon the rocks again where he could be seen. Garth piped on the summit of the island, with his single drone resting on his shoulder and sticking into the air. His fingers played upon the double drones, and he looked like a red-faced chicken with his left arm wiggling to press upon the bag. The boy was truly playing beyond the ability of his lungs. Caygek stood next to him.

Merlin tramped over. "*Stop!*" he shouted, but Garth ignored him. Merlin was about to plug the hole in the intricately carved drone when someone called behind him.

It was Natalenya, who had also climbed out of the hollow with Arthur. She pointed to a high window in the wall of Dintaga, maybe thirty feet up, where a banner of some kind fluttered in the wind.

Ewenna, Gorlas's mistress, stood in the window, silently holding some cloth, and then let go of it. The wind took it, raised it up for a brief moment, and then whisked it out, away from the wall, and it fell upon the rocks.

When Merlin looked back at the window, Ewenna was gone.

Colvarth was there first, and Merlin and Natalenya joined him. Garth kept piping. Colvarth turned the cloth over — and revealed the tapestry of Vitalinus, High King of the Britons. "This depicts Vortigern's grandfather," Colvarth said. "She has now given us warning. Vortigern will soon cross the causeway."

"But the tide …" Natalenya protested.

Colvarth rolled up the tapestry. "The tide was shallow, and

departed half an hour ago. Gorlas went and met with Vortigern while you two were absent. Our time is at an end."

Merlin drew his sword. "Then we should find a defensible position. Maybe the hollow Natalenya and I found."

"Fighting is useless now," Colvarth said. "Better to parley and hope for life. Maybe we can convince the warriors that Vortigern killed Uther—"

"No," Natalenya said, pulling Arthur close. "Vortigern will deny it and will kill us."

Garth stopped playing and began to holler from the summit. "Come! Everyone!"

Caygek stood beside him and waved his arms to beckon them as well.

Merlin shook his head. "Now what do they want?"

But the two were insistent, and finally Colvarth said, "Let us go to them," and walked off with the tapestry under his arm. Natalenya followed.

Merlin was about to go as well, until he heard a noise toward the coast. A host of men crossed the causeway, at their front marched Gorlas next to a bearded man Merlin assumed was Vortigern.

Merlin ran after the others to find Garth piping again while Caygek pointed out to sea.

Merlin followed his gaze.

"A boat is coming," he said. "Garth called it using his bagpipe!"

And sure—it was true. The lone sailboat Merlin had thought too far away to shout to was heading straight for Dintaga and getting close.

"What? How did you—?"

Garth no longer appeared comical to Merlin. With his red hair blowing in the wind over his handsome brow, he was dignified and reliable. His noble bagpipe's polished wood shone in the light, and the music seemed to float on the wings of angels. Garth stopped playing, caught his breath, and smiled. "Us fishermen use bagpipes to talk to each other. That's why me father piped. I used the song for distress."

"You're a saint," Merlin said and banged him on the shoulder, sqwonking the bagpipe.

Behind them, the sound of men's feet echoed over the rocks.

They all scrambled toward the edge of the island where the boat approached.

And Merlin gulped. The shore lay thirty feet down a cliff. Colvarth and Natalenya would have trouble getting down beyond halfway, where the rocks became steep.

Behind them, the footsteps of the men grew louder, and there was shouting.

"Down on the rocks, everyone!"

Merlin assisted Natalenya with Arthur, even as Caygek and Garth assisted Colvarth. Together they made it to the midway point while the boat sailed within a stone's throw of the island.

Garth hailed the fishermen as the boat drew nearer. "*Dynargha!* Hello! Caught much fish today?"

There were three fishermen, and a tall one nearest them stood up near the mast. "Not caught much!"

Merlin rapped Garth in the head. "Don't talk about fish. Tell them — "

Garth glared back, but called out, "We need help!"

"What?" the tall fisherman said. "You're on land. You think we loiter? We've bellies to fill ... we fish!" He turned back to the other men.

Colvarth nudged Merlin. "Tell him we have silver ..."

"We have coins," Merlin yelled. "We need passage to Kembry."

The fisherman started at them. "How much? It would take five screpallow."

Merlin told them they had the coins, and the men conferred together.

"As long as you don't care where we drop you off, I agree," the fisherman called.

Colvarth cupped his hands to project his voice. "Not to the Demetae?"

"Too far. I'd rather fish, but Crothak's uncle is sick, and we'll go and visit him in Baegower."

The big fisherman at the rudder steered the boat closer as Garth and Caygek lowered themselves down to the waterline.

"Throw a line to us," Merlin called.

Caygek leapt on board and passed a rope to Garth.

Garth tossed it up to Colvarth, who asked, "What is this for, my Merlin?"

Merlin slipped his tunic off and joined the long sleeves in a knot to make a loop. Next he tied the waist off. Taking Arthur from Natalenya, he placed the child inside the shirt through the neck hole. Then Merlin slipped the rope through the hole created by the joined sleeves.

"Pull it tight!" he called.

Once the rope was taut, he slid Arthur down to the boat, and the fishermen grabbed the squirming bundle.

While this was happening, Natalenya climbed down with Garth's help. Pulling on the rope, he brought the boat close enough for her to leap in.

Colvarth tried to follow, but his foot slipped, and he tumbled upon the rocks, scraping his chin and gouging his right eyebrow. Garth helped him up, but the old man was dazed and held his shoulder.

Behind Merlin, someone shouted, "A ship ... They're getting away!"

Garth urged Colvarth to climb into the boat, but he shook his head in pain.

Six men appeared at the top of the cliff, ten feet above Merlin. Three of them sheathed their swords and pulled bows from their backs. The others began to climb down the cliff.

They were caught.

Gorlas stood near Vortigern, and his wide jaw flapped with his words. "You see, Prince of Vitalinus, we have them cornered on the far end of the island."

Vortigern grogged down wine from a silver cup, and burped. "Your welcome has always been gracious," he said. "Handing over my foes is your greatest kindness yet."

"Look," Gorlas said, "your men shout. The bastard shall die, and your sister, my new wife, shall be cleansed of Uther's filth."

Vortigern spied Gorlas out of the corner of his eye. "We will kill them all ... all, of course, but Arthur. You must know that these men are loyal to Uther."

Gorlas pulled a short blade and pointed it at Vortigern. "But you promised me!"

"He will die, yes," Vortigern whispered, grabbing Gorlas's beard and pulling his fluttering eyes close. "But not here, you fool, unless by accident. You must be patient. The High Kingship isn't won through haste."

Gorlas ground his teeth. "You must promise me — "

"You think I am a fool to let him live?" Vortigern said, letting go and draining the cup.

"And will the girl live?" Gorlas said. "Did not your son say that he plans to marry her?"

"Ehh. If it is her, yes, I have to let her live for a time — but I cannot trust her. She won't live long, that I swear. I have my own way."

"If you will not hurt him again ... then hold out the orb!" Mórganthu commanded. "I want to see what is happening."

Ganieda refused, keeping a tight hold on her bag.

"If you decline me this, then you are a traitor to druid craft, and party to those who murdered your mother and uncle ... yes, murdered my son ..." The corners of Grandfather's mouth curved downward in a snarl.

Ganieda froze. Every fiber of her body wanted to obey and please her grandfather. And she did hate her brother—but she would not willingly suffer again in order to harm someone. It had hurt too badly to use the green fire of the fang. And since wielding the fang and growing in physical stature, she felt stronger, able to speak her mind and desires as well.

"Just the orb," she said.

"We will begin with that, yes," Mórganthu said, smiling now and stroking her hair.

She reached in, drew it forth, and held it up before him. The cold light flickered, enflamed, and finally showed an image of two men.

The first was a tall warrior who had a thin, yellowish beard. Upon his back lay a dark red cloak with a pin of pure gold at the shoulder bearing the likeness of a boar. In his hand he lazily held a silver cup, as if it were empty.

The other man wore a finely embroidered tartan of blue, white, and teal along with a silver torc and many rings on his fingers. His face was dark, his beard darker, and he grinned widely, showing his teeth.

He reminded Ganieda of Tellyk, her wolf, only this one would have black fur if he were a wolf, she decided. His eyes completed the picture—alight as of a hunter with his prey in sight.

Grandfather breathed heavily. "The warrior is Vortigern, who is already under the power of the Stone. Though he has gone his own way, he has been useful, yes, very useful for us."

"Maybe he can hurt Merlin ... so I don't have to."

"Perhaps," he said. "Or maybe you can command him. Would that ... would that be easier?"

"Who is the other?" Ganieda asked.

"You think he may serve us too? He is Gorlas, king of the people of Kernow."

The air felt suddenly thin for Ganieda, and the ground beneath her tilted and swirled. She saw Gorlas as through a long tunnel—and he was older, with gray hair. He called to her from the top of a small cairn of stones, a grave. "Help me ... help me find my love ... my Igerna. She is dead, and I cannot find her."

Just like Ganieda had imagined, his face changed into that of a ravenous wolf, and yet he still spoke, his teeth gnashing. "I will make a pact with you," he pled, "only help me find her."

The vision faded, and the purple flames of the orb winked out.

Ganieda felt weak. "Yes, he will serve us," she said, "but not for many years." These images swirled through her head. Too much, too soon, too fast, and she was scared. Scared of what was happening to her. Scared of the orb and the fang, but not wanting to give them up.

"Why will he not serve us now?" Grandfather asked. "What have you seen?"

She fell to the fur, hid her face, and wept until Grandfather pulled her hand away so that she saw his curled lips. "What have you seen?"

"Many years from now, when he's a gray-hair," she said, "I will make his grief full and then he will beg for my help. Only then will he serve. Leave me alone!" She tried scratching Grandfather's hand, and he pulled it away.

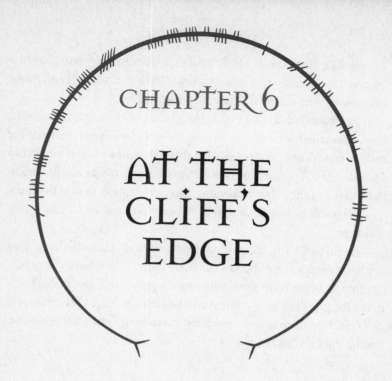

CHAPTER 6

AT THE CLIFF'S EDGE

As Vortigern's warriors notched arrows in their bows, Merlin panicked, grabbed the rim of the cliff, and dropped. He skinned his shins and left knee, but landed in one piece. Together with Garth, he helped Colvarth stumble into the boat.

An arrow whizzed by right where Colvarth had stood a moment before.

Merlin jumped in as two arrows struck the boat, and then helped Garth clamber in.

"The *last* one in," Garth said. "I can't believe it."

The fishermen turned the sail to catch the wind. But as they pulled away from Dintaga, two of the warriors jumped into the water and grabbed on to the edge of the boat.

Caygek hit one over the head with his pommel, and the man fell into the water.

Merlin had more trouble with the second warrior, who was able to pull himself into the boat.

Merlin pointed his blade at the man, but hesitated. Besides fighting the Eirish warrior and Mórganthu to save his father's life, Merlin had never killed a man.

Seizing the advantage of Merlin's delay, the warrior hammered him across the ribs with his forearm. Merlin fell to the deck, hit his head, and dropped his sword.

The warrior unsheathed his own blade and raised it to jab Merlin through the chest. His dripping face was red with fury, and his black hair wild.

Merlin recognized him — it was the same man he'd knocked from the horse.

"Die, druid-murderer of the king!" he yelled.

The sword stabbed forward, but then faltered. Colvarth, who had been laying between Caygek and Merlin, pulled hard on the man's foot. The warrior wavered and plummeted — the blade's tip still falling toward Merlin.

Merlin rolled to his right, and the blade sliced the skin of his left arm. He sat up, spun, and jammed his elbow into the fallen warrior's face. "Vortigern is lying," Merlin yelled. "We're *saving* Arthur."

But the man kept struggling, and so Merlin, Caygek, and the tall fisherman wrestled the warrior and threw him over the side. He dropped with a splash, leaving his sword behind.

Still, a spear hurtled over Merlin's head and ripped a hole in the sail. More arrows fell, but the boat left the island — and the shouting warriors — far behind.

For the first time in two days, Merlin sighed in relief and looked at his surroundings. The boat that had saved them was very different from the boats built for Bosventor's marsh.

Unlike the flat-bottomed, squat, or leather-sided coracles Merlin was used to, this boat was big. From its thick keel to its raised prow, seven men could lay down — if they didn't mind the pile of fish that had been netted and thrown into the center on top of the stone ballast. The ship was twelve feet wide, and its hull was made of two wooden skins — an outer chinked with pitch and wood shavings, and an inner, both of which had been nailed to the thick ribs made of curved oak. The single mast was placed part way to the front of the ship, and its old sail stood twenty feet high.

But on a second look, Merlin was surprised how old, worn, and cracked the decking was, to the point some of the the nails were missing. This boat was originally built to be seaworthy, but now its timbers creaked, and the accumulation of water in the bottom worried him.

The tall fisherman they'd bargained with saw Merlin's face and bellowed, "What? Don't like my boat, uhh? You think we sink and become little pyskow — little fishies, uhh?"

Merlin flinched.

"I tell you, this boat was my grandfather's, and it's as solid as the day he inherited it from my great-great uncle. So you want to swim instead?" Over his solid frame was wrapped a blue and brown plaid, and his balding head and chin were fringed with grayish-orange hair. His nose was hooked, maybe from having been broken, and his skin was tanned by years on the open sea.

His dark eyes studied Merlin.

"Thanks for taking us on board," Merlin said, still wondering if the boat would hold together for their journey.

Natalenya, with Arthur in her arms once again, wiped blood from Colvarth's face using a rag and some water from a cask.

"No more," he said, wincing. "That stings."

The fisherman examined the damaged sail. "You have nice friends on Dintaga, uhh? Our fee just went up another three silver." He pulled a large needle and twine from a wooden box at the side, climbed up, and began sewing the tear to strengthen the cloth and prevent it from ripping further.

"I'll pay you fifteen," Colvarth said as he held out the silver coins. "Five for each of you. For risking your lives to save us." Colvarth then introduced the traveling party, explaining their plight only as much as was needed, leaving out the fact Arthur was the son of the High King.

"Sure, an' your piping was true," the youngest fisherman of the three said to Garth. He had a full head of brown hair, thrashing in the wind, and he looked like a younger version of the tall fisherman. "You *were* in trouble — but not the kind of trouble we like to deal with."

"This is my son, Henktor," the tall fisherman said. "Hard worker, him — makes me proud. Crothak, however" — he thumbed at the heavy-set man tending the rudder — "is a lazy dog who fiddles with his nets."

A broad smile, with a few tooth gaps, spread over Crothak's face. "Don't mind Inktor. If I am a lazy dog, then he's a barking one who scares all the fish away."

The three fishermen laughed.

Merlin and the others gathered together at the middle of the deck, where the boat was steadiest. The sail stood forward from this point, and they were in no danger from the boom. Natalenya passed out some barley bread, cheese, and dried meat.

"May I have more?" Garth asked. "Me tummy's awful empty after these last two days ridin' hard an' such."

Natalenya gave him a double portion, and he smiled. When she finished her own food, she sang a song in Latin, which Merlin only understood a portion of. But she began to cough after a few verses, and stopped singing.

Inktor stepped up to the group and furrowed his brow. "No Roman talk on my ship, uhh?" he said.

"You don't like the Romans?" Natalenya asked, coughing again. Her eyes narrowed. "They used to patrol these waters and protect the likes of you. Aren't you afraid of sea raiders?"

Merlin remembered that her father, the Magister of Bosventor, had been descended from Romans stationed on this very coast. He put a hand on her arm.

"Sea raiders?" Inktor said, jutting his chin out. "I can outsail any of the Eirish or Scoti. But you land-tillers should worry about the Prithager."

Natalenya smirked at him. "Really now ... Picti?"

"I said *don't speak Latin.* That's how I got hurt — curses on the Romans, making us like slaves in their army."

"What happened?" Merlin asked.

"Forty years ago I fought under Servyt up on the wall before the last remnant of the Romans left. My patrol, we were ambushed, and the Prithager sliced me up to find out how much the soldiers had dwindled." He lowered his plaid and showed them his back.

Merlin sucked in his breath. He knew his own back had been scarred from being whipped, but this man had nearly been flayed alive.

"Would have died if Crothak's brother and his men hadn't saved me. I say worry about the painted ones. The sea raiders won't come inland, but the Prithager will. With nothing to stop them, a horde could swarm down from the north, right over the silly, broken wall that the Romans built. Bloody devils."

"Me father an' I were fishermen," Garth said. "Did you ever meet Gorgyr of Porthloc?"

"Can't say I have. Why aren't you with him, uhh? Fathers can always use a stout lad."

"He's dead ... a storm."

"An ill fate, that'un." Inktor said. "Happens to the best. Anyway, we're headed for Baegower, where Crothak's uncle lives. We've got a long journey, uhh? So no more Latin." He pulled up his plaid and stomped off to tend the sail with his son.

They all rested as best they could. Arthur tried to curl up in Natalenya's cloak, but her coughing made him cry, so the boy finally settled down with Garth. It was painful for Merlin to hear Natalenya, who coughed badly until falling into a wheezing sleep.

Merlin's slumber was poor as well, what with the boat rolling and the occasional spray of water over the side. And his dreams were filled with the spectre of a ship chasing them. As fast as the western wind lifted their sail and pushed them along, the pursuing boat still gained. Soon it came within hailing distance, and at its prow stood Vortigern with a bloody blade in his hand.

Bedwir stood near the shore holding a borrowed spear, cursing his swollen nose and wishing his clothes were dry.

Before him, Vortigern, Vortipor, and a few select others prepared two sailing boats. It had taken nearly an hour of riding down the coast to get to the nearest fishing village, and then they had to negotiate the borrowing of the boats. When the fishermen refused, Vortigern had commanded that their nets be shredded — and only then did they relent.

Bedwir wrung the bottom of his pant leg out again and remembered the scuffle onboard the ship with the fugitives. If only he hadn't struggled, perhaps he could have learned more. What had Merlin said before they threw him overboard? That Vortigern was lying and that they themselves were trying to save Arthur?

Bedwir looked warily at Vortigern. Sure, Bedwir had followed him since Uther had put the battle chieftain in command that fateful night in Bosventor. Bedwir had even trusted Vortigern, in a way. But every time something important happened, Vortigern would do something odd.

The worst was that Vortigern had not picked Bedwir to go along with the main party. Of the forty or so warriors present, only half could fit on the boats, and Bedwir was deemed unworthy to come along.

What if Merlin *was* right — that Vortigern had lied to them? What if the fugitives were trying to save Arthur? Was Vortigern more interested in his own kingship than his nephew's? The only way to find out would be to go along in the boats.

And if Vortigern wasn't loyal to Arthur, then the child was in great danger. But what of the druid who had helped dump Bedwir into the water? Oh, the madness of it all. He'd just have to find a way to go along.

"What a lousy, liquid lot," the warrior said next to him. His name was Penkoref, Bedwir remembered, and he liked to stay up late drinking with the other warriors.

"What's lousy is getting thumped, losing your sword, and being thrown in the sea," Bedwir said. "What's your complaint?"

"I get seasick, that's wot," Penkoref said. "All I ask for is a fire and ale, a dry place where I can curl up, and Vorty-growl sez I'm goin' fishing. Well, I'll be sicker'n a squid, I sez, but he don' care, I gotta go."

Bedwir had found his chance, but knew he'd have to take hold of it with both hands. Turning on Penkoref, he shoved the man down to the ground with a snarl. "Son of a disloyal weasel, I'll not have you speak against Arthur!"

The man blinked up at him. "Wot? I said nething o' the kind—"

"I'll trounce any man here who isn't willing to sacrifice all for Arthur." Bedwir shook his spear at the other men around him, and they backed off. "Get up, Penkoref. I challenge you for the right to save Arthur."

"A duel! A duel," the men shouted.

Penkoref stared at Bedwir, and their eyes locked.

Bedwir winked.

A slight smile spread on Penkoref's face as he picked himself up off the ground. "You do, eh? Well, I challenge back. I'm ez loyal to Arth' ez any warrior hereaboots."

"A duel!" the men shouted, and someone threw Penkoref a spear.

"The winner goes after Arthur, and the loser stays back," Bedwir shouted.

The warriors began chanting, "Winner for Arthur. Winner for Arthur!"

Bedwir crouched, leveling his spear.

Penkoref did the same, and the two charged each other.

Bedwir turned his spear to the left, dodged right, and jabbed it into the ground in front of Penkoref's running legs. And for once in this dreadful day, it wasn't Bedwir who went down.

Penkoref sprawled to the dirt.

Bedwir brought his point to the man's chin. "Yield."

"I'll only yield if ye'll acknowledge me honor," Penkoref said, and then *he* winked at Bedwir. "That I'm ez loyal to Arthur ez any."

Bedwir pulled Penkoref up. "I'll acknowledge your honor, but not your skill."

Just then Vortigern burst into the clearing. "What's the meaning of this?"

"Bedwir for Arthur," the men shouted. "Bedwir's taking Penkoref's place on the boat."

"What?" Vortigern said, shaking his head.

And so the men shouting louder, "Bedwir for Arthur!" and they picked him up, carried him to the shore, and placed him triumphantly in a boat.

Penkoref bowed his head before Vortigern, looking very sorry.

Bedwir watched as Vortigern backhanded the defeated man, and then punched him in the gut. Penkoref fell back, sucking air. "Weakling," Vortigern said, and stomped off to the boats — and Bedwir.

"I don't want you," Vortigern shouted. "Get out."

But all the men shouted, "Bedwir for Arthur ... Bedwir for Arthur!"

Vortigern's lips turned sour, and he turned on the men. "Get in the boats, you lazy louts."

Then he turned back to Bedwir. "I've got my eye on you," he said, his hand on the hilt of his blade. "Any trouble and *your* fish guts will join the ballast."

The men who had been picked filed into the boats, taking care to keep their cloaks from touching the filthy deck, and then they shoved off.

The owner of each boat had been forced, along with a helper, to navigate. The sails went up and the two ships were away.

Per his typical bad luck, Bedwir ended up in Vortigern's boat.

"Where are we going?" Vortipor asked his father as they set the lines and sailed out of the small cove.

Vortigern shook his head. "Eeh … Kembry. We're just going to Kembry."

"But where? The coastline's forty leagues long here."

"I'll worry about *where* after we land. Sure, the hens slipped the net, but we'll get 'em."

Ganieda tried to put the orb back into her bag, but her grandfather grunted.

"We have watched for hours, yes, but we are not done, my daughter's daughter," he said, his voice shaking with excitement. "We have learned the secret that Merlin and Arthur will land at Baegower — but where is our servant, Vortigern, going? How will he find his way?"

"We could tell him ourselves," Ganieda said, as if she knew how to do such a thing. Had the voice told her how? That low whisper she heard in the back of her head? The voice had begun speaking to her in her dreams over the last two weeks ever since she saw the Stone in all its magnificence — but now she only heard it whenever she held the orb or the fang.

Did the voice come from the orb? The longer she looked into it, the more she felt that *it* looked at her. But that was silly. It was just a ball, a ball with power. A ball that gave *her* power.

But the voice knew about the orb. Sighed, even wept about its secrets.

"How? How can we tell Vortigern where to go?" Grandfather asked. "I see him at the prow of his ship, but he is not here in our tent to glean our knowledge."

"I can talk to him. The voice has told me so."

Her grandfather sat back. "You? You have heard the Voice? I, too, heard it when I would touch the Druid Stone, our Stone of

Abundance, which Merlin has intruded with Uther's blade. Since then, I no longer hear it."

"But I hear it. And other voices, who are in pain," Ganieda said, as her hand holding the orb shook. "I hear them crying in the dark..."

"Vengeance, yes, yes. The Druid Stone too seeks vengeance for the offense committed against it. Do it. Tell Vortigern where to go — tell Vortigern to kill Merlin..."

Ganieda looked into the orb and saw the warrior Vortigern, his chin uplifted and his beard blowing in the wind.

The orb grew in her hand, until it became heavy, so heavy. It expanded until she could hold it no more and it rolled off from her hand. Soon it was larger than Ganieda, and it split and opened up like a maw with great teeth. She felt a tug on her heart to lean forward and look at it, but she tripped and fell.

Ganieda screamed, her chest frozen and her arms outstretched to push the evil teeth away. They clamped down, and a great tongue swept her down its slimy throat.

The world went black.

A dank light appeared, and Vortigern loomed suddenly above her. Ganieda could breathe now. She tasted the salt, smelled the foaming waves, and felt the breeze in her hair. The now-bright world rose and fell with the flowing boat, and she stood before Vortigern, whose eyes grew wide and whose jaw trembled. She pointed beyond the prow, and said to him, "Baegower. They land at the village of Baegower."

She wanted to tell Vortigern to kill Merlin, to kill Arthur — but could not bring herself to say it. Why did she ... hesitate? Did not her mother command it? Did not the Voice require it? Did not Grandfather seek it?

Death hunted her, hunted her family — her father buried in the cairn, her dead mother — and now her brother. Did she really want him to die?

Despite the curses of her mother, Merlin had rarely been unkind to Ganieda. He had even brought her gifts now and then — a boat folded out of a bad parchment from the Abbey, or a honey-scented flower. He would hold her hand when she was scared. Caress her hair as if, just maybe, she meant something to him.

She drew in a breath, and Vortigern faded … falling to his knees and dropping his spear … faded. The fresh air was sucked away, and the rolling of the boat steadied. Only the shade of her grandfather's tent remained, the bones tied to its ceiling cackling in the wind.

"I have told him," she said.

Grandfather coughed in glee.

CHAPTER 7

UTHER'S MYSTERY

Merlin awoke to someone nudging him. His bed swayed, and his gut wished to empty itself.

Colvarth's face appeared, too bright for Merlin's tired eyes, and the old man nudged him again. "Awake, my Merlin. You and I must speak in private while the others sleep."

Sitting up, Merlin rubbed his eyes, and they felt gritty. "How close are we?" It was still day, but the sun had begun its descent in the west. Perhaps six hours had passed during their journey across the Kembry Sea.

"If I judge correctly, we will sight land soon. I have something to show you ... and we must have a plan."

Merlin followed him to the prow of the boat where they could be alone, and there, with their backs turned to the fishermen, Colvarth pulled a dull, tin metal box from his leather bag. It was about as long as Merlin's hand, and slightly wider. For height, it was no more than the length of his index finger.

"This was found by Uther before he died," Colvarth said. "But I know not its contents. Will you help me open it?"

Merlin touched it, and felt a strange tingling in his palms. He let go, and then touched it again. This time, the feeling was gone. Strange. He held it up. The box weighed very little, but something clacked inside when he turned it. Inscribed shapes formed complicated patterns across its sides, and on the back lay the cross of Jesu between two odd-looking trees.

"It is tin," Colvarth whispered. "But old, perhaps from years beyond our lifetime."

In one corner the metal lay brighter where it had been scratched. Upon the front, there was a small, rusted, rectangular iron plate with a hole for a sliding key that must unlatch the box. There was writing as well, but Merlin couldn't read it.

"Where did this come from?" he asked, feeling the weight of the box.

"From the island of Inis Avallow. It was buried inside the old tower. Uther had a vision — but to my shame, I thought he was drunk."

Merlin examined the narrow gap between the lid and the base. "Shall I try a blade to force it open?"

Colvarth hesitated, and then closed his eyes. "You may try — only be careful. It was bought with the blood of Uther and his wife."

"So Arthur owns it now?"

Colvarth nodded.

Merlin took out a small knife and slipped it lightly into the gap near the latch. Pressing gently, he heard a click, and the lid loosened. Not opening it, he handed the box back to Colvarth, and the old man received it with trembling hands.

Colvarth opened the lid — slowly.

Inside lay a small wooden bowl, dark from age, and it was cracked on one side. Merlin reached in and took it up, and its base was covered in a band of gold with more writing.

"That is all?" Colvarth said. "A circlet of gold, and black dust?"

Merlin looked inside, but saw no dust — the box lay empty. The wooden bowl in his hand did not have any dust in it either. "I see no dust, Colvarth," he said, "but the bowl is very old."

Colvarth squinted his eyes. "I see no bowl, but you hold an empty circlet." The old man reached out and took the band from Merlin — but his hands passed right through the wooden bowl as if it didn't exist.

Merlin blinked. He grabbed Colvarth's wrist to hold the man's hand steady. He felt the bowl again — and sure, it was there, rough, solid, and wooden.

"You can't see the bowl?" Merlin asked. "I can see and feel it. And your hand passes through it." Merlin received the bowl back, and held it by its wooden edge.

Colvarth gasped. "The ring floats! You are not touching it, yet it floats before your hand. Truly this is a mystery. And you say you cannot see the dust in the box? The bottom is filled with it." Colvarth reached his hand in and stirred around the nothingness.

Inktor, who'd been chatting with Crothak and Henktor at the rudder, stood and began walking toward them. He ducked under the sail, stepped over the sleeping, and sauntered over, whistling.

"Hide this mystery," Colvarth whispered. "Put it back ..."

Merlin returned the bowl to the box and closed the lid loosely. Colvarth hastily threw his cloak over it just as Inktor came close.

"With wind like this, we'll land before sunset," Inktor said. "You a little sick, uhh?"

Merlin forced a smile. "We're fine," he said, hoping Inktor would leave so he could look at the strange bowl again.

"If you're Christian and need help," Inktor said, "there's a church near the village. You might consider there, uhh? But if you're all druidow ..."

"I am a *former* druid, but am now Christian," Colvarth said. "Do you know of a priest?"

"What? You think I live in Baegower? You think I know everything, uhh?"

"Surely —"

"Just cause I say *there's a church*, you think I know all about it, uhh?"

"Well, no, but —"

"His name's Anfri, and he lives up the hill beyond the village. Take the main road a good walk, and you won't miss it."

With that, he walked back to the sail, adjusted a line, and then joined his companions at the rudder.

"So we make for the church, and get help there?" Merlin asked.

"I am not sure," Colvarth whispered. "If this Anfri is one I have heard of, it may be better to ask the nearest thief." Colvarth brought out the tin box again and opened it. "Now help me — what can this be? In my lore as a bard and druid, I have heard of such things, mage-made things. By the power of demons I would now say. But this is not pagan — it has the cross of Jesu Christus upon the box."

Colvarth felt inside, his fingers passing through the bowl and stirring the "dust," as he put it. He sighed, and then prayed aloud in his slow and halting speech. Merlin closed his eyes and lowered his head.

Father of rich wisdom — we beseech thee in poverty.
Spirit of bright power — we call thee in weakness.
Son of high royalty — we call thee in humbleness.
O hear our praying — you who dwell on the mountain.
O hear our calling — you who sing upon the thunder.
O hear our weeping — you who reign over the whole earth.
Reveal to us thy mysteries — mighty Father of the fathoms.
Reveal to us thy secrets — sweetest Spirit of the whispers.
Reveal to us thy riddles — gentlest Son hiding in shadows.
For we praise thee — in our rising we praise thee.
And we praise thee — in our journey we praise thee.
Always we praise thee — in our resting we praise thee.
O God — to your Threeness we lift our voice.
O God — to your Oneness we lift our eyes.
O God — to your Glory we lift our prayer.

Colvarth finished and held the open box out to Merlin. "Tell me what you see," he said.

Merlin lifted the bowl and studied it carefully. He described its grained ridges, flecks of wood, and texture. This was all amazing to his newly healed sight, and he wondered if the miracle had given him the ability to see spiritual things as well. Either way, he hoped his wonder would never fade at being able to see again after seven years of blindness.

Next he described the bowl's shape as simple, even plain. He himself had drunk from many carved bowls in his life. But the wood of this one was unique. He told Colvarth he couldn't guess the type of tree, or its age. "If only we could read the writing on the box," he said.

"Would it hold water?" Colvarth asked, pulling a draught-skin from his belt. He pulled the stopper with his teeth and poured a little into the bowl — but it passed right through the bottom and splashed his knee.

Merlin was surprised — the bowl felt so real to him! "It must be for some other liquid — heavenly, maybe," he mused.

Colvarth held the box out again, and Merlin put the bowl back inside. Colvarth then closed it, wrapped a twine around to keep it closed, and placed it carefully in his leather bag.

Merlin remembered his awful dream about the boat pursuing them. "Do you think Vortigern will follow us?"

"This man is the grandson of a ruthless, usurper High King who slew Uther's grandfather. He will not rest until Arthur is either out of his reach or is dead. We must ride north and hide like the wren — with those loyal to Uther's house."

Merlin grimaced, for the time had come to tell Colvarth of his decision. Natalenya's mother had asked them to bring news to their uncle, but Merlin had wondered if it was best, in light of the dangers ahead, to leave Natalenya with him instead. Now that Merlin knew how ugly his face was, he had to release her from their betrothal.

"First I must deliver Natalenya to her relatives in Oswistor ... to her uncle Brinnoc."

Colvarth squinted. "Why? Will you two not marry?"

A lump rose in Merlin's throat. "You think I don't … want to? I saw my scars for the first time, and I can't subject her to — "

Colvarth waved a hand. "Nonsense. She does not see your scars, she only sees the love in your eyes."

Merlin swallowed. "I won't talk about it again. It's best this way. She'll understand."

When Vortigern collapsed to his knees, Bedwir started to run to him, but stopped. He feared the battle chief's anger if anyone thought him weak-footed in such placid waves.

After Vortigern found his feet, Bedwir picked up the fallen spear and handed it back.

Vortigern beat his chest and blinked as if a salt spray had stung his eyes. "Where? Where did the witch go?"

Bedwir looked warily at the crew and warriors. A witch? There wasn't even a woman among them. "What did you say?" Bedwir asked, but the battle chief pushed him aside and stepped over to the fisherman who manned the sail.

"Take us to Baegower."

Vortigern's lips nearly frothed, and the fisherman studied him with a wrinkled brow.

"Take us to Baegower!"

"All'un right," he said. "Nay need fer yellin a' me." After signaling the man at the rudder, he adjusted the sail until the boat cut northeast. The other boat saw their veer and followed suit.

Like most of the other warriors, Bedwir settled down and leaned back against the side of the boat. In some ways this was best — you couldn't lose your footing. But it didn't help the stomach any, and Bedwir's gurgled.

Vortigern kept pacing, his eyes darting here and there. No doubt looking for his witch. The man even poked his head into a deck hatch. After a short inspection, he walked back to the fisherman managing the knotline and scowled at the limp sail and quiet wind. "How long to Baegower?"

"May'en be four hours, I'd conject."

"You can't go any faster?"

"Nay, unlessen the wind bites a mite more."

A gust suddenly snatched the sail, and one of the ropes whipped loose and welted the fisherman across the face.

Vortigern grabbed the snaking line and pulled it tight. The boat sped now across the sea, and Vortigern's laugh was lost amongst the waves.

"Tell me ... what it was like?" Grandfather asked her. "How did you tell Vortigern where to go? You never left here, yet when I looked into the orb at Vortigern, I saw *you* standing in front of him."

Ganieda blinked. "I was only there. The orb ate me ... Didn't you hear me scream?"

Grandfather clucked his tongue. "Yes, yes, of course you screamed ... but the orb didn't eat you. You embroider the tale, my daughter's daughter."

"It was scary."

Grandfather patted her on the head. "Well, it is done, and now that Vortigern has been told, you don't need to do it again."

"Why do you want my brother to die?"

"I?"

Ganieda slipped the orb back into her bag and wrinkled her nose at him. "You said I should tell Vortigern to kill my brother."

Grandfather's lower lip wrinkled, and he lifted his bloody, bandaged right forearm and thrust it toward her face. "You ... you want to know *why*?"

Ganieda tried to step back, but the hot fabric of the tent pressed against her hair. "You want your hand again ..."

"I want your brother's neck to look like this." He stripped off the bandage and revealed his arm, with the skin dying and red at the stump of bone where his wrist had been sliced through. He fingered its end with his remaining hand, disturbing the scabs that surrounded the wound.

She couldn't look anymore and darted to the side.

Grandpa caught her by the shift and pulled her back.

She screamed.

"I want revenge. I want Vortigern to kill him and Belornos to afflict him evermore."

Ganieda beat at Grandfather, but his hand wouldn't let go. "I didn't tell that warrior to do it. I couldn't."

Grandfather shook her like a rag and then dragged her to the center of the tent. "Then you ... will ... go ... back to him. Bring forth the orb!"

She remembered the white teeth. The leeching, slavering tongue. The scaly throat that had sucked her down. She wanted to shout, "No!" but the Voice called to her instead. Its words coiled in her head like smoke, and she shut her mouth.

Reach out thy hand, small one, and take this orb.
Behold, I have called my servants from the north.
Without rest they pillage, burn, and capture.
Call them to strike, with sharpened spear and axe,
Against our foe who has stricken us down.
Against Merlin — death to Merlin the fool!

The bagged orb grew warm at Ganieda's side. Before she knew it, her hand had reached in and taken it out.

Grandfather fell to his knees before it, and she held the sphere aloft. Purple light streamed from it, and mist rolled inside. The image cleared, and before her rushed two hundred warriors. They wore loincloths and leggings, and their lean, muscled bodies shone in the light. Blue paint striped their limbs and naked chests, and feathers decorated their long spears and bows. Most of them bore a round shield, bronze-spiked and dangerous. Their greased hair lay dark, and over each of their shoulders was draped a cloak of checkered cloth.

They chanted as they ran. Ahead of them rode two leaders in chariots made of wicker, pulled by sweating horses.

"Who are *these* warriors?" Ganieda asked.

Mórganthu sneered. "Prithager from the north, a brutal people, backward and with only rumors of the true knowledge of the druidow. The Romans call them Picti. Why does the orb show us these ... these swine?"

"They are near to Baegower. Near to Merlin. So very near."

"They must be raiding Kembry. The Saxenow invasion has taken the British warriors away to battle there, leaving the heartland weak."

A purple flame snapped inside the orb, and its focus changed to the bristly face of one of the Prithager leaders. He had dark eyes under a bony brow. His nose was lumped, with a deep scar across it, and his lips sneered in anger.

Grandfather clapped his hands. "Tell *him* to kill Merlin. Tell him to kill Arthur! With Vortigern behind, and these warriors in front, our foes cannot escape."

Ganieda pulled the orb close and ran to the water bucket. "I can't." And she doused the orb in it, causing steam to whirl upwards and fill the tent.

The world turned white and spun around her. Ganieda tumbled into the empty air.

CHAPTER 8

BROKEN PROMISES

Natalenya tried to sleep but for her hacking cough. She had cried at first, but now with the sun well below the sail, there was nothing left of her tears except dried salt on her cheeks. If only she could catch a little sleep before dark — but no, it felt like a thistle had been jabbed inside her throat.

The sailors had given her a small mat stuffed with flax to sleep upon, but it was damp and stank of fish. Worst of all, Merlin hadn't even said good night to her. He had slept for a long while — until Colvarth had come. The two had talked privately at the far end of the boat, and then Merlin had gone silently back to bed.

Apparently Natalenya wasn't wanted.

She didn't understand him anymore. Everything made sense back in Bosventor. Even when his eyesight had been healed, he had looked upon her with such love and devotion that it made her ears hot and her nose itch.

When had it changed? Had it been yesterday on Dintaga? At the pool in the cleft of rock? He had been crying. She had tried to cheer him, but he would hardly look at her. And then that pain had ripped into her gut like a gladius from hell. Worse, he hadn't comforted her the way she had wanted. After making sure no insect or snake had slithered behind her, he had wrapped his arms around his own selfish knees and looked away. He had rejected her, and she didn't know why.

When had she offended him? What had she done? What had she said? A thousand questions raced through her mind, but there was no answer that made sense.

Only that she was ugly.

Now that he could see her, he didn't love her anymore. He didn't love the mole on her cheek, the way her eyebrows grew together, her teeth. The hundred little things she didn't like about herself. And his perfect, blind dream had been shattered by the reality of seeing who she was.

And then she had gotten sick, and he hadn't even found enough love in his heart to help her. To find something to soothe her cough. To pray over her.

He had withdrawn his love just that fast, and she wanted to sob, and the tears came pouring out once again. Maybe he had never loved her. Maybe in her haste to flee from Vortipor's slobbering flattery she had misjudged Merlin's desire to marry her. Better if he had never brought her. She could be home comforting her mother.

The sun slowly lowered in the west, and Inktor finally hailed the sight of the Kembry coast. Natalenya overheard him and the other fishermen determine their location based on the familiar hills and cliffs.

Natalenya dried her tears as Merlin woke from his slumber. He pulled off his cloak and stood unsteadily as the waves rolled the boat. After speaking with Inktor, he went to wake them all, but chose Caygek first, perhaps because he snored the loudest.

Once up, Caygek grabbed Merlin's arm. "I have a bone of yours to pick at," he said. "Seems like you'd be in trouble without me helping."

Merlin glared at him. "What do you want with us?"

"A little appreciation and understanding. I've taken a liking to Garth. The boy doesn't have a father, you know."

"And you think you're his guide in life, yes?"

"Without my private advice before Uther was captured, I doubt Garth would've saved Arthur. He's told me himself. Your precious quest would have died before it ever began."

"Caygek the hero ..." Merlin said. "What will you think of next?"

"Maybe saving your skin again the next time you foul up."

Natalenya saw Merlin tighten his jaw and take a deep breath through his nose. "Listen, I appreciate everything you've done to help. But the difference between you and us is that we've pledged our fealty to Christ's kingship."

"And what kind of king is this Christ? What is his claim?"

"He claims the hearts of all the Britons."

Caygek stood and pinned his cloak once more over his shoulders. "So you want me to bow down, eh? You're starting to sound like Mórganthu and his Druid Stone, deciding what we all must do."

"Me? Those are the words of Jesu. And do you know why I can trust them?"

"Tell me."

"Mórganthu wanted revenge, but Jesu gave up his life so we could be forgiven."

Caygek said nothing more, yet his eyes narrowed and he turned away to look out over the sea.

Merlin went to Natalenya and shook her shoulder while she feigned sleep. When she sat up, a coughing fit took hold. He gave her a sip from his waterskin, and she smiled up at him. "Are we there?"

"Soon." His hand hesitated on her shoulder for only a moment before pulling away.

"Merlin," she said.

He turned to face her, and though he didn't smile back or show any other emotion, his eyes were red-rimmed. "Yes?"

"Could you sit and talk a bit?"

He glanced away. "I ..."

"I know something's wrong."

He locked gazes with her and his lips parted, but he didn't speak. Even so, there was longing in his eyes.

"Merlin?"

"Yes?"

"Were you going to say something?"

"No ... not at all." But there was a catch in his voice and he gulped. Turning away, he woke Garth, who slept soundly with Arthur's head poking out from his cloak. When Garth sat up, his right cheek was red with the imprint of the wood grain from the deck.

"We're almost to shore, sleepy," Merlin said, and mussed Garth's hair even more.

Natalenya turned her face away, confused and alone.

Before long, they landed the boat on a broad and gently sloping beach amidst ten or so other fishing ships, all pulled beyond reach of the tide. Above them on a cliff lay the village, and Natalenya disembarked with the others, happy to be on solid ground once again.

They all thanked Inktor, Henktor, and Crothak, bidding them farewell as the fishermen sorted their catch.

The evening sun gave them maybe an hour before it went below the hills. They walked up the strand and soon arrived at the rock-cut stairs that led to the village. Natalenya coughed all the way up and became dizzy by the time she reached the top. Just in time for Garth to hand Arthur to her. The world went black for a moment, and she feared falling over, but it passed.

Arthur clung to her hair and began sucking his thumb.

The village was half the size of Bosventor, with the houses tightly packed due to the cliff edges on three sides. Smoke rose from the centers of the roofs, and a few men could be seen in the lanes.

Natalenya hung back while Merlin approached the nearest two men, who sat chatting on a log. When he approached, they both stood to greet him.

"What do you need?" the first man said, fear in his eyes as he studied Merlin's scars. He wore a leather tunic covered in wood shavings. "Odd folk aren't welcome here." He spoke with a slight Kembry accent.

"We're looking to buy five horses."

The second man spoke. "We don't sell our horses less'n they're near to useless. Try our priest, Anfri, who's bought a few off a traveler or two. He's uppa the village a bit."

Merlin looked to Colvarth, who blinked but then nodded.

They thanked the men and skirted the village, heading inland and away from the cliffs until they found the priest's dwelling set off to the side of a heather-covered hill. A large cross cut from limestone marked the spot, and the forest grew close behind his dwelling.

Loud cracking sounds echoed from inside.

Stepping near the door, they heard shouting and more crashing. They all paused, and Natalenya listened carefully.

"Useless pots," yelled a man's voice, and out through a window spun a broken amphora, which landed with a dull clunk on some grass and leaves.

The man, who appeared to be a priest, was tall and skinny with long brown hair. He sprinted out past the travelers as if they were trees grown up near his door. Catching up with the pot, he crushed it with his tattered boot. "Useless. Useless and empty!" He kicked the shards away.

Only then did he realize he was being watched.

"Excuse me … my apologies … *mea culpa* …" He gave a deep bow and flourished his lanky arms. "And for what *honoris* does the humble Anfri owe your esteemed company, kindly souls?" He spied Natalenya. "And may I not forget my lady of benevolence?" The man straightened up, raised his left eyebrow, and bunched up his thin lips. His baggy frock had been woven with silver threads for accents — but the bottom fringe was dirty and stained.

Colvarth cleared his throat. "We are travelers from Kernow looking to purchase five horses, and we are in great hope that you might have so many available."

"Lodgings? You say you need lodgings? I have just the place, a mite dusty perhaps … but soon spiffed up to your lofty expectations. It is in fact … my loft."

Colvarth took hold of the man's sleeve and shook it. "We must ride tonight, and will not be staying."

The man clapped his hands and winked at Colvarth. "Then mayhap some refreshment? My wine is sadly and sorrowfully gone, but I have some succulent … ahh … half-malted ale that your excellencies would find most refreshing." He made a pouty face, closed his eyes, and held out his hand as if to collect some long-expected coins.

Merlin stepped forward. "Horses. We want to buy some horses."

The priest hopped and pointed in the air. "Ah, yes. Just the thing, I mean, just the horse, I mean, just the *equi*. A nice band of … merchants … rode here just two weeks ago. The coats on these horses are most … brilliant, and their hooves are … quite remarkable. Over this way."

The priest stomped off on his gawky legs toward the woods.

The others followed, but Natalenya felt tired and lagged behind. She wished for a place to sit down. A fly buzzed around Arthur, and he began to fuss in her arms. She wrinkled her nose at him and forced a smile between coughs. "I need to get you a snack from Garth's bag, I do. We'll buy the horses first, and then I promise."

She stepped forward, felt dizzy, and fell to her knees in the mossy shadow of a tree. This journey had been too hard on her: not enough sleep, the fear of being chased, and caring for Arthur almost constantly. And now her sickness. Very soon they would have to find a place to *really* rest. Inland, away from questioning ears. She had hoped it would be at this church, but Colvarth wanted to ride through the night. How could she keep going?

Her arm itched, and she scratched it. These buzzing flies! She pushed up her sleeve so she could scratch it better — and froze. There on her arm lay a large boil. About an inch from the boil her skin was normal, but then it paled to near white before rising in a purplish, oozing mound. She wanted to shriek, but instead yanked her sleeve down. It will go away, she told herself … if she could just find a place to rest. But there was no resting until after they bought the horses and rode toward somewhere safe. Raising herself, she hefted Arthur and ran after the others, her breath now a wheeze interrupted by deep coughs.

When she arrived, the priest was showing them a set of eight horses, all grazing the short grass from tethers tied to different trees.

"This fine specimen has great heft about him, and his legs are stout and strong. But pick any of my unsurpassed horses you like — they are all of the same quality and the same price, ten silviquii apiece."

Colvarth cleared his throat. "You call yourself a priest? Why, this is robbery. A good horse costs only three in Londinium."

"Londinium, you say? You are from Londinium?" The priest cracked his knuckles. "Ahh, how I long to see that blessed fortress again. My father was born there. For his sake … and just for you, just for you, mind, I will lower the price to eight silviquii. There are no better horses for that price in these parts."

Garth stepped forward. "If these were the finest horses o' Kembry, they wouldn't be worth half that. But look at these — they're nothing but worn-down, mangy shipwrecks."

The priest bunched his eyebrows together and frowned at Garth.

Natalenya saw the horses now too. She had been so focused on the priest and his antics that she hadn't looked properly at them. The first one — the "fine specimen," as the priest called it — may have had stout legs, but his back was so curved, his rotund belly almost touched his hocks. The second horse limped, and the next was hairless and thin — his ribs looked like they would break if she sat on him.

In fact, Natalenya couldn't find a sound, healthy horse among them.

Merlin inspected one and found its right eye had been gouged out, possibly by a branch. "The only thing unsurpassed about your horses is how much pity they need."

"My horses are the finest for sale in Baegower."

Merlin strode over to the priest and grabbed his frock. "If you weren't a priest, I'd throw you in the manure."

The priest brought his hands together in prayer, his eyebrows beseeching heaven. "Two ... two ... s-s-siliviquii apiece ... any of my horses for two silviquii."

"I'd say that's a good price," someone said off to Natalenya's left. She turned, and saw Caygek leading five horses from a thick stand of pines. "And there's more where these came from." The new horses he had brought were straight-backed with a solid gait. They were strong and their coats flashed in the filtered sunset.

Colvarth stepped forward and quickly inspected them. The old man's shoulders straightened and the brightness returned to his eyes. He took out his money bag and counted out ten silviquii and held them out to the priest.

"But that price was for *these* horses. You cannot possibly—"

Merlin shook the priest by the frock. "You said *any* of your horses for two silviquii. We all heard it."

The priest pulled sideways to get away from Merlin and then stumbled back, nearly tripping over a fallen tree. Regaining his balance, he looked into each of their eyes. When he found no solace even with Natalenya, he said, "But ... but ... those aren't *my* horses, you see—"

"Ahh, that is good," Colvarth said. "No payment is required. Wild horses are for anyone to catch, and we caught them." He opened his money bag and was about to pour the coins back in when the priest jumped forward and grabbed his arm.

"Well ... now that you put it that way, my good friend, I do sort of remember them. Oh yes ... these ones *are* mine after all. How could I be so daft? Dim light and all."

Natalenya hoped Merlin would come and help her mount— but again he ignored her. Garth helped instead, and soon she and Arthur sat on a white mare. At her request he passed up some food from his pack.

After the others mounted, Colvarth threw the ten coins to the ground.

"Thank you, thank you." The priest scrambled to gather them. "Don't take the valley," he yelled after them as the party rode off. "They say it's haunted by *bogeys* ..." This last word echoed through the trees.

They ignored him and found a track that led eastward down the cliff and into a valley where a stream ran toward the sea. After the track turned north to head into the heart of Kembry, Merlin rode his horse next to Caygek's. "How did you know he was hiding better horses?"

Caygek glared at Merlin. "Those that have the sharpest wits get the best trade."

"C'mon, what tipped you off?"

"You really want to know?"

"Sure."

"He was a Christian."

Merlin stared for a moment, then he shook his head and rode forward until he was just behind Colvarth.

Natalenya had been ignored yet again. She let her horse fall to the back of the line, fed Arthur some dried oatcake ... and wept.

CHAPTER 9

RHYMES AND RUINS

Merlin rode with the others as the sun set. At first the track on their side of the stream was almost too slippery for the horses to traverse, the valley being so narrow. But it broadened out, and the footing soon became firm. Dead gorse bushes, dry and brambled, cropped up along the edges of the stream, and the air smelled sour.

Having left the sea behind, Merlin had hoped he'd feel safe. Nevertheless, he had the feeling that faces hid in the shadows of the trees, watching their progress. It felt as if Vortigern and his men were going to ambush them. But that was silly.

Darkness fell quickly as the sides of the valley rose to become tree-studded cliffs that marched past like gloomy sentinels. The gorse thorns faded to black, and the stream continued its dirge down to the sea.

When the sun fell below the cliff tops, a thin fog poured down the valley and encircled the legs of their horses, slowly rising until all the gorge was covered with the dank whiteness. It filled not only Merlin's vision but also his lungs, and he shivered.

Birds flew across the expanse, caw-cackling their disdain upon the travelers. They were magpies, black as night, with the tips of their wings a ghoulish white. Natalenya sang out the old "Rhyme of the Magpie," her voice weak and alone from the back.

> One for sorrow ... Two for bliss ...
> Three is snake's deceptive hiss.
> Four for silver ... Five for gold ...
> Six for secrets never told.
> Seven you live ... Eight you die ...
> Nine dead ghosts of the magpie.

Merlin looked back at Natalenya, and then at where the magpies had landed — a stand of pines that had leeched themselves to the sides of the cliff. How many magpies had flown past? Seven? Or eight? He didn't know.

They continued up the ravine, the fog thickening. The urge came upon Merlin to flee — to get out of the valley as fast as possible. He felt vulnerable, and he wanted to break out onto higher ground where clean air and the open land waited for them. He hailed the group, and then kicked his horse to a gallop.

The others followed, and he led them up the ravine until a large hump of ground arose from the white fog of the valley like the back of a giant boar. Ancient standing stones surrounded the mound, and each one was engraved with the symbols of the druidow: serpents, birds, giant cats, cauldrons, and antlered men. A low doorway had been cut into the side of the mound and the tunnel lined with massive stones to hold back the smothering earth. The right side of the hill lay almost in the stream, but there was room to pass on the left.

Behind Merlin, someone cried out. It was Natalenya. She held out her hand, beckoning someone, anyone. "Please, take Arthur ..." Her eyes were glazed.

Caygek rode up quickly and took the child from her trembling hands. Natalenya tried to climb down from her horse but swooned and fell.

Merlin jumped off his horse and ran to her. He pulled her cloak back, to reveal the pale skin of her face — almost deathly. Her lips quivered as if she were trying to speak, and her breathing was shallow.

"Natalenya!"

He took her delicate hand and patted her cold fingers. He put his hand to her cheek, but she didn't respond. What was wrong with her? "Natalenya … Natalenya …" he called, the love he'd withheld welling up inside him.

Colvarth joined him. "She is bad, yes?"

Merlin lifted her up and carried her to a large standing stone and set her down on some soft grass. "We camp here tonight."

Colvarth shook his head. "We cannot. Not here. This is an evil place."

With all his will, Merlin wanted to agree. He could lay Natalenya over his horse and they could walk out of the valley. But with her sickness getting steadily worse, he knew she needed rest. He had ignored it too long already. "We have no choice. We're staying."

"Next to a burial mound? In all God's creation, I would not choose to camp here."

"God is here too," Merlin said, but he wasn't fully sure if he believed it. "Garth, Caygek, get some wood — we're lighting a fire."

Colvarth sighed. "A fire? You would reveal our presence to all eyes?"

"She needs warmth and hot food."

Colvarth set his bag down, and then his harp. "I don't like it, but I will follow your lead. May God protect us this night."

The tunnel in the mound began to groan, and hundreds of bats poured from its doorway. They flapped all around Merlin, and he covered his head with his arms until they spiraled away into the darkness.

Bedwir had dozed off, unaware how close to shore they'd come until the boat bumped the sand and the men leapt out to pull it up the beach.

The sun had set sometime during his nap, and Bedwir shook his head to chase away the gloom that had filled his dreams. He got to his feet, and his legs felt cold and stiff, but he was glad to slip down to the beach and gather with the other warriors.

Without delay, Vortigern had torches lit from a coal box and began climbing the rock stairs that led to the village. Bedwir and the other men followed to the top, where all was quiet, save a dog barking in the distance. Vortigern went straight to the nearest crennig and banged on the door with the hilt of his blade. When a man cracked open the door, Vortigern slammed it wide and quickly had the man on his knees begging for mercy, the blade near his chest. His family screamed behind him.

"Five travelers and a child? Have you seen them?"

"I . . . I . . . sent them to the priest's house to buy horses — "

The man flinched as Vortigern lowered the torch. "Tell me what they looked like."

"Two men, one with scars on his face. An old man. A boy. A girl holding a child — "

Vortigern smiled. "How long ago?"

"A little . . . little over an hour . . ."

After getting directions to the priest's house, Vortigern led the way.

Bedwir hung back and helped the man up, slipping him a coin for his trouble. By the time he caught up to the others, they were already halfway to the priest's house. When they arrived, the priest was singing inside.

O the jolly-hey, do-diddly-i-merry-o,
With a hey to left, jo-jarry-o-wine-o.
O the jolly-hey, bo-bibbly-by-berry-o,
With a hey to right, go-gibby-o-fine-o.

Vortigern thumped on the priest's door, the singing stopped, and the man poked his head out the window and stood, guffawed at all the torches. His long locks nearly covered his eyes and his skinny lips formed an *O*. His face was flushed, and his nose a bit red. In his right hand he held a small, unstopped amphora, whose red liquor was spilling to the ground.

Vortigern stalked over to the priest. "Do you have any horses for sale?"

The priest's eyes brightened up, and he put his finger to his mouth. "Shah … don't say it too loudly, my lordly lodgings, winely souls. They might hear the other horses hiding in the pines."

Vortigern directed one of the warriors to slip inside and check the premises while he talked to the priest. "How many horses do you have for sale?"

"Ahh, my Londinium, blest friend of my fortress, juss for your sake, mindy-mind, I will lower the price to eighty silvi-quarts o' wine. Fer the whole lot o' em."

Vortigern grabbed him by the frock and pulled him out the window. Somehow the amphora didn't spill, and the priest took a big swig before he acknowledged Vortigern again.

"Mayhap some regurgitants? My wine is sorrowfully not fer you, but I haf malty ale yer eggs-gallantsy might like." He stuck out his free hand and started shaking the bag of coins hanging from Vortigern's belt.

Vortigern slapped the priest across the face, and he fell to the earth. Once the warrior returned, shaking his head, Vortigern turned back to the priest. "Show us the horses, and no more prattling."

The priest made a long face, closed his eyes, and hiccupped.

"Vortipor! Get your sea-stinking legs over here and help him stand."

Vortipor stepped through the crowd, stood the priest up, and slung the man's arm over his own shoulder.

But the priest could hardly stand, so Bedwir shifted his spear to his other hand, stepped up, and took his other arm.

"That's-a-way ..." The priest pointed toward the woods, and then reached around Bedwir's head and grabbed his nose. The priest's fingernails were dirty, and his breath stunk of sour wine.

They made their way down a narrow path until they arrived at a clearing where eight horses chewed the grass. Vortigern took his torch around and inspected them.

The priest let go and tried to walk, but after a few wobbly steps he grabbed Bedwir's hair and hung on. "Thith fine speck-ilady haf great hefty legs which're never strong. But pick any horse's nose you like — they're all filled with the same quality stuff."

Coming back to the priest, Vortigern snorted, and then yelled, "You call these *horses*, you donkey of a priest?"

Mercifully, the priest let go of Bedwir's hair — but then grabbed his spear and hung on. "Wellky ... nowen you push the tail switch-way, my goofing friend, I do sorta resemble them. Yes ... those horsies over in'a the pines *are* mine too, after all. I'm so drafty."

"Ehh?" Vortigern said just as a faint neighing sound floated from the trees to the left. Two warriors were sent to investigate, and came back with six horses, all fine and high-stepping. Vortigern portioned them out, taking a large black mare for himself.

Vortipor left to mount his horse, and Bedwir was stuck with the priest hanging on and hugging him. The other warriors quickly jostled for the sad-looking mounts, no one wanting to foot it after Vortigern.

"Which way did they go?" Vortigern asked the priest.

The priest looked up at him, a bit slack-jawed. "Bogeys be in the valley. Don'th go there, I sez, but they did. They followed the stream, that-a-way. Now pay eighty silvi-keys fer me horsies." He held his hands out and made a long face with one eye closed.

Vortigern clouted the priest on the head with the pommel of his blade, and the priest collapsed.

Bedwir had to drop his spear and grab him to stop the fall.

Vortigern rode off with the mounted warriors, and the others ran off on foot carrying the torches.

Bedwir was left alone holding the unconscious priest. The forest was dim, but enough moonlight slipped through the canopy that he could see one old nag of a horse no one had wanted. The horse's spine was so curved that her belly lay halfway to the ground. The horse pulled up some grass, lifted her head, and studied him.

Bedwir looked down the trail to where the warriors had gone. He looked at the horse. Setting the priest down in a nice patch of moss, he dropped a coin into his hand. Retrieving his spear, he untied the horse's rein and pulled himself up. If she could go faster than he could run — that was all he cared about.

He whacked the horse, and away she went, a little unsteady, maybe, but faster than he expected. So what if his feet almost touched the ground? Who cared if he looked silly? Out past the priest's house and down into a shaded valley where a stream gurgled in the darkness, he followed the others. Soon he was passing the stragglers, who jeered at him. The main host was next, and he ignored their hoots and heckling. He left them all behind — but was still far to the rear of Vortigern and the other mounted warriors.

Alone, he followed the stream northward with the moon at his back. One time his horse strayed too near the bank and his right thigh was gouged deeply on a gorse bush. He cursed, and, after directing the horse closer to the cliff, he held his ripped breeches against the wound to stem the blood.

Fog was everywhere now, and Bedwir wished he sat higher on his horse.

Somewhere nearby, an owl's chortling call bounded throughout the gorge, echoing into twenty owls, which all seemed ready to dig their claws into his back. Why hadn't he grabbed a torch from one of the others? His heart beat faster, and he hefted his spear to feel its balance.

His horse neighed in terror, and then reared up — if you could call it that.

Bedwir hung on to the reins. The horse, after righting itself, ran off at a gallop down the valley. Ahead, he saw the dark forms of Vortigern and his mounted warriors standing still as statues behind a large rock.

Bedwir reined his horse to a stop at the far end. Down the ravine, a campfire sputtered ghostlike through the fog. It was lit next to a humped, grassy mound surrounded by standing stones. And in the far distance beyond that one lone fire, Bedwir saw ten fires burning in a line across the valley from cliff to cliff — blocking their way north.

Vortigern spat. "What devilry is this?"

Ganieda moaned herself awake, fluttered her eyes open, and found she was in complete darkness. One moment she had been in Grandpa's tent, dunking the orb in a water bucket ... and then what?

She remembered. The steam had poured forth from the sizzling orb.

It had filled the tent, and its smell had made her dizzy, like her head was a feather floating up and blown by the wind. She had fallen asleep, and now she was here. But where was here? She sat on her knees, with her hands pressed on a cold and rocky floor. The air felt chill and damp — not like Grandpa's tent. Had he moved his tent onto a granite slab while she slept, and it was now a moonless night? She crawled forward, her knees pressing into sharp gravel, and the palms of her hands scraping the rough stone. She reached ... ... reached ... to find anything to give her a clue as to where she was.

She found something at last. It was long with rounded edges, like the slim hilt of a dagger, but rough and dry. She pulled at it, and it cracked loose. She felt it now with both hands and could tell it wasn't the handle of a blade. She reached forward with her free hand and felt something else ... round like a ball. She probed further, her mind trying to remember when she had last seen an object shaped thus. Holes ... rough edges ... round bumps that were ... teeth.

Teeth? It was a human skull. And that meant her other hand held a ... a bone. Her lips contorted for a scream, but she held it in and flung the bones away. She wiped her hands on her shift, sat back, and cried. Where was Grandpa?

"He is not here ..." came a voice.

It echoed around her.

"But I am ..." it said.

Ganieda pulled her feet under her skirt and felt for her bag. Her fingers wrapped around the fang. "Who're you?"

"What you possess cannot protect you from me, for they are my gift to you — "

In that instant, a face appeared in the air, and a man stepped forth. He held no torch, but his dark robe shimmered a pale blue like the most beautiful sky she'd ever seen. His face was handsome, and somehow it reminded her of her father's, with the cheeks angled just so, the nose shaped thus, and with a brown and curly beard. But his eyes. Covered by heavy eyebrows, they were dark, and she couldn't see their color. She looked and looked, but only a shadow lay there, so deep that she felt she could tumble in and be lost.

He smiled. "Beautiful one, do not be afraid. I have a quest for you ... and I will send you forth from here to do my bidding."

She wanted to run both to him and away from him at the same time, and this perplexed her. "What do you want?" she said, combing her hair with her hands.

He studied her and considered a moment. "I want you: your service and your heart. Your soul and your love ... only for me, pretty one."

"Why?"

"Because."

"Why?" She stood now and glared at him, still hoping to catch a glimpse of the color of his eyes.

"I will give you many things. Love in your lack. Comfort in your suffering. Power in your anger. Beauty in your flesh. All things that the world can give ... and yet more."

"Give me back my mammu …"

He paused and studied her tears. "Take forth your orb. Do not be confused, dear child — yes, you tried to douse it in the water, but I have put it back for you."

She opened her bag, looked inside, and found he told the truth. She held the orb forth, the man said a strange word, and it came to roaring, glowing life, pulsing in her palm. There, within the orb, she saw her mother. Mammu lay sleeping by the spring where she'd died, only her flesh was hale. Her lips smiled and her raven hair had the glorious luster of life. Her dress was new and pretty.

"You see, my very own child, that your mother is there, and you may see her. Only bind yourself to me and it will always be so."

Ganieda's heart beat faster. "May I go to her?" Above all things she wanted to lay there with her beautiful mother. To be hugged and loved. To play and dance among the flowers that grew by her side. To sing with her again. To —

"Only at the end of many delightful years of service will I grant this to you. At that time, if you have been faithful, you will receive your mother's reward — and be with her forever."

Ganieda peeled her gaze from the orb and looked at the strange man, hope nearly bursting her pattering heart. "Tell me … tell me what to do."

"Nothing but what you already want to do. You must be my and your grandfather's messenger this night."

"What message shall I carry?"

"Only this: go to Ealtain and Scafta, the leaders of my Pictish warriors. I have led them to this valley. You must tell them to destroy our sworn enemies."

CHAPTER 10

SNARES AND SECRETS

In disbelief Merlin looked at the line of campfires in the distance. It had not been more than an hour since they had made their own fire and set up camp near the burial mound when Garth came rushing to them from his lookout.

"Someone's lightin' a fire. Down the valley!" He was breathless and his cheeks were flushed. And then he marched over and stirred the pot of soup Colvarth had made. "Is the bracken broth ready?"

Merlin grabbed Garth's arm and pulled him away. "What do you mean there's a fire?"

Garth pointed, and then he, Merlin, and Caygek set off to see what was happening. By the time they stepped beyond the edge of the mound, there were five burning. Soon it doubled. The light from the flames cast an eerie glow through the fog, and the shadows of many men walked among them.

Garth tugged Merlin's sleeve. "Who are they?"

"We've got to get out of here."

"Back to the sea?" The last word was spoken a little too happily.

"No. Just out of the valley."

Back at the camp, Merlin hastily explained to Colvarth what they'd seen. The old man's eyes went wide and he almost jumped up, but instead held his place by the fire so as not to disturb Arthur, who lay asleep in his arms.

Merlin threw their bags back onto their horses.

Garth started kicking dirt on the fire, but Merlin stopped him. "Leave it. If we keep it burning, it'll hide our departure." Garth nodded, and threw an armful of cut gorse branches onto the fire, which crackled to life.

The horses were ready, and Merlin was just about to pick up Natalenya when Colvarth stood, astonishment on his face. Arthur awoke and looked around, blinking his eyes.

"Look, my Merlin. We are trapped!"

He wasn't pointing north toward the ten fires — where Merlin expected — but south. Just a moment before there had been an open, fog-cloaked path of escape for them, but now about three hundred feet away a lone fire had been lit. A torch was taken from it to another, and that fire sprang to life. Within a short while there were fifteen fires to the south, and the way out of the ravine was completely blocked in both directions.

Colvarth's hands shook as he held Arthur close. "Oh, God," he prayed. "Let us know where safety lies."

Little Arthur reached out and pointed to the fires, his small eyes squinting. Merlin himself was in shock. There was a force of men at both ends of the valley.

Caygek joined them and drew his blade.

Garth was practically hopping.

The sides of the valley were steep, and their dark edge jabbed upward against the night sky. Merlin took the bags down again from the horses and handed his to Garth. Kneeling, he picked up Natalenya, her arms limp over his shoulders. Her face was still pale, but the fire had given her some warmth. She weighed enough that the task ahead wouldn't be easy. And what of Colvarth? "We'll climb. We have to try."

"The horses?" Garth asked.

"Leave them picketed."

After gathering most of their belongings, Merlin led them westward to the nearest cliff, only a stone's throw from their fire. The sheer limestone crumbled off in Merlin's hand. "There has to be a path up," he said, and searched northward.

Pines and oaks grew on the sides, and using their branches Merlin could scale up a few feet, but it was too dangerous with Natalenya and he had to drop back down.

He continued along the bottom of the cliff, searching for a path up, a ledge, anything, but it was all the same. After the search proved fruitless, he rushed them across the stream, avoiding the gorse bushes, and sought a way up the opposite cliff.

But there was no way up. "We only have one choice," he said finally. "We can't get out of the valley, and there is only one place we can defend."

Garth looked at him, his eyes reflecting the white of the fog. "Where?"

"The mound. With an entrance that narrow, only two men could squeeze through at a time, giving us a chance. It's even possible they won't dare search for us inside."

Colvarth started to stutter. "B-but, you propose entering the pagan burial mound?"

Merlin answered by carrying Natalenya back to the stream and crossing back. The fog swirled around him as he forced his way through the grumbling water.

"I will not do it." Colvarth ran after, grabbed him by his cloak, and pulled him around. "A grave should not be disturbed, much less the graves of the ancient pagans who have been buried in the name of their gods. Once I spoke in praise of these gods — but I will not seek protection from them."

Merlin pulled away and slogged up the opposite bank. "Then stay outside and tell Vortigern where to find us."

"You think it is Vortigern? Hah!"

"Who else would it be?"

"But ... but he could not have followed us." With one hand Colvarth wrung out his cloak, which had slunk into the water in his rush.

Merlin turned and looked him eye to eye. "Stranger things have happened in the last week. If it's not Vortigern, maybe we'll wish it was."

Their horses nickered as Merlin approached. He drew his dagger, cut their reins, and sent them off into the pallid gloom. If they planned to hide in the mound, they needed to make it look like they had left. He took a torch from one of the packs, lit it using the fire, and gave it to Garth. He then kicked the moist dirt over their campfire.

Merlin finally approached the burial mound, its distended belly pressing down and threatening to strangle the throat of the low stone doorway.

A muffled scream echoed from inside.

Quickly, he closed his eyes and turned his right ear toward the sound to verify that it had come from the mound. His hearing, once his sharpest sense, had dulled somewhat since his eyesight had been restored, and he didn't know if he could trust it anymore.

The scream warped around the standing stones and faded away.

Merlin looked at the dark maw of the mound. Had the sound come from there? Surely not. There was nothing in there but the bones of the dead. They had worshiped pagan gods, yes, but the one true God still reigned.

Even in a place like that?

Was he making the right decision? The others gathered behind him, Colvarth's cheeks puffing in and out under his wrinkled brow. A cloud covered the frown of the moon, and the valley grew dark.

Caygek strode forward, ducked, and entered the mound. "Ah,

the bravery of Christians," he said, his mocking voice echoing from the darkness.

Galloping horses could be heard approaching from the south. It was now or never. Merlin followed reluctantly, and he had to crawl on his knees to get through the small doorway without hurting Natalenya. She moaned and shifted her head on his shoulder. The air was cold and smelled of dead worms, lifeless mushrooms, and bat droppings.

Thankfully, Garth was right at his heels carrying the torch. The stacked limestone walls lit up, revealing to Merlin's left a grotesque, ancient painting of wolves that stood on two legs. They were clawed with needle-like teeth protruding from curling lips. Severed limbs of warriors lay hacked at their feet. One of their victims had red ochre scratched across his face.

Merlin's own facial scars suddenly hurt as flashes of memory came back to him: The wolves circling around Ganieda. He had run to her, kicking and yelling. The wolves backed away. But a dark one pounced, ripping into his arm. He was pinned to the ground, and then the long, broken nails of the wolves scratched him. Their teeth ripped his flesh — until his father had finally come and scattered the pack. Merlin's eyesight had been ruined, and his face scarred.

And Ganieda had never been touched. Had the wolves been her friends even at that young age? Was *she* somehow responsible?

He shook his head and tried not to think about his sister. He focused on the rocky floor before him, and the roof of the tunnel finally raised high and broad enough for him to stand.

Behind him, Colvarth rushed inside. "Quick, farther back … before they see the torch!" He held wide his black cloak to block the light.

They ran — and after about twenty feet farther, a four-way intersection appeared with sloped tunnels. Caygek beckoned them to the right. They turned, and soon the tunnel ended in an arched chamber: a tomb, low and foul smelling.

Colvarth gathered them into a circle — Caygek a pace away — and prayed:

O Father with thy mighty shield — protect us now.
O Spirit with thy brilliant wings — gather us now.
O Jesu with thy zealous whip — guard us now.
To the Threeness — we call in hope.
To the Threeness — we turn for help.
To the Threeness — we send our prayer.
May thy strongest wood protect us.
May thy sharpest iron fight for us.
May thy vast, strong hands conceal us.
O God of the night — see for us.
O God of the day — forgive us.
O God of the dusk — rescue us.

Merlin breathed deeply of Colvarth's prayer, but the air was still unclean, and the torch smoked. He suddenly felt weak. Natalenya had grown heavy, and he fell to his knees and set her down. It was then Merlin noticed that Garth had brought the pot of soup along. The boy sat down and poured some of the bracken broth into his bowl and began sipping it with his eyes closed.

"How can you be thinking of soup right now?" Merlin asked.

"No sense leaving it behind. Smell it." Garth held out his bowl until it lay just under Merlin's nose.

The salty smell of the broth surprised him in its richness and notes of garlic, leeks, and fiddle head ferns. And this dredged up memories of the simple things of life: the winter nights with his family sitting around their hearth sharing bread and stew, the days with his father chopping wood for their fire, chatting with villagers as they waited for something to be forged.

He reached for his pack to find his bowl. He wanted to get it out and fill it with hot soup from the pot and remember these things. But then he spied above his pack — painted in red ochre on the tunnel wall — a dragon. His hand fumbled at his bag, and he forgot the bowl. Forgot the soup. The beast's mouth spewed forth noxious breath, and its claws held a dark stone. *A stone?*

Merlin's head filled with memories of the last time he'd seen the Stone. It had been in the smithy, and the blade — the blade he and Uther had shared — jutted from its craggy surface where he'd hammered it in. He last glimpsed the accursed rock while pulling his father out, with the flames devouring the roof of the smithy. Merlin's simple things would never come back; they had all turned to ashes. All that remained for him was the face of his father. He had known it while young and had never imagined that one day his own vision would be gone. After that, he knew his father's face only in shadow and by the touch of his hands. Then, as Merlin grew older, and their relationship became more distant, not even that connection remained.

After God had restored Merlin's vision, he had only moments with his dying father — and the image of that man's face now burned in Merlin's mind. The dark beard that hid the strong jaw. The slightly curved-up nose. His bushy eyebrows. The burn across his right cheek. The eyes that had seen too much sorrow. The eyes that had seen his own love — Merlin's mother — drown, or so it he had thought.

Natalenya stirred a little, and in her sleep spoke some words inaudibly. Merlin felt her forehead and was distressed that the warmth imparted by the fire had faded so quickly. The clamminess of the tunnel was creeping into her flesh, and Merlin knew they shouldn't stay long.

Caygek glopped down his share of the soup, braided his long blond hair, and then hefted his sword again. "I'm going for a look out."

A deep tiredness in Merlin's bones kept him rooted to the floor, his hand on Natalenya's forehead. He knew he should follow, but he wanted to sleep and forget about their danger.

"Are you coming?" Caygek asked. "It will take two to guard the door. Or should Garth take your place? I've been training him, you know."

Merlin forced himself up and drew his own blade. "I'm ready."

They walked back to the junction of tunnels, and just as they were turning left into the passage that opened to the valley, voices came from the other direction — from deeper in the mound. The sound echoed from the dark — from farther in.

The blood in Merlin's face drained, his spine tingled, and his feet felt suddenly numb.

Caygek halted, and they both looked at each other in the distant torchlight.

Merlin motioned toward the entrance. "You guard the door ... I-I'll investigate ... farther in."

Caygek's brow was knotted. "We should go ... together."

"Someone has to guard the door. It was my choice to enter the mound — I'll handle it." The truth was that he didn't want to go alone, but the danger of leaving the tunnel entrance unguarded was too great. He wished, above anything else, to get the others and run like a rabbit from a badger's nest. But with Vortigern possibly outside, there was nowhere to go.

Nowhere but deeper into the burial mound to make sure they were safe here.

Caygek nodded and slipped off to guard the entrance.

Merlin turned to the utter darkness, blade drawn and heart racing.

Vortigern pointed to the line of fires in the distance and cursed until even Bedwir blushed. "Who in the name of Taranis is that?" was the only repeatable thing he said, and even *that* called on the name of a pagan god.

Vortipor, his horse next to his father, said, "What are we up against?"

Vortigern turned in his saddle. "Fire for fire. Everyone, gather branches and wood. I want fires all across the valley."

Raising his hand, Vortipor backed his mount up. "Father, isn't secrecy best ... considering our goal?"

"We have less warriors than we did in Kernow," Vortigern said, "but we're not weaklings who skulk in the dark. This may be just a trick by Colvarth."

Vortigern lifted his foot and kicked Bedwir in the side, shoving him precariously over.

Bedwir tried to catch himself, but the leather reins had rotted and they tore. He toppled to the ground — not too far down. But then his horse stepped on his right shin, and he yelled in pain.

Vortigern laughed. "Gather wood, you spineless, horse-faced louse."

Bedwir stood, using his spear as a crutch, but his leg throbbed sharply. Between the horse stepping on him and the thorn jabs from earlier, his leg was in bad shape. While most of the warriors chopped branches from the dry gorse, Bedwir headed in the other direction and gathered deadwood from among the roots of the trees. He carried six armfuls back, and they quickly formed up their fires across the valley. One of the men lit the center fire, and from there it was transferred to the others.

Only then did Bedwir get a chance to breathe. He nursed his leg while leaning against his horse and studied the one lone fire in the middle of the valley. What he saw concerned him. There were figures moving around it, a torch was taken away, and then the main fire was snuffed out. Only the flicker of the torch remained, and then it too was swallowed by the death shroud that filled the valley.

Where had they gone? And did that single fire represent those who had taken Arthur hostage? Who were the men that had lit the other fires way down the valley? And what if Arthur was about to be slain? Who would help him?

Bedwir looked to Vortigern.

The man leaned against his horse and adjusted a large golden ring adorning his finger. He then took out a bag of smoked meat and sliced off a long lump and began chewing it. Never once did he even look down the valley. Did the man not care what happened to Arthur? Until now, Vortigern had seemed to pursue Arthur with a zeal unmatched by anyone else in their warband. Why was he waiting now?

Vortipor's thin frame slid over from beyond the nearest bonfire and approached his father. His meager beard was wet with dew, and he looked worried. "How long do we wait?" he asked.

"Till daylight, when we can see what devilry is afoot." Vortigern sliced off more meat and began chewing.

"A scout could answer our questions."

"Nah. I'll not chance it in the dark. If Colvarth has raised some warriors, then we're probably outnumbered. If he hasn't, then Arthur's not going anywhere, now is he? I have waited too long for this moment to lose it in the dark."

Sticking his chin out, Vortipor said, "And what of Natalenya?"

"There is the torc of a king to think about here — and you still want the girl, eh?"

"The kingship isn't my concern. The girl. All I want is the girl."

Bedwir wanted to limp over and grab Vortipor by the tunic and shake him. He wanted to shout, "Arthur *will* wear his father's torc!" But he held back in the shadow behind his horse and watched the two — as bile burned in his throat.

Vortigern shook his head, dewdrops flinging from his long moustache. He glanced around as if to make sure they were alone, and then lowered his voice.

Bedwir strained his ears to snatch the words from the mist.

"Are you the great-grandson of Vitalinus, High King of the Britons?"

Vortipor said nothing, but the firelight glinted off his eyes like daggers.

"Then forget Natalenya. Rebuild with me the feasting hall at Glevum, thrown down by that cursed Aurelianus. In a few hours, we will secure the High Kingship for ourselves."

Vortigern put his arm around his son and walked him away into the darkness, whispering.

Bedwir heard no more. He was about to shout and denounce Vortigern before his fellow warriors, but something gave him pause. How many were secretly loyal to Vortigern? After all, those who crossed the channel had been hand-selected by the battle chief. Perhaps all of them.

Fire in his veins and a spear in his hand, he leapt onto his sorry horse and kicked it into a gallop toward the dark center of the valley. He had to warn those who held Arthur — wherever they were.

A yell went up from the warband as he left them behind. Soon, other horses galloped in chase. He turned to see Vortigern in the lead, along with Vortipor and two others.

Bedwir kicked his horse harder, and she increased her galumphing to a speed that surprised even him. But it wasn't enough. Vortigern was gaining on him — fast.

Bedwir hefted his spear, shook it, and felt the vibration of the heavy tip. He might only get one chance. The mist bent away from his horse's legs as they cut through the valley. The cool, water-laden air flew past his cheeks and soaked into his skin. Droplets formed on his brows and threatened to drip into his eyes. He wiped his forehead and saw the dark mound rise out of the fog, much larger than he had thought it to be. From here, the standing stones looked like the teeth of some giant serpent whose open jaw was swallowing the mound from below.

He galloped past the nearest, and saw nothing but the smoking remains of a fire. Colvarth, Merlin, and Arthur were gone — but where? There was no time to investigate, for Vortigern was riding fast upon him, his sword aloft and a deadly pallor to his face.

Bedwir scamped his horse forward, across the stream and into the open — and stopped in alarm. Down the valley rushed hundreds of men holding torches. Their fierce and feral screams echoed through the gorge, and their short spears jabbed past their shields as they ran. In front of them rode a huge man in a wicker chariot. The blue paint on his body shone in the torchlight, and he bore a spear with feathers flying from the haft behind the bronze point.

They were Picti — Prithager from the north. Bedwir's fingers froze on the reins, and he had to fight his own hands to get his horse wheeled around — only to see Vortigern and his warband riding down on him.

CHAPTER II

THE FATALITY

Ganieda took a deep breath as she stole one last glance at the man, whom she now knew was the Voice. He faded until only the spectral light of his robe remained, and then that too vanished.

Although left in complete darkness, somehow her eyes could see. It was almost as if her own skin, hair, and clothing cast a glow upon the floor before her.

The instructions were simple, and after she obeyed, then she could see her mother again. All Ganieda had to do was walk straight through the tunnel until it opened upon a valley. There she must speak with the two leaders of the Picts and tell them to kill Merlin and all who were with him.

Kill Merlin?

Grandfather wanted that.

But Ganieda had decided *not to* and had defied her grandfather. Why had she changed her mind again so quickly? The words of the Voice echoed through her remembrance.

"Why me?" she had asked.

"Because you are destined for greatness," he had said, kneeling down and holding her hands. "I have chosen you until my two other servants are free."

She had looked at him, cocking an eyebrow. There was a scar on his forehead, almost hidden by his hood. Its meandering, furrowed line ran into his hair — as if his skull had been savagely broken once, but now it was healed.

"You must bring the Pax Druida back to my land. The time of the Romans is over, and they served me well ... for a time. But now I am doing a new work, and many enemies stand in my way. You must help me drive out the Christians — who stain my soil with their diseased feet and invade my people's minds with their jaundiced teachings."

"Who are you?" Ganieda had asked, afraid that the man's long fingernails would dig into her flesh if he didn't like the question.

"I?" And then he had laughed as if she'd probed some place of hidden delight. The sound echoed through him like he was a hollow tree struck by lightning, old and rotten.

"That is a secret," he had said, "a mystery that you will one day unravel. But know this — that I have been the very Lord of the Britons for time beyond your ability to count, *and I will allow no other to take my place.*"

Once again the Voice had shown her the image of her mother sleeping peacefully. Only now she lay under a tree bearing strange, elongated red fruits. Ganieda longed to eat of the fruits and sleep in her mother's embrace. She was so beautiful that Ganieda could almost smell her dark tresses. Safety. Love. Abundance. All these Ganieda wanted, but they were just out of reach.

She shook her head, and the remembrance fled. The dark tunnel lay before her, and she took a step, determined to have her mother back even if it meant Merlin's death.

Merlin took a few steps and then stopped, hearing the echo of his own boots on the rock-scrabbled floor. Ahead of him, the bowels of the tomb sucked away all light, and though he wished for their only torch, he would not leave Colvarth and the others in darkness. Besides, the blindness was not unfamiliar. He turned his head to the side and listened, trying to discern what — or who — lay ahead. At first there was only silence, but then he heard something move. A footstep perhaps.

He sniffed the air, and the faint stink of some sort of animal — perhaps a wolf — made the back of his throat crawl. Walking forward again, he waved his blade back and forth to ward off any hidden menace. Something echoed ahead of him, and he stopped to listen. Almost like someone had caught their breath.

And then he saw her. The form of a woman with glowing skin floated from the shadows. Her black clothing drooped from her figure in great swathes, and it too burned with a pale light. Her face reminded him of Môndargana, his stepmother, yet it was not her. Attractive, like Mônda, sure — yet dread filled him when he beheld her. Merlin's strength drained from his body. He fought to raise his blade to strike the witch, but his arm lay fast at his side.

She saw him, and her eyes lit with a smoldering fire. The corners of her lips turned upward in a snarl, and she let out a scream that pierced the air.

Merlin's heart stopped beating for a moment, and his chest tightened as if a pair of massive blacksmith tongs squeezed him. He tried to speak, but couldn't. His legs felt weak, and he fell to his knees, all the while staring at her face as she said his name. His name. She knew it.

"Merlin ..."

But when she said it, her figure shrunk for an instant, and then grew again to her former size. And that brief glimpse was all Merlin needed, for he knew her now. Her distinctive scream. The face. His name. She was Ganieda, his young sister, grown to maturity by some evil art.

She couldn't be ...

Merlin had asked Troslam and Safrowana, a couple in his village, to care for his sister back in Bosventor. Troslam, with his golden beard and ready smile, had promised him he would seek Ganieda out and bring her into his home. Had he failed? How could Gana be here in Kembry? And why did she scare him like ... a witch?

He shook his head, mumbling, "No-o-o-o." But he saw that it was true.

She raised her hand to strike him, and her fingers held a long, radiant spike — curved and sharp.

He tried to shield the blow with his sword, but his hand would not obey him. His blade clattered to the ground.

Her blow fell, scratching him across his right cheek and nose. Green lightning, like flames in a copper furnace, jumped from her hand and jabbed deep into him. He yelled, but there was no sound.

She twirled around him, brandishing her white dagger and flinging scornful laughs from her lips.

Blood began to drip down his face and nose, and he finally took a breath. Gathering all his strength, he covered his eyes to protect them from her next blow.

It fell quickly, slicing across his left cheek and hand.

Hatred and anger boiled up in Merlin. This time it was neither wild wolves scratching him — or even *her* wolves. It was Ganieda herself.

His hands accidentally smeared the blood up into his eyes. Redness, shadow, and the dizzying, ghostlike form of Ganieda filled his gaze. He fell to the stone floor and everything went dark.

Merlin felt himself falling, falling, spinning, and tumbling through the air as the lights of countless stars rushed past. It was cold, and he knew nothing more until he found himself standing upon a wide, bouldered plain surrounded by hills, and beyond them, mountains. A wind arose and then died after touching tufts of grass that had dared to lift their brown, stunted heads from the sand. No bird could be seen, or any other animal, and a profound silence filled the land.

He stood, sensing something wrong, some doom approaching.

The ground shook, and he heard cracking behind him.

Merlin turned to see a roof and thick timbers breaking up through the soil. Sand slid down the roof as they thrust up to a neck-bending height of sixty feet. The ground fractured, and black walls shoved up and clacked onto the timbers. Massive stones skittered across the ground and formed an arch just as the planks of a huge door rattled from the soil and latched into place.

The clouds overhead rumbled, and Merlin shivered. From the distance came the sound of marching feet, and then a voice, strong and deep:

Rash, ram — crash and slam;
Ache, axe — break your backs;
Slack, slink — clack and clink;
I am Taranis.

A man rode a steed over a low hill, and he led warriors in the thousands. His arms were like oaks, and he held in his hands a large bronze pot and stone hammer. His skin was golden, and his plated armor gray. The horned helm upon his head that hid his face had been fashioned of a darker metal.

The horse below him had a coat the color of ashes, with a black mane. Smoke rolled from its nostrils, and its furred hooves sent sparks into the patchy grass, lighting it on fire.

The man hammered upon the pot, and lightning burst from its surface — skyward in a great arc. Thunder, in turn, beat upon the earth like a drum. The army marched closer, and the man called out again:

Bake, blast — snake and asp;
Thick, thunk — split your trunk;
Snip, snap — trip and trap;
I am Taranis.

Merlin hid behind a boulder as Taranis rode closer. The hammer smashed again upon the pot and lightning struck out once more, riving the ground and sending the clouds into a roiling tumult. Now only twenty paces away, Merlin shrank in terror, for Taranis was five times taller than any man he had ever seen. The horse he rode was truly a monster, with swelling muscles, pulsing veins, and teeth that could pluck Merlin's head as if he were some weed.

Gnash, gnaw — croak and caw;
Bleed, blood — spill a flood;
Nick, neck — pare and peck;
I am Taranis.

When he dismounted, his metal-shod boots sent cracks through the rocks. He set down the pot and hammer and pulled a large axe from his belt. The house that had risen from the sand shook as he walked toward it, and he unlatched the wooden door. With the groan of timber cracking, the portal swung inward and Taranis entered.

With the man's back turned, Merlin prepared to flee, but realized that the army, of shorter stature than Taranis, had begun to surround him. Each of them had spears with long golden blades, and they beat them in time on their gray shields as they marched. Golden nose rings had been driven into their nostrils, and from each ring hung an iron chain down to their belts.

The only escape now lay beyond the house, and Merlin ran, his legs shaky and his breath forced.

But Taranis reached out from the door and snatched Merlin by his tunic and swung him up into the air. "Our business with you isn't finished, little trespasser." He carried Merlin into the house and slammed the door with a booming crash. Merlin was flung onto a high table, and the man leaned over to peer at him through the eye slits of his helm.

Merlin's head spun as he tried to pick himself off of the rough wood. He had just sat up when Taranis reached up to his helm, snapped it into two pieces, and pulled it off.

Merlin backed up, his pulse racing — for Taranis had the face of a bull. The red-tipped horns entered his skull just above the bovine ears, and his luminous eyes burned fiercely.

Taranis laughed through his stunted snout, saliva dripping from his lips. "You must pay me for trespassing on my land!"

Only then did Merlin notice a huge balancing scale standing a few feet behind him. In one wide pan sat a large pile of gold coins, and the other lay filled with the heads of men.

Taranis dumped both pans out and brushed the contents off the table. The heads fell thudding to the floor even as the coins scattered and rolled away.

Merlin felt for his sword and found it missing. He had dropped it when he was with Ganieda, and now he couldn't defend himself. He ran to the edge of the table and looked down, considering his options. But many of Taranis's warriors had now entered the house and surrounded the table.

"You can only get away, little man, after you pay my tax." Taranis banged his meaty fists on the table, and the shock sent Merlin to his knees. "Whom shall it be?" he asked, and he lifted up to the table a cage, and within it stood Merlin's companions. Colvarth, his black cloak torn and his arms covered in welts, held Arthur, who screamed. Garth's face was white, and his lip had been split and bloodied. Caygek's beard had been ripped out.

Natalenya was also there, half hidden behind Caygek. Upon her cheeks lay a black rash, and she glanced at him, looked down in sorrow, and then covered her face.

Taranis clinked into the left pan the largest gold coin Merlin had ever seen. "Which shall you sacrifice to pay me? One *should* be enough to equal the weight of this coin."

Merlin hesitated.

"Or shall it be *your* head?" He hefted his axe, and swung it downward. Merlin jumped to the side just in time, and the notched blade nearly split the tabletop, sending huge splinters flying in his face.

"Which head shall it be, little man?" Taranis said, bringing his noisome snout down to Merlin's face.

"None!" Merlin yelled, and he grabbed one of the splinters and drove it into Taranis's oily nose.

The beast yelped as blood poured onto the table. He swiped at Merlin, who ducked and ran to the cage, trying to free his friends. But he could find no lock or mechanism to open it.

The shadow of a giant hand fell upon Merlin and slapped him away from the cage. Merlin flew back, slamming into the pans of the scale and slumped to the table. His head buzzed, and the world faded and reappeared. He felt the rough wood to assure himself he was still alive, and then slowly climbed to a sitting position.

"I will overlook your insolence, and give you *one* last chance to choose my payment." Taranis picked up from the floor another cage and banged it onto the table.

Merlin blinked at the person standing alone in the new cage.

It was Ganieda.

She stood there, her small hands trembling upon the bars. Her hair was knotted, and tears streamed down her bruised face. "Help me, Merlin," she called. "Don't let him kill me!" She fell sobbing to the floor of the cage.

"Whose head shall be my payment?" Taranis said, holding his axe between Merlin and himself. *"Choose."*

Merlin looked to the faces of his friends, desperate, and pained. He could never choose any of them for death at the hands of Taranis — not even Caygek.

Then Merlin looked at Ganieda. She had tried to kill — nay, *was* trying to kill him. If she were dead, then he might live. Live to carry Arthur to safety. Live to see Natalenya home with her family.

The sad remembrances of his childhood with Ganieda flooded back to him. Memories of her screaming at him for nothing. Of her spitting in his face when he wouldn't obey her. Of her cruelly tripping him in his blindness. In all these things Ganieda imitated Mônda, her mother and Merlin's stepmother.

Mônda, the daughter of Mórganthu, hated God whom Merlin clung to — and she had made it her goal to make her stepson's life miserable whenever his father's back was turned.

Merlin felt his face flush with anger. He wanted to say the words, "Kill her ... kill my sister" — but he couldn't. Despite her cruelty, she had also been like a shadow to him all his life, following him, needing his help, running to him when she was scared. Even needing his protection. Did she not deserve it now? Had she not been deceived by Mônda?

How could Merlin abandon her? How could he even think such a thing? He prayed for forgiveness, even as he prepared for action.

"Enough. What is your answer, little man?"

Another splinter lay nearby, and Merlin jumped and snatched it up, shouting, "None! I won't give you anyone!"

But Taranis only snorted.

Merlin lunged at him, hoping to drive the wooden spike into a chink in the armor at his waist — but Taranis swatted him away.

Merlin rolled across the table, his skin stinging and ripping. He slid to the edge and began to fall, grabbing the lip just in time and hanging on.

The warriors below screamed for his blood.

Using all his strength, he slowly pulled himself up and onto the table.

But it was too late. Taranis had ripped open Ganieda's cage, and she lay on the table underneath his hand, screaming. He raised his axe and looked at Merlin. "Since you will not choose, little man, I have chosen, and she is mine!"

The axe fell.

Merlin collapsed at the sight, every fiber of his being in shock. He beat his fists and wept — wept until his vision failed and the cruelty faded.

Ganieda laughed at Merlin, who lay in the dark like a lifeless eel. She scratched him again, feeling the power of the fang and the weird new strength in her arms. Where had her might and new determination come from? She did not know, but she silently thanked the Voice — who had chosen her.

Merlin seemed to stir. Maybe it was the blood dripping from his scalp, or maybe the kick she had given him in the ribs. Ahh, he was reaching for his blade, the lout. She stepped upon it, hoping it would snap, but it did not. He slipped it from under her foot as she cursed him with all the wicked words that her mother had ever taught her.

He raised the blade and looked at her, a fierceness in his eyes that she had never seen before. She tried to rip him again, but he feebly blocked the blow with his blade.

She spit at him. *She* was the strong one, and he would not stop her. For she was Ganieda no longer, but rather Gana the great. Yes! She would call herself, in the Eirish of her grandfather and mother, *Mór*-gana — High servant of the Voice, True Master of the Stone, the Fang, and the Orb — and Merlin could not prevent her from returning the rule of Britain to the Voice.

But her brother did something altogether odd. He flung his blade away, and with a look she had never seen in her life, he leapt at her, grabbed her wrists, and held them at her side. The two were now face to face, and she strained against him with all her will. Although Merlin's grip was strong from years of work in the blacksmith shop, she was stronger.

Gritting her teeth, she broke one wrist free — and then noticed his eyes. They were weeping. He blinked to clear his vision and said the last thing she expected.

"I love you!"

His voice broke, and he sobbed. Letting go of her other wrist, he hugged her.

An uncanny wind arose in the tunnel, fresh and clean, and it blew upon her, sapping her strength, her power. She slowly shrank and became as she once had been.

Ganieda the little.

She pushed Merlin away, slipped from his grasp, and ran down the dark tunnel. Flying past a startled man who hid at the entrance, she burst into the cold night. From her own eye, a single tear fell.

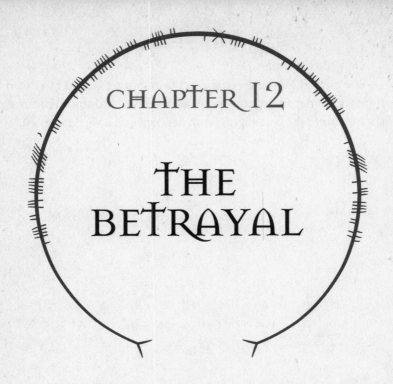

CHAPTER 12

THE BETRAYAL

B edwir would have been slaughtered on the spot if it hadn't been for his horse.

Having been in many battles during his years in Uther's war band, his bravery had won him the slim torc of a chieftain. Yet there he had sat — his legs unwilling to even kick his horse. Normally, flanked by fellow warriors, they'd face the enemy together. Here he was utterly alone, with death on both sides.

Sure, he'd raised his spear and aimed it at the blue-painted war leader bearing down on him, but the slicing screams of the Pict had filled Bedwir with such fright that his wits had flapped off into the night.

And with Vortigern hurtling toward him from the other direction, he'd just frozen up.

Thankfully, his horse had better sense.

It bolted back across the stream to the circle of stones and clambered up the mound until they reached the summit. From that vantage, he turned in his saddle to see the war leader of the Picti slow down, knot his brow, and peer through the fog. It was then Bedwir realized the man had thought *Bedwir* his personal challenger. As if *he* was leader of the High King's armies.

Hah! And when Bedwir's horse turned tail and ran, the brute couldn't make sense of it.

Vortigern, however, realized the dire position he and the few with him found themselves in — and he took his great horn from his belt and blew it. Bedwir had often admired this horn, gilt with ancient runes from the house of Vortigern's grandfather, and even in the darkness Bedwir could see it shining above the battle chief's head. All of Vortigern's remaining warriors rushed down the field as he shouted his battle call.

"*Havoc ... havoc!* To battle, men of valor!"

The Pict now spied Vortigern and charged his chariot directly at him. They met with a crash of weapons — Vortigern's shield shoving the spear to the side, and the Picti leader blocking the carefully timed chop with his torch.

But after they passed each other, the Pict's chariot hit a large stone, and his wheel separated, rolling off into the fog. The man jumped down, bellowing a Pictish curse, and turned to face Vortigern.

Vortigern ignored him. He scanned the field of battle and saw what Bedwir saw — that their men, though far outnumbered, fought bravely. Not only were they taller, stouter, and better armed, but they had more men horsed, bringing strength and speed to their attack. None of their own had gone down yet, though many of the enemy had fallen to the foggy ground, bleeding.

Vortigern finally detected Bedwir perched up on the mound. He shouted at him, snatched up an enemy spear, and spurred his horse upward.

Bedwir turned his mount, intent to dash down the other side — and found six Picti racing up at him, their spiked shields foremost. *Six?* He turned back to Vortigern, leveled his spear, and went whooping down. If he died, then none would ever warn Colvarth of Vortigern's treachery. But what if Vortigern died? Aha! Bedwir smiled as he sped his horse downward.

He had the high ground. *He* had the longer weapon. Vortigern would perish under his bright lance, and then Bedwir would reveal the treachery to all. He would hang Vortipor's headless body on a tree and restore Arthur to safety.

Bedwir the great, they would cheer. Bedwir the faithful!

But then his horse lost its footing. In one step, its right foreleg sunk into the rain-soaked earth of the mound, the beast rolled, and the world flipped. When next he looked, Vortigern's horse had thundered upon him, and the man drove his spear into Bedwir's side. At first, it felt like a hammer had rammed into his thick leather armor, but then the blade ripped through and pushed on his rib. The pain seared every fiber of his body, burning and burning. And yet harder Vortigern drove the spear, until the evil tip sliced through his skin and out of his side — and struck his faithful mount. The horse screamed, bucking and chomping.

Bedwir clamped his eyes shut as pain racked his body.

Merlin's wounds stung. He pulled the stopper from his waterskin and washed the blood from his face as best as he could in the dark. Putting the stopper back, he found his way back down the passageway. As he passed the tunnel where the others hid, he could hear Arthur crying, and Colvarth trying to comfort him. Merlin called to them. "It's just me ... I'm going to Caygek now."

Colvarth's voice spoke from the darkness. "That scream has awoken Natalenya and scared Arthur. Who was it, my Merlin?"

"We'll talk later. We're safe." But Merlin wondered if it was true. With Arthur crying, their hiding place was in danger of being discovered.

Moving down the main tunnel, he found Caygek crouching to the left of the door.

Caygek jerked his blade at him. "Don't scare me," he said.

"What's to be scared about?" Merlin said, feigning ignorance.

The moon lit up the fog outside, and Caygek studied Merlin's face in the half light. "You're bleeding."

"I had a little tussle back there."

"The witch?"

Merlin shook his head. "My sister."

"Your ... *sister?* Here in Kembry? Here in this tomb?"

"She's Mórganthu's granddaughter ... *you* tell me how she got here."

Caygek cursed under his breath. "I wasn't a follower of Mórganthu. I don't pretend to know his arts."

"But you're a druid."

"Not all druidow are alike. I am a *fili*, and a follower of the arch fili until Mórganthu cut him from this world. We opposed Mórganthu and his plans for a human sacrifice. It's been against our laws for the last ten generations of the druidow."

"Tell me," Merlin said, "why do you think human sacrifice is wrong?"

Dew drops hung from Caygek's brow, and he shook them off. "Life is sacred. The soil, the trees, the animals, the gods. The knot-work of nature re-creating itself, and man is part of that in a mysterious way, if you will. One of our brihemow has said:

The Sky and the Blessed Earth bear witness,
The Sun and the Sated Moon bear witness,
The Rocks and the Wildish Wood bear witness,
The Living and the Loyal Dead bear witness!
Without a blade — from foulness we climb,
Without a blade — through water we swim,
Without a blade — to daylight we fly,
Without a blade — no need for sacrifice!
To thee, Fair Esas, I bring my life
From Spring's Beauty unto Summer's Bounty,

131

To give an Elated Servant for thee,
To offer to thee my Unblemished Life!

"Thus we have corrected our old errors. We are always perfecting our truth. You know, *truth against the world*."

"Do you know why Christians say human sacrifice is wrong?"

"I've never thought about it."

"God requires the blood of all who fail to obey his laws. Yet he created us and loves us like children." Merlin paused here and thought about his sister: so frail, so confused, and so ensnared. "So God sacrificed himself for us, so our blood doesn't need to be shed. Not even the blood of animals — "

A clanging of steel from outside caught Merlin's attention, and he and Caygek crept closer to the mouth of the tunnel. Three men with spears stood in the circle of stones, fighting a warrior on horseback. It was Vortigern, swinging like a madman — his strokes fell true, and soon two of them lay dead.

Colvarth's voice echoed from deep within the tunnel, soothing Arthur's cries. The words of scripture floated to Merlin:

Only to thee, my King, have I pledged my fealty. Neither let wicked men strippeth nor mocketh me.

Hear, O Lord, my earnest plea, and in thy righteous anger send out thy bright warriors to rescue me.

Give unto thy seneschal the command to open thy tall gates, O Lord, that I may enter in and find refuge.

Cut off the clutching hand of the wicked, for they graspeth for my blood.

Merlin noticed the third man was huge, with a bare chest and massive arms. His hair was greased back, and he had no beard. Blue whorls had been painted on his torso, and he hefted a long bronze-tipped spear.

"Picts!" Caygek said.

The man crouched, jabbing toward Vortigern to keep him and his horse back.

Nevertheless, Vortigern charged at him.

The Pict backed up and leveled his spear at Vortigern's throat.

Vortigern raised his shield to block it, his horse thundering forward, blade held high.

Colvarth's voice called out again, and now Merlin recognized it as one of the Psalms:

For all my hope, High King of heaven, is in thee.

Yea, even as a babe fresh from thy hidden palm, verily even then my lungs sang forth thy praises.

And though I now pronounce to mine enemies thy judgments and thy splendorous majesty, yet even then thou protectest me.

But soon I will be old, and they will cast nets for my feeble feet.

Vortigern rode down hard upon the Pict and ducked at the last second.

The Pict's spear point missed.

Vortigern swung his blade.

The Pict reversed his spear, blocked the sword, and rammed the butt into Vortigern's side, nearly unhorsing him.

Vortigern howled as he rushed past, then turned and charged again. This time the spear hit square upon his shield, piercing it. He howled in pain, backed up his horse, and chopped at the shaft until the Pict wrenched it out.

The Pict dove closer in with the spear, trying to jam it into Vortigern's face. Four more Picti joined him from behind, all whooping, holding their shields up and brandishing short spears.

Colvarth spoke again, this time quieter, and Merlin barely discerned the words:

For they speaketh lies, and their words pierceth my heart, saying, "God hath forsaken him — thus we shall make him a slave."

O my King! Set thy standard above me and place thy shining blades around me!

Give a pox unto mine enemies, and throw their corpses into a pit!

*But give me hope forevermore, for it lies faint within my breast,
and I cannot see the fullness of thy strength.*

Vortigern grimaced and reared his horse up and to the side,
blocking the spear with his blade. Blood now spattered his ringmail
under his shield arm, and he rode off into the fog blowing his horn.

Caygek shook his head, a smile on his face. "They're *retreating*."

"Only Vortigern," Merlin said, and he looked with dread on the
Pictish war leader who soon gathered hundreds of torch-bearing
men near the edge of the stone circle.

Colvarth's words once more echoed down the tunnel:

*Open my mouth, Lord of the Feast, and place therein fat words,
fare and sumptuous, of thy righteous acts.*

*String my harp, Sovereign King, so that I may sing of thy mighty
deeds to the very ends of the earth.*

His voice trailed off, for Arthur's cries had turned to nothing
but sniffles. Merlin hoped now that their position would remain
unknown — but his optimism was ill founded, for he had momentarily forgotten Ganieda.

She now stepped into the stone circle. Though small of stature,
the light from her dark cloak was menacing, and the fog churned
around her like wolven wraiths. The Picts, astonished at her presence, fell back until only two Picts remained: the war leader who had
battled Vortigern, and one other, with a large knot of hair perched
upon his head.

The war leader threatened Ganieda with his spear. "Thusa
back'ive, she-witch!" he growled. Merlin understood the man's
speech, though barely. The words felt twisted, and they were spoken
with a strange, guttural accent.

The other man, with the pile of hair, took a long stick with bells
and shook it at her, calling out a throaty chant.

Ganieda did not flinch. Instead, she raised her arms. In her left
hand shone a burning ball of purple flame. In the other, the white
dagger with a sickly, greenish glow.

Merlin touched the stinging wound on his nose; the blood had just begun to scab over.

Caygek placed a hand on Merlin's shoulder. "What's she doing? Is she giving us up?"

Merlin sighed. He couldn't believe it either, but it was true.

"Then we have to kill her."

"I've already done what I can," Merlin said. "Run out now, and they'll know for sure that we're here."

"If I had a bow, I'd — "

She raised her voice, and in a language Merlin did not understand she proclaimed something to them. Then she turned, and pointed at the mouth of the tunnel where they hid.

Merlin's heart began to beat wildly.

The Picts roared at her words and looked toward the entrance to the tomb.

But she screamed, and they all shut their mouths. She said something more, and then to emphasize her point, she took her dagger and pretended to slit the throat of the war leader. He snarled and backed up.

And then she disappeared, dissolving downward into the fog.

The Picts, stunned at first, searched the ground where she had been. Satisfied she was gone, they finally turned to face the mound and walked slowly toward Merlin and Caygek's hiding place, the light from their torches floating through the fog.

If Troslam could have complained out loud without giving himself away, he would have. Why had he ever promised Merlin that he'd look after Ganieda? So here he was, holding a spear and hiding behind a thick bush not twenty paces from Mórganthu's tent.

He had been looking for the girl ever since Merlin left, and had almost given up when his wife reproved him for failing to see if she was staying with the old arch druid. To be honest, Troslam had been avoiding the area, not wanting to deal with the druids gathered there. Now, as he approached, he could hear the voice of a young girl arguing with Mórganthu inside the tent.

Troslam ducked down and snuck over to a leafy oak. From there he dove next to a bush much closer to the tent.

Was that movement behind him? Or was it just the wind in the leaves?

He stiffened, sensing something approaching softly — secretly.

Troslam spun, his spear ready.

Something dark and furry leapt at him, baring its teeth and snarling. A wolf!

Troslam's heart vaulted inside his chest and his hands stiffened on his spear.

The wolf's sharp claws were on his arms now, its head turning sideways as it went for his throat.

Troslam twisted the spear upward, tucked his chin, and arched his back to get away.

But the beast's full weight slammed him down as the fangs clamped on to his bearded chin.

Troslam screamed and jabbed the spear at the beast.

The wolf tried to rip below his beard, and then yelped, jerking and writhing in pain.

"Get off!" Troslam yelled, rolling and slamming his elbow into the wolf's head.

The beast fell to the side, snarling.

The tip of the spear had jabbed into the wolf's belly, but not far.

Troslam tried to stab it in deeper as he pulled himself up, but the wolf flipped over, found its feet again, and ran off into the woods, whimpering.

CHAPTER 13

CHILDREN OF THE SALMON

With hundreds of warriors bearing down on their hiding place, Merlin knew this was the end. Imitating Caygek, he put his back to the opposite wall of the tunnel and tried to meld into the shadows. He drew his sword and held it before his eyes one last time. This had been his father's treasure, and now he would die with it. The braided iron of the guard curved outward from two small, yellow gems that shone at the center. The leather-covered hilt felt thick and strong in his hands, and the dim sheen of the blade reflected the fresh cuts that lay across his face.

He took a deep breath, and sent a prayer heavenward — ahead along same the path that his soul would take to the Almighty.

The first of the Picts arrived in the fog outside the tunnel — faces pale as the walking dead under their dark, greased hair. Their bodies likewise, with the blue of the frozen north swirled upon their limbs like wind over a barren plain of hoarfrost.

Their spears were short, else he and Caygek would be easy pickings in the confines of the tunnel. Spurred by the shouts of their leader, two of them advanced through the low doorway. Thankfully, the darkness made them abandon their shields and take up torches to illuminate the room.

Caygek whistled, and he and Merlin leapt out. The warrior on the right stood before them, his dry and cracked lips agape as Merlin swung his blade.

The warrior recovered his sense just in time, and used his torch to block the blow, but sparks flew into the man's eyes as Merlin thrust his blade through the man's chest. The Pict screamed and fell back. Another warrior took his place, stepping on the fallen man's bloody chest.

Merlin was only vaguely aware of Caygek, who was a very whirlwind of braids and blade. He had already dispatched two Picts, and was fighting a third.

The Pict in front of Merlin jabbed his spear at Merlin's throat.

Merlin spun to the right, grabbed the haft with his free hand, and struck the man through the belly. The man's form fell back, howling, toward the entrance of the tunnel, nearly blocking it — until a massive arm reached in, grabbed the man by his hair, and dragged him back out.

The torches hissed amongst the dying, lighting up the stone ceiling. In this waving, crimson glow, the massive leader — who had felled Vortigern — stooped into the tunnel. His long, bronze spear was clutched in his hands, and its tip and feathers were stained with Vortigern's blood. Dark were his eyes, with a lumped forehead. His nose had once been shattered by a sword, for it lay cloven across the bridge, with a deep scar.

He roared like a frenzied bear and rushed at Merlin.

Throwing himself to the rock wall, Merlin used his blade to parry the blow, but the man kept coming and smashed a fist across the Merlin's jaw.

Everything turned white: The stones of the ceiling, the Pict's snarling face, the walls, and Caygek's face, open-mouthed. Even the warrior's dark hair had gone pale, though it was now smeared —

blurry. The tunnel tilted, bent, flew from Merlin, and everything disappeared in the whiteness.

It was fog. And he could touch it, hold it, shape it, breathe it deeply into his lungs, and yet he could not feel anything about it except its heaviness. The fog thinned, slipping from his fingers like sand. Merlin stood upon the shore of a lake. It was night, but no stars burned in the sky. Clouds hung upon the edge of the horizon, and lightning flung from their lofty thrones down to the earth.

Music. A lilting tune flitted through the air. Drums rolled in the deepest glens of the lake. The waters roiled, splashing up. Ten feet from the shore, a hand broke the surface. An arm rose. Shimmering. Sleek and silver. Red hair, finer than fired gold, parted the waves, and the oval face of a woman ascended underneath those beautiful tresses. She floated now upon the water, and a glow of coppered-silver shone from her wrap. Above her collar lay a gilt torc with inlaid stones, white and dazzling.

It was Merlin's mother, Gwevian, smiling at him. "Do not fear," she said.

Merlin's tongue was loosed now, and he spoke. "I'm never afraid in your presence, Mother." He wanted to hold her — to remember and live again his young childhood, now lost in shadow.

"I speak not o' me, or of here, but o' what has befallen ya … and what shall soon take place. Do not fear, but arise and go forth ta where ya are taken."

"What shall I do? Where am I going?"

"The only instruction tha' I have received for ya is this: *Depart.* Go where ya are led, and God Most High will provide and support ya. Once there ya must perform, by faith, the tasks set before ya."

The water boiled again, and his mother began to sink. Tears fell from her eyes as she slid back into the waves.

Merlin ran out into the water, and his boots filled with liquid, cold beyond his imagining. He paused. "No! Don't leave me again." But she was gone.

He rushed forward, deeper, and soon he was swimming. But

the water was cold — so cold. His breaths came quick and fast, and the chill numbed his thoughts of everything but his mother. "Come back," he yelled, flailing at the water that separated them.

From the mist, his mother's voice called out again. "Depart, Merlin ... ya must go ..."

He sank into the freezing water, and his sight failed. There in the murk, music flooded back, the high notes calling him to the waking warmth of the world, and the low notes giving him strength.

It was a harp playing. The music floated above him — now around him — a beautiful melody plucked from heaven that filled his soul. He opened his eyes, and a man in a black cloak stood above, straddling him. Merlin lay on the ground, and the light of many torches filled the room. But it wasn't a room, it was the tunnel, and Colvarth held the Harp of Britain in his hands. A song, deep and rumbling, flowed from his old but tender lips. He sang, and the words were thus:

Over an lhand, from mhount and ghlen
Chame we peiple, across am fhen.
Where is an king, O where is he?
Tha' fhights for you, tha' fhights for me?
Chame we to Tull, to Twilloch-Scwane
To shee his light, our fleish and bain!
To mhake a king, a king to thrain
To shwear our aith, air hill and plain.
Upon am mhound, upon an shtone
Bhled he his blood, our hiearts to own
Crithan-Tuath! Crithanas-Mor!
Mhade we a pact, in diays of yhore.
Member'ive, sons, member'ive, men:
Yiur king, yiur oath, yiur fealty ken!
Take'ive yiur shpears! Take'ive yiur bhows!
And come'ive now, to Duntarv Ros.

During the course of this song, Merlin's senses sharpened, and he became aware of the massive Pictish warrior standing before Colvarth, ready to spear him — right through his harp strings. But the man hesitated. He cocked his head, rolled his lips, and blinked his eyes. Soon, he stepped back, listening, and the other warriors did likewise.

The fighting stopped. Caygek, blood spattered on his arms and breathing heavy, stepped next to Colvarth as the song ended.

The Pictish leader shook his spear at Colvarth. "A bhaird ... who are yiu tha' know an song o' our peiple?"

Merlin pulled himself to a sitting position. His jaw was swollen and his head felt like a melon.

Colvarth continued to pluck his harp slowly — but his right eye blinked as he spoke to the man. "O Child of the Blue Salmon — hear me. I did not know your sovereign of many years ago, yet more than once have I visited Alba, met your people, and learned your songs. I bid you peace in the name of Prith-Tyritha, whom you call Crithan-Tuath."

"Are southeirn doigs, and na friends o' Chrithane! She-witch shaid make yiu thraill, so gut yiu unless agree'ive be thraill." The man sucked a wound on his hand, and the redness smeared his bristle-bound lips.

Merlin did not understand this last demand, but the man's flinty eyes told him he was serious.

Colvarth nodded slowly. "A pardon, Ealtain, Mighty Chieftain of the Prithager, we must all speak together to determine our answer. We will either fight, and no doubt you will gut us, or we will agree — but give us time to for counsel."

"Give I yiu till burnig my torch ris nothing. Then spear or thraillring — you choos'ive." His warriors removed their dead comrades, and then he stepped outside. But before disappearing into the night, he forced the handle of his burning torch into the moist soil. He leaned over, snarled at them, and then left — his heavy footsteps echoing into the night.

"What did he say?" Merlin asked as Colvarth helped him stand.

"He will either kill us, or make us slaves. We must decide before his torch goes out."

Oh, Natalenya! She held the fears of all the world in her dark eyes as Merlin returned, jangled as he was from the blow by the Pictish leader's fist. He longed to go to her, to comfort her and be comforted in their last hour. But he knew he couldn't break his personal oath to distance himself from her. Even now he needed to keep her free from a man as disfigured as himself.

Garth, holding Arthur, asked a lots of questions, and Colvarth explained as best he could.

"We are trapped, but have been granted the strange choice of our escape. Either through choosing to fight, and thus the sure light of heaven, or else the dark path of slavery and thralldom — a captive without hope of being free. In the first, our hopes of granting the High Kingship to young Arthur will fail, but yet we will die belonging to and defending our land — men of freedom, able to hold our heads high at the feasting hall of our Father. And yet in the second, though surely filled with sorrow, even death, there is yet a small hope that our oath of fealty to Britain and the High Kingship shall be fulfilled."

Caygek spoke first. "To me, I will submit to no man, and be no man's slave. My father once was a slave to the Romans building their roads. He escaped, yes, and then fought against them until they killed him. I've heard his tales, and I say we fight."

Garth took hold of the corner of Colvarth's cloak. "I don't want to die. But I don't want to be a slave neither. Less'n they make me fish for 'em, I s'pose. Do the Prithager make soup?"

"Oh yes, but not the kind you'd like to eat."

"What's in it, sir, if'n I can ask?"

"Don't."

"Cabbage? I don't like cabbage much. Me father always said — "

"Shush."

Merlin wanted to speak but didn't know what to say. Being caught and made a slave was something that had haunted his mind from childhood because he had heard too many stories of raiders taking away young men and women. The people simply disappeared, never to be seen again. And Merlin had no hope that this chieftain of the Picts would treat them well. Thus he felt that Caygek was right — they should fight.

But what had his mother said — it seemed only moments before? Her words echoed through his soul: *"Do not fear, but arise and go forth to where you are taken."*

Taken? Did God want them to hold on to hope and trust Him? Merlin felt like he was leaning over an open pit, about to fall into its black and stenching depths — and God wanted him to jump? To become a slave — maybe for the rest of his life? How would that help Arthur? How would that help anyone?

But if they fought the Picts, what then? Two warriors, a boy, and an old man against hundreds? Impossible odds, and they would all be killed. But maybe not ... What of Arthur? Natalenya? No, they would take her, and ... they would probably take Arthur as well. He would grow up as a Pictish warrior, fighting *against* Britain.

If *they* were taken as slaves, then someone would need to protect them, if possible. The only way to do that would be to become a slave himself.

So that was it. *"Depart. Go where you are led,"* his mother'd said. But where was God? Where was *His* protection? Merlin slammed his fist on the stonework, bit his lip, and closed his eyes as tears threatened their way out. Merlin would just have to trust, but it was hard ... so hard.

The debate had gone on without him, but now Colvarth saw him and silenced the others. "Though we all have strong feelings in this matter ... as we must ... I take the right as eldest here to place this grim decision in Merlin's hands. I am old, and whether I depart now or delay my death shortly through toil, it will not matter so much for me. But I trust that Merlin, who loves each one of you" — here he looked to Natalenya — "will make the best decision for all of us."

Caygek snorted at this, and Merlin looked hard at the druid.

Blood had flecked Caygek's cheeks, and he flared his nostrils. They stared at each other, eye to eye, until Merlin finally turned away to look to the torch dug into the ground at the mouth of the tunnel. The bottom had cindered, sputtering down to its last few flames. Their time was almost up.

Taking a deep breath, Merlin's words came out thick, due to his swollen jaw. "Caygek, you are wrong. Fighting ends all hope we have of fulfilling our oath and raising Arthur to be the next High King. *We will not fight them*, but will seek our freedom as soon as we may."

Colvarth slowly nodded — while Garth and Natalenya's eyes glistened in the dark.

Caygek swore. "Son of a fool! I've made no such oath. I will be free or die."

Merlin grabbed the man's tunic and pulled him close. "Then you endanger all of us. You've tagged along this far, and now you will abide by our decision."

Caygek bellowed and clouted the injured side of Merlin's jaw.

The pain shocked him, and he let go of the man's tunic. His vision blurred for a moment, and the next thing he knew, Caygek had drawn his sword and the death tip prodded Merlin's chest. He held his breath.

"Who gave *you* leadership?" Caygek sneered. "Those that are fastest make the decisions, I say."

A loud thump came from behind Caygek, and he dropped to the ground.

Colvarth stood behind him, holding a hefty stone. "No, my difficult druid ... you are wrong. Those that stay awake make the decisions."

Merlin breathed again. "Thank you, Colvarth."

Now for the hardest thing he had ever done in his life — facing the Picts and the long death of slavery, for himself and those he held most dear.

Ganieda awoke in the most creamy warmth she'd ever known. One moment she'd been shivering before the Pictish leaders, and now she was … where? She turned on her side and felt with her hands the fur of an animal skin wrapped around her. The smell of oats baking made her stomach growl … and she opened her eyes.

Grandfather leaned over some bannocks, which lay on a flat rock nigh the embers of their fire, and poked them with his jagged fingernail. The orange light flickered on his forehead, lighting up the inside of his eyes in the near-darkness of the tent.

"Ah, my daughter's daughter — you awake at last. I tried to use the orb while you slept, but could not make it show me what I desired. Thus I despaired of learning what happened to our enemies until morning, yet now I have your attention once again. I hope this time you will be more … *obedient*."

Never taking his eyes off of her, he drew forth the brass sickle blade from his belt with his one good hand and sliced a bannock in half, flicking a crumb into the coals. It flared up for a moment and then died. "There will be consequences if you betray me again."

Ganieda shivered, despite the warmth of the fur blanket.

"Would you like a bannock? The oats are old but still have some life."

"No."

Outside the tent, a yelp was heard, a scream of some animal, and then loud whimpering.

Grandfather caught his breath.

Growling mixed with a whine, and then faded, loping into the distance. It was Tellyk; Ganieda knew it. Something was wrong. She had just stood when the ties to the flap began to rip, the shining steel of a spear point slicing them through. Blood lay on the tip.

Grandfather jumped. The brass blade shook in his hand.

The door of the tent flipped back and a spear pushed through, followed by the huge shadow of a man.

Grandfather backed up. "Who … who are you? What do you want?"

145

The man said nothing, but stepped forward and slammed the butt end of his spear into Grandfather's head.

Ganieda screamed as he crumpled to the ground.

The man turned toward her.

She reached for her bag, tied near her hip. *Her fang.* She would cut him! But the strings ... they were too tight to open quickly.

The man stood over her, his cheeks puffing above his thick, golden beard. She stared at him, wondering if she knew him, but darkness filled the tent as he blocked the light from the hearth. Without a word, he bent down, grabbed her, and picked her up.

The ground fell away. She screamed again and tried to scratch him with her fingernails. But he lifted her farther into the air, swung her upside down, threw her over his shoulder, and then walked off into the coolness of the night.

"Let me go!" she screamed, but he would not.

She tried to reach for her bag — her fang that would slit him — but it lay on the other side of his shoulder near his neck, and his hand lay upon it, holding her waist.

In the distance, the camp of the remaining druidow stirred, and a few of them lit torches and began shouting out her grandfather's name, asking if all was well.

She pounded her captor with flailing fists, even tried pulling his hair, but he all but ignored her as he sprinted down the dim alleys of the deep and ever-shadowed forest.

PART TWO
FOOL'S LOSS

Sharp as talons, the captors cutting;
Black and blacker, the fang death spreading;
Glop as glutton, the eater eating;
Drowse as dreamer, the sleeper sleeping;
Fortress on hill, ware the wicked guise.

CHAPTER 14

TAKEN NORTH

Vortigern swore as he wrapped a cloth rag around his bleeding arm. The spear had cut deep, but he'd been hurt worse before and lived to slice the heads off of his enemies. The problem here was that there were just too many wretched heads.

The mist had thinned, and he spurred his horse forward to get a better view through the large clump of trees. In the distance, the torches of the Picts parted, allowing Vortigern to see the entrance to the burial mound. Some figures stepped forth, holding their hands aloft. Vortigern squinted, but couldn't make out who the fools were in the dark.

"Ehh ... Vortipor, is that them?"

Vortigern's son covered his eyes to block the moonlight. "It's them, sure. One's holding Arthur." And then his voice faltered. "I even ... even see Natalenya."

Vortigern loosed the reins of his horse. "We can leave, then. I couldn't have wished a better end for Arthur. No blood on my hands, and we'll never see him again."

"Leave?"

"We have lots to do. Gorlas is raising men for us, and we have the Saxenow to fight."

Vortipor grabbed the leather brace of his father's good arm. "We can't just leave!"

Like an owl to the kill, and just as silent, Vortigern slipped out a short sword and held it at his son's throat. "There's a new High King to swear fealty to, if you haven't noticed. Choose the girl, and *your* eyes will never see your great-grandfather's torc on my neck. I swear it."

His son hesitated.

Vortigern's anger rose. A squanderer for a son, he was. Always chasing the beauties — and his head so loose it was just *waiting* to fall off. He twisted the blade, but not enough to cut.

His son sucked in his breath and flared his nostrils.

Perhaps there was a better tact, Vortigern mused. He withdrew his sword.

"Imagine old Glevum rebuilt ... and you sitting around the feasting fire in the great hall. You sit upon a pile of skins after a great victory, and a boar, roasted and sweet, lies before you. Its haunch is in your teeth, with the fat dripping down your beard. A thousand warriors raise their bowls of ale and shout your name. 'Vortipor ... Vortipor the Great!' they call. The kingly torc of our family line lies upon *your* neck, bright and shining, and the bards sing your praise."

His son's eyes went glassy. "And I'm married, right?"

Vortigern repressed a snicker. "To anyone you want. They'll all be yours once I'm gone, but I need your help *now*." He pointed toward the Picti. "Over there is only death. Come on." He turned his mount and rode away. The other warriors followed, but Vortigern's son stayed behind.

Curse him. The stupid fool.

But before Vortigern had spurred his horse out of the valley and down toward the sea and their waiting boats, his son rode at his side again. Vortigern smiled. All his long years of patient suffering under

Uther were over. It was time to gather his warriors to Glevum and declare himself the High King.

Just as the torch went out, Merlin led them out of the mound and gave themselves up to the Picts. Of course Caygek had to be trussed with a rope from Garth's pack and pulled out against his will — cursing Merlin all the way.

Ealtain, the chief of the Picts, presided over the slave taking. For his first act he approached Merlin and reached his right hand toward Merlin's bloodied face and scars. His huge fingers stunk of sweat, leather, and the bitter woad they used for war paint. Merlin flinched, and in response the chieftain backhanded him across the face and wrenched the torc from his neck. The falcon beaks on the ends of the torc scratched his skin.

Merlin staggered, fresh blood coursing down from the facial wounds Ganieda had given him. And when the pain eased and he could see again, Ealtain had placed the gold torc upon his own neck, tossing his dirty, old, bronze one to the dirt, where a nearby warrior scooped it up.

Next, Ealtain called out for a broad, dark-haired man to step from the ranks, presenting Merlin and the others to him as if they were a gift.

But someone else pushed his way through, shouting. This man was even taller than Ealtain, though not as thick, and he shoved the dark-haired warrior back with the haft of his spear. His orange-red locks were coiled into sullied braids, and his nose was long. His eyes, unblinking, were dark green, and they dared the dark-haired man to defy him.

Shouting erupted among the warriors, but Ealtain roared until they quieted. Turning to the red-haired intruder, Ealtain snarled, his lip upturned in contempt, and bid the two to fight.

The dark-haired warrior picked up a spear and stepped forward, jabbing.

Red-hair flinched back, knocking the blow aside with his spear.

All the warriors gave them a wide berth. Merlin motioned for their band to back away too, but they only managed a few steps before the spear points of the warriors stopped them.

Red-hair, who had the longer reach, countered with a quick strike to the head of his opponent. The man ducked and struck out with his shaft, thunking red-hair in the ribs. Red-hair answered with a vicious kick to the man's stomach — then, while the man was momentarily stunned, red-hair cracked him across the back of the head.

Dark-hair slumped to the ground, falling across his spear.

Red-hair laid his foot on the man's neck and let out a quavering victory yell, the feathers on his spear vibrating in the midnight breeze.

Behind him, Ealtain charged forward, his teeth bared, and slammed his shoulder into red-hair's side, knocking him flat. Ealtain's own spear now hovered over the man's eyes.

"Keepa an thrails by right-ah — but if thwarta mo again, fight'idh yiu, and then eat-idh yiur liver — like yiur fatheri."

By this, the Pictish chief had given Merlin and the other's as slaves to red-hair, whose name was Necton — but Ealtain was not pleased that his choice had been frustrated. Indeed, he drew a thin, bloody line across Necton's chest, and spit on his face before backing away.

Necton rose, eyes unblinking, watching Ealtain. He wiped the spit from his face with a handful of grass and then approached his new slaves with a grim smile on his lips.

"Ealtain must have killed Necton's father," Colvarth whispered to Merlin. "There's bad blood between those two."

"Could that help us ... or hurt us?"

"We'll see."

Necton stripped them of all their weapons, food, and belongings, even their boots and cloaks. Only their basic clothes remained.

When Necton came to Colvarth, he stole the white-gold torc from his neck and placed it upon his own. Colvarth's torc ends were formed with the heads of moor cats, each with a sparkling white eye, and this pleased Necton.

To Merlin's surprise, Colvarth didn't seem to care about the loss of his torc. "I am old," he told Merlin later, "and cannot take my torc with me to God's kingdom. Such things are understood only when one realizes this island is not our true home."

For Merlin it was harder, though. His own torc had been given to him by Muscarvel, that marsh-dwelling, prophetic madman with a rusty blade. A kingly gift the torc had been too. Merlin had worn it as a sign of God's promise to him of his role in protecting the new High King. To see it on Ealtain's neck was almost insufferable, but Merlin held his tongue.

Merlin also realized how frail Colvarth was. The bulk of his cloak had always hidden his thin frame, but now he stood before them, aged and taking deep breaths from the chill night air.

One thing did grieve the bard though ... for he moaned when Necton stole the tin box containing the strange bowl Merlin could see but Colvarth could not. Thankfully, the Pict just tossed it into a bag and didn't examine its contents.

"We must get it back," Colvarth whispered to Merlin, "for this is a mystery of the Christ and should not fall into other's hands."

Merlin nodded, but this wasn't his present concern: Necton was studying Natalenya. Merlin's throat burned hot, for this was something he hadn't considered properly. He had decided to deliver her to her mother's kin. Even though he was alive — which meant there was a chance he could protect her — how could he *really* prevent Necton from making her his wife? He should have never allowed her to come along. Never.

Thankfully, Necton turned and sorted through the rest of the party's belongings, and these he distributed to the men under him. A difficult time for Merlin was when his father's personal longsword was taken by Necton. All his Pictish warriors marveled over the blade's workmanship and eyed Necton with wonder as he strapped it on.

When Necton unrolled the tapestry of Vitalinus from Colvarth's bag, he dropped it and jumped back. He yelled for the other leader with the bulky hair. "Scafta, come'ive here!"

Scafta ... Merlin worried as he thought about him. Where Ealtain was brutal, Scafta slithered. The man's hair was long, matted into coils, and balled up into a great mound over his head. It was held there by two great combs made from the shoulder blades of a deer. And to protect this mass he had a strangely patterned hood held up by a framework of curved branches. Though his face had been shaven, his eyebrows grew so densely they merged into one long line, and his bony cheeks and thick lips added to the fearsome visage. His boots had a network of metal spikes tied onto them, and he wore a necklace of bones, bags, and scraggly feathers.

In his hand he held a long stick carved with human images. At its base and top hung cleverly crafted bells amidst human hair tacked on by their thin strips of scalp. When Scafta had first seen Merlin, he had pressed this stick in his face and shaken it, whooping a dance of victory. It had smelled foul, and Merlin had turned his nose away, only to invite a beating from the man.

"He is their *shaman* ... their witch doctor," Colvarth said. "The druidow of ages ago were thus, or so is whispered in our rare-spoken lore."

Scafta stepped over at Necton's call and studied the tapestry, his feet tense and ready to jump as if it would strike him. The wind blew, and the tapestry flapped a bit, causing Scafta to grab a spear. With a cry the witch doctor drove the point through the image's chest, and he danced around it shaking his stick, warning all the warriors of its danger.

When this ceremony was done, Scafta threw the tapestry into a nearby fire, and Merlin was glad to see the near likeness of Vortigern go up in flames.

There were exceptions to Necton's theft, however — for apparently the Picts had a love of music. Necton let Colvarth and Merlin keep their harps, since Necton was unable to play them himself.

When Necton pulled the sack with Garth's bagpipe out of the pile, however, Scafta's eyes lit up, and the witch doctor started pawing the leather bag, its drone pieces, and the chanter.

Garth stepped forward, his cheeks red, and he tried grabbing it from them. "Leave that alone, you ... I'll not lose it again!"

Necton, still gripping the bagpipe with one hand, slipped his new blade from his belt and pointed it at Garth.

With the blade threatening him, Garth let go and jumped away. "I mean ... I mean ... you can have it ... if you insist!"

Necton sheathed his blade, and then tried to put the bagpipe together. He dropped some of the drone pieces, however, and couldn't figure it out. With a bark, he motioned for Garth.

Garth, puffing his cheeks in and out, put it together. And when he was finished, Necton yanked it away and tried to play it. When only squeaks came out, he threw it on the ground and lifted his foot to stomp on it.

Rage rose up in Merlin. Would this Pict ruin everything dear to them? Garth prized nothing if not his bagpipe. Before Necton's foot came down, Merlin leapt forward and pushed him back. Necton slammed Merlin in the chest, knocking his breath away and sprawling him in the mud.

That was when Scafta intervened. He pulled from his bag a single, shiny gold piece and offered it to Necton, who shifted his eyes from Garth, to Merlin, and then back to Scafta and his coin, now spinning between the man's fingers like a toy.

"Keep'ive foir song magic," Scafta said, and he stepped on Merlin's fingers, which happened to be resting on a sharp rock.

Merlin wanted to shout but had to suck air instead.

Garth dropped to his knees and begged Necton to let him keep it. "Please, sir ... I'll play it for you, promise!"

Necton pushed Garth away, shook his head until another gold coin joined the first, and then took both, allowing Scafta to scoop up the bagpipe and walk off with it, a wicked glint in the witch doctor's eyes.

Garth wept.

Merlin pulled himself up, cradling his bleeding fingers, and saw warriors had brought a set of slave collars. Every fiber in Merlin's body wanted to resist, but surrounded and weaponless, he had no choice.

Each collar had been made of two pieces of wrought iron, joined at the back by a bent pin. The left side of the collar ended in a small link. The right side ended in a large link and a chain attached just before it. The small link was threaded through the large link, and then the chain was threaded through the small link, securing it. The chain was then slid onto the next slave collar. Thus they were chained together into two groups; Colvarth led the first, followed by Natalenya, and Caygek. The second group was only Garth and Merlin — or so he thought.

Garth, in particular, looked down at his slave collar a long time as if there was something funny about it. Merlin tried to ignore him.

Necton dragged forth another man with long black hair. His face was swollen, bruised, and bloody from a beating, and he lay there, dazed. His eyelids puffed out grotesquely, and he could barely open them.

As Necton ripped off the man's deep green cloak, Merlin spied there a brooch — the golden boar that Uther's warriors all pinned on their cloaks.

He was Vortigern's man.

Necton also stripped him of his shirt of iron scales and put it on himself. The stranger bled from his side — a sword or spear had sliced near his ribs. The blood had dried down his tunic onto his breeches. If the wound was deep, the man would probably be dead within a few days.

And then Merlin recognized him. He was the warrior Merlin had battled on horseback, as well as on the fishing boat. He alone of all Vortigern's warriors had been taken by the Picti.

Necton clapped a thrall ring upon him just ahead of Garth, and the man groaned, trying to pull it off. For this he was beat with a stout club until he collapsed to the ground, his legs jerking. They locked it by bending a thick iron pin with a massive hammer.

A little later the man awoke.

Merlin helped him sit up and asked his name.

"Bed-dwir," the man said, his tongue thick, and then Merlin truly knew him. He wasn't just a warrior, but rather one of the war chieftains underneath Vortigern. Merlin had met him at Uther's war council held in the king's tent. But Merlin had been blind then and hadn't seen his face. Uther had asked for their advice in dealing with the villagers' disloyalty, and Bedwir had recommended holding a dance with music and mead to win over their hearts — clearly the kindest approach given by one of the war chieftains.

So here before Merlin sat a man who's heart brimmed with grace and forgiveness — but also dauntless courage, for Bedwir had been the first to attack Merlin twice. Was he loyal to Arthur ... or Vortigern?

"I'm Merlin. I met you in Uther's tent, and we've fought twice near Dintaga." He half-expected Bedwir to become enraged, but instead he grasped Merlin's hand and squeezed.

"Is ... Arthur safe?" he asked, his head lolling to the side.

Merlin motioned for Garth to hand Arthur to him, and he placed the boy in Bedwir's lap.

Arthur eyed Bedwir silently and folded his small hands, not knowing who the strange man was or why he should be put in his grasp.

Bedwir kissed Arthur's head, and tears streamed from the slits of his eyelids. "He's here ... O blessed God, he's here!"

Colvarth stepped close now, Natalenya and Caygek chained behind him. "Follower of Vortigern, do you know me?"

Bedwir reached out and found the bard's shoulder. "Colvarth, I do know you — at least your voice — and I doubt no longer your loyalty to Arthur."

"We fled from Vortigern and his blade."

"Justly, for this n-night I finally overheard him plotting ... with Vortipor to k-kill Arthur."

Bedwir swooned, and Merlin steadied him. "Are you all right?"

"Vortigern speared me, but I think my ribs saved my life."

"If God has saved you," Colvarth said, "there is a blacker thing than death at hand."

The sun rose, red as blood, and Merlin yanked at the slave collar once again, hoping beyond hope that it would loosen and he could slip it off. But it was not so. Indeed, the thrall rings were heavy, and Merlin's had already begun to chafe his collarbones. He tugged at it again, feeling the iron with his fingertips to find any cracks or flaws in its forging, but there were none. He studied the chain likewise but found no hope of breaking it without tools — and being the son of a blacksmith, he would know.

Necton stepped over and pulled Arthur from Bedwir's hands. Holding up the boy, he studied Arthur for the first time, almost like a trinket he might keep or throw away. Arthur's lips pouted, and the boy was about to cry, his legs wiggling so high above the ground.

Setting Arthur between his feet, Necton pulled off the boy's shirt and then whistled for a warrior to come over. The warrior brought a leather satchel and untied it. Necton knelt down, dipped his fingers in, and smeared greasy woad paint over Arthur's chest.

The warriors around him shouted and shook their spears. "Chrithane! Chrithane! Now ish boiy an Chrithane Mor!"

Merlin cringed. Necton intended to raise Arthur to be a Pict, a warrior of the mountainous north — and unless Merlin could free them somehow, Arthur would fight *against* his own people.

And even though the boy was given back to Garth to be cared for, Merlin worried how long that would last.

Merlin saw among the Picts the same horses they had set free in the dark. These were prized because they helped the warriors carry home more plunder, and Scafta-big-hair took the honor of doling them out to certain warriors that pleased him. Necton didn't get one, but he traded with one of the lucky warriors for it. Caygek's sword was part of the bargain.

A moan escaped Caygek's lips as his blade disappeared into the mass of warriors.

During this time, Ealtain reattached a wheel to his chariot with a hammer.

They marched when the sun rose above a distant hill, and their pace was brutal. Merlin was grateful for his position at the back of the line because it allowed him to see the needs of those in front — and pray for them.

Natalenya — she could barely handle the walk and stumbled often. Merlin longed to help her but was glad when Colvarth allowed her to lean upon his shoulder.

For Bedwir, the man had trouble keeping up at first, but rallied to prevent Necton's spear from jabbing another slit in his side.

Garth, the saint that he was, carried Arthur most of the time and tried to keep him happy. Between all of Garth's funny faces and his alternating sad and cheerful demeanor, the two had clearly bonded.

"Arth, you're better'n a bagpipe, that's for sure," Merlin overheard him say. "But it'd sure be nice to have both. I'd teach you to be a piper like me father, that's what I'd do."

For the most part, the Picts ignored them, but now and then Merlin, at the back, would get rammed by Scafta with his witch doctor stick. He would lean over his chariot, leering, and say foul things, spittle slipping from his dirty teeth.

From the position of the sun, it appeared they were heading northeast, and Merlin pled with God that a band of warriors from Kembry would accost the Picts and set he and his friends free. During the warmest part of the day they rested and drank in a deep forest. Necton ate fish and smoked meat but only offered his slaves dried bread.

Before they left again, Ealtain came up. "Joined us yiu an right time. Now go back'idh north we are to homes — and begin we an thrail taking."

"This is a common practice," Colvarth explained to them later. "Raiders sweep down from the north, pillaging as they go, but don't take any slaves until they turn back toward home."

They marched for five more hours that day, and it was mercifully cut short well before dusk. All of them had held up well except Natalenya, for by the end she had to be helped by both Colvarth and Caygek. Merlin ached to help her, but Necton's spear kept him bringing up the rear.

They retreated into the woods again, and the warriors seemed tense, sharpening their spears and chatting in low, excited whispers over their meal.

Colvarth, with the sharpest ears for their strange tongue, told them what was being said. "Ealtain has requested to attack a nearby village. To decide the matter, Scafta has studied the flight of birds to and from the otherworld — or so he says. Because of this, he has authorized the attack. The birds tell him it will not rain ... apparently he does not consider fighting in the rain to be auspicious. And the men hope for treasure and to add new slaves for the journey home."

Merlin shifted his slave collar. "Do you think there's a force in Kembry large enough to stop them?"

"Perhaps if many villages banded together ... but that is unlikely since most have gone to fight the Saxenow on the coast. The High King will not return there to lead them, sadly."

"Yes he will ... but the torc of the king will be worn by Vortigern." Merlin regretted saying it, but it was the truth.

Colvarth sighed. "My great failure, yes ... O, God, I did not see the scoundrel, even while he was nesting in my beard!"

"At least our heads won't be on *his* spears."

"And for that, let the Lord be thanked."

"I wish the Romans were still here keeping the Picts in check. I never dreamed they raided this far south."

"Ah but the *Pax Romana* is gone, and do not wish for it again, for it was really nothing but the *Pretium Romana*, the Bribes of the

Romans ... and so now the Picts take by blade what they'd been given by the Romans to keep the peace. What we need is a strong High King to prevent such brazen attacks."

"We must find a way to free Arthur."

"Yes."

Necton stepped up to them. The scale armor he'd stolen from Bedwir was now smeared with blue woad, and some of the paint had mixed with Bedwir's dried blood. Next to him stood a smaller warrior holding a spear with a barbed tip. "Watch'idh guard yiu while attack-i we this village. Stay'ive here yiu, or slit'idh guard yiu."

They figured out Necton was leaving to attack a village, and a guard — who looked like a shorter, younger Necton — was going to watch them. Soon the warriors formed up a long line, and after crashing their spears together, they raced off through the woods due west.

The guard tossed his red hair out of his eyes and laughed. To reinforce his new power over them, he ripped Merlin's tunic with the end of his spear.

Ganieda screamed, her back to the rock wall of the crennig.

Strangers surrounded her, peering at her. Ah, they tried to smile, but she could see through it — their quick glances and their smirking faces told all. That cruel man had hit her grandfather, the only family she had left, and had stolen her away.

He stood in front, with thick, fox fur boots wrapped over his brown pants. The man's tunic was woven finely with many different colors, making up a plaid she hadn't seen before. His big hands still held his spear, and Ganieda could tell he was just waiting to skewer her with it. He had a red-yellow beard, and she could see his sneaky eyes just under his dark eyebrows.

Next to him stood a woman, her hair hidden in a striped white-and-orange wrap. Her hands were stained a light brown, and she had a long wooden spoon in her apron. Behind her peeked out three girls. One was younger than Ganieda, one was about the same age, and the tallest was older. Those frog-eyes, why wouldn't they look away?

The woman stepped over and knelt before her.

"*Tellyk*," Ganieda screamed. If he were here, he'd rip them with his fangs, he would—

Fangs? How could Ganieda have forgotten so quickly? She slipped her hand into her bag, and pulled out her long fang.

The woman reached out to her. "There's no need to be afraid ..."

Ganieda scratched the woman's arm, and a stirring of power climbed up Ganieda's spine.

The woman screeched and pulled back.

But Ganieda wasn't through yet, and she leapt forward, raising the fang.

The man, however, bent down and seized her wrist, bending her arm away from the woman. "Imelys, get the rope. I told you she was wild!"

Ganieda pulled the man's hair. "Let go! Where's my wolf, and where's my grandfather? I'll kill you!" But she realized she had spoken in the tongue of the druidow, and these foolish people wouldn't understand her.

The man twisted her hand holding the fang until her elbow and shoulder burned. She tried to get her hand free, but unable to do so, she let go of his hair, and tears began pouring down her cheeks. She didn't want them to see her tears, and tried to brush the wetness away with her sleeve, but the man wouldn't let go.

"That hurts," she screamed.

One of the girls brought a thin rope, and the man grabbed it and wrestled Ganieda until he had tied her left wrist.

She shrieked.

"Troslam, don't do this!" said the woman.

He wound the rope around the other wrist and yanked it tight. "We have no choice." The man finished with a messy knot, and then bound her feet with the remaining length.

The rope burned her skin. Ganieda thrashed her body and pulled to get free, but couldn't. She tried digging the fang into the rope to cut it, but the man snatched the fang from her grasp. So quick, and it was gone. She screamed. "Give it back — give it back!" She would kill him if she got free. He would regret this. They would all weep in their regret.

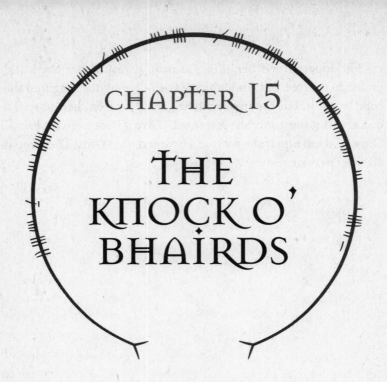

CHAPTER 15

THE KNOCK O' BHAIRDS

Merlin thought they would all get to rest while the warriors were off raiding, but he was wrong — very wrong. The guard forced them all to a nearby stream where clothing had been strewn around in piles.

The guard commanded them to start washing the clothes in the stream, and then he sat on a rock with his sharp spear across his lap.

Merlin looked at the clothes and realized *why* they needed washing. They were soaked in blood — all of them. The clothes had been stripped by the Picts from their victims, whose blood had dried onto the cloth.

Merlin glared at the guard, who pretended to gut Merlin with the tip of his spear. The thought of attempting to escape flitted through Merlin's mind, but he let it go. There were five other warriors left in the camp, and he and his fellow prisoners would never make it. So submitting, he bent down, and began scrubbing a horrific, bloody tunic, whose previous owner had been stabbed three times.

The rest followed his example, picking up whatever cloth lay near. Before Garth began, though, he set Arthur down in the grass with a piece of bread, and the boy alternated sucking on the bread and playing with the stalks, here and there pulling them up in fistfuls.

This went on for an hour, and with each garment, Merlin began to despair a little more — for their future, and for the future of the villagers who were being attacked by the Picts. He wanted to pray but found it hard, what with the red-stained brook slowly flowing past and the slave collar noosed around his neck.

Natalenya began to sob.

Merlin looked over, and in her shaking hands lay a little tunic. Some boy, maybe three winters and not much older than Arthur, had been slain by the Picts, and then stripped of his clothes. Her tears fell upon it, and she tried to scrub it, but could not control her trembling.

Merlin wanted to comfort her, but did not know how without angering the guard. Then an idea struck him. He dried his hands on his pants, pulled his small harp from its leather satchel, and began plucking a hymn he'd learned at the chapel in Bosventor.

The guard stood and watched Merlin intently, but then sat down again on his rock and listened.

This is what Merlin sang:

O great Father, dark in thy thunder,
Come now, forgive us, turn wrath aside.
Thee do we worship, thy strength a wonder;
Come now and help us, thy hand a guide.

Colvarth knew the song, for he joined in, and Garth must have heard it at least once, for he tried to sing a little. Natalenya sucked in her sobs and, breathing hard, paused as if listening to the words.

O high, holy Son, red in thy blood,
Come now, forgive us, cover and save.
We are thy people, drown'd in the flood;
Come now and pull us from death's dark wave.

165

It was hard to trust God while wearing a slave collar, so as he played and sang, Merlin tried to think of God's goodness and of his own need for forgiveness. Thankfully Natalenya finally found her voice, and raised it shakily on the last verse.

O sweet, blessed Spirit, high in thy halls,
Come and forgive us, from deepest shame.
Wash us, cleanse us, for we are but thralls;
Come now and free us, whisper our name.

Even with the verses sung, Merlin still played the tune, humming it to himself.

Natalenya nodded to Merlin with a thankful expression, and he returned the gaze, allowing himself for a moment to enjoy the beauty of her eyes again.

But he had to look away or his heart would melt, and so he focused back on the harp. And just when he thought that he, as well as Natalenya, had found the strength to continue scrubbing the awful, spear-ripped clothing — Scafta arrived.

Apparently he'd come back early from the raiding and had heard them singing. In particular, he'd heard Merlin singing.

"Yiu doig with scars," he said, pointing at Merlin with his witch doctor stick. "Yiu stop!"

But Merlin defied him and kept on playing, if only to gall the man.

"Yiu think yiu am bhaird?" he yelled as his nostrils flared and the veins pulsed on his neck. "Airson challenge-amsa yiu before our wiarr-band for am Knock o' Bhairds."

Hitting Merlin over the head, he stumped off.

Merlin looked to Colvarth for an explanation, but the bard only hummed while he scrubbed a blood-soaked scarf upon a rock.

"Colvarth? What was that all about?"

The man stopped his humming, sat up, and bit his lip. "You have been challenged."

"And ...?"

"And you and Scafta will each stand on opposing hills ... *knocks*, as they call them. There the war band will judge between you and Scafta. This is an old practice of one bard challenging another."

"Judge us?"

"Yes. Judge as to which of you is the better bard."

"But I'm not yet a bard, how can I ..."

Colvarth frowned. "You have a strong, bardic voice, and you will be a bard after many years, God willing, but I regret that I've taught you precious little in these few days we've had together. I hope your innate wisdom is enough."

With one eye on the guard, Merlin picked up another bloody tunic and began scrubbing it. This one had a hole in the side. Then he whispered to Colvarth, "Can't you take my place? Why'd he pick me?"

"I am old and threaten him little. You, however ..."

"What?"

"The Picts fear you."

"Necton sure doesn't."

"Ah, but he does. Have you not heard the whispers of the warriors, and seen Necton's glances at you?"

Merlin leaned closer to Colvarth. "No, I ..."

"Your scars mark you as a great warrior, fearless in many battles, and to them your harp marks you as holding the secrets of the other world. And Scafta, too, fears you. He fears for his position, and he hopes to make you out to be a fool. Every Pictish king requires a bard, and Ealtain has chosen Scafta, but could just as easily choose another."

"If I were Ealtain, I wouldn't choose Scafta as *my* bard."

"Ah, but you don't understand. A Pictish king requires a bard to make the people afraid. Without Scafta, the king would lose his authority. The people fear Scafta, and therefore fear Ealtain. Take the bard away from a Pictish king, and you chop off his right hand."

"But I'm a fool if I have to pretend to be a bard. I can't challenge Scafta."

"Ah, but you must. Sometimes to be a fool is a wise thing," Colvarth said, and then he winked. "Being a fool might save your life."

Merlin and the others continued scrubbing for another hour. Arthur grew restless after crawling around as far as Garth would allow, and the clouds seemed to match Merlin's mood, gathering darkly overhead. Soon the warband returned, whooping and shouting. They carried sacks full of plunder, and at their spear points walked seven villagers to be made into slaves. Merlin's heart beat rapidly as they put these new villagers through the same grueling process, and he could hardly look.

So he turned and watched Natalenya, and that was almost worse. She was so tired, worn out more than the wet rag hanging from her hands. Her skin had gone pale, and yet Merlin could tell from her shallow breaths and droop of her eyes that she must have a fever.

She was getting worse, and what could he do to help?

Pray. He could pray. So he did, asking God to heal her, to give her strength. Earnestly — his heart secretly full of hot tears — he prayed during the slave-taking. And when he looked upon her again, she was worse, now laying in the dirt with her eyes barely open.

God? Won't you heal her? he pled, but no answer came; no healing, no balm, no miracle.

And around him the Picts celebrated their victory. Grotesquely stained spears clacked, bags clinked, and blue-painted bodies danced.

It was only then that Merlin noticed that a young man had been chained behind Caygek. One of his front teeth had been smashed, and blood still stained his fuzzy cheeks. He stood shorter than Caygek by a forehead, and Merlin learned his name was Peredur, the skinny son of a horse trader. Just fifteen winters, and already a slave.

But now was not the time to be focusing on the new slaves, for Scafta conferred with Necton and then pointed at Merlin.

"Whenna?" Necton asked, and Scafta shook his fist and slammed it into his hand. Necton nodded, and, raising his hands, stopped the celebration of his fellow warriors. Then he gave a long speech, most of which Merlin could not understand.

Colvarth gripped Merlin's shoulder. "It is now. You are to stand on that hill, and Scafta will be on the other. You will each take turns trying to impress the Picts with your bard craft."

"But ..."

Colvath shook his head. "I am sorry, my Merlin, that I have failed to prepare you. Simply play a song that you know."

"But — "

"It is supposed to be a song of a true bard, but they might not understand anyway — "

"Colvarth!"

The bard stopped speaking and looked at Merlin.

"Besides a few prayers and a worship song, I only know two children's rhymes."

Colvarth opened his mouth. He shut it. He opened it. "What? No praises to a king? No battle songs? No festals? No laments? How long have you been playing the harp?"

"Barely two weeks ... Natalenya hasn't even had time to teach me." A cold shadow fell on Merlin, for the clouds had now covered the sun, and they brooded over him.

"The Christian prayer songs you know might anger or confuse the Picts. Do what you can with the rhymes. I will pray."

"A lot of good that will do ..."

Colvarth glared at him, but said nothing.

Necton came with the great hammer and pushed Merlin down next to a rock. With four clanks upon the pin, he freed Merlin from the others. Necton started to pull Merlin up, but he refused the help and stood on his own.

Colvarth offered his large harp, but Merlin shook his head. He had only plucked Natalenya's large harp once, and he would be more comfortable playing the small one that Natalenya had given him.

He stepped onto the small hill knock Colvarth had indicated, and found that the warriors had formed a wide ribbon around the two. Scafta stood on the other hill, his hands holding a harp made from the upper skull of a buck, with the strings tightly wound onto the antlers and down to holes carved into the skull. It was a crude instrument, but Merlin recognized the elemental power it would hold over the Picts compared to Merlin's ten-string lyre harp, which had been purchased from a Roman merchant. While Merlin's was a fine instrument with a carved wooden soundbox and bronze tuning pegs, Scafta's skull "sound box" had sharpened teeth and strange designs carved and painted into the bone. To the bottom of the skull had been attached many bells and other metal trinkets.

Scafta went first. He held his harp high, and, jangling it, pranced around his mound, faster and faster, his feet kicking into the air. All the warriors beat their spears together in time to this — until Scafta jumped into the center at the same moment that they slammed them together in a final, teeth-chattering blow.

And then Scafta began to play. His harp strings were thick, making the melody resonant, and this matched his voice. Merlin could not make out the words, but it was clearly an old song, for the older warriors among the group dropped their eyes in respect.

But as the song went on, the darker notes began to rule, and this matched the thickening cloud cover. The pace quickened as well until Merlin felt as if the devil himself would soon emerge from Scafta's mound and join in. When it ended, a few of the warriors had tears in their eyes. Clearly Scafta had chosen his song well.

All eyes turned skeptically to Merlin, and he could only think about tuning his harp — but what a fool! He knew no bardic lays, no ballads of consequence, no songs of history, and certainly nothing the Picts might understand or know.

His mind raced among his meager set of songs — then thunder clapped in the distance, an edge of black clouds approaching from the west — and he suddenly knew which children's rhyme to sing. He could hear the sound of his mother singing from so many years before, and his fingers began plucking out the tune. His throat twitched, making him cough before singing out:

The land be green and the hills be brown,
For the wind doth make the moon to frown.
For this is the way the thunder chants,
And over the world his dark feet dance.
The sky be dark and the clouds be gray,
For thunderstorms roll the sun away.
For this is the way the thunder chants,
And over the world his dark feet dance.
The sea be green and the depths be black,
For lightning falls and the earth doth crack.
For this is the way the thunder chants,
And over the world his dark feet dance.

At this point Merlin was supposed to sing, "Sleep, sleep, little babe sleep," and he paused in order to figure out how to avoid embarrassing himself completely. At that moment lightning burst from the sky, shaking the air — and so he sang out:

Grief, grief, you'll come to grief,
For God throws down the thunderstorm's lance.
You'll all come to grief.

The warriors had up to this point been looking on with some attention, but when a new blade of lightning shattered a tree just behind them, they ducked, covered their heads, and called out Merlin's name in their strange tongue.

Scafta would not have it, though, and ran screaming at Merlin.

They were only twenty paces apart, and Merlin had almost no time to react. He turned to the side to ram Scafta with his left shoulder, cradling his harp in the other hand.

But it didn't work, for at the last second Scafta whirled aside and booted Merlin off the hill. Merlin fell, and before he could recover, his harp had been yanked from his hands. Scafta dropped the instrument to the ground, smashed it with his boot, and then turned upon Merlin.

Raindrops fell upon his cheek as a sharp pain cracked his temple — the echo filling his head like bees in a hive. He covered his face with his hands, but Scafta kicked him again, and again.

Ganieda slept, uncomfortable as it was with her hands and ankles tied. Images floated through her dreams of the man attacking her with his bloody spear — and of the woman screaming and scratching her with long, orange fingernails. Once she dreamed that a dark beast had come and hung her upside down by her feet and dangled her over a pit of snakes whose glowing tongues spat fire through their flashing white fangs. Ganieda called for help, but none came. She called for her mother and father, weeping and struggling against the grip of the beast, but no one ever came to save her.

She awoke, suddenly, upon a feather-stuffed mattress. A thick blanket covered her, and she felt warm. Someone must have moved her in the night, for she had fallen asleep on the hard, earthy floor. The sun shone through the shutters and onto a nearby stone wall, but Ganieda could tell neither the time of day nor how long she'd slept.

She rested while scheming her escape from the ropes. Soon the blankets became too warm, and she wanted to thrust them off. She thrashed wildly and unsuccessfully until her frustrations came out in a scream. And slowly the blanket crept up until it covered her face and stifled her raw voice. She wanted to hurt these people — to kill them and run away back to Grandpa.

The blanket was pulled back — and there stood Ganieda's mother, Mônda, come to rescue her. Ganieda tried to breathe the fresh air, but could not make her lungs move from the joy and shock. Her mother's dark tresses hung down toward Ganieda, and she wanted to touch them with her hands, to have them trail across her face, to smell them once again. Only the hair smelled different than her mother's, like rotten bark … with a hint of onion?

Ganieda's vision changed, and her mother was replaced by another woman — the one whom Ganieda had scratched the night before. Her headwrap had been removed and Ganieda saw that the hair was not quite as dark as her mother's.

"Are you hungry?" the woman asked, and only then did Ganieda notice the smell of bread, yeasty and fresh. Beside the woman sat a tray of buns, and a steaming mug. The smell of salty boiled carrots and cabbage wafted over her.

"You let me go," Ganieda yelled, fresh tears streaming from her eyes and running across her nose and cheeks.

"And what will you do, lass? Will you hurt me again?"

"Yes! I'll kill you ..."

The woman arced an eyebrow. "Will you now? Then I shouldn't let you go, should I?"

"Let me go. Let me go, and I'll scratch you again!" Ganieda would find the fang and then ... but she knew her words didn't make sense. With these threats, why would this stranger ever let her go?

"Well then, I only have one choice, don't I?" The woman's lip trembled — and she shucked off Ganieda's blanket.

Ganieda braced herself for the blow. The woman would beat her, and Ganieda would scream. She filled her lungs for it, waiting.

But the woman picked at the knot holding her legs tight. Soon Ganieda's ankles moved free, and she considered kicking the woman, but decided to wait and land the blow when it was least expected after her hands were free.

The woman's fingers shook as she undid the knot at Ganieda's wrists.

Ganieda tensed. Why was she doing this? The woman's arm was wrapped in a thick bandage, with dried blood soaking one side where Ganieda had cut her. Didn't she know Ganieda would hurt her and then run away?

The smell of the soup filled the small room fully now, and the bread with it, and Ganieda's stomach growled. Maybe she would eat first ... and then shatter the empty bowl in the woman's face ... and then run.

The knot slipped away, and the rope was set down, and the woman kissed Ganieda's wrists where the skin had been chafed. "I'm sorry," she said, and her hair teased Ganieda's arms and knees. Ganieda wanted to feel those locks for just a moment, but then they slipped away and the woman brought the tray of steaming goodness and set it before Ganieda.

"My name's Safrowana, and it's going to be all right."

CHAPTER 16

THE WOUNDED KING

Scafta finally stalked off, leaving Merlin hurting and stunned. Colvarth and the others helped Merlin to stand and guided him over to a spot under a tree. There he rested while the warriors hunkered down until nightfall, when they would travel again.

Merlin's dreams were strange, beginning with a reliving of Scafta's attack. The witch doctor's boot, sharp like a broken rock, came down again and again on Merlin's head, and he was kicked until he shrunk so small that he tumbled into a tiny crack that opened in the ground. He fell into smothering earth, which covered his face. It became impossible to breathe. He flailed for a handhold, anything, to pull himself up, but the soil came off in lumps. Darkness took him.

When he awoke, it was night and he lay in the bottom of a small boat, its wooden ribs creaking and water lapping the sides. Merlin sat up. A thick, peat-scented fog covered the world, and though he could see neither oar nor sail, the boat plied through the water on a will of its own. Hazy reeds passed by and frogs drummed their throats in the distance.

A loud splash fell near the front of the boat, and Merlin's heart skipped a beat. He tried to calm himself, but his skin prickled as if a hundred centipedes crawled inside his tunic. He leaned over the edge of the boat, and there, deep down in the water, he saw two large eyes staring at him, luminous with green fire. The creature's white hide covered it like scabbed bark, and it was larger than any living thing Merlin had ever seen, maybe forty feet long. It swam below the surface, mostly in the shadowy depths, and its tail knocked Merlin's boat to the side with a loud crack. The boat tipped, but did not capsize. Water began to fill the bottom of the boat and wet Merlin's boots — the creature's blow had sprung a leak!

He grabbed for his sword, only to find it missing, and he couldn't find his knife. But then the fog parted and another boat appeared. A man rowed it, whistling quietly. Didn't he see the creature?

"*Stay back,*" Merlin yelled, but the man ignored him and rowed his boat nearer. Then the man set his oars down and stood in his boat, a dark, hooded cloak upon his frame and his face in darkness. He held in his hand a fishing net, and tossed it into the water using a long rope. He was still whistling.

The creature below the water paused, the green fire of its eyes glaring upward. Then, as if spooked, it shot away into the depths.

Merlin's boat had now sunk partway into the water, and Merlin abandoned it, swimming over and grabbing onto the net, still dangling from the man's hands. "Help me up," he called, looking frantically into the water to make sure the creature wasn't returning.

The fisherman reached down and pulled him into the boat. He then lifted the net in, and it was filled with seven large perch, gray-green with black stripes.

"Where am I?" Merlin asked, his wet clothes dripping on the bench.

The man did not answer. He took hold of the oars and rowed. Merlin tried to glimpse his face, but the hood drooped too low for that.

They rowed through the fog for a long time, and yet it seemed to Merlin that they stood still. Nothing could be seen on the left or the right, and time slowed until Merlin felt they would go on like that, the man bumping the oars, splash into the water, raising them — dripping years across the surface of Merlin's life — and then back down again for another row. Perpetually.

Just as Merlin began to shiver, the boat bumped something. Turning around, he saw a wide shore, gray with rocks. Merlin climbed out and pulled the boat up the shingle.

The fisherman gathered his catch, still flopping slightly, and climbed onto the shore. He lit a small lantern from a tinder box, and then led the way up a narrow track.

"Who are you?" Merlin asked, trying to keep up, but the man ignored him. Merlin wanted to grab his sleeve, turn him around, and pull back the hood — but began to fear what he might find.

Soon they passed through a forest of stout but short trees, their wide, pointed leaves motionless in the lifeless air. A stone fortress loomed out of the thinning fog. Its granite blocks had been weathered from hundreds of years of wind and rain, and they towered over Merlin, more imposing than even Dintaga. To the left stood a high tower with a conical roof, its windows black. The gate was open, but it was dark inside, and a stillness pressed down over the place like a blanket, thick and moldy.

The man entered, his lantern too small to light up anything beyond the gate but for a foot or so.

Merlin hesitated. If he stepped inside, would the doors close behind and trap him?

The fisherman turned and beckoned him. His hand was thick and calloused, and there was no hint of evil in his motion — but could Merlin trust him? Yes, he had seemed to scare off the creature in the water, but what if it was for some fouler purpose?

Merlin turned back and looked the way he had come. He knew the boat was still there on the shore, and he could take it and — but the creature was there, so he could not go back.

"There is nothing to fear," the man said, his fish gleaming in the lantern light.

Merlin had forgotten about the fish, and that is what made his decision. The simple act of catching fish hearkened back to his own memories as a child, when his father would take him out on the marsh. They would spend hours filling the bottom of the boat, cleaning their catch, smoking them, and hanging them from the ceiling to provide meat through the long winter.

How bad could this man be? Merlin stepped forward, and together they entered the shadowed interior of the fortress wall. The man walked slowly across the courtyard and to a timbered hall where they entered. The floor was littered with rocks, and the hearth in the center lay dead, its ashes sodden and the charred logs old and broken. On one end of the room lay a dais, and upon it stood two granite thrones whose stonework was cracked. They were framed by blood-red vines that grew up the wall.

The man handed the net of fish to Merlin, and though it was heavy it gave him something to do — something to hold on to — and that net of fish felt more real to him than all the rest.

The fisherman stepped up to the dais, turned, and sat down heavily upon the throne. And in that instant, all the world changed. Lights burst out in the room. The net of fish changed suddenly to a tray of salted and baked fillets. Servants appeared dressed in finely woven clothes of yellows, blues, and crimson, and they carried platters of steaming breads, troughs of meaty stews, and crocks of spicy soups. Above the blazing hearth lay a spitted boar, roasting, with fat sizzling and dripping.

The fisherman had changed too. His dark cloak was gone, replaced by a mantle of plum and argent. His tunic was plaid, like the princes of Kembry, and his pants made from handsome gray leather. Next to him, upon the other throne, sat a woman. Her hair was red like a flaxen fire, and her elegant dress was the most brilliant blue Merlin had ever seen. Upon her head and the king's lay simple silver circlets with neither gem nor ornamentation.

A servant came and relieved Merlin of the tray of fish. He was hungry but didn't care, for the sight was feast enough. He dropped to his knees before the king and queen, wide-eyed and open-mouthed.

"Rise, Merlin, and be at ease, for you are an honored guest," the lady said, and her voice was like a songbird freshly lit amongst the dew-dripped flowers.

Merlin looked up, and her face was radiant such that he had to turn away lest she steal his very soul. That was when he saw the man's face. His jaw was strong under a handsome nose, and his brown hair fell thick past his shoulders. But a sadness hung upon him unlike any Merlin had seen before. His lips hung down at the corners as if a smile had never been seen across his face. The skin of his cheeks lay tense and brooding, and his eyes — the sadness was most pronounced in his eyes — they were sunken as if all the tears of the world had been shed through them and had left them hollow. The crease of his brow was so pronounced that Merlin shuddered.

"My lord," Merlin dared utter, still on his knees, "what burden do you bear, and how may I cheer you?"

The king said nothing, but only pointed to the plaid of his chest ... and there Merlin spied a stain. Blood it was, trickling down from his heart, pooling in his lap, running down the throne, across the dais, and soaking into the ground. There was so much of the blood that it was a wonder Merlin had not seen it before.

Even the queen was concerned now, and she rose to help her husband, but he waved her back. "Nothing can be done for my wound, and you know it well," he declared.

"That may be," the queen said, "but that is why Merlin is here. He holds the power to heal your wound, if he is willing."

Merlin felt himself go pale. If he was willing? Heal the king's wound? Merlin had no power to heal. His prayers for Natalenya's healing had gone unanswered. His prayers for release from their slavery had gone unheeded. A fool he was. A powerless fool, with a God who had abandoned them to sickness and death. He wanted to believe — to trust — but his faith was beginning to fade as the trials mounted and the impossibility of their situation pressed upon him.

But the queen spoke again, her voice soft as the waters of a gently flowing stream. "Do not doubt, brave Merlin, but believe the gospel! Within the bag at your side hides the power to heal the great wound of my husband."

Merlin did not even bother to look down at his waist. He knew there was no bag there — he had already searched himself when the creature had slunk by in the marsh. But ... what was this knot at his elbow? He felt with his hand, and sure, a bag was mysteriously present where none had been before. He untied it and reached inside, felt something wooden, and pulled it out.

It was the small, strange bowl he and Colvarth had found in the tin box. The bowl Necton had stolen from them without knowing what it was. Its wood was aged to a deep brown, and its base was covered in a circle of decorated gold.

"You hold the *Sancte Gradale*, the Sangraal," the queen said, stepping down from her perch and falling on her knees beside Merlin. "The cup of the Christ! At the Last Supper, it held the wine that was poured out for us all, and the *Pergiryn* who built this fortress, this shrine, used it to catch our Lord's blood when he lay dying upon the cross. It is most holy."

Merlin studied it again, holding his breath, for now its bottom was filled with blood, dark and dread. He almost dropped the thing, his hands shaking, but the queen reached out and steadied them, her eyes shining with wonder.

"To think that you have brought it here again," she said. "To think that I have now touched the cup of the living Christ. May I bring it to my husband? For his wound is grievous."

Merlin stood, and giving her the Sangraal, she held it out to the king's lips, who drank of the blood, all of it, and in that instant was healed. The stain upon his tunic faded and was gone, the pooled blood evaporated, and a joy filled his face. Raising his arms to heaven, he sang forth a song Merlin had never heard:

Trust not in guile, or in a hoard —
trust in the power of Christ, your Lord.
Not in the wood, or in a sword —
here lays the blood of Christ, yes poured.
Let death break forth, and blade's bright rust —
at the judgment they turn to dust.
And when you fail, in thick disgust —
there, in the Christ of heaven, do trust.

The light of the Sangraal flashed then, more intense than any light Merlin had ever seen. The world was covered in that light, and the dream faded away.

Merlin opened his eyes to a world unlike the one he had dreamed about. His head felt like a dead fish — bloated, washed ashore, and ready to pop.

Colvarth was there, trying to rouse him with insistent whispers. "He has taken Natalenya! Awake!"

"I know. I know ..." Merlin said. Of course Scafta'd taken Natalenya's harp and smashed it. Even in his drowsiness, Merlin's heart began to burn in anger at such a desecration.

"Not the harp — Natalenya herself, Necton has ..."

"Necton?" This didn't make sense to him. Necton couldn't play the harp, certainly not a broken one. Merlin sat up, the world tilting around the rock steadiness of Colvarth's hand.

"You must be up — Necton has taken Natalenya to make her his wife!"

Ganieda ate and was satisfied, wondering who these people were such that they treated her so harshly ... and yet so kindly. Her mother had always warned her to avoid the other people of the village. None of them were descended from the glorious Eirish, like her mother. They were cruel, ignorant, and foolish. Certainly the tall man's treatment of her grandfather had been cruel — but the woman treated Ganieda gently despite the fact that Ganieda had cut her.

Wasn't that how the world worked ... cut those who cut you? Why did Safrowana unbind her while being threatened? Ganieda had fully expected to be beaten, and yet here she sat in the woman's lap — dallying over her bread, smelling her hair, and feeling warm and truly safe for the first time in many weeks.

But what of the others? Those girls? That cruel man?

Someone knocked on the door and entered. It was the man.

She wanted to scream, but her mouth was full of bread, so Ganieda stuffed the remaining piece in and clung to Safrowana. That man wouldn't dare hurt her then!

"It's okay, little girl. I'm called Troslam, and I'm sorry for the rough handling. I've made you a dress, and I hope you like yellow."

He laid upon the bed a bright yellow dress, cross-woven with orange and red strands. It was more beautiful than any dress Ganieda had ever seen, and she just stared at it as the man left and closed the door.

Ganieda reached out and felt the cloth, smooth and soft. *Is it mine?* she thought to herself, but didn't realize she had spoken it aloud until the woman answered her.

"Of course it's yours, dear. Let's try it on."

Before Ganieda knew it, she was dressed and feeling beautiful.

The woman left to get some ointment for the small cuts on Ganieda's legs. While she was gone, Ganieda flopped back on the bed and repeated the woman's name out loud to herself. *Safrowana ... Safrowana ...* It sounded similar to her mother's name *Môndargana*, but of course not half as special. From her vantage point, Ganieda looked up at the cast-iron lamp hanging from a hook nailed into a beam running across the roof. The oil had nearly run dry, for it sputtered in the still air. And just as she was about to look away, the wick flared up, revealing a line of white nearly hidden on the lamp's ledge. White? Could it be?

She jumped up, almost losing her balance on the stuffed feather mattress. She leaned forward to see what the white thing was, but the wick was too dim. Blowing at it as hard as she could, she couldn't make it flare up. Looking around, she found her old dress, nearly rags now, and she waved it at the lantern until the wick flashed, revealing what lay on the edge of the lamp ... and it was ... her fang!

She reached forward, straining, tilting, but the bed was too soft and too far away. She spied a broom in the corner, and jumped off the bed to get it. She had just returned to the center and raised the broom handle toward the lantern when someone knocked on the door.

She froze. What if she were caught? They would take the fang and hide it somewhere else. Maybe break it. Maybe bury it in a hole where she would *never* find it again.

The door began to open. She dropped the broom to the ground and pretended to sweep.

It was Safrowana, come back with a small crock of ointment. "Ah, lass, there's no need for that," she said, and she gently took the broom away.

Ganieda let it go, for she could grab it if only Safrowana would leave again. But for what excuse? Ah, that was it. Ganieda picked up the empty soup bowl and held it out.

Safrowana smiled. "In a moment, lass, let me put this on your cuts ... That's it, hold your leg out. So many scratches. You must have run for hours through the woods to look like this."

The ointment felt cool as it was spread on Ganieda's leg, and it smelled of thyme and lavender. Safrowana smiled, picked up the bowl, and left.

Ganieda ran to the broom, grabbed it, and went swinging at the lamp. She hit it once, but the fang didn't fall. A second time, but still nothing.

Ganieda banged the lamp hard, and the fang fell to the rushes that covered the floor. She seized it and tucked it into her shoe—

just as the door opened. The three girls entered the room, the tallest of whom was in front — her with the maroon, green, and white plaid. She had a funny look on her face, and the two in back were whispering.

The front one stood there, looking down her nose at Ganieda, who could almost feel the scorn. The girl held her hands behind her back, hiding something.

Stay away from the other girls, ya hear? Ganieda's mother had said. *They hate ya and they'll hurt ya.* The words rang through her head, and she repeated it to herself.

The big girl made a hesitant step forward.

Ganieda tensed, holding the broom ready to defend herself. She would hit the tall one in the head and throw the broom at the others. Then she'd pull the fang from her shoe. They would learn not to hurt her, for she'd teach them the power of the fang, and they'd never forget.

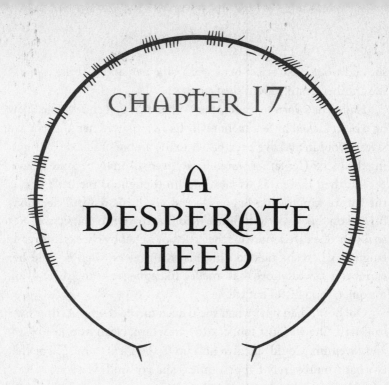

CHAPTER 17

A DESPERATE NEED

Natalenya ran crying to Colvarth and Merlin, the slave collar's chain banging into her shins. She had escaped, by God's grace, from Necton, but at what cost? He knew now the depth of her sickness, for he'd seen the black boils gathering on her upper arms, and he had shoved her away, yelling at her as if her life was worth far less than the mud beneath his feet.

Strangely, she had begun to place her hope in him — that if she fell too ill to keep up on the trail that he would put her on his horse. But now that he knew about the boils he would never help her — and if she faltered, she would be killed or left to die.

But even as her itching sickness condemned her, it had also saved her from an unholy marriage, for once Necton saw the truth, his interest faded and turned into anger. Maybe fear.

And in her disgrace, she barely had the courage to go back to her friends. To Merlin. Especially Merlin. She had hidden the boils from him, but now she couldn't conceal them anymore. He would see and would also reject her, even loathe her, and their love would die another death. Could she face that?

Hadn't he sworn to protect her? When had that ended? She knew he'd been kicked by Scafta, but why had he allowed her to become a slave? Wouldn't it have been better to die an honorable death fighting the Picts? Her father would have never willingly become a slave.

But then there was Arthur. Merlin thought of the little boy as the future king of the Britons — and all of his painful decisions hinged on that uncertain future. Did that matter to Natalenya? Not so much. She cared more for the little boy's chubby cheeks, his ready laughter when she tickled him, his soft fingers when he held her earlobe, his sweaty toes that smelled like vinegar — and most of all, his quiet, thoughtful nature.

Oh, how it had hurt when she'd been forced to give Arthur over to Garth. She was just too sick to carry him, clean him, feed him, and love him. Could she give him up to the Picts to raise? For that is what would surely happen unless she got well ... and ... what? Would that really change anything? She would probably have to marry Necton simply to take care of Arthur. But could she? That beast of a ruddy-haired pagan? And maybe he was already married, and that sickened her. No, she could not. Never. But what then? Would she ever get well? Or would she die, overcome by the black, encrusted boils beginning to cover her body?

As she ran, the questions swirled around her, calling out, clawing at her ragged clothes and trying to pull her down to a quick grave. For such questions she had no ready answers, and she stumbled — and stumbling again she passed through the ranks of the Picts, over a small hill, and finally collapsed at Merlin's feet. Her whole body ached, and her sobs rolled in and out of her throat like jagged stones.

At Colvarth's urging, Merlin had finally found the strength to stand on his wobbly legs — and then Natalenya had come to him and fallen at his feet. He knelt down to her, but pain throbbed into his eyes and blinded him for a moment.

"Are you all right?" he asked, but it was a stupid question, for she was sobbing. Of course she wasn't all right.

"I'm … I'm …" but she didn't say more, so he reached out and touched her shoulder to offer some comfort, and found she was trembling.

"Don't touch me!" she said, and slapped his hand.

Merlin recoiled just as his vision cleared. Her sleeve had been ripped open past the upper arm, and the skin was covered in black and purple boils. Her sickness wasn't just making her tired, or giving her a fever. It was infecting her flesh.

"Did Necton hurt you?" he asked, not knowing what else to say.

She shook her head, and Merlin took a deep breath. He'd been unable to protect her, sure, but at least he didn't have to add that to his list of failures. But her sickness — this black death creeping over her body — it made his insides churn in wrath until tears slipped from his eyes.

He had to find a way to help her … but how? Then his dream floated back to him of the fisherman who had really been a king, wounded and bleeding … and the Sangraal had healed him. All this time Natalenya'd been sick. and they had held this relic in their possession — the very cup of Christ!

Merlin needed to get it back from Necton.

Now.

Her suffering must end.

But how could he retrieve it while he was chained to Garth and Bedwir? He turned to talk to them — only to find that Necton had failed to pin his collar on again. He'd been set free to challenge Scafta, and so for the moment he was still free. He saw Necton's tent within a stone's throw, and the man himself nowhere in sight. Most of the warriors slept on the ground in the open, but Necton, along with a dozen others, had been afforded the privilege of a tent.

Around Merlin, the Picts milled about their newly lit campfires preparing food and laughing. But Merlin needed a way to hide his face, or else one of the warriors would stop him. At his feet Colvarth and the others were sorting through a new pile of tunics, breeches, and cloaks taken in the raid, and Merlin found a tunic with a hood. He slipped it on, ignoring the lifeblood spilled through a rend in its side.

Garth stood up from talking to Peredur, the young man who'd been chained behind Caygek. He tugged at Merlin's elbow. "What're you doin'?" he asked.

"Quiet."

"I said, what're you doin'? We're supposed to be sortin' these." He pointed to the clothes.

"Since when do *you* care about work?"

"Necton's not goin' to like it, and I don't want'a miss dinner." Garth sniffed the smoke wafting through the camp from the many spits of roasting meat.

"You think you'll get anything other than dry bread, huh? Well, I'm going to get something from his tent."

"Food? If'n so, then we'll come with." He made to grab a few tunics. "Maybe we can get me bagpipe from Scafta's tent while we're at it."

"No! I'm not getting food, and you're staying put. If you want any kind of dinner, then distract Necton if you see him."

Merlin slipped off toward the tent. He tried to appear as relaxed as possible, and this suited him for it minimized the pounding in his head. A strong urge to glance left and right came over him — to see if anyone was approaching to stop him — but the hood blocked his vision.

He was now only ten paces from the tent, and still no one had noticed. He walked forward and ducked under the opening. The air was hot inside, and he tied the flap behind him. Before him lay an unfolded cot, an empty pewter mug, a small cask of drink — and a large bag.

Merlin knelt down and began sorting through the bag. It contained items of plunder, including rings and jewelry, clothing and cloaks, a leather satchel of dried meat, a woven bag with ground horseradish root, various coins amounting to a small fortune, and many other things stolen from the people of Kembry. At the very bottom Merlin discovered Colvarth's tin box.

He pulled it out from the bag, but found the box had been locked once again. Not having his knife, he needed something to unlatch it. Looking through the bag, he found a slim but large coin, and attempted to slip it into the gap near the lock and wedge it open. This had worked before when he and Colvarth had first examined the Sangraal — but this time it didn't open.

Sweat began to form at his hairline and trickle down to his eyebrows. He dug back into the bag and found a woman's copper hairpin, with many tines, and using that began working at the lock, but still the box would not open.

Outside, he heard some footsteps.

His heart began to beat wildly, making his cheeks hot. He blinked away sweat dripping into his eyes and tried to remember the iron locks his father had made in their blacksmith shop. They had different kinds of mechanisms, and that gave him an idea. Taking the hairpins in his teeth, he bent it and tried fishing it deeper into the mechanism.

Necton's voice called from near the tent entrance, and a distant warrior hailed him.

Click. The box opened. The bowl was still there with its golden circlet upon the bottom, but he'd be caught with it and ...

Necton began untying the tent flap.

To get away, Merlin tried to find a place to slide under the side of the tent, but there were too many tent pegs, and the fabric was held too tightly to the ground.

There was no escaping before Necton entered.

Ganieda pulled the broom back, ready to swing it upward at the tall girl, who wouldn't expect something fierce like that from one as short as Ganieda. No one ever did, and Ganieda prided herself at that.

The tall girl stepped forward again.

Ganieda knew it was the last time the girl would look at her like that. The broom would strike her in the face before she knew what was coming.

But the girl acted quicker than Ganieda … and pulled a rag doll from behind her back. She held it forth, saying, "We made this for you, and want you to have it."

Ganieda gulped. She still wanted to strike the girl, but how could she do that now? Maybe if the doll were ugly, but it wasn't. The cloth was a bright blue, maybe the brightest blue Ganieda had ever seen. Bluer than the flax flowers that grew near her house. Her house that had burned down such a short time ago.

Ganieda had no doll. Had nothing to love. Not anymore. And these horrible girls had made it … for her? She wanted to reach out and touch it, take it, hold it, but she was afraid it would become smoke, like everything else in her life.

The girl gave it to her, and then knelt down and tried to hug her.

Ganieda scrunched up her shoulders and stepped back. She'd sit in Safrowana's lap, receive the dress, and maybe even a doll — but she surely wouldn't hug this strange girl.

A look of pain — of fear and confusion — passed over the girl's face. The smirk was gone.

This girl had been afraid too, Ganieda realized.

Safrowana returned with the second bowl of soup and exchanged it for the broom.

The earthenware bowl felt warm, and the steaming goodness wafted upward. Ganieda sniffed deeply. After replacing the broom in the corner, Safrowana left the room with the girls, and Ganieda was alone.

She set the soup on a small table next to the bed, bent down, and pulled out the fang from her shoe. What was this thing? This white length, sharp as a needle, that could hurt those who tried to love her?

Even Grandpa had been hurt by it, for she remembered clearly his pressed lips and blinking, tightened eyes when she had first cut his remaining hand. She had betrayed him in that moment ... had cut her own grandfather.

If she kept the fang, would she keep hurting people? Would she hurt this family that was trying, however awkwardly, to love her?

But the Voice called again.

Take it and use it, dark haired one,
And you will have power over your enemies.
Consume it, my beloved, and take it into your life,
And it will consume you with a fire
more dear than even your family,
more dear than all who call themselves friends.

The sharp fang vibrated, pulsed, and slowly writhed upon her palm, making her itch to close her small fingers upon it. Making her want to grow again into Gana the great. To become *Mórgana*. To take hold of the vigor and power of a life obedient to the Voice.

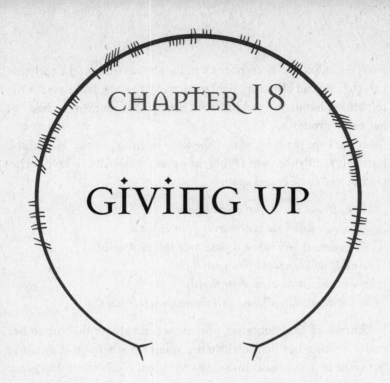

CHAPTER 18

GIVING UP

Garth's voice rang out, and Necton paused from untying the tent flap.

Merlin let out his breath. The boy had bought him a few moments. He pulled at the side of the tent again, but couldn't make a space big enough to slip out.

Necton yelled at Garth to get back to work and commenced untying the last set of laces holding the door flap closed.

Remembering that the wooden bowl portion of the Sangraal had been completely invisible to Colvarth, he yanked at the gold circlet, but it refused to come off. Pulling furiously now, he bent it, wedging it from the bottom of the bowl.

The tent door flapped wide.

Merlin hid the bowl under his tunic, between his belt and his breeches. Then he quickly dropped the circlet back into the tin box.

Necton roared, grabbed Merlin by his hood, yanked him to his feet, and slammed his fist into Merlin's face.

A crunching sound came from Merlin's nose as pain jolted through his head. Crumpling to the ground, he tried to make sure the Sangraal stayed in his belt, but his arms buzzed and he could barely move them.

Necton dragged him out and across the field by his hood, and threw him to the ground at Peredur's bare feet. Someone brought the hammer, and within thirty heartbeats Merlin found himself chained again to Garth and Bedwir — and only then did Necton begin searching him.

Merlin panicked as he felt the Pict's fingers on him, not wanting the Sangraal to be taken. He just *had* to heal Natalenya. He couldn't fail her now. The Sangraal was his only hope, his only way to heal her, and this Pict couldn't have it.

Necton ripped off Merlin's tunics and began violently searching him. The Pict's fingers were rough and his nails scratched at Merlin's skin, but Merlin didn't fight back. Instead, he slipped his hand to his belt and pushed the Sangraal out from its place where it was wedged. The wooden bowl fell softly to the grass, and he hoped Necton wouldn't notice it.

When the Pict couldn't find anything hidden, he ran off to a roaring campfire, snarling at Merlin as he went. A warrior with long black hair sat nearby gutting a young boar in preparation for roasting it. Necton yanked a sizzling iron spit from the fire, ignoring the complaints of the warrior, and marched back to Merlin.

Merlin blanched. Instinctively, he reached out to where the Sangraal had fallen, pulled it into his hand, and hid it behind his leg. It had healed the Fisher King — could touching it shield him from injury? Maybe.

Necton approached the place where Merlin lay on the grass. His face was red, his lips were pulled back from his teeth, and his neck was knotted with bulging veins. The iron spit smoked and hissed, and Necton brought it down at an angle across Merlin's bare chest.

Agony poured from where the spit touched his skin, a river of blazing fire. Merlin screamed and tried to wriggle away, but Necton jammed his boot onto Merlin's neck and pressed. Quickly, Merlin was worried more about getting air. He twisted to get out from under the boot, but this pressed his chest harder into the burning spit.

Necton removed the spit but then rammed it down again, this time diagonal to the previous burn, but higher up. And he didn't let up on his boot.

Merlin wanted to call for help, but nothing came out but tears stealing from his eyes. The light began to fail.

"In the name of God, leave him alone," Colvarth said, trying to pull Necton away. "You will kill him!"

Necton backed off, but not before slapping the bard and knocking him down.

Garth was crying nearby, and Bedwir sat behind him. Natalenya — who had crawled behind Colvarth so his chain could reach Merlin — pleaded with a rasping voice. Caygek stood in the background, aloof, and Peredur had closed his eyes.

Merlin sucked in the air, a brutal, choking effort. He glanced down at his new wounds, and they were ugly. The spit had not just burned him, but had charred his skin, leaving it red, black, and bloody. He had endured it for Natalenya. He loved her so much. But the Sangraal had failed him. It hadn't protected him from the branding ... could he trust it to heal Natalenya? Anyone?

"Next time-an, kill-idh yiu I will," Necton said, and then marched off.

Merlin lay there breathing and weeping for some time, until Colvarth crawled over. His cheekbone was red, and some blood had dripped from his nose into his moustache and beard. "You are marked now ... as one of God's servants," he said, helping Merlin to sit up.

Merlin couldn't answer him, but shook his head to disagree. He wanted to keep crying, but tightened his throat and wiped his eyes on the torn edge of Colvarth's sleeve.

"It was and is and will be ... painful ... yes," Colvarth said. "But look ... it is the sign of the cross ... the sign of the name of Christus."

And it was true, for Merlin could see it now. Necton had branded him twice, each time diagonally across his chest ... and what was Merlin to make of this? Suffering! And more suffering. "It is the mark of a slave," he said, pouring out his anger like sickened, sour milk. And what good was the Sangraal? What good had his dream accomplished? Not only did he have scars on his face and his back, but now he had them on his chest as well. How much could he endure?

He looked at Natalenya now, and saw that she lay propped upon the pile of clothes, coughing. A new boil had formed on her neck, and so no matter how upset Merlin was at his new misfortune, he still needed to try and heal her. Retrieving the Sangraal had cost him greatly, and so he would at least try. He slowly unstrung Colvarth's waterskin from the man's belt and tried pouring it into the wooden bowl.

Like before, the water poured right through as if it didn't even exist, but when he finished, he looked inside, and there, in the bottom, remained a single drop of water. This he brought to the coughing Natalenya, and gently pulling on her chin, he poured it from the bowl into her mouth.

She swallowed, looking up at him with puzzled eyes. And then ... nothing. He waited, enduring his own burning pain, but nothing changed with Natalenya. She coughed some more. Her forehead felt as hot as ever. And the boils ... the boils still infected her skin in dark, rumpled masses.

The Sangraal had failed to heal her. Had failed him when it was needed the most. He wanted to chuck it into the woods. Throw it in the nearest campfire. Bile rose in his throat, and he lifted the Sangraal and cocked his arm back.

But Colvarth grabbed his wrist. "Though I cannot see it, I know what you hold. You shall not do this!"

"Why not?"

"It is holy."

Merlin shook his head. "It mocks me. You mock me."

"Have you forsaken God?"

"If this is holy, then God has forsaken *me*." Merlin pulled harder to break Colvarth's grip.

Colvarth increased his hold on Merlin's arm. "Are you yet blind?"

That was it. That was enough. Merlin stood, roaring, and he pulled Colvarth up until the old man lost his footing, let go, and slipped back to the ground. Merlin stepped forward, tugging the startled Garth and Bedwir along with him. He approached the same campfire Necton had taken the spit from, now temporarily unattended, and he dropped the Sangraal into the flames.

Colvarth called out, still winded, crying for him to stop.

Merlin waited for the old wood to catch fire and turn back to the dust Colvarth claimed that it was — but it did not. The flames didn't even seem to touch it, and yet it began glowing, brighter and brighter. Golden it was, now shining with a living splendor that filled all of Merlin's vision. What was this thing? Like a star, clear and beautiful, yet its dazzling light became so intense that he had to shut his eyes lest they be burned.

He fell to his knees, then, and reaching out blindly, he felt for the Sangraal until he found it and pulled it from the flames that wanted to scorch his flesh. The bowl was strangely cool to his touch, the light faded, and he was once more able to look upon its dark wood.

"Though I cannot see it, I know that it is holy," Colvarth said. "It was bought with Uther's blood, and perhaps others. Do not destroy it. Do not cast it away."

Merlin, ashamed and yet full of wonder, gave up. After he tied it inside a cloth from the pile, he gave it back to Colvarth. "I'm sorry," was all he could say.

After all this, Natalenya still coughed.

Merlin didn't understand. He just didn't understand.

The Voice spoke once more to Ganieda, the words breathing upon her ears like soft rain. "Come, my little servant, claim again that which has been taken from you. Strike, and do not desist! And all that you desire will be given to you."

But Safrowana had already offered that. Love. A place to stay ... and belong.

She looked at the fang once more, and a shadow crept over her heart. And in that chill she made a decision that she knew deep down, somehow, seemed right. It rested upon the hope of being loved by Safrowana, her second mammu — and for that chance she rejected the fang.

She held her palm out, placing the fang as far from her body as she could get it, walked over to the window, and dropped it upon the dusty sill behind two old loom shuttles. The sun was setting outside, and for a brief moment its light shone brightly through the slats of the shutter — and upon her hope of a new life.

Ganieda turned her back upon the fang. "May a raven take it away!" she said. Then she ran to the feather bed, threw herself upon it, and began crying.

Mórganthu gulped the air in, hoping he had not been seen. If that man caught him hiding here, he would be beaten again, and then how would he fare? More precisely, what would happen to the worthy cause of all the druidow? Ah, to be younger, with two stout hands, and be able to defend oneself with sword or club. Mórganthu would have to be spry, even sneaky, to accomplish his goal, what with his right hand cut off by the scheming of that Merlin — curse his body to burn over the fires of a thousand solstices.

Ah, but that weaver was the true thief. Stealing into Mórganthu's tent and taking his granddaughter away. Such a gangrenous worm as that would curse the day he crossed the arch druid, his gods, and their blessed followers!

Hah, and did that weaver forthrightly think he could get away with such insolence? Did he imagine Mórganthu was so ignorant as to not know him, his name, and all the names of his family? *Troslam*,

Safrowana, and *Imelys* they were, for Mórganthu knew the names of everyone in the village as well as their business and history. It was his duty to know everything, and he had paid good money for the information from Connek and a few others when he had first come back to the stone circle.

Mórganthu steadied himself against the cold rock wall that surrounded Troslam's pasture. Thankfully no one lived on this land adjoining the weaver's, making it the ideal spot for him to spy from. He had discovered an old kiln built into the far back corner of the wall, and the stones were a bit loose there. He inched his eye downward toward a hole which allowed him to spy on the back of the crennig. The weaver's house was silent, and Mórganthu watched until dusk fell upon the mountainside like the shadow of a vulture.

The time had come to sneak into the pasture, so he tried pulling the stones out from the kiln, but found it too difficult with only one hand. Perhaps he could kick them out, but that would make far too much noise, so he abandoned the idea.

Ahh, maybe he could slip *over* the wall if he could find something to help him climb. Sneaking into the doorway of the old, abandoned crennig next door, he sorted through the rubbish, broken furniture, smashed pots, and rat-eaten old clothes until he found an old bench and barrel. Taking these one at a time, he set them upon each other next to the rock wall and slipped over, the clever fox that he was. Getting out again might be harder, but he would see to that once he located Ganieda — and her fang — and verified that both were safe.

Pattering feet were heard inside the house, and Mórganthu slunk over to the shuttered window where the sound had come from. Peeking inside he saw … yes … Ganieda laying upon a bed, crying. These devils who worshiped a foreign god had hurt her, and druidic anger rose in Mórganthu's chest. He started to form her name on his lips to call her quietly over to the window when a woman walked into the room, thumping her feet across the floor. The witch.

But he saw it before he ducked down below the window. There, on the sill in between the shutters, lay the fang! He had almost missed it there in the dust, but it glimmered, long and white in the glow of the moon. He reached out his hand to pull open the outer shutter, and —

The woman turned around and faced the window.

Mórganthu bent down and slunk against the wall of the house. Had she seen him? Had she heard him?

"I thought it was a beautiful night ... but there's a foul stink on the wind," she said. And then she pulled the shutters tight. Something clicked.

Mórganthu bit his cheek, for she had locked them, and he would not be able to take back the fang without making a great deal of noise. But she must not have seen the fang, for the sound of her footsteps brisked away from the window, and he heard her talking quietly to Ganieda.

Daring a little, he lifted his head and peeked through the now narrower slit that remained at the bottom of the shutters — and he jerked back, for now four people had gathered around Ganieda. Mórganthu looked again: the mother, that cursed Safrowana, was still there, but now she had been joined by her daughter, Imelys — and two other girls. Two? Who were these? Some local urchins, no doubt ... but no! Their garments were too fine — too fine for such as this somnolent, filthy village.

He squinted, and started to gasp before he stopped himself. They were Uther's daughters — alive! Mórganthu's Eirish warriors had lied to him, yes, lied about their deaths. Just like Arthur, claiming the girls were killed at Inis Avallow as Mórganthu had demanded. Yet here the girls were, right within his grasp. He raised his eyebrows and wiggled his jaw, imagining all the wonderful possibilities this new truth offered him.

Yet he was torn. He wanted to free Ganieda and get the fang, but now he needed to think. If he freed her now, then the weavers would know their secret had been found out and this glorious opportunity would be wasted.

Ganieda could wait... And the fang could wait. Just a little. Maybe Ganieda might use it to free herself. He needed time to think.

Backing away from the window and ducking around the left side of the house, he found the gate and slipped quietly out to the road. But he was on the wrong side of the house for going back to the stone circle and his tent, and didn't want to walk directly in front. So he snuck across the road, past a huge boulder, behind a bush, and worked his way across.

A hand came from behind a tree, grabbed on to Mórganthu's tunic, and jerked him sideways. "Got you at last," the man said, his voice hissing.

Mórganthu tried to push against his grip, but couldn't break free. He found his feet and used his nails to gash at the man's face instead. For his efforts, the man hammered Mórganthu in the stomach, and he fell to the ground like a dry leaf.

"I should have skewered you the first time I saw you," the man said.

Mórganthu lay in the dirt, gasping. He looked up to see who it was, but the moon, like a halo behind the man's head, veiled his face in darkness. A long white tunic lay upon the man, stained with soot, dirt, and blood. The bottom hem was wet, and stunk of fish.

The man spit on Mórganthu. "What a liar. You promised gold, and where is it?" He dropped and pinned Mórganthu's good arm with a knee. Then he jerked a Roman-forged *gladius* from his belt and stuck it under Mórganthu's nose. Froth fell from his teeth, and his thin lips quivered. "The Stone doesn't call me anymore... doesn't make gold for me anymore..."

It was Tregeagle, the village Magister, the once-fearsome overseer of the village and father to that wretched girl, Natalenya.

"You duplicitous imp," he yelled. "Have the stone make gold or I'll cut your nose off."

"I cannot. The Stone is hurt ... The blade ... the blade prevents it."

"Then pull it out, curse you. Use your druid arts."

"I cannot. I have tried."

"Then give me *your* gold. You must have a hoard of it stashed away ... buried ... hidden."

"I have none." He wished he did, but the Stone had been injured before he'd thought to make his own coins into gold.

"I don't believe you." Tregeagle pressed the gladius into Mórganthu's nose, and blood snaked down from the wound.

Mórganthu lowered his voice so no one would hear. "Wait ... wait ..."

"Why? Your ability to smell means nothing to me." He grabbed Mórganthu's hair and pressed the gladius harder against the bridge of his nose.

Mórganthu sucked his breath in. Only a bit more pressure and his nose would be sliced off. He squirmed, but there was no getting away. At least not without giving something up. An idea came to Mórganthu — how to free himself from the beastly Magister's blade as well as exact vengeance upon Uther's daughters.

"I can get you gold ... let me speak!" Mórganthu voiced, barely a whisper.

Tregeagle's lips bunched up, but the gladius didn't move.

"Vortigern will pay you gold for the information I will give you."

"Vortigern?"

"Yes ... Take your sword away, and I will tell you."

The gladius moved away an inch, but Tregeagle still had Mórganthu's arm pinned and held his hair..

"Uther's daughters ... are in the weaver's house ... hiding there. Vortigern will pay you dearly for this information."

"Why?"

"He wants all the heirs of Uther dead." And Mórganthu wanted them dead too, but didn't say it. Revenge upon that man's entire house because Uther had murdered Mórganthu's son and caused his daughter's death.

Tregeagle drooled on Mórganthu's neck. "You know this? He will pay gold?"

"Happily ... happily, O Magister. All the gold you can wish for."

Tregeagle fell back, freeing Mórganthu. He dropped his sword clanking upon a rock. "Gold ... I shall have gold again ..."

Mórganthu pushed himself up and held his arm, which was stiff and painful. He would neither forget Tregeagle's infractions, nor forgive, for Mórganthu never let any trespass go. "Take your warriors and capture Uther's girls ... and keep them until Vortigern comes."

"No, but I will send Erbin to fetch Vortigern."

"Troslam might take them somewhere else and hide them ... No, you must capture them!"

"And then have to feed them? Are you mad? Let Troslam give those leeches his crumbs, I say. You'll keep watch, now, won't you?"

"I?"

"Yes, you and your druidow," Tregeagle said, picking up his gladius again. "And if the girls get away, you'll pay with your nose ... and then I'll kill you for being the clumsy imp you are."

Mórganthu rubbed at the cut on his nose and backed away, nodding.

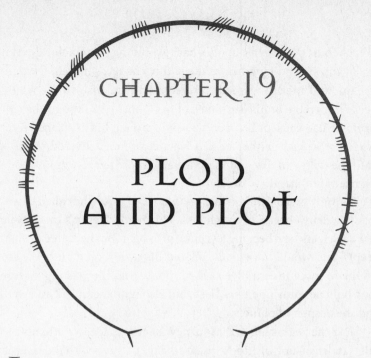

CHAPTER 19

PLOD
AND PLOT

The slaves' trek north took over a month. The Picts raided, pillaged, and burnt their way home, encountering no group of British warriors large enough to stop them. Over two hundred other slaves had been taken during the course of their sojourn, and they trailed behind Merlin with clanking chains, moaning and huffing.

Natalenya fared the worst of them all. She started out each day walking strong, but then when the sun became hot, she would weaken. By the end, she would be helped along by Colvarth and Caygek until she would faint. That was when Merlin would bear her in his arms, for no one else of sufficient strength would carry her for fear of catching the sickness of bloated scabs that covered her arms and legs. Thankfully, the chains attaching him to Garth and Bedwir were long enough to allow him to do this penance.

And with each step, each raw stride upon Merlin's aching legs and bloodied feet, he carried her. Up hills and down valleys. Through streams, and under the dark canopy of forsaken forests. Past raided villages where the old women cried over their dead. Each day when he picked her up, his back would begin to ache. Soon it would throb. And long before the end of the day's march, it would scream, and Merlin wanted to scream with it. Instead, he would weep in regret — of his decisions, of his foolishness, and of the suffering he had caused. Yes, and he would lament his misplaced trust in God who had neither healed Natalenya nor delivered them — until the tears ran dry and there were no more left to wet his growing beard and her dirty dress.

The only grace — if horrible, awful grace it could be called — was that Natalenya began to weigh less. This made Merlin's impossible task easier, and she became less painful to bear. But he feared for her, deeply, and would have gladly shared his own food with her if she would do more than nibble at her rations. And the wasting disease took hold not only upon her flesh, but also upon her mind and soul, and she despaired of life.

Near the beginning of the journey, Necton made two attempts to kill Natalenya, not wishing a diseased slave to travel with them. Each time, by some grace, Merlin was alerted in time to gather everyone around her and prevent him. Over the next few days, when Necton saw that no one else had caught the disease, especially Merlin, he relented and left her alone. His malevolent stare, however, hinted that he wished her to die and disappear.

Colvarth tried his best to help her, but no matter what chance herb he found while marching, none could halt the spreading boils or draw out their dread pus. The old man would shake his head, close his eyes, and pray, but there was little else he could do.

Bedwir also fell under Colvarth's care, and to Merlin's amazement, the man slowly healed of his wounds. By the end of their journey, he began to look again like one of Uther's warriors: stern, determined, and deadly. If only he had a blade. Though obviously grieved at their predicament, the man had an inner joy at finding Arthur — and Merlin resented this. Finding Arthur as a slave? There was little hope in that. Very little, as far as Merlin could see.

And Arthur himself would hold on to Garth's neck through the long marches. Always quiet, always watching, he seemed to somehow understand their danger and did not add to the burden by crying without warrant. During rests he would crawl about, laugh, play with Colvarth's beard, pull himself up on Merlin's knees, and even take a few faltering steps.

Garth held up the best of them all, and though he complained bitterly about his lost bagpipe and the lack and quality of their food, he somehow thrived. To Merlin's amazement, he grew taller, and though thinner, it allowed his strength to show through the more. What did concern Merlin, however, was his long, whispering talks with Caygek, and his willingness to serve Necton — even when the man was cruel. Garth even tried to learn the Pictish language. Was he seeking better rations, which he rarely got, or was he hoping to somehow get his bagpipe back? Or worse, was he just avoiding Merlin and his sullen, scarred face?

Caygek, ahh ... now he was a puzzle. If Merlin had been made of straw, then Caygek would have set him ablaze. Yet, the two-faced lout that he was, the druid would let Colvarth lean upon him as needed during their long marches — yes, Colvarth, the man whom all druidow hated because he had left their ranks and taken the Harp of Britain with him. Ah, they itched for his natural death and the day they could rightfully reclaim the harp. So why did Caygek help him? Merlin would have thought that Colvarth's swift death would have pleased Caygek more than anything in that man's miserable, sour life.

Peredur helped Colvarth as well on the rough journey, and more than once remarked how the old man was like the grandfather he'd never had. During the journey, Merlin gleaned some details from the young man's life ... growing up in Kembry, his father having gout, his older brothers fighting the Saxenow. Him not being allowed to fight because of his small stature. And now he was a slave, and unlikely to ever see his family again — if any of them even lived after the Pictish raid. And it angered him to see their family's horses being used as pack animals. "Those horses were imported, bred, and trained for war. And the Picts don't even know!"

Colvarth tried to keep their spirits up during the march by leading them in prayer and worship, especially on every Lord's Day, but Merlin found it hard to focus on God with the slave collar pressing upon his shoulders. Raw wounds had formed, and as much as he tried to shift the iron band around, the sores never seemed to heal.

They marched northward over seventy leagues and finally passed the first wall built by the Romans — of stone stacked to the height of three spans and on top wide enough for two men to walk abreast. Such a foolish emperor to think he could keep the Picts out of Britain. Keep them from swooping down and taking slaves. At least this first wall, the *Vallum Aelium* built by Hadrian, was mostly intact despite it being abandoned many decades earlier. But what good did it do without warriors to guard it? None — and the Picts took Merlin and the other slaves through one of the many broken-down gates with neither hindrance nor challenge.

But they were not yet in Pictish lands, for the vast, trackless Kelithon Forest still lay between them and the second Roman wall — the point of no return. Merlin asked Colvarth who ruled the land between the two walls.

The bard blinked before answering, his wrinkle-lined eyes sunken now after so much exertion. "This is Guotodin land, and King Atle rules here. He has been a sometime friend to Uther's house — and sometime enemy."

"Atle?" Merlin asked. "You mean he's still alive?"

"Alive? Oh, I would not be surprised. And that is more strange than you can know."

"He was old when my father visited there, but why is that strange? You are old yourself."

Colvarth sighed. "And shortly to die."

"I didn't say that."

"But it is true. And here is the peculiar part: The tales when I was a youth told that even then Atle was very old."

Merlin shook his head. "Huh."

"And years later I consulted with his advisers over a dispute with the druidow. I beheld him myself then, and he seemed even younger than I, which makes little sense to me even now."

"But my mother was —"

"Yes, I am familiar with the story of your father … with your story." Colvarth looked at Merlin, his eyes alight. "You are Atle's grandson, and that may be worth something to us."

"But he doesn't even know I'm alive. I can't prove the relation. And my father and mother ran from that man's wrath. What makes you think —"

"Yet I am filled with hopefulness, for you resemble him in some ways."

Merlin pondered that thought for awhile, but dismissed it as folly. Why would Atle care about his fate? The man had tried to kill Merlin's mother, his own beloved daughter, when she became a Christian. Unless Atle had changed, and drastically, then he might hate Merlin all the more.

From that point on the terrain grew more rugged and the trees thickened. Merlin's job carrying Natalenya became harder. And her strength flagged — so that now Merlin had to carry her more often. As she lay in his arms unconscious through those arduous hours, he hoped she wouldn't remember that it was he who carried her, for he wanted to set her free from her promise to him, foolish him who had enslaved them, scarred and ugly him who did not deserve her love.

And as he plodded the ridgeways with Natalenya hanging limp in his arms, forded streams at shallow spots, and slogged through the tree-thick vales, all became a mashed pottage of pity, sadness, and anger — with a finger of madness stirring at the edges. Chains. Moans. Clinking. Aching. Slipping. Bleeding. Scabbing. Collapsing. Death. Dying. Desperation. These woods — this Kelithon Forest — became to him, and always would be, the forest of his penance, and the forest of his inner screams.

Finally, with deep exhaustion beyond anything Merlin had ever felt, they arrived at the second wall, the long-abandoned *Vallum Antoninus*, a broken and menacing barrier of turf and rocks whose scattered bones marked the entrance into Pictish lands. Merlin had heard of this ruined wall — and the living death its passage represented — but had never imagined he himself would one day cross it.

And gratefully, after only a few more leagues, they reached the tribe's lands, the entrance of which was marked by a line of large, stone monuments decorated with decaying skulls of men and horses.

The village lay on the western shore of the largest lake Merlin had ever seen, its reaches stretching beyond his sight to the north. And beyond the village lay a high mountain range skirted by gray and brown-topped foothills with colossal, moss-bound pines.

The village itself was larger than Bosventor — perhaps three hundred domed huts made completely of stone, including the roofs. And the Picts had their own fortress built into the side of a glen not far away, and in the glen there flowed a stream that emptied into the lake. The surrounding farmland had not yet been tilled, as spring came later in the north.

"We are all blessed," Colvarth said to Merlin after they arrived.

"Blessed?" Merlin said, hardly comprehending the word. He set Natalenya down on the grass and fell on his side, sucking in air.

"Yes, the land of the Picts goes another seventy leagues north ..."

"We'd still be walking for a long while, sure. I'm glad too."

"You would still be walking, yes. But I ... I would soon die."

And it was true, the old man had spent himself on the journey. Merlin rested a hand on Colvarth's shoulder and felt what little was left on his bones.

A celebration ensued for the warriors, victorious over their soft, southern enemies and rich with slaves and plunder. They feasted long into the night while the slaves' camp lay quiet like a corpse. Only one guard was posted, for no one, including Merlin, had the strength to flee.

But a thought bothered Merlin as he fell asleep in a drafty stone hut that had been given them: The village appeared to own no previous slaves. If the Picts captured slaves every year, what had become of them?

The next day, about midmorning, Necton came, took Arthur from them, and painted new designs of blue paint upon the young boy's chest. His wife, whom they later knew as Gormla, was standing to the side of the crowd, and he gave the child into her arms. Arthur cried as they carried him away. Merlin wanted to stop him, but there was nothing he could do. Not yet.

The warriors assembled all the slaves, and Ealtain addressed them. "Anns Tauchen-Twilloch be village-i, and airson bless'ive yiu ris our gle ghodis, and ris our peiple. Reborn is now an land, and be'ive yiu our offering ris it."

Ealtain droned on, but Merlin ignored him. What did it matter? At least he understood the part about where they were — the village of *Tauchen-Twilloch* — and as far beyond the end of the known world as Merlin could imagine.

Garth stepped next to Colvarth. "I'm startin' to understan' their speech ... Did he say they're goin' to sacrifice us?"

"No ... at least not yet." Colvarth answered. "It means we will be the ones working their land, their offering to it."

Garth shared the translation with a slave next to him, and so the word spread.

And Merlin soon learned what Ealtain meant: Breaking up the soil with ard and hoe, even if their backs nearly broke. Digging out thousands of rocks until their knees were numb. Planting the crops of barley, oats, wheat, beans, and turnips, even in the pouring rain. Weeding until their fingers bled. Hauling water on aching shoulders whenever the summer wind raked the top of the land with its dry talons.

Merlin wanted to close his eyes and wish it all away, but couldn't. Slowly, he became numb. Numb to the work. Numb to the beatings when he didn't go fast enough. Numb to the deaths. Numb to everything except Natalenya. Merlin worried for her. With her sickness, no one wanted her working in the fields, and so she was relegated to a mold-and-slime-encrusted rock hut far away from the others. This was the "hut of the dead," he had been told, and here she rested and, if it was possible, improved a little.

And some of the other slaves did give their very life blood, for they were whipped if they didn't work hard enough, and some men died at the hands of a merciless Pict and his ripping, choking rope. Necton himself was harsh to his slaves, especially to Merlin.

"Lazy doig, yiu!" Necton yelled at him one summer day as he clouted Merlin on the back for the third time with the haft of his spear.

Merlin had done nothing but stop to let Garth and Bedwir catch their breaths while the three were carrying water. Now Merlin had paid for it with a bruised back and a welt on his neck.

"Thusa work-ha harder yiu, or make-idh yui an Scafta thrail, and then yiu'll pay-sa."

Merlin cringed at this threat to make him Scafta's slave, for Necton meant it, knowing full well Scafta longed to beat Merlin into submission and remove completely any threat from someone the people considered a rival bard.

For if he ever became Scafta's slave, he wouldn't last long, as the witch doctor was brutal. One poor slave found out the hard way by misplacing his wooden comb. When he found it again, it was helping hold up Scafta's voluminous hair. The man, indignant of having lost everything else, could not stand this final outrage. He snuck up behind Scafta and pulled it out. Scafta whipped around, grabbed the man's wrist, pinned him to the ground, and slew him.

Merlin had to find a way for them to escape — and soon.

His first break came when Bedwir found an iron-plated wooden hammer left behind beside their oat field when some workers had finished repairing a cart axel. Merlin hid it underneath a rock just behind a tree. And so he began to plan.

But was Natalenya too sick? She had improved a little, yes, but enough to survive such a journey? They had to try, even if going slowly was the only way.

As summer's frenzy rusted away to fall's exhaustion, no opportunity to escape presented itself. At lest the weeding became less, so Garth and Colvarth were given the job of helping prepare food for the slaves, as well as the Picts. To do this more effectively, they were chained only to each other, and even had the privilege of handling some old knives to cut up the food under the watchful eyes of one of the Pictish guards.

One day Merlin was carrying a heaping basket of oats to a storage hut, and he passed Garth stirring a pot of old, weevil-infested beans over a fire. The boy said to the Colvarth, "It's all wrong." A few tears had rolled down his cheek, and he wiped them off.

Colvarth arched a dirty eyebrow. "The soup will taste better than it looks."

"Not the soup," Garth said, dropping in some long fetticus weeds pulled from the wheat fields. "This slavin' an all o' Scafta's killin' ... an their pagan worship. It's all wrong. I saw a lot with the druidow, an' I'm sick of that witch doctor even more than I was o' the ard dre."

Scafta walked by with Garth's bagpipe under his arm, as he often did in the evenings. He turned a wicked eye at Garth, fuffed up the bagpipe with air, and began playing. To Merlin it sounded like Scafta was squeezing a sick rat to death. The boy played much, much better.

Garth clenched his jaw.

"There is something we might do," Colvarth whispered, "besides pray and hope."

"What?" Garth asked as he leaned forward to hear the reply.

A warrior yelled at Merlin to get moving, and so he never heard Colvarth's answer.

It had only been two days since Mórganthu's pact with Tregeagle, but he was already fretting the decision. He ground his teeth while walking back and forth outside his tent. Around his tent. To the stone circle. Around the stone circle. To the southwest to gloat over Uther's cairn. Oh, how he wanted Ganieda. How he wanted the fang — desperately. But if he made any move to take either back, then Uther's girls might flee and hide. If so, then Tregeagle and his warriors would try to exact the gold debt upon Mórganthu and his precious nose.

Surely he could just leave and Tregeagle would never find him. But he couldn't abandon his daughter's daughter to these worshipers of a foreign god, never, so he had to stay. And not only that, but he wanted to see for himself this honey-dipped retribution upon Uther's children.

But the fang? Was there any way to get the fang? No. Even going back to see if the shutter was unlocked was too chancy. And Ganieda could use it to defend herself, if needed.

He would have to wait until Vortigern came, and then make sure the oaf knew that *his* granddaughter was also in the house and she was not to be touched. There must be no confusion.

If only he had more than four of his druidow to help. The rest had dug the Honor Pit, set their dead brothers's bodies in it, and left. So only two could be called upon to take turns watching Troslam's house. Mórganthu vowed to make them vigilant, for these remaining scums of Uther would not escape before vengeance had been exacted.

And the orb, aha, the orb would help him keep watch. Since Ganieda had used it so effortlessly to see places far away, even visit them, could Mórganthu learn its secrets too? If so, then he could scrutinize those around Ganieda to make sure she was being treated well. And he could also quite possibly see and observe other things happening in Britain, Erin, and even across the sea. With the orb he could devote his time to learning the secrets of the world, expanding the knowledge of the druidow, and thereby increasing their power.

He ran back to his tent and took out the orb from the deep barrel where it had been hid. It felt somewhat soft to the touch, which was strange since he could see into one side of it like it was made of glass. He fingered the fibers coming out the other end, and they had stiffened over the last many days. Some of them had even broke off. What was this thing? He held it up before his eyes, and commanded it to show him where Merlin was. Mórganthu wanted to gloat over that meddler's squirming slavery.

Tendrils of a black smoke swirled inside and then lit up with a dim, purple radiance. Soon the image cleared, and he spied Merlin, a stubbly beard on his smudged, sweating face. The man trekked north with a slave collar pinned around his neck, and his skin bled under its heavy grip. He'd even been chained to other slaves. And though Mórganthu could clearly see all of Merlin's suffering — and the suffering of that wretched Garth and the wicked Colvarth — Mórganthu became so incensed that the scoundrel lived that he wanted to smash the orb against a rock. But he dared not, for with the orb he could see many things.

And so as the leaves turned from summer's green to autumn's brown, he spent his time absorbed with more important visions, such as that traitorous Vortigern. There he sat, with a majestic torc around his neck as he began his reign as High King of the Britons. Thousands of warriors lauded him, each one bowing before him and kissing his boot. The flat-nosed Vortipor stood beside him, only half interested in the proceedings. The hall around the new High King was being rebuilt, and Vortigern smiled like a buffoon at the masons and carpenters busy at work. Ah, but he would come to Bosventor soon, like a dog to its vomit, and kill Uther's daughters on Mórganthu's behalf. What a nice thing for him to do. Mórganthu didn't have to lift a finger. Only watch. And wait.

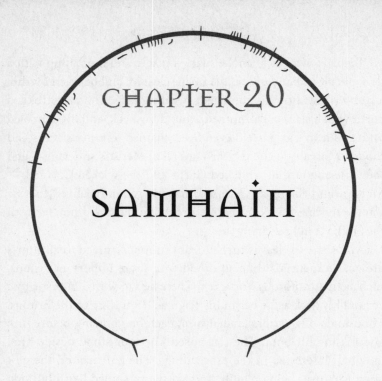

CHAPTER 20

SAMHAIN

W eeks passed with Merlin waiting for the moon to go from full, to half, to a cold crescent, to nothing but a hoary sliver — and the time to act had arrived. With the nights getting fridgid, they couldn't wait another month, guards or no guards.

So early the next morning, before the warriors drove them from the stone huts to work, Merlin rolled over to Colvarth, woke him, and told him of the secret mallet and of his plan.

The bard's face flushed in the thin light filtering through the door, and he motioned Merlin closer. "It is all I could hope for, but it will be difficult."

Merlin tensed his neck, thinking of the risk. "I know."

"You do not. Tonight, when the moon is dark, the Picts will celebrate their pagan harvest feast of Samhain. Have you not known why they work us to the bone to finish the harvest?"

"Perhaps they will be careless."

"Perhaps not. To them, it is a night when the otherworld bleeds through to our own to work its mischeif. They will celebrate, certainly, but they will be afraid, and more than likely post more guards around the village."

"They're that afraid?"

"They fear the otherworld. And because of that, many fear you."

"Still?"

"Scafta is afraid."

"He hates me, sure — "

"Lately, he has been observing you more. The last few days I have often seen him standing in the woods, studying you. Watching from the shadows."

Just then, a darkness fell over the door.

Merlin sucked in his breath and bit his lip.

"Thusa get-a up yiu!"

It was just one of the guards, come to wake them up.

That day the Picts worked the slaves many extra hours to finish cutting and threshing the wheat crop. Necton took particular interest in driving Merlin to the breaking point and brought a whip to keep him moving. It didn't matter if Merlin's left calf had cramped up, that his blistered hands wept their pus onto the wheat, or that his right elbow throbbed in pain — he had to keep loading the wooden carts with sheaves until they could hold no more, or else endure additional scars added to his back.

Merlin was thankful Bedwir was chained beside him and did his best to help, despite his right foot having been injured on a thorn the week before.

The slaves then pulled each cart over to a large, flat rock where Caygek, Peredur, and many others threshed the sheaves. From there they sifted the grain into hundreds of baskets and clay pots for storage inside a row of stone crennigs. The Picts hoped that these grains would last the village through the long, snow-deep winter.

Merlin cast a heavy bundle of sheaves onto the nearest cart and then turned to pick up another when he saw Colvarth and Garth, chained together, walk toward the woods with a guard at their heels.

Merlin's tongue felt thick and dry, but he called out anyway, "Where're you going?"

Garth waved. "A hunter got a deer, an' we're s'posed to skin it an' roast it."

"Did you sharpen your knives this time?" Merlin called.

"Yesterday's boar taught me. *Always sharp yer knives* is me new motto!"

Hopefully, the boy had learned a different lesson as well and wouldn't get another bashing. Earlier in the day a Pictish cook had punched Garth in the eye for tasting the roasted boar's crispy skin so he could "make sure it'd been salted right."

Merlin shook his head at the boy. What a trial it must be for Garth to cook up big pots of grouse and oat porridge soup … without being able to taste one spoonful. To bake baskets and baskets of steaming barley rolls … without being able to eat one crumb. To boil and mash great tubs of honeyed sloe and rowan berries … without being able to even dip his thumb in. To fillet heaps of pike and smoke them … without being able to nibble the smallest morsel.

Thinking about it made Merlin hungry too, for he and the other slaves would get their same, worthless fare: moldy bread, and if they were lucky, some old, dry meat only fit for a dog. He was glad Garth could get away from the cooking for a bit — at least he wouldn't be tempted.

But lack of food meant nothing to Merlin. He just wanted their escape to succeed.

And the other slaves? They just wanted to survive to the feast, for Scafta's lust for blood made him hunt among them for any infractions worth a beating. And he found such a violation in a bare-chested, older slave who he caught sleeping under a pile of sheaves.

"I … I was jus' … checkin for bugs!" the man said as two warriors stood him up and shoved him toward Scafta.

The others backed up, and a circle was quickly formed. Necton stood nearby, and he secretly scowled at Ealtain when the chieftain stepped over to see what was going on.

Scafta crouched, ready to spring, one hand balled in a fist, and the other holding his shaman stick.

The slave backed up, but a warrior shoved him forward once again.

Scafta struck, lunging to the man's left and cracking him over the head.

But the slave fought back. He shook his head and picked up a wooden hay fork. He held it up and jabbed it forward.

Scafta turned to the side, and as swift as a fox he slid off a secret cap on top of his shaman stick and swung the stick toward the slave. An iron-tipped, crude dart flew out and punctured the slave deeply in the chest.

The man staggarred back, dropping the pitchfork. He looked down at the dart and screamed. His hand drifted up unsteadily, took hold of it, pulled it out, and then his face turned white.

He fell to his knees then, just in time for Scafta to kick the slave twice in the gut with his spiked boots. Blood poured out as the slave collapsed, moaning.

Scafta retrieved the dart, put it back in his stick, and then strutted near Merlin with that enormous shrub of hair massed upon his head, all the while picking at his teeth as if he'd just eaten Merlin's liver.

Clenching his fists, Merlin wanted to rip each one of Scafta's ribs out, and he would have if it hadn't meant certain death at the hands of the Pictish warriors, who looked at Scafta with awe on their faces. Even Necton, who stood nearby, had a look of shock. And Ealtain, the man who derived a portion of his authority from the witch doctor, walked away from the fight with a fearful, backward glance. Who could stand up to such a one? All Merlin could do was glare back until Scafta tired of his gloating, turned on his heel, and left.

The slave died that hour: shaking, vomiting, and mumbling about strange colors.

Later that day, Merlin, Bedwir, and a number of other slaves were given the task of dragging logs to a clearing in the middle of the village where the Samhain fire would be lit. All around, the Picts worked on masks made from the dried, thick hides of large turnips: ghoulish, horned, sooted black, and grinning. They planned to wear these while dancing, and so smeared ashes on their bodies to make them as white as ghosts. Their practiced chants reminded Merlin of a cross between the guttural howls of wolves and the warning cacaphony of crows.

And whenever Merlin looked into the face of a fellow slave, there was a tightness about the eyes. They were afraid, all of them, for their usefulness would soon come to an end. Only one hundred and fifty or so remained of the original two hundred slaves; some had given in to disease, some had been killed, some just suddenly died from overwork. None had escaped. What would the Picts do with them when the work was done?

And so Merlin wrestled with his desire to free all of the slaves, and not just his own little band — but decided it was too risky. His oath had been to Arthur, and to that he would be true — even if he was a fool to try even that. Could Arthur really come to the throne of his father? Could the island be ruled by justice, and *every* slave set free?

Deep down, Merlin doubted, for the months of suffering and the sickening stupidity of his decisions had grown a callus so thick that he could hardly feel his soul breathe anymore. The only dim hope he had was to escape. But would they all just be dragged back before morning? If so, would Necton give Merlin over to Scafta so the witch doctor could exact his ultimate revenge?

In the midst of his wood hauling, Merlin spotted Arthur playing outside Necton's hut under Gormla's watchful eye. He wanted to go over and hug the boy, talk to him, and tell him it would be over soon — but he couldn't arouse suspicions. He needed to wait until tonight. And there was work to do, so he and Bedwir stacked the wood for the fire to the height of a man and then some.

Dusk fell, and all the slaves were sent to their end of the village, along with five guards set as watch. Most of the slaves retired to their stone huts for the night, but Merlin gathered his band together and had them light their own small fire about ten paces from the edge of the Picts' feast. All, that is, except Natalenya, whom Merlin would warn of their plan in a short while.

Thankfully, the six of them were chained in pairs now, and not three together: Caygek with Peredur, Colvarth with Garth, and Merlin with Bedwir. This would make it easier to attack the guards, if they could somehow get them down to three.

"This night is special for the Picts," Colvarth explained to Peredur, who had been brought up ignorant of the old ways, "because for them it marks the death of the season of light, and the birth of the season of darkness."

A man stepped up to them, the firelight making shadows play on his face. It was Necton, and he held a hammer in his hand. He pointed to Garth and had him kneel as he unbent the pin holding the boy's slave collar to Colvarth.

He grabbed the boy by the tunic and began dragging him toward the feast.

Merlin jumped to his feet and began to follow, motioning for Bedwir to join him — until Colvarth grabbed their chain and stopped them.

"Do not interfere," he said. "I have witnessed this celebration once before, and I think the boy is safe."

"You think?"

"I cannot be certain."

"Then I — "

Colvarth yanked the chain. "If I am wrong, there is nothing you can do. There are too many warriors."

"But I — "

"If something must be done, then wait and pray, and I will tell you when."

Merlin sat down again and tried to take a deep breath, but his heart sped up instead as he watched the proceedings before him.

Necton took Garth and made him kneel before Scafta, who rubbed his hands together in glee, and then strapped to the boy's back a wooden saddle from which hung, on his left and right, two large bronze circles emblazoned with the image of the sun. The saddle had a wooden statue shaped like a rider that held a large drinking horn.

"This is the Sun Horn," Colvarth explained, "and it holds a special admixture of ale and … other things."

The horn itself had been taken from some massive beast, and Merlin could only fathom how dangerous hunting it must have been. Its drinking edge had been circled in gold, and golden wires spiraled down along the horn's sides to the sharp tip.

After Garth was positioned and given instructions, he pawed forward on all fours, pretending to be a horse — a very careful horse — and delivered to them their ale. The Picts' voices rose in uproarious laughter at this spectacle, and Merlin thought Garth would turn red from embarrassment, but for some reason, he did not. He held still on all fours, first before Ealtain, then before three other leading warriors whom Merlin did not know, then before Necton, each one lifting the horn from its socket, drinking a long draught, and then replacing it.

Last, Garth waddled the horn before Scafta, who lifted it high and babbled on before the crowd about the sun's death and how they would celebrate that night to assure its warm return. Then he drained the horn before placing it back in its socket in the wooden saddle.

General merriment ensued, with the Picts passing around bowls of ale, along with baskets of little biscuits shaped like the sun, and these they ate with relish. Garth was released from his saddle, and he ran back to Merlin and the others, picking up along the way two biscuits that had been dropped.

Merlin realized he'd been holding his breath, and knew why when he saw Garth's face.

It was white. "Scafta said he'd cut my throat if I spilled the ale."

Merlin turned angrily to Colvarth. "Did you know this?"

Colvarth sighed. "I suspected, but I did not know for certain. At the Samhain feast I witnessed many years ago, the young boy did not spill the ale either."

"You risked —"

"No, I trusted in God ... You are the one who would have risked."

Merlin crossed his arms. "Well, we're all going to risk it tonight. Is that understood?"

Everyone nodded, including a still-pale Garth, who ate one of the biscuits. After finishing it, he handed the other to Merlin. "It's sweet, but I'm not hungry anymore," he said, wiping the crumbs from his mouth.

Merlin then explained as quietly as he could the full plan — and finished just before Necton returned to fix Garth's slave collars on again.

After this was finished, Merlin made his exit, taking Bedwir along, to visit Natalenya. And he brought with him the biscuit to give as a gift.

As they approached her hut, a pang of guilt swept over him because he only visited her once every few days or so, not wanting to keep her heart entangled. Colvarth continually reprimanded him for this, and made sure to visit her twice a day. Even though this made the burden lighter for Merlin, it was not enough to ease his conscience.

Looking inside her hut, he saw her kneeling next to a flickering fire of bramblewood. Why wasn't she resting? She needed to gather her strength, especially if they were to escape in the middle of the night. As he ducked under the low doorway, leaving Bedwir outside, he prepared to scold her — but then he heard her whispering in prayer. He shut his mouth and stood there while she finished.

Even in her sickness, with her cheeks sunken and her body so frail, she was beautiful. When he was blind, he had tried to imagine what she looked like, but never thought he would see her one day … nor hear her say that she loved him. From her sweetly curved eyebrows pressed across her closed, caring eyes, past the tip of her impertinent nose over those tender lips moving quietly in prayer, down to her small, pretty chin — he loved her.

After a short while, she sat up, saw him and then faced away. "You're here."

"We're leaving tonight. All of us."

"Not me."

"Yes. All of us. We're going to take Arthur and head south."

"I don't know if I have the strength," she said, a hint of a tremble to her voice.

"I brought you something."

"I don't need it."

"It's sweet … it might give you strength." He held the biscuit out.

"Eat it yourself."

"It'll help."

"That's not what I need."

Merlin looked down. "What do you want, then? I'll see if I can get it."

She turned then, and her reply was cold. "I want some beef, braised and roasted in carrot gravy and served in a silver chalice. A warm blanket and a fine dress. Servants to wait upon my every wish. A comb for clean hair and oil for my unblemished skin."

Merlin felt his soul begin to rip apart.

She sat in silence. When he glanced up, there were tears streaming down her face.

"I'm sorry," was all he could say.

"No, you're not."

"I am," he choked out. "You've lost all those things, and I can't promise them. We might not make it tonight."

She bared her teeth. "I don't want those things, and what I do want you won't give me."

He broke the biscuit in his hand, not knowing what to say. He wanted to whip it against the wall, but he cradled it in his trembling palm instead. "Let me know what it is ... I'll give it."

"You."

CHAPTER 21

ESCAPE

Back in his hut, Merlin's muscles ached to the point that he had trouble resting. His calf hurt in particular. Not that a bed in the dirt with a rumpled-up ragged tunic for a pillow helped any. Most of all, his heart hurt ... for Natalenya. What was he to do? She needed him, but he had vowed to free her from her promise.

So he got up and sat in the shadow of the hut's doorway, the others snoring around him, and watched for the Picts to settle down for the night. But his wait stretched on because they danced for hours like spinning phantoms with their ash ethereal bodies and black masks. And they chanted, screamed, and beat the ground with spears while Scafta pranced around the Samhain bonfire like a demon-horse, calling on their gods for protection and for the death of enemies.

By the time the villagers retired and slunk off into the darkness, the stars had whirled far from where they had appeared at sunset, and though it worried Merlin that dawn wasn't far off, he breathed a sigh of relief when the five guards turned in and only two took their place.

And these two, who were all that prevented their escape, spent some time rekindling the fire that Merlin had lit earlier and settled down on the large rocks that surrounded the fire. This was exactly what Merlin had hoped for, and he had positioned the fire so that the guards would have their back to Merlin's hut.

It was time.

He alerted Colvarth and the snoring, snuffle-mouthed Garth so they could keep watch. He then woke Caygek, Peredur, and Bedwir, and they stripped off all their extra, ragged clothing and snaked them through the chains as best they could to keep them from clinking.

Merlin directed them to leave the hut in absolute silence. Once outside, he and Bedwir stretched their chain taut between them to remove all chance of noise, and Peredur and Caygek did the same. They then approached the guards with muted footsteps. Slowly. Crouching. Pausing. Walking.

Ahead, one of the guards finished chewing on a chunk of meat and threw the bone behind him. It landed a few paces from Merlin with a dull thud — giving him an idea. He bent down, picked up two rocks with his free hand, and then directed them forward.

When they got to within lunging distance of the guards, Merlin threw the two stones over their heads and into the darkness. The guards grabbed their spears, and, blinded by the campfire, stood to peer toward the sound.

Merlin made eye contact with Bedwir, Caygek, and then Peredur. Nodding twice, they lunged forward. Merlin and Bedwir wrapped their chain around the nearest guard's neck and throttled him so tightly that only a muffled gasp came out. Caygek and Peredur did the same with their guard, and soon, both were dead.

Not wanting to see the man's face, Merlin closed his eyes as he let the body fall to the ground. And even though he picked up the spears and started to rush back to get the others and escape, Caygek halted him.

Carefully, the druid and Peredur sat the bodies upright by leaning them against the large rocks to make them look as natural as possible. Then Caygek took some other rocks and used them to brace up their heads.

As a final touch, he threw a few more logs on the fire, and then they stole off into the darkness to get Garth and the bard, who had both been watching with wide eyes. From there, it was a short walk to Natalenya's hut, where she was waiting with a small bundle of cloth.

"Leave it," Merlin said.

She shook her head. "It's for Arthur. We might need to change him still."

Merlin led them out to the field, and to the tree where the hammer lay hidden. He had no trouble finding it in the dark, for the trunk was much thicker than its companions. The hammer was still there, and its heft felt like a promise of freedom in Merlin's hands. From there, he led theme into the woods a good distance, and with as little noise as possible, he unbent the pin that kept Caygek and Peredur's collars chained together, and then the pin that held him and Bedwir's.

Natalenya, of all them, did not have a slave collar because no one cared whether she lived or died, whether she stayed or went.

Turning to Garth, he was surprised to find the boy already free and his slave collar laying on the ground. "It never fit anyway," he said with a mischevious grin.

But to free Colvarth, he still had to unbend the pin, and he did so with Garth's help. And just as Merlin lifted the slave collar off of the bard's shoulders, the man let out a stifled screech.

"Shah!" Bedwir said.

"But my harp! In my excitement, I forgot my harp!"

Merlin thought for a moment before answering. "We'll have to leave it. We have no choice."

"You do not understand ... it is the very Harp of Britain!"

"Arthur's more important!"

"But I —"

Merlin waved him to silence. Now for the most dangerous part of their escape: sneaking into the village, finding Necton's hut, and stealing Arthur back. All without being discovered.

Merlin tilted his spear down and knelt behind a bush at the very edge of the village. Garth joined him, with Bedwir staying in the shadows just in case something went wrong.

Now where had he seen Arthur playing ? He tried to remember the shape of Necton's hut ... was it slightly oblong compared to the others? No! It was taller to accommodate the man's height. So he looked out over the village, but everything looked different at night. Many of the doorways were covered by a large flap of leather, but some were not, and the nearest one's black interior gaped at him like the frowning mouth of a giant, eyeless skull.

Merlin held his breath. All it would take was one hound to start baying and they were dead. He pointed around one side of the nearest hut, crept out with Garth, and then began walking quietly, yet as normal as he could, trying to pose as one of the villagers.

Garth tumbled over a tripod holding two chains attached to a spit, but Merlin caught him. The spit still had a roasted bird on it, half eaten already, and it swayed dangerously toward the bars. Garth grabbed it, steadied it, and pulled off a wing.

"No," Merlin whispered.

Garth shook his head and held the wing behind his back.

Merlin huffed but chose to ignore it. Up ahead was Necton's hut, a little to the left. He led Garth around to approach it from the side. Now for the trickiest thing he had ever done. If it was only one man inside, he might rush in, spear him, and hope for the best — but with Necton and his wife both there, surely someone would yell and they'd be caught.

No ... Merlin had to *sneak* inside and steal Arthur without them knowing.

Just then, behind Garth, the leather flap of a hut's door was pushed aside.

A little boy stepped out, and, ignoring them in his bleary-eyed state, ran over to a rock and relieved himself. The child was older than Arthur, but not by much if you counted his size.

Garth tapped Merlin on the shoulder.

"What?"

"Watch ..."

Garth walked over to the boy and offered him the wing, holding the roasted meat right under the boy's nose and whispering something in Pictish. The boy took the wing, a confused look on his face as he nibbled at the greasy skin. Garth then took the boy's other hand and walked him toward Necton's hut. He opened the hut's flap as quietly as he could, and stepped inside with the boy.

Merlin crouched down in the shadow of the hut. This wasn't how he'd planned it — Merlin was supposed to go inside while Garth kept watch. His heart hammered against his ribs, and he felt his arms pulse with fire. In contrast, the spear felt cold in his hands. Time, measured in heartbeats, throbbed painfully slow.

A noise. Scuffing feet. Garth appeared before him holding a sleeping Arthur, who wore nothing but a deerskin loin cloth. He was sucking his thumb as he snuggled into Garth's tunic.

Merlin dared a breath.

They fled, yet Merlin's legs felt made of mud. Finally to the woods, where Bedwir joined them as they made a hasty and silent retreat to where the others hid. Merlin told the story, and everyone hugged Garth, including Natalenya.

Southward Merlin led them, following the lake shore until they neared the edge of the tribe's lands, marked by a line of large, stone monuments adorned with mocking skulls.

But something pricked Merlin's ears, tuned as they were by his years of blindness. He halted the party next to some bushes and they ducked down.

Ahead, a shadow stepped out from one of the stones and moved stealthily toward them.

Merlin tensed.

Footfalls. A whistling call. Murmurs. Shouting.

He looked between the branches and spied ash-grimed warriors running toward them.

While having his four druidow take turns obeying Tregeagle's demands to keep watch on the weaver's home, Mórganthu passed his time spying, calling up scenes through the orb. Among many other things, he examined the state of Erin, his homeland, including its king, named Ailill Molt, that ruffian of a Christian with hair growing out of his ears. He stood among the king's monkish counselors, who traipsed about in their rotten robes. Mórganthu wished for the fang then, that he might cause as much pain to the king as possible, for the memory burned in Mórganthu's mind of the killing of the Brotherhood of True Seers, and of their heads upon poles. After Pádraig had given over the church to be ruled by that simpleton of a singer, Benignus, the king had declared war upon the druidow who would not convert. Mórganthu yearned for both men's death upon the stone at the hill of Tara, so that the isle might be given a new birth.

He also saw the Saxenow hordes pulling their boats up on the shores of Britain. Mórganthu thought deeply about these strangers for many weeks. How might they be used to further his purposes in Britain? No, they did not honor the druidow, but neither did they worship the Christian god. Many a night Mórganthu sought to study the leader of these beasts, a young man named Hengist, with a horse-hide cloak falling across his sinewy arms. He was deadly with a blade, and there were none his equal among the many skirmishes with the Britons. Vortigern, the new High King, surely had a mess, for while the Saxenow camp grew larger, Vortigern's grew smaller as some of the men stole back to their homes after hearing the news of Uther's death.

Mórganthu prayed to the spirits of the nine sacred woods that this wouldn't slow Vortigern's arrival in Bosventor.

Inis Môn, the druidow's blessed isle off the northwest coast of Kembry, was one of Mórganthu's favorite spots to view. Its brown shores rose up to green grassy hills and the burned trees surrounding the broken stone circles — all desecrated by the Romans. How he wished to replant its sacred groves and renew its sacrifices conducted there from beyond remembrance. The Stone had given him a vision of the renewal of the sacred isle, but so far, it had amounted to nothing. How could the Stone have been wrong?

He spied out the druidow in distant lands. Yes, these were the places he remembered from his journeys as a youth. His father took him and his older brother to visit Brithanvy, Gaul, and Kallicia for a time. But these places brought him no peace, for he saw these druidow suffering as well in poverty and neglect. The Christians were everywhere, rotting the golden apple of his comrades' world like insatiable worms.

And, of course, he looked in upon Ganieda and the wicked Uther girls to make sure they were still present in the weaver's house.

But it was tedious, for they stayed indoors:

Cooking soup, roasting fowl, and baking bread.

Spinning yarn, dunking them into dyes, and learning to weave.

Playing games with colored shells, hopping up and down — giggling — all the things little girls do that Mórganthu could not comprehend.

But despite these outward things, he could tell Ganieda was lonely and unhappy. She often sat in her room weeping and demanding that her curious visitors leave her alone. Four times did Mórganthu see her hit and scream at one of the other girls, and each time she had to be restrained by the mother.

But worst of all were the times when a monk would come and ply his witchery upon Ganieda. Mórganthu recognized him as Dybris, the monk he had caught trying to free the other monks on the night of Beltayne, the night the druidow would have risen to power if not for Merlin and that impudent, parchment drooling, bilious fool. And this man had the stupidity to lead the family in worship of their strange god, and Ganieda had to sit through it! And what bothered Mórganthu the most was that his granddaughter actually seemed to be considering this god, for she would sit raptly as the foolish brown-headed monk droned on from his scroll.

Mórganthu's temples throbbed, and his bowels ached to view such profanity. He wanted to sickle out the man's liver and feed it to Ganieda's wolf, wherever the fanged thing was hiding.

And that insipid, sluggish Vortigern couldn't come soon enough to end this mockery.

Among all the people, places, and things Mórganthu requested to see, the orb would sometimes show him things unbidden. The most prominent of all was a white-bearded king, old beyond most men's reckoning. He sat upon a wooden throne inlaid with sapphires and held in his hand a rod carved with the severed heads of boars, deer, wolves, and hawks — and at the very top, the head of a dragon, its pearl-like eyes shining back at Mórganthu through the orb.

The king had a pock-marked, age-spotted nose and dry lips that were pinched in a scowl. He wore a dusty robe of badger fur over a thin, red tunic made of a strange, shiny cloth embroidered with bone-white thread. At the man's feet, upon a dais covered with gold, sat a misshapen lump of a woman in a shabby, jester-like outfit. Her nose was crooked, and she drooled from broken teeth. Her back was horribly bent and twisted, and it was a marvel she could walk and fetch the king's dainties of cheese, fruits, and succulent meats from a large feasting table. Many warriors lounged around, lifting high their silver bowls.

One of these warriors stood and addressed the king — a young man of particular note because, to Mórganthu's shock, he resembled Merlin — except for the scars, of course. He had dark, wavy hair over a handsome nose and a strong jaw. He wore a tunic similar to the old king's, but his had been dyed black on his left half and red on the right. And he was also strong, like Merlin, easily able to wield the shining blade that hung from his waist. This blade was broader than most British blades, with a shorter handle, and it reminded Mórganthu of a sword he'd seen in the far north — a Lochlan blade brought from a distant land across the northeastern sea.

"Loth," the king said, tapping his curled fingernail on his rod to get the youth's attention, "the ninth year es upon us ... and I begin to feel etts weight." His accent was definitely Lochlan, Mórganthu thought.

"But where will we get the child?" the young man asked.

The king looked at him, perplexed. "Have none been orphaned in de village?"

"None, father ... none of the young ones, I should say."

"Plenty children are available en de vorld, and so one vill come to us ... dey always have. But I vill study de matter afresh, and if none are found, ve can always give a child de ... proper qualities. Fetch my charts and books."

"Yes, father." The young man bowed and then exited the feasting hall.

And as the image faded, Mórganthu received one more view of the old king, and could see the resemblance ... father and son, yes, it was true.

And so the months passed for Mórganthu, lost in thought, deep in spying. Waiting for Vortigern. Waiting.

CHAPTER 22

REVENGE

R un!" Merlin called, but it was too late. Fifteen warriors surrounded them, all with spears leveled, and Scafta among
them.

"I told you they'd set a guard," Colvarth said.

"So many." Merlin instinctively dropped his spear. Their was no
other choice. Arthur must live, and they must live to free him.

Bedwir hesitated, but then followed Merlin's example.

Scafta snatched up the two spears and stepped up to them,
mouth open in awful triumph. His breath smelled like rotten fish,
and he pointed both spears at Merlin's chest.

"Thusa back-ive ris am village!" the man screamed. "Now!"

They were marched single file all the way back to the center of
the village, where the heaped and dying embers of the great bonfire
still burned. When the dead guards were discovered, a great cry rose
up among the warriors, and soon all the village was roused.

Necton, at the discovery of Arthur having been taken from his hut, was furious, but controlled his anger and gave Arthur back to his wife, who sobbed into the child's bare chest.

Ealtain swung his massive fists, struck Caygek down and then Bedwir. Finally, stopping before Merlin, his chest heaved in and out and his lower lip knotted in fury. The veins on his arms throbbed, and he held up a hand to smash Merlin.

Scafta clicked his tongue, and Ealtain jerked his head around. Scafta stepped over, his massive ball of hair looking more scraggly than normal, and whispered in the chieftain's ear.

Ealtain smiled and shouted for everyone to back up.

Merlin backed up too, but Ealtain grabbed his tunic and pulled him to the center.

"Given-sa ris Scafta Merlin is, air escape, that airson killed-ar might be. Thusa say-idh yiu air him yiur curses!"

Merlin didn't understand this exactly, but could tell it was serious by the whiteness and shock that came over Colvarth's face.

Scafta stepped into the ring holding a spear. But not just any spear: a jagged, wicked-looking thing with a collar of what looked like human hair tied on just beyond the black tip. The shaft was stained with blood and gore, as if it had already been used that night to gut someone. That was when Merlin noticed a sharp iron hook on the other end.

Merlin was weaponless.

Ealtain sneered and then stepped to the edge of the ring of yelling, angry Picts.

Garth peeked out behind Ealtain's elbow with his eyes squinted and his jaw set. Natalenya stood behind him, her white fingers gripping the boy's shoulder.

Scafta advanced, the spear end jabbing toward Merlin's throat.

Merlin backed up, but there wasn't far to go before he'd —

Something hit his ankles hard, and his legs flew out from underneath him. He fell to the hard-packed dirt, and his head spun. A three-foot log lay under his feet that someone had rolled out to trip him.

The crowd erupted in laughter, as Scafta jabbed the ground repeatedly just inches from Merlin's arms, chest, and head.

Merlin sat up, dazed, then quickly got to his feet. Where had Scafta gone?

The back of Merlin's tunic ripped, and Scafta laughed as he waved the cloth he had cut like a flag of triumph.

Merlin jumped away and spun, only to find the iron hook around his right ankle.

Scafta pulled.

The world turned sideways as Merlin fell again, this time hard on his shoulder.

Scafta flipped to the spear end and stabbed it downward.

Merlin rolled, feeling the dirt crumble on his cheeks and hearing the crunch of the spear only inches from his side. Kicking Scafta's leg, he yelled, rolled again, and stood to a crouch.

The Picts cheered Scafta on, now even louder.

Merlin snarled.

Scafta backed away, a wicked grin on his face. Letting go of the spear with his right hand, he reached to his scraggly set of necklaces and yanked off a small, leather bag.

With the spear off kilter, Merlin leapt and threw a punch right at Scafta's fleshy nose.

But the witch doctor backed up and threw the contents of the bag in Merlin's face.

It was dust — blinding, choking dust. Merlin's swing missed, and he almost fell. His eyes stung, and he tried wiping the dust off his face with his sleeve, but it was no use. He tried to open his eyes to see where that brutal man stood, but he only saw smears of light, shadow, and his own bitter, blinding tears.

Merlin heard a footfall, and he turned toward it, but then he heard another from behind, and he spun in that direction. Where was Scafta? Laughter swirled around him as he groped and swung toward every sound.

Merlin tensed his body to be skewered, for Scafta would gut him at any moment. He wanted to raise his hands, give up, and end it. End it all. They would all die. He had failed them. There was nothing he could do to defend himself.

Or could he? A calm fell over him, faint at first, but then stronger — a sureness, a confidence, a normalcy — even in his temporary blindness. Seven years he had been blind. He had fought Rondroc blind. He had fought Connek blind. He had fought the giant warrior blind. He had fought Mórganthu blind. He had driven the sword into the Stone — again, blind.

He closed his stinging eyes, ignored their pain as best he could, and focused. He crouched. He yelled at Scafta with all his breath, venting his anger, and trying to scare him. A hush fell over the Picts. Time slowed. He listened with every skill he had ever learned, turning his head back and forth to locate any sound of Scafta.

A scuffing. Beside him. To his right. One pace away. A brief chuckle of derision. Scafta was righthanded, wasn't he? The spear, with its hook on the end, couldn't be turned as quickly. Scafta wouldn't suspect —

Merlin lunged, reaching for the spear ... and touched the wood with his right hand.

Scafta jerked it up ... directly into Merlin's left hand. He grabbed it.

Scafta tried to gore him with the hook, and the sharp tip jabbed into Merlin's belt and cut into his hip — but it was caught there, allowing Merlin to seize the shaft with his right hand as well. He yanked the hook free from his belt, stopping it from cutting any deeper.

The two fought for mastery over the spear and rammed heads twice. The awful smell of Scafta's ratted hair almost made Merlin retch.

Making a small trench in the soft ground with his bare feet, he shoved as hard as he could. Scafta stepped back, and fell, pulling Merlin with him. As he dropped forward, Merlin's shin hit the log that had been rolled out earlier — Scafta had tripped over it, and was momentarily stunned.

Merlin pushed the spear down with all his weight, and he shoved it onto Scafta's bare neck. The witch doctor gurgled in anger, and even tried to spit on Merlin, but he wouldn't let go.

Merlin heard something near Scafta's head, and then the witch doctor began screaming as if Merlin was killing him.

"Hold him still," came a voice. A boy's voice. It was Garth!

Scafta kept screaming and began to buck wildly. Merlin had a hard time holding him.

"Almost done!"

Scafta's strength increased, and the man lifted the spear off of his neck. Merlin kneed him, and the spear dropped back down, yet Scafta screamed all the more.

What was the boy doing? Merlin's vision was clearing, but not enough to see. He heard a strange noise, like ripping wool.

"Done!" Garth yelled, and Merlin heard him jump up. "Let him go!"

Scafta went limp, yet Merlin could tell he hadn't passed out.

Merlin dropped back to his haunches and stood, taking the spear with him in case Scafta attacked. His full sight had began to return, and he wiped his eyes again. Scafta still lay on the ground, but something about him looked odd. Merlin turned to Garth, who stood above the witch doctor — holding the man's huge knot of hair!

"'*Always sharp yer knives*' is me new motto!" Garth said as he brandished a long cooking knife in the other hand, which, Merlin surmised, he must have hidden in his waistband. Colvarth, standing behind Garth, was pursing his lips in a silent whistle and he tried to look innocnent of the matter.

A shorn Scafta rose up, looked at the crowd of astonished Picts, and ran away yelling. It was awful, like a rabid lynx shrieking to escape a vat of boiling water. He pulled at his short, scraggly hair, shaking his head, and jerking his arms up and down as he ran off into the woods.

Ealtain pounced into the ring, brandishing his own spear, which was longer than Merlin's. His lip twitched as he yelled a battle cry.

Merlin had just enough time to deflect the thrust and step to the side.

Ealtain swung, and Merlin ducked.

Merlin countered by jabbing the hook end at Ealtain's leg, but the big man grabbed Merlin's spear and yanked it out of his hands.

So quick, and Merlin was defenseless again. He prepared himself for the inevitable.

But Ealtain screamed and stuck his chest out as a spear point came ripping through his gut. Blood rushed down his legs, and he fell to his knees. He looked down at the spear and tried to turn to face his killer, but the shaft of the spear prevented it, and he fell.

Necton stood behind him, his teeth clenched and his head shaking while he pulled the spear from the dying man.

Merlin backed up and Colvarth pulled him close, whispering, "The Picts have a saying: *'Fallen the bard — fallen shall the chieftain be.'* Necton has now slain his father's killer. And you and Garth have made it possible."

"Necton! Necton mac Erip!" the people shouted as one, hailing their new chieftain, who had just taken Merlin's old torc from Ealtain's neck and put it on his own, so that now he wore two torcs.

Suddenly, a skirling was heard from the right, and there, upon a small hill beside the lake, all alone, stood Garth playing a happy tune on his bagpipe. And he wore, balanced upon his head, the bulbous hair of Scafta.

Merlin almost laughed.

The people gathered around Garth — slave and Pict alike — and the boy played until they were all present and staring at him — this strange being in their midst.

After a big mouthful of air, he addressed the people — and not in the language of Kernow and Kembry — but in a halting sort of Pictish, which when translated, went something like this:

"Good people of *Tauchen-Twilloch*, hear me! With the help of my God, this day I have sent away your witch doctor in shame — expelled your priest in disgrace."

The people looked on him in awe. Even Necton had his mouth open.

"No more do you need to sacrifice your animals and dance to the Sun. It shines upon you strong and bright even now, and my God promises that its cycles of warmth and cold will not fail you, or your crops, or your children's children for as long as your village may last."

It looked like he wanted to say more, but couldn't think of anything else. So he put his blowpipe to his mouth and started playing again.

The people looked at him, smiles on their faces, and the Pictish women started chanting *"Mungo! Mungo! Mungo!"* And the others joined in, picked him up, carried him to Scafta's hut, and bade him enter and live there.

It was a wonder to behold, for everyone was overjoyed to see Scafta go, and though they didn't know what exactly to do with Garth, they honored him for his feat. *"Mungo! Mungo!"* they shouted, and the Pictish grandmothers pinched his cheeks, thinner though they had become, until he blushed.

Merlin stepped up to Colvarth and asked him what the word meant.

"It means '*dear sweet one*.' I think that's his name now, at least among the Picts."

With a bit of ceremony, Garth threw Scafta's hair into the burning Samhain embers, and its odor filled the village. "I thought it smelled bad before," he said, holding his nose. Soon, though, the wind blew the stink away, and everyone felt relief—Pict and slave alike.

CHAPTER 23

THE BITTER TREK

With Scafta gone, the elderly began asking Garth for help healing their sicknesses. The mothers had him bless their children. The shepherds sought his advice for how to care for their cattle. But mostly he liked to help the fishermen, showing them what he knew from growing up on the Kembry Sea.

In all this, Merlin shook his head in amazement, seeing Garth not just as an orphan who'd lived at an abbey and now was a slave — but as a sort of missionary among these people. He prayed over them and taught them what he knew from scriptures he'd memorized. He even instructed a group of the younger Picts to sing a few psalms.

Of course, there were benefits to all this; the most important to Garth was that his cheeks were rarely absent a morsel or two offered from the Picts' hearths. But he also helped the slaves, imploring their masters to let those who were injured to rest. And in all this he had freedom to move as he willed without his slave collar.

And Merlin began to see a different side to the Picts. They could be generous, even loving. They laughed and played games. The people sang and danced, celebrated and mourned together. None of their own people starved. The wives cared for their young, provided for their families, and kept their homes warm and clean. The fathers watched over their children, taught them how to survive, provided food to eat, and built their homes strong and tight.

Every Pict worked hard, from the oldest to the youngest. Despite having slaves to work the fields, there was plenty for the Picts to do: hunting, fishing, smoking meat, pelt-making for boots and cloaks, spinning wool with rock and reel, weaving, repairing shelters to house their animals, stowing their boats for the winter, blacksmithing, making baskets, furniture building, creating useful things out of antlers and horns. And that was besides the crafts and artistic things they created: bead-making, pottery, embroidered hats, along with silver and gold-smithing.

Sure, they were pagan, but hadn't the people of Bosventor been pagan just a generation or two ago? Could these people change as well, Merlin wondered, and turn away from superstition?

But it was hard to accept these things, and he didn't swallow them easily, for he and the others had been made slaves again. Garth was revered, sure, and Scafta was gone, along with Ealtain's tyranny. But that didn't change their future prospects.

In this way another cycle of the moon passed, the nights grew cold, and then the hammer fell, confirming all of Merlin's suspicions.

Despite what Garth had done, they were all to be sold to Pictish tribes farther up in the highlands. Those tribes couldn't raid as easily as Necton's, who lived on the border, and they would pay gold, silver, gems, and other precious things, including cattle, for the chance to own slaves who would work their land.

Apparently, this was the pattern: The border tribes would raid and find new slaves, work them, and then trade them north before winter. In this way, the slaves found themselves farther and farther from home, working until they died — and the pattern would repeat itself.

Garth did everything he could to stop it, but the Picts were unbending. The slaves were thought of as cattle, and they wouldn't even consider losing their profit from selling them. When pressed too hard, Necton even slashed Garth on the forehead and threatened to put his slave collar back on, tighter, if he wouldn't stop in his demands.

Merlin's spirits fell. Not only was freedom impossible with an ever watchful and strengthened guard, but they would be separated from Arthur. As the weather turned drab, and the day of their departure approached, Merlin descended into a deep sadness.

Colvarth tried to talk to him, but Merlin ignored him, preferring instead to stare into the burnt remains of yesterday's fire and the ashes that had become his life.

Finally, the bard kicked him. "Awake, thou son of a mushroom!"

Merlin jumped up and grabbed Colvarth by the shoulders. He wanted to shake him, but stopped himself when he saw the man was smiling.

"What?" Merlin said. "Out with it."

"There is hope."

"Hah."

"There is always hope. Garth has, with my help, negotiated where we will be sold."

"I don't want to hear it."

"But — "

Merlin yelled. "I said *I don't want to hear it.*"

"You don't, hmmm? Then hear a word from Isaiah mab Amoz:

O boar-headed one with a rebel heart,
Remember well the ancient scripture:
That I am God, and there is none like me,
That I am God, and none may change my course,
For I hold thy death, and also thy birth,

The furthest past, and all unfinished deeds.
Trust in me — my joy cannot be thwarted:
From far away I summoned a mighty hawk,
A man of strength to fulfill my purpose."

Colvarth hesitated, and when Merlin chose not to look up, he walked away.

The next day the journey began for Necton's slaves. He took an escort of ten spear-wielding Picts, and, curiously, his wife Gormla came along on horseback, carrying Arthur in her arms.

Natalenya was provided for, thanks to Garth, who had borrowed a donkey from a Pictish grandmother, with the condition that an old blanket lay between Natalenya and the beast, something she was more than willing to do. Riding was still a trial, however, for the boils on her legs hurt terribly, and by the end of each day's march, she could barely hang on to the donkey's neck.

Necton brought two other donkeys for carrying food, a tent, and the plunder from his raiding that he wished to sell. To make the journey faster, each slave was chained to the same partner they'd been with during their labors: Caygek with Peredur — and Merlin with Bedwir.

When they left, all the people gathered to see Garth off, and the people shouted, *"Mungo! Mungo! Mungo!"* as he passed, and he received more kisses and pinches that morning than Merlin thought the boy could bear. Garth had been given the choice of staying or going, and though he chose to go with Merlin and the others, he was overheard saying he'd like to come back one day and help these people. He also was allowed the privilege of not having a slave collar, leaving Colvarth unchained, but still with his collar on. Necton wasn't worried about the old man with the harp.

But what was the use? For Merlin, it was awful — worse than even their original slave-taking, for it sealed their fate and meant escape would be nearly impossible. He marched with the others, head down, keeping the tears at bay. Plodding and plodding. Foot over foot. Mile after painful mile. Bedwir tried to talk with him, but Merlin ignored him. It wasn't until they came to the Antonine Wall that Merlin realized they had been going south rather than north.

"What?" he exclaimed as the moss and vine covered ruins appeared over the hill.

Peredur slapped him on the back. "Where'd you think we were going?"

"To the highlands."

"Well, you're wrong." He gave a nod and walked on.

Merlin jogged to keep up. Bedwir matched his pace to keep the chain from swinging.

"Where *are* we going?" Merlin asked.

Peredur grinned. "Ask Colvarth."

The bard was at the front of the group, and Merlin and Bedwir had to catch up with him. Colvarth turned when he heard Merlin coming, amusement in his eyes. Merlin was huffing, but he managed to say between breaths, "You didn't tell me."

"You didn't listen. Necton has finally agreed to sell us as slaves to King Atleuthun."

"Finally?"

"Ah, but Necton didn't want to go. It seems Atle has been a harsh bargainer in the past."

"But King Atle? Why did you — "

"What did you expect? We told Necton you were the king's grandson, and that he would pay handsomely for you. And so we owe a great thanks to Gormla. With the expected reward, she wants to visit their market, and so she was the one who convinced Necton."

Merlin had to think about this. "But — "

"Yes, it is true, Atle knows nothing about you, but hopefully I can convince him of your parentage. Leave it to me."

"If Atle *doesn't* consider me his grandson, then Necton will be furious — "

"Shush ... do not say that so loud."

"—and if Atle *does* consider me his grandson, then Atle himself will be furious. He tried to kill my mother!"

"Perhaps he has softened."

"Perhaps!? You're betting our lives on a *perhaps*? This might be worse than if we'd been sold north."

Colvarth strummed his harp, held tight in his other hand. "Tsk."

Merlin and the others marched nearly twenty-five leagues over the hills and across the lands of the Guotodin, and no one harassed them. Arthur took in all the sights quietly, sometimes riding on Garth's shoulders or hanging from Bedwir's arms. One night they stopped near the outskirts of Dineidean, a major hill fort in the region, but did not enter. The land to the east grew flatter under their feet and the forests thicker beside them until one morning at sunrise they at last spied Dinpelder in the distance — a strange hump of rock rising from the woods like the back of a gigantic boar.

But Merlin had been fooled by what he thought was just another hill. It took far longer to reach its base than he expected, and when they arrived, he opened his mouth in awe and craned his neck. Everything else lay relatively flat for as far as the eye could see, but here stood this massive rock jutting out from the earth and towering over him ... one hundred and fifty feet, if not more. It was similar in width and breadth to the Meneth Gellik mountain at home but was shaped more like a flat bulge with sheer sides. The stone was different too; not the hard granite of home, but rather a gray stone flecked with white, which turned brown when weathered. Scraggly grass and mosses covered the hill, with pines and oaks clinging to its dangerous drop-offs. A wide path wound its way up the western side, leading to a fortress at the top that had been built of earthworks, timber, and stone — thick and strong as the mountain itself.

As Merlin followed Necton and the others, he cast wide eyes at the serrated cliffs. His mother had been thrown off one of these when King Atle had discovered she'd become a Christian. God had saved her miraculously, sure, and without injury — but King Atle's anger wasn't sated, for he then tried to drown her by tying her in the bottom of a leaky boat as the tide let out. And there it was — the ocean — only half of a league to the northeast where a river emptied past a village and its crowd of boats.

And on that second attempt upon her life, Merlin's father, Owain, had saved her by braving the arrows of Atle's warriors and swimming out, plugging the leak, and sailing away.

Merlin had been told this tale of his parent's courtship only six months ago, before his father died, and here the story was, coming to life before his very eyes. He could picture it all ... including Uther's wrath at Owain for abandoning him on the eve of battle.

And now Merlin was here, and quite possibly about to meet his grandfather for the first time. A chill ocean breeze burst across the path, smelling of salt and filled with blowing flakes of snow. Merlin and the others hunched against the cliff face until the gusts died away.

Soon they came to the open gate, and it towered above Merlin — planed wood and banded iron at least ten feet tall and a foot thick. The guards were neither dressed like Britons nor like Picts. Each wore a roundish, hill-shaped helm engraved with coiling sea serpents. The guards' armor was made from overlapped bronze scales, each molded like a salmon diving into the water. And the leather work — gloves, greaves, and boots — had all been dyed to a green reminiscent of the sea. At each of their black belts was tucked a long, curved axe, and Merlin didn't doubt that each man knew how to use it.

But there was trouble gaining entrance. Necton explained his errand to the chief of the guards while he pointed at Merlin.

The guard shook his head.

Banging the butt of his spear repeatedly on the ground, Necton said it again.

The guard backed up, and ten more appeared at the doorway brandishing their axes.

Colvarth stepped between the two groups and held up his hands. "Let me explain," he said. "I declare before you the son of Gwevian myr Atleuthun. She was lost to your sovereign many years ago, but now her son has returned."

"Gwevian?" the front guard said, his thick, red moustache puffing out with the word.

The man's accent was one that Merlin had not heard before ... or had he? There was something similar in the way that one word was vocalized to the way his mother spoke.

The front guard consulted another of his kind, and soon both of their eyes lit up. "*Theneva!*" they said, turning back to Colvarth and Necton. "Sure, an we hae heard o' the lass."

"Then I suggest you do not keep your lord waiting, since his grandson stands before you."

"I'm named Digon," the red-moustached guard said, "and I'll bring yer message tae the king." He turned and ran up the stone walkway. The other men stood at the ready with their axes, eyeing Necton and his warriors.

While Merlin and the others waited, huddling in the cold wind, Garth passed around some oatcakes and a little water. Merlin felt better for it, and he could tell by the way Natalenya ate hers that she welcomed it as well.

When the food was gone, and the guard still had not returned, Necton began sharpening his spear with a smooth rock he found on the path. The other Pictish warriors did the same, all the time eyeing Atle's men and their axes.

The gusts blew with a vengeance, and a deep chill set in Merlin's bones.

Finally, Digon returned. He had brought twenty more men, all dressed the same.

Necton leapt up and raised his spear, a snarl on his lips.

But Digon held up his hand. "The king hae requested an audience with ye, but first ye must set aside yer spears an other sich weapons."

Necton grumbled at this, but discussed it with Gormla and the warriors. Finally, he tacitly agreed by throwing his spear down with an impressive flourish. As he did so, Merlin noticed him push a knife into his belt where it would be hidden behind his cloak. The other warriors threw their spears down as well, and a few were able to hide their knives in similar fashion.

Digon grunted and motioned for them to follow. Necton went first, pulling the reins of Gormla's horse, followed by two warriors leading the donkeys filled with plunder. Merlin and the slaves went next, and at the very back marched the final group of warriors. They soon found themselves on the very top of Dinpelder — a gently sloping plain surrounded by a thick rampart, with guards stationed at different points to keep watch over the surrounding countryside.

In front of Merlin lay a large village of timber huts. People milled about in the weak light of the morning, carving wood, tending sheep, weaving, chinking the cracks in their dwellings, and many other tasks.

As their party passed through, they came to a small market with wares of pottery, baskets, dried meats, and other things for sale. The owners looked upon them expectantly, and some even called out. Gormla slipped down from her horse, and one of the sellers grabbed her by the sleeve.

"Ye like jewelry, yes? Here, me lass, try a bracelet on!" And the man slipped a fine bracelet made of silver wire and dangling seashells over her wrist.

Necton stepped in between, ripped off the bracelet and threw it back. "Must sell-ametch first!" Gormla complained bitterly to him as he pulled her away from the booth.

As they walked on, one of the children, a youth with disheveled black hair maybe ten winters old, came out of his family's hovel and stared at Merlin like he were a convicted thief come to steal the family's lamb. The slave collar probably didn't help any.

When they neared the far end of the village, Merlin took his gaze off of the silent inhabitants and saw their party's destination. On the highest point of the hill stood the strangest wooden longhouse Merlin had ever seen: It had nine levels, each with steeply sloped gable roofs, and each level progressively smaller until the top could hold only a single man on lookout.

The wood was dark, maybe pine, and this was used for roof tiles as well. The lowest level was huge … bigger even than King Gorlas's fortress, Dintaga — and the height of the building astounded him. The beams inside must be massive indeed to support such a structure. It was stave-built, with vertical timbers held together by sawn wood bands. At the top of every roof peak jutted out a fish, carved to look like it was jumping out of the foaming waves.

As they climbed up the hill and approached the hall, Merlin spied strange gods carved in relief into the cornice, jambs, and the huge doorway itself. These gods were giants who fought each other — their hammers swung by muscled arms. Each one blew storm clouds from thick lips, and lightning flew down to their feet, which stepped upon piles and piles of skulls.

Natalenya dismounted, and the horse and donkey reins were tied to the rail. Necton and two of his warriors took the bags of plunder and hefted it over their shoulders.

The guard knocked. "Open 'er up," he called, "this be king's business!"

CHAPTER 24

THE BITTER SCHEME

Vortigern shook off the snowflakes dusting the sleeve of his disguise and urged his horse up the road. The sun had just risen, revealing a burned-out abbey building that hugged the mountainside just ahead. What a rot, this trip was, coming back to that stinky little village of Bosventor to find and get rid of Uther's daughters. Didn't he have enough to do as High King? Wasn't rebuilding his war host enough? Wasn't fighting back the Saxenow on the coast enough?

Ah, but that druid, Mórganthu, had failed him. Hadn't gotten rid of the girls, and now Vortigern had to endure this nasty trip in cold weather. To make it yet worse, his back bothered him. Five days of hard riding had jolted him wrong and the pains shooting through his hip and spine made him feel like he had the horse on *his* back, not the other way around.

And why was Tregeagle so insistent? The man had sent his blithering servant twice, whining out of his puckered little mouth,

"Come and pay me for finding your nieces." Pay him? Stick a sword through Tregeagle's flapping tonsils, more like.

Couldn't the man wait for the fighting season to end? For the Saxenow to settle down at winter's coming and leave the poor Britons alone? Leave the overworked and underpraised Vortigern alone?

A barn-muck of a mess, it was.

He really just wanted to rest for once in his life. To recline in his newly built feasting hall at Glevum. To eat and drink. To celebrate a little. But no ... here he was, digging after Uther's little rabbits like he was still a common warrior.

He cursed out loud.

"What is it?" Rewan asked, his horse riding next to him. "Don't like the snow?" He brushed off the flakes that had gathered on his thighs.

They had ridden up to the burned-out buildings, and the road didn't go any farther. Vortigern had taken the wrong path, so he stopped his horse and ordered them to turn around. At least the monks were gone, and good riddance.

Before they rode back to the crossroad, Vortigern studied Rewan to see if the man's disguise was good enough. He didn't want anyone knowing the High King and his men had come. Their task would have to be secret. An old cloak, and even older tunic ... but at his hip a tear had opened up and some of the leather showed through. "Tuck your tunic in, you fool."

Rewan complied. "There's something else botherin' you. Is there unspilt blood left here? Something tells me we didn't finish our work last time." He drew a dagger, put it between his teeth, and smiled at Vortigern.

As his new battle chief, Rewan would certainly understand because he had a mind for such things. Maybe now was the right time to talk about it. At least Rewan had some sense of what was right and wrong for a king to do.

Thankfully Vortigern's hapless son, Vortipor, had agreed to stay at home and spend time with the fawning ladies. If he'd come along, he certainly would've cringed at what Vortigern planned. Vortipor would never understand this gift to him and his heirs.

Rewan and the three men with him had been handpicked by Vortigern for this task. He turned around and looked at them as they gathered their horses around him. Ruthless men, all, and willing to do anything for a bright coin and a full cup.

Vortigern cleared his throat. "The bottom of the bag, my men, is that I don't want Uther to have any brats who can stab me, or anyone from my house, in the back."

Fest, one of the twins, spoke first — a brutish man with a chin sticking out so far that his little brain must have rolled down and stuck there. "So Arthur's back, huh? I thought he'd been taken by the Picts."

"Not Arthur," Vortigern sneered, "but his older sisters. I don't want Uther grandchildren running around either. His father killed my grandfather ... I know how it goes."

Enison smiled, showing the gap where his two front teeth had been knocked out. He was the smaller twin brother of Fest, and not nearly as smart. "So we's takes 'em, eh? And then we's does ... what wi'em?"

Rewan kicked out and struck the man's shin. "We kill them, dolt."

The third man, Tethion, pulled his horse around, one hand fingering the feathered arrow shafts hidden by a cloth covering his saddle bag. "And that's why we're in disguise ... so no one knows it's us — true?"

Vortigern nodded. They were catching on. "Not a soul here knows any of you four ... at least not by name. Me, though, they'll recognize. So call me *Ivor* while we're here ... catch it?"

"Listen up," Rewan said so everyone could hear. "Nobody's to know the High King is here. Got that stuck in your noggin?"

Fest and Enison both nodded.

"And what's your problem, Tethion?" Rewan asked.

Tethion squinted his left eye and studied Vortigern. "These your sister's kids, an' she was killed by them druidow, right? And now you'll have us kill your nieces? I don't get it."

Vortigern paused. Igerna, his sister. He hadn't thought about her these many months. Of course he'd wanted her to live. She was descended from Vitalinus, wasn't she? But the spit started gathering on his tongue, and he ground his jaw.

"My sister was a traitor to the house of my grandfather," he said. "She sealed her fate when she married the son of that butcher."

Vortigern had wanted her to finally see things clearly ... see her brother become High King ... see the glory of their grandfather's house restored. He'd asked Mórganthu *not* to have her killed along with Uther, and Vortigern had made the arch druid promise. But it was an accident. Mórganthu had told him so. And now her tainted daughters would follow her to the grave. The bloodline of Vitalinus would be pure once again.

Vortigern reached out and grabbed Tethion's reigns. At the same time he drew his blade and jabbed it toward the man's stomach. "Do you have the guts for this? If you're not sure, I can spill 'em on the ground and check."

"No problem," Tethion said, holding up his hands. "As long as I get some ale soon. Get me more 'n a drop and I'll be jus' fine."

"A drunk archer misses the target." Vortigern said, sheathing his sword once more. "You'll be quick, silent, and accurate. *Got it?*"

"Some ale afterward? Even some sweet mead."

Vortigern snorted and chewed on his moustache. "All right ... When this is done, we'll all see what we can find on the way back."

Vortigern and the four rode their horses no more than ten paces back down the road when an old man wearing a snow-covered hood stepped from the bushes and held up a hand.

"I see ... I see you have come back to claim your own," the stranger said.

Vortigern spit at the man's feet. "Get out of our way."

But the man wouldn't move. "I know your errand, and I must speak with you."

"Who are you and what do you want?"

The stranger's sleeve slid down a little on the upraised forearm, and some blue scar lines became visible in the morning light. "I am the one who sees all, O High King. By my druid arts I even spied your coming two nights ago, camped secretly as you were in the valley near the lake where you slept under the pine tree. Did you think I wouldn't know you in your disguise, Vortigern?" The man pulled back his hood, revealing his face and black-and-gray beard.

Vortigern dropped his reins and shook his head. It was Mórganthu, that renegade of a doublecrossing druid. How had he known who they were? Surely he hadn't been on the trail spying on them for the last few days ... Vortigern had purposefully chosen empty lands for their path and had seen no one on the way from Glevum.

Vortigern's face turned hot, and he scowled. "Out with your words. And then get out of my way."

"O King ... O King Vortigern, I tell you that the ones you seek are near, and that *my* granddaughter is staying with them. She is not to be touched."

Vortigern sniffed. "Why should I care?"

"Because we have something in common, you and I ... a love for the Stone. It has given you power over the people, yes. For me, I want power over the very stars of heaven."

The mention of the Stone piqued Vortigern's curiosity. He still felt its pull and the dreams of majesty it had given him. "What of the Stone ... is its power restored?"

"No, no ... not yet, but I assure you that one day it shall be ... of that you have my word. But you, O King, might try to pull the sword from the Stone yourself ... you have two good hands and are strong ... yes, and you are the High King now, the rightful heir to Uther's sword."

This intrigued Vortigern. Could he, through brute strength, do what Mórganthu could not through his druidic arts? But that wasn't what he'd come for. Maybe after the girls had been taken care of. "I don't have time for this," Vortigern said. "Now get out of my way."

"Patience, O King, for I must speak with you about my daughter's daughter. She is black haired, so you'll not mistake her for Uther's, or the weaver's. I need your solemn promise —"

"And you'll trust me more than I trust you?"

"Ah, you refer to our previous disagreement. Know, O King, that all is forgiven. After all, we are a forgiving people."

"And a thieving people too. Uther's torc was missing when I buried him. Give it to me."

The druid looked down. "I ... I do not have it. What does it look like?"

"It had two eagle heads with amethyst eyes."

"A warrior must have stolen it."

Vortigern took in a breath. He had his own torc from his grandfather and didn't need Uther's. What he wanted was to make sure that it was never worn by a rival. No matter. If he had success in getting rid of Uther's daughters then he never need worry about that again, at least from Uther's line.

Eh, but how fun it would be to run the old man down and see him scream under the sharp edges of his horse's hoofs. It would be so easy. One less thieving druid in the world. But what of the Stone? What if Mórganthu held the Stone's secrets? What if he alone could restore the Stone to its power? A longing filled Vortigern to see the Stone again. To touch it. To experience again the ecstatic visions that'd driven him to reclaim the kingship, to kill Uther, to kill anyone in his way.

Did Mórganthu stand in his way? Perhaps not, but Vortigern hated him all the more because he needed him. "You have my promise, but nothing more. Now get your muddy legs out of here or I'll kick you into a ditch."

Mórganthu bowed and stepped aside.

Vortigern and the others rode around an arm of the mountain, bringing the village into view on the southern slope. Smoke trailed upward from the holes in the crennig roofs — half of them anyway. It seemed the village wasn't as bustling as last spring. Had the people moved away? Died? Hopefully not of sickness — that was the last thing he needed, catching ill after finally claiming what was rightfully his.

He led them onto the village green where they watered their horses and ate a small meal of smoked meat before remounting and heading up the main track that led to the old fortress — and Tregeagle's house. Finally they arrived, trotted the horses into his yard, dismounted, and tied up the reins. Vortigern banged on Tregeagle's door with the antiquated Roman eagle carved into it. What a joke, he thought. *Vortigern* was the real power in Britain now — not Uther, and certainly not the Romans who would never return. *He* was the High King.

"Open up," he called, "I've got business here!"

After Vortigern and his men rode off, Mórganthu slipped into the forest at the side of the road — when he heard a curious noise behind him. It was a distant scuffing of feet. Someone — a figure in a dark robe — was standing outside the charred remains of one of the abbey buildings.

Mórganthu crouched behind a fallen oak with branches full of dead leaves, and waited, watching. The person was looking around, listening with a hand cupped near his ear. Finally, he began walking on the road toward Bosventor — no, he was half limping, in an urgent-yet-wary sort of way. Had the man been injured at some point?

When the man shambled past the fallen oak, Mórganthu bit the end of his healed stump of an arm. It was that Dybris fellow ... that prying, foolish, interfering, and altogether death-deserving monk. What had he been doing in the abbey's ruins? Scavenging, perhaps? For what? Mórganthu wondered at how he could have missed spying such a thing with the orb. The monk lived in the old chapel in the village proper, that he knew, but was there something else, something secret, that drew him here?

And how had the monk become hurt such that he limped now? Ahh, on Beltayne night when the sword had been sunk into the Stone ... that had to have been it. Mórganthu remembered seeing the monk's body crumpled up against the wall of Owain's smithy — perhaps McEwan's club had performed that magnificent bit of work.

Mórganthu dearly wished that this Dybris had fled along with the other monks when Tregeagle had driven them all away after Merlin left.

But the perilous question was ... had Dybris overheard?

Mórganthu gulped. Did the monk know about Vortigern and his plan to kill the girls? If so, he would go straight to the weaver's and —

Mórganthu's heart began beating fast. This was the undoing of all his patient plans, and he would have to act swiftly. Vortigern, that oaf of a king, would go to Tregeagle's first — which meant it was up to Mórganthu to stop Dybris.

He sat down on the snowy grass, took out the orb ... and put it back, realizing his mistake.

Seeing wasn't enough. With such short notice, there was no stopping the girls from escaping. He had to deal with it on his own — and get Ganieda out of there *now*. If Uther's girls escaped, and Ganieda was left in the house, then he could not predict what Vortigern would do in his rage. He might kill Ganieda. He might burn the place to the ground.

And then the fang would be lost as well. The fang ... oh, the fang!

Dybris had gotten ahead, but his limp slowed him, and the road meandered the long but easy way around the mountain. Could Mórganthu get ahead of him by taking the high path? He crept from his spot and ran as fast he could, away from the road and up over the northern side of the mountain. Oaks, pines and beech, ashes, and rowan — he felt as if all his snow-dusted friends cheered him on as he ran as fast as his burning lungs and aged feet would carry him.

With the monk limping, perhaps Mórganthu could get there first.

But what then?

Mórganthu stepped out of the woods next to the fortress and saw the village below him even as a daring plan formed in his mind. Dybris wasn't even in view yet.

He rushed down the hillside, avoiding the path to Tregeagle's, and finally slunk in the shadow of a huge rock where two of his four druidow hid. They were watching the weaver's house at his command.

"Are they still there?" he rasped, and both druidow nodded in answer.

"Keep watch, but make no move, and do not ... do not show yourselves. The cat has arrived to eat the mice, yet a dog approaches and we cannot risk a disturbance. Come if I shout."

He snuck across the road to the abandoned crennig next to the weaver's land. He slipped inside. This would have to be quick.

Where had he seen those rags? Ah yes, precisely where he remembered the last time he came here to spy on the weavers: in the corner lay a pile of old clothes, next to the smashed old chair someone had lit a fire with on the hearth. He evicted some impudent rodents from the pile's center and shook out each piece: a few bags, worn and dirty; three tunics, each more shredded than the last; two breeches, both shabby; an old lumpy hat, chewed but serviceable; and a pair of well-woven gloves, in decent shape. Some women's clothes were mixed in, but those were useless to him, and he dropped them to the dirt.

Doffing his own, druid-designed cloak and clothing, he shivered as he put on everything. One of the pants had lost its tie, and so he put the other over it and tied it tightly. He put on all three tunics, the worst on the outside, and this hid the blue scars on his arms perfectly.

His beard — what about his beard? Would they recognize it, so long and illustrious? He had always prided himself in it, yet he had no choice. He pulled out his curved knife, and, pressing the length of his beard against his chest with his bad arm, he cut it as short as he could. A painful, uneven sort of shearing, it was, but that would aid his disguise. Then he rubbed ashes in to make what was left more gray.

His long hair he could not cut easily with one hand, and so he stuffed it down the back of his tunics and hoped no one would notice it under that insufferable hat. He dearly hoped that Belornos, his god, would honor him for this extraordinary sacrifice, for the clothing smelled dreadful.

Now for some mud, which he found in a corner of the crennig where the roof sagged. This he smeared lightly on his hands, forearms, feet, ankles, and a little on his face — all to cover the blue whorls and lines that marked him as a druid. He had to appear thoroughly like a poor beggar to incite the sympathies of those hypocritical Christians.

Ah, but his missing hand … had Troslam seen that it was missing? Did he know? That would give him away for sure, and nothing could be done to hide the fact — or could it? He examined the gloves. One had holes chewed into it, but the other was untouched, and it was the correct hand. He found some thin sticks, and shoved them into the five fingers of the glove. Then he filled it with a little sand he found near the hearth — just enough. With some cloth ripped from an old dress, he tied the glove onto his stump using his good hand and his teeth. Thankfully, the bump of his wrist bone still protruded out, or he would never have made it stay.

The hand didn't look real, of course, but if he put on the other glove and made that hand stiff, then they might not notice. Maybe he'd stiffen his entire body to incite more sympathy from the fools.

Grabbing one of the old dresses, he wadded it up and stuffed it into a bag. This he slung over his shoulder before peering outside. Dybris was nowhere in sight, so Mórganthu shuffled out to the road, hunching, and started walking away from the weavers. If he could get the monk's sympathy, then maybe the man would take him with — right into the weavers' house.

And it didn't take long, for Dybris came up the road, scuffing one of his legs. Mórganthu positioned himself in the way, bending over to appear shorter.

"Please, please, good man," he called, disguising his voice to hide the Eirish lilt, and pretending to shiver in the swirling snow. "A cold beggar needs help!"

When Dybris stopped and looked at him, Mórganthu wanted to clap in glee, but instead put on a sad face. There was pity in the monk's eyes, yes, and something indecipherable. The odd thing was that the left half of his face sagged just a little ... the same side that he limped with.

"I can't help you now," Dybris said as he placed a small coin in Mórganthu's good hand. "But take this and find yourself a cup of good cheer." His words had a slight slur.

Mórganthu exaggerated his shivers. "But ... I am quite cold, and need a warm hearth to sit by ... even fer a moment. I've been walking night 'n day for days 'n days, and — "

Dybris shushed him. "I'll hear your story later. I haven't time now." He pointed down the lane to the far, far end, where the chapel sat against the mountainside. "There, in the last crennig — our chapel — should be a small fire, with more wood outside. You are welcome to stay there, and I will come soon and share a warm crust with you, but I have an urgent errand to attend to — "

"Ah, ah ... but my lungs!" Mórganthu feigned a wheeze. "I'm wore out, ready to die, and my breathers are all but frozen! I don't think I can walk that far." He wheezed twice more. "Is there perhaps a place ... nearer by?"

Dybris looked at him quizzically. "You've come this far, surely you can make it to the chapel. Now, excuse me," he said, and he began to limp off.

But Mórganthu snatched at the monk's robe, gripped it tightly, and stopped the man. He pretended to be jerked nearly off his feet by this action, and fell to one knee.

"Mercy ... mercy upon me, a frozen icicle of a worm, good monk."

Dybris tightened his lips and turned around. "Oh ... all right, then. A fire?"

"Nearby, yes."

"A few moments only? Just so you can make it to the chapel?"

"Oh, yes, you are a kind savior in my dark troubles, my ... my good monk."

"Come along then, I'm going to the weaver's, but you'll have to leave *very* quickly. It may only be a short visit."

"Oh, thank you, thank you," Mórganthu said, turning his laugh into a wheeze.

They went together: Dybris limping, and Mórganthu gasping out his frosty breath. When they came to the weaver's gate, Mórganthu kept walking, pretending he didn't know where he was going.

Dybris patted his shoulder. "Here, good man ... come in and warm yourself."

"Ah yes, ah yes ... just the place for me frigid breathers." Mórganthu swallowed. He'd better not overplay it.

Dybris knocked on the door. "Open up, I have important news!"

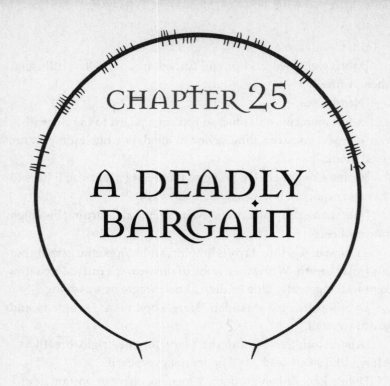

CHAPTER 25

A DEADLY BARGAIN

Hearing no sound from King Atleuthun's hall, the guard knocked again on the door, this time louder. "Open up I says, open uppa!"

"Shut yer gull beak," came a voice from within. "We kenna."

The doors clicked open, and two warriors stood at the ready. The guards led their party into a large, smoky hall past a blazing hearth.

Merlin looked up and squinted his eyes. The center of the hall went upward to the very top — the ninth level. Massive beams had been mortised and tenoned together to support the structure, and here and there, bars had been crisscrossed to hold it all together. The lower levels had rooms around the central atrium, with doors opening outward toward the railings. The height made Merlin's head spin.

Colvarth elbowed him. "Pay attention."

Merlin blinked and looked around. Unbeknownst to him, they had halted before a low table, both wide and long. Many warriors reclined around it, and they all stared at the party. Their long hair — either red or golden — was held in place by silver clasps that reflected the dim light. Iron plates over leather covered their chests, and nearby stood a rack of spears, barbed like harpoons. Their helms, each of which had been set on the table near to their drinking bowls, had small fins riveted onto them. Each man's gaze flicked from Necton's Pictish warriors with their blue cloaks, to Merlin and the other slaves who stood together.

One of the warriors stood out among his peers. His hair was long like theirs, although black and curly. His eyebrows pressed down as he studied the party — Merlin in particular — and there was some secret concern there. Something seemed familiar about him, though Merlin could not put a finger on it. Certainly his tunic wasn't familiar — a rich, shiny material of black and red, the like of which Merlin had never seen.

A screech filled the room, but Merlin could not tell who had made it.

"Cease thy kries, *mine mor*," came another voice.

And only then did Merlin see the man seated on the throne at the very back, for the smoke had obscured his presence. A long and curly white beard fell down from his aged and frowning, face. A fur of black and white lay heavy upon his shoulders, and over his chest he wore a red, shiny tunic decorated with white thread. The man was mostly skin and bones.

Merlin sucked in a breath. This was King Atleuthun, his grandfather, still alive.

Atle's hand held forth a rod, and he bent over and hit a bent and twist-backed person on the head with it — a woman, if Merlin's guess was right. She wore a knobby, garishly purple hat, and this must have softened the blow.

"Cease! Stoppe!" the old man said, and hit her again.

But she cried out in a blubbering sing-song. "Theneva ... Theneva Gweviana!"

This time he took his rod and smashed her across the face, and the woman's bulbous nose began pouring forth blood. It dripped onto her already stained purple tunic. Only then did she cease talking and pinch her nose to stem the flow.

The king looked up and scanned his visitors.

Merlin felt like an intruder. He didn't want to be here — yet here he was.

"Vich o' de young men among ye dares claim he's me grandson?" the man bellowed, his lips curling in disdain and his sunken eyes smoldering in the dim morning light that was able to penetrate the building.

Merlin swallowed and stepped forward as far as the chain to Bedwir's collar would allow. "I am he. Merlinus mab Gweviana, who, I am told, is your daughter." Merlin wanted to kick himself ... why had used his Latin name? The king had a strange accent. Was it Lochlan? Either way, it certainly wasn't Roman.

All the warriors turned to look at him — especially the young man with the black hair, whose gaze fell upon Merlin like a razored arrow.

In the silence, Merlin decided to continue. There was nothing else. "I was born near here, though I know not where, and then my parents moved to Kernow, where I grew up."

The young man stood and swaggered over to Merlin. A short blade lay at his hip, broad and sharp. "And sae ye, a youth, hae come from Kernow in the southwest — as a slave?" The last word had a mocking tone.

"Loth! Sit, and I vil handle de imposter," King Atle said.

But Loth ignored the king and just stared at Merlin, a challenge in his upturned nose.

Two things surprised Merlin. First was Loth's speech, which was different from the king's — the man rolled the "r" in *Kernow*, which reminded Merlin of his mother's accent. Second was Loth himself — he stood exactly Merlin's height and could have been his brother. It was like looking into a mirror of himself, only older, and without the scars.

Natalenya gasped.

Merlin continued. "Our party of seven was taken captive in Kembry, and this eighth man was added to our number later." Merlin tapped Peredur's shoulder, and he gave a slight bow.

"Seven?" Loth said. "Not only are ye sich a liar, but ye canna count, either." He yanked Peredur's chain until the man fell to his knees. "With him included, I see anly seven."

Merlin's hopes rose. Even though Arthur sat in Gormla's arms, Merlin wanted to make sure that Atle knew of the boy's existence — while still keeping his identity a secret. "The one you have missed is but an orphan babe, yet is loved by us all." He pointed to Arthur. Gormla jerked to the side as if to hide the child from view.

King Atle cleared his throat and looked to the child. Then he turned his gaze to Merlin and Necton, and finally back to the child. And he was silent, considering them like they were wooden pieces on a gameboard. Finally, he and Loth exchanged a strange glance, and then the king spoke. "Yerr klaim to be me grandson is impossible." His next words slipped out one by one from underneath his snarling upper lip. "Andd ... I ... know ... dis ... for ... I ... haf ... no ... *daughter*."

Necton grunted and his nostrils flared. He turned on Colvarth and grabbed him by the tunic. "Told-ha yiu to me, pay-idh he would ... give-idh he to me gold ans abundance!"

Merlin signaled Bedwir and prepared to pounce if Necton tried to injure the bard. But Colvarth took a deep breath and whispered to the Pict, "Let me speak. I can convince him."

Necton released him.

Colvarth handed his harp to Caygek, approached the throne, and fell to his knees. "Oh great King of the Votadin! Lord of the wood people, and lord of the sea people, hear me! I am known to you as Bledri mab Cadfan, and many years ago, during the reign of Rhitherch the Old, King of Rheged, I once visited your grand *hof* and enjoyed the bounty of your hearth. Then I was in the service of the druidow. Although that is no longer the case, I am still chief bard of this island of the Mighty. In those days you held my word in esteem as a seeker of truth, and as a speaker of truth — and in the trust that you once bestowed upon me, I ask you to hear me now."

Atle snorted while petting a dog that yapped at the base of his throne.

Colvarth continued. "As servant of High King Uther, I came to know of this Merlin, and of his father, Owain. This Owain was in Uther's warband nigh on twenty years ago, and they sought your succor in time of dire need, and you granted it ... *You must remember this*, for Owain it was that took in marriage your daughter, Theneva Gweviana. It is thus — "

Atle leaned forward, and with his rod attempted to smite Colvarth in the head, but the bard ducked just in time.

"No more vil I hear o' yerr foolishness," the king bellowed. *"I haf no daughter!"* He snapped his fingers, and two of his guards stepped forward and raised their axes. "If ye spekk thus again, ye vil lose yerr tongue — and yerr head vith et. I neither vant ye, nor any other slaves, and vil not pay forr dem." The king cackled until a coughing fit overtook him.

Colvarth shuffled backward on his knees until he was out of reach of the guards. Then he quickly stood and joined the others.

Necton cried out and tried to leap at the king, but his own warriors held him back.

King Atle waved his age-spotted hand toward the Pict. "Neferless, we are villing to see yerr plunder andd consider payment for sich dat we deem useful."

Calming somewhat, Necton shook off his warriors. He brought the first of his sacks and dumped it upon the feasting table ... then the second ... and the third. Each time a clatter filled the hall as the mound grew larger.

Merlin's opened his eyes wide, for there — amidst the jumble of jewelry, plenteous Roman-made silver dishes, fine clothes, bronze lamps, cloaks, armor, scrolls, and many other blades — lay Merlin's sword. To think of it now, the last time Merlin had seen it was at their slave taking when Necton had strapped it on his own waist. Why was it to be sold? Here lay one of the finest swords Merlin's father had ever forged — and Necton was going to sell it?

He nudged Colvarth and asked him why.

"The Picts prize spears above all weapons, and though they amuse themselves by pretending to take swords for their own, they do not know the art, nor desire to learn it. They sell such to others and reap the coins instead. Only in their spears do they trust."

Now that Atle had rejected purchasing them as slaves, would he buy Merlin's sword? What of Merlin's torc? He looked, and that still rested around Necton's collar. In either case, they were lost to him.

The warriors began sorting through the pile, considering each piece and passing to others what they weren't interested in. Atle himself shuffled over, and threw things into the hands of his servant woman. One of these was Merlin's sword, snatched from the hands of a lesser warrior who nodded his head to the king, eyes downcast. The king nodded while inspecting the blade's edge and strength, its iron crossguard braided like the horns of an ox, as well as the yellow gems and the leather-wrapped hilt.

When all had been sorted through, only a few notched blades were left, along with the worst of the clothing and jewelry. The king conferred with his warriors at length about the value of the items, and finally sat upon his throne. Loth passed some guards and disappeared into a distant room. When he walked back, he shook in his hands two bags filled with clinking coins. He handed them to the king, and then sat once more at the head of the table of warriors.

The king cleared his throat and then spoke. "I haf counted out ferr ye twelf geld pieces, andd tirty silver — "

Necton stepped forward, his hand open to receive the bag, but the king jerked it back.

"I vil not give dese coins to ye unless ye make one more bargain vit me. I desire to buy de orphan child for me househeld, andd vil pay ye dree more geld pieces ferr him."

Gormla shouted and tried to run from the hall with Arthur, but guards jumped in her way and grabbed them. Other guards held their axes at the ready.

Necton's fury rose, and he lunged at the king, the hidden blade drawn from behind his cloak and jabbing toward the king's heart.

But Loth was quicker — he stuck out his leg and tripped him.

Necton crashed to the stone floor, and three guards quickly restrained him, wrenching his arms behind his back and then pulling his blade away. The other Pictish warriors hadn't had time to react, and before they knew it, they had the harpoon-like spears and axes pointed at their backs and necks.

Loth held his sword point at Necton's ribs and forced him to kneel before the king.

Atle smiled down at him curiously. "De child? I haf made an ofer ferr him, and I vil haf yerr answer."

Necton looked sideways at his warriors plight, and then at his wife's. Finally he turned his gaze upon the king. "May I, gle servant-i of yiur, make-idh an offer?"

Atle chuckled while he tapped the sole of his red-woolen shoes upon the gilt dais underneath his throne. "Ya, ye may make counter, but me answer may be yerr blood."

"Sell-i yiu an child ..." Necton began.

Gormla struggled against the grip of her captors. "No! Sell-i canna!"

Necton ignored her and flinched at Loth's blade. "Sell-i yiu an child ... and all an plunder ... for an price named yiu ... plus three more gilt coins for an thrails."

"I do nott vant de slaves."

"Want you an child? Then take-a yiu an thrails."

The king shook his head. "Loth ...?" The blade bit into Necton's side.

"Two coins for an thrails — "

The blade bit deeper.

Necton jerked away. "One gold-ah coin ... *one coin only!*"

The king nodded. "Ve are in agreement. One geld coin ferr de slaves and tree ferr de child. Do ye see how easy dat vas?"

Gormla sobbed uncontrollably as one of Atle's warriors seized Arthur from her. The child screamed all the way to the king's lap. Gormla covered her face with her hair and wept into it.

Two bags and a single gold coin were tossed to Necton, who snatched them and retreated from the feasting hall with his warriors and howling wife. The door slammed shut behind them. Necton was gone. But Merlin's joy was short lived, for now they had new masters.

Atle called Loth and a few warriors to approach him, and he spoke to them in a low whisper. Loth questioned his father, but finally nodded.

The king's warriors brought forth hammers, and, without any words, they unbent the pins that held the slave collars together. Unthreading the chain through his collar, Merlin shucked it clanging to the floor. Confusion filled his heart as he looked at the king … his grandfather.

Atle stepped forward and placed his thin and slightly trembling hands upon Merlin's shoulders. "I know who ye are — me grandson — an' so ye are free."

At the same moment, the old woman with the bent back shuffled forward and took hold of Merlin's left hand, all the time saying, "Theneva Gweviana's … Theneva Gweviana's!"

Merlin pulled his hand away and wept. He didn't know what else to do — because all his pain, all his frustration, and all his many months of suffering poured forth from his soul, blurring his vision.

Atle touched one of the scars on Merlin's face. "Vat is dis? Tears? Did ye nott know dat I always play a hard bargain?"

CHAPTER 26

A DEADLY RUSE

Vortigern banged again, and finally Tregeagle opened the door. When the Magister saw Vortigern, his jaw fell open, and the light of the morning sun reflected strangely in his eyes.

"Ehh, shut your mouth," Vortigern said. "You smell like a dead lizard."

Over Tregeagle's shoulder, he spied the man's wife about twenty paces back.

"V-v-vorti—" Tregeagle stammered. His hair was long and matted, and the man hadn't shaved his white beard in weeks.

Vortigern clamped his hand over the man's filthy lips. "My name's Ivor, yes?"

Tregeagle nodded.

Vortigern took his hand away and wiped the spit on Tregeagle's tunic—once brilliant white, now soiled with dirt and oil.

"Ivor... Ivor," Tregeagle said. "I'd been expecting you... months ago."

Vortigern grabbed Tregeagle's shoulder, pulled him outside into the falling snow, and closed the door. "It's hard being a traveling merchant. Do you know if anyone in the area has something to sell? Perhaps *two* of something?"

"Two ... yes, two."

"Where would I find them?"

Tregeagle pointed down the mountainside. "There ..."

"Ehh, which crennig?"

"The one with the high stone wall. The weavers live there, and you'll have no trouble buying *two* yards of cloth from them."

"Ah ... so I can purchase two yards there," Vortigern said.

"And how much *gold* will you pay them?" Tregeagle asked, holding out his empty palm.

"No payment until my goods are received."

Tregeagle gritted his teeth and contorted his bottom lip. "B-but —"

"No payment until *receipt*, I said."

Tregeagle started pawing at Vortigern's money bag, which hung from his right hip.

Contempt filled Vortigern, and he backhanded the man's face, slamming him into the door. Tregeagle slipped in the snow and fell to the ground. "I-I was just making ... sure ... sure they were there. I —"

"Try it again and you'll get no gold from Ivor, do you hear?"

Tregeagle's right eyelid started fluttering.

What a wretched, skulking, skunk of a man, Vortigern thought. Vortipor should be glad he wouldn't have *him* for a father-in-law.

Vortigern turned to his men. "Let's get down there and purchase our cloth," he said.

Mórganthu nearly jumped when Troslam opened the door with his sharp spear in hand. Did he know? Or was this his usual precaution? Perhaps Mórganthu hadn't watched him quite enough with the orb.

Dybris raised his hand through the falling snow, "Peace, Troslam. It's *urgent* we talk."

"And who's this?" Troslam asked, pointing his spear at Mórganthu.

"An old beggar who needs to rest his lungs by your fire. We *need* to talk."

"What's his name?"

"Ahh ..." Dybris turned and looked at Mórganthu. "You're not Muscarvel, are you?"

Mórganthu panicked. Why hadn't he thought of a name? He shook his head no.

Troslam tapped his spear impatiently. "Look, of course he's not Muscarvel. He doesn't smell like a marsh rat, does he? The answer, Dybris, is that you don't know this fellow."

The first thing that popped into Mórganthu's head was, "Hobble, my name is Hobble." He had barely remembered to hide his Eirish lilt.

"That's not a proper name ... Where are you from, and who's your father?"

Dybris was now waving his hand. "*Troslam* ... I need to speak to you *now*."

Any delay was good, and Mórganthu spun his tale quickly. "My name is Hoyt mab Hagan, but my friends call me Hobble. I am journeying to Isca from the northern coast. I have family there. My father — "

" — has lungs colder than yours," Dybris interrupted. "Troslam, there is no time!"

Troslam nodded. "All right. I have to be careful."

Mórganthu entered after Dybris, and Troslam barred the door. The room felt hot, almost stuffy after having been out in the cold wind. The aroma of a rich pea soup assaulted him, and he breathed it in with vigor.

"The fire's back there," Troslam said, pointing to a central room with a hearth. Mórganthu shuffled past Dybris and sat down next to the flames. He held out his good hand to warm it, keeping the false hand resting on his leg. The enticing pot of soup hung from a chain over the fire, and he was tempted to take up one of the nearby mugs and fill it — when three girls ran through the room, followed by a slow, somber Ganieda.

The three jumped up and down. "Dybris, Dybris, Dybris!"

But Ganieda did not. She sat near Mórganthu, looking at her shoes.

"Why are you sad, little one?" Mórganthu whispered in the druid language that only Ganieda would know.

She stood up, her eyes wide open. "Grandpa," she whispered back to him in the same tongue. Then she sat down again and looked away, blinking rapidly.

He switched to the language of Kernow so as to avoid attracting attention. "You are wise," he whispered, "yes, wise to not betray me. It is not safe here."

She turned and stared at him. Her dark eyes were so deep. "How did you find me?"

"The orb."

"I thought you might have died. Or left me. Or forgotten." She looked down again and scuffed the heel of her shoe in the dirt.

"Where is the fang? Is it where you left it before?"

"I won't tell, Grandpa." She looked up then at Safrowana, who was walking quickly through the room in answer to her husband's summons. "I-I think . . . I think I like it here."

"Why? Why not with me, my daughter's daughter? I have come to take you away."

"I'm not afraid here."

He arched his eyebrow and said in as insinuating of a tone as he could, "Is not *Merlin* behind this? Did not *he* arrange this?"

She swiveled toward him, and curled her lips. "No!"

"Are you . . . are you quite sure?"

"If he were," she said loudly, "I would kill them all."

"Shah!" he said, "Keep your voice down, they will—"

But it was too late. Troslam had heard, and, leaning in from the other room, was looking at them with wary eyes. "It's the druid," he yelled.

Mórganthu only had a moment to act. Ganieda would not go with him willingly, and this outraged him. If that was her choice, then fine, let her die with the dogs. But he could still recover the fang if he could get it from behind the loom shuttles on the windowsill. Then that devilish Troslam would pay dearly for his previous violence against his personage.

He jumped up and ran past a huge loom toward the back ... but there were two doorways. Which one?

Behind him, Troslam shouted.

Left? Or right? He reversed the image in his mind and tried to picture the outside of the house and where he had stood.

Troslam thumped past the hearth and was nearly upon him.

Left it was! Mórganthu jumped through the door and flung himself toward the window. And there, still sitting in the dust behind the shuttles, was the fang — white, and sharp as death.

Troslam yelled behind him.

Mórganthu reached for it — but the weaver had grabbed him by the tunic. He was pulled backward.

Mórganthu's hand swiped out, but he couldn't reach the weapon.

"What are you doing here?" Troslam yelled.

Mórganthu leaned forward, reaching, but missed. In a last, swinging effort, he popped open the iron lock of the shutter just before Troslam yanked him away.

"You'll not leave that easily!"

Mórganthu was dragged into the main room where the hearth lay. He kicked and scratched at Troslam, but the man pinned Mórganthu's arms and tied a cord tightly around his wrists. Mórganthu struggled against this at first, but then realized the man wasn't accounting for his fake hand. To make sure they didn't realize this foolishness, Mórganthu clasped the fake hand in his good one.

Troslam had just finished tying up Mórganthu's feet when

Dybris rushed into the room, shouting. "They're coming down the road … Vortigern and his men are coming!"

Merlin stood in the doorway to Atle's private chamber. For the first time in many months he felt clean. They had all been offered baths and clothing, and Merlin chose a long blue tunic sewn with a thick sea-green thread, as well as black leggings, leather boots, and a broad sash of white fabric for a belt. And his sense of cleanness went yet further, for the awful monster of slavery had been pulled off of his back, slain, and thrown into a deep pit, never to escape.

Atle beckoned. "Kome in … kome in," he said. "Ye haf refreshed yerself, I see, andd are now kome to dank me fer yer freedom."

Merlin entered, and dropped to one knee before the king. "That I am, and most gratefully." Atle's dog came from around the corner, barked, and then sniffed him.

"Rise, Merlin, andd sit before me."

Merlin took his place on a padded chair, smaller than the king's, though of similar design, with fish and sea creatures carved upon its surfaces. Though it was only late morning, the room was without windows and very dark, and a white, tallow candle sat in a golden stand on the table directly between them.

King Atle leaned forward, into the light, and his eyes looked even more sunken, if that were possible. A torc lay upon his throat, but of different design than Merlin had seen before — it was made of solid gold, not twisted wire, and the two ends had been fashioned into disks, each like the giant eye of a silent, hungry sea creature. The thought of four eyes staring at Merlin unnerved him, and the bright candlelight had already begun to make his head hurt.

"King Atle … sir, I …"

"Enough formalities. We are family, ye and I. Ye may call me Atleuthun, or simply Atle." The king's words were soft, but his face showed little emotion.

The candle light still hurt Merlin's eyes, so he reached out to slide its golden base to the left and out from between them.

Just as he touched it, Atle put his hand out and stopped it. Merlin tried to keep sliding it, but Atle was too strong.

"Ye are a guest here — no? We are family — ya? Does dat mean dat you vil inherit the tings of me house? Dat ye can touch dem as if dey are yer own? No."

Atle's arm lay skinny upon the table. How could he have such strength at his age?

"Loth ess me heir … He has served me vell, and participates vit me by blood. Ye are a beggar here, andd ye shan't forget it." The king withdrew his hand as quickly as it had come.

"Of course … of course. I did not presume I would inherit anything simply because you have freed my friends and me from slavery."

"Ya, ya, ya … ess true. Ye'f been bought vit me geld, and should be me slave. Never presume. Neferless, I haf freed ye, against de vishes o' some, and alotted ye all a sum to help ye on yerr vay." He threw a small bag of coins on the table in front of Merlin.

"Et ess not much," Atle continued, "but de least I can do … considering yerr great help to me. But" — and here he wagged his finger — "nefer presume et ess as great o' help as I daily receive from me son, Loth. I am most proud o' him."

Much of Atle's words puzzled Merlin. He was grateful for the gift, but didn't want Atle to think he was greedy for anything that belonged to the king. "You do well to be proud of Loth. As a faithful son, he will inherit all that you own when you die — "

The king laughed then, long and loud, and the dog barked too. "A good jokke, yes. Yerr muther must haf thought de same … or she wouldn't haf run off. May I ask how she fares?"

Merlin paused. How could he explain that he'd thought his mother dead for fourteen years — drowned — only to find she was alive? That she'd been changed by the Stone's enslavement so that she could only live in water?

"She's fine," was all he could think to say. "She's ... ahh ... staying in Kernow."

"She has drifted so far, den? And vat has she told ... about me? And me house's history?"

"Nothing ... only your name and the name of your fortress." She'd given him some vague instructions as well, but Merlin couldn't remember them now. What had she said? The candle continued to burn, but Merlin's headache had eased. The chair felt so soft, and Merlin's limbs ... so tired. He needed sleep after their long march.

"And yerr father? Vat has become o' him?" Atle leaned forward and turned his head a little to better hear the answer. There was an odd, burning gleam in his eye.

"He's dead ... six months ago."

"The judgment o' de cursed always katches up vit dem, does et not?"

Merlin bit his lip and said nothing, though he wanted to defend his father and his heroic death. If Atle hadn't just freed them from slavery, Merlin would—

"Ah, but I like ye. Ye have a different sort o' pluck, and ye have also brought de child. I am indebted to ye. De villagers will be happy too, and ye haf saved me much trouble vith dem. So tell me about de boy—about his parents. I must know everything."

"You mean Arthur?" Merlin blanched ... for he realized he hadn't consulted Colvarth about what to say. How much should he reveal?

"Yes, dis Arthur ... How did his parents die?"

"They ... uh ... were killed."

Atle clucked his tongue. "Both o' dem? Yes?"

Merlin's throat felt suddenly dry. "Yes."

"Are ye sure? Derr couldn't be a mistake?"

Merlin had to think. He hadn't personally seen Uther die, having been blind. But his father had witnessed the king's death, and Colvarth had witnessed Igerna's. "No mistake. Why does it matter?"

"The boy has had lots of de anguish, and I vant an end o' suffering ferr him."

"Our slavery's been quite hard. Arthur had it easier, though."

Atle clasped his hands and smiled — each of his gray teeth had been worn flat as if he ate the shale from the cliffs for dinner every day. "Today at de mid-meal ve are having our ninth year celebration, and dis boy vit-out a father — "

"Arthur."

Yes ... de boy ... and ye ... haf come just in time. I am most grateful. Ye won't leave until after de feast?"

"Of course not. We will be honored to be your guests."

The dog yapped as if he wanted to be included as well.

"Ah, but ye are nott de guest o' honor, and should nott presume such. Velcome, ya. Honored, no. De little one, Arthur, ess me guest o' honor, and shall feast by me side in great finery. Et ess a ninth year celebration, after all."

"Ninth year?" Merlin asked. The candle had burned lower now, and he could hardly keep his eyes open.

"Ah, but dat's right," Atle said, relaxing his smile. "Yer muther hasn't told ye dese dings. Every nine years ve hold a vonderful feast. Et ess our oldest tradition on Dinpelder, we say."

"I saw the preparations going on in the kitchen," Merlin said. "It looks like you've been preparing for many days."

Atle nodded to Merlin, then he leaned forward and blew out the candle. Merlin was blind for a moment and saw only a hazy floating outline of Atle in the darkness.

"Ye are tired from yer travels, " Atle said, "and now our audience ess at an end. I shall see ye shortly at de feast."

Merlin rose, took the small bag of money, bowed in thanks, and left.

As Merlin closed the door, something fell into his hair. He shook his head and brushed it out — a small piece of wood. Rotten, it was, and it crumbled in his hands. He looked up, and, in the dim light coming from the main hall, noticed that the log above Atle's doorway looked peculiar. He touched it, and sure, it was rotting away. In fact, as he made his way to his assigned room, he noticed other logs that had the same decayed appearance. Funny, but it seemed to him like the whole building might come down soon under its own weight. How old *was* the place?

He tried to put it out of his mind as he closed his door, wearily flopped onto his heather and fern stuffed mattress for a quick nap, and fell asleep. But visions of Atle's face haunted him, and in his dreams he couldn't get the king's hand to let go of his arm.

CHAPTER 27

THE MORTAL THROAT

Panic ensued all around Mórganthu as he pretended to struggle against his bonds. If they would leave him alone for even a few breaths, he could slip his fake-handed-stump out of the cords and free himself. But no, they all had to run around in fear of Vortigern like the little fools they were.

At least Troslam had some wits. He gathered the others and presented a plan. "There's five of them, and we've no choice but to escape."

Safrowana could hardly catch her breath, and made it worse by covering her mouth and nose with her hands.

"But how?" Dybris asked. "They'll see us climb your wall, and they'll guard the gates."

"Not if we go *under* the wall. We've never used the old kiln built into our land's wall. The stones in the back are loose, and I can push them out."

Dybris shuffled them all toward the back of the house. "Then go! I'll guard the door and give you time to get away."

"No," Safrowana said, finding her voice, "I'll stay as well — with Ganieda and Imelys. We'll pretend you're on a journey, and that the girls never lived here ... won't we?"

Imelys nodded.

Ganieda looked confused but nodded anyway.

Troslam took hold of his wife's hands and shook his head. "I can't let you do this."

"You have no choice. You're the only one who can protect them."

Troslam closed his eyes for a moment and then embraced her.

There was a knock on the door, and everyone jumped.

"And Mórganthu?" Troslam whispered. "He'll tell."

"I'll gag him. Now go!" Dybris handed over the spear.

While Troslam and Uther's girls snuck out the back door of the house into their high-walled pasture, the monk made good on his word and tied the gag firmly around Mórganthu's head. It hurt, and so Mórganthu pretended to shake his head in protest, but knew he could take it off quickly when needed.

There was another loud knock at the door.

Safrowana set Imelys to spinning in the corner, told Ganieda to pretend to stir the pot of soup, and set herself on the loom's bench and began unwinding the shuttle. She nodded to Dybris and took a deep breath.

Vortigern and his men were banging now. "Anyone home?!" they called.

"Pray," Dybris said as he went to the door.

Mórganthu swiveled his body on the floor to get a better vantage point. Dybris had just begun to lift the bar when someone rammed into the door from the outside. One of the hinges cracked away from the frame, and Dybris fell to the floor with the bar on his chest.

Three men burst in — one with a spear and two with swords.

Safrowana screamed, and the girls both jumped.

Ganieda ran to Imelys, and the two held hands behind two wooden vats of dye.

The spear came within inches of the monk's belly, and the monk flinched. "Peace!" Dybris yelled. "We are Christians here and mean you no harm."

The two swordsmen charged into the room. One went straight for the girls, and they screeched as he cornered them. The other warrior sought out Safrowana, who, after her initial fright, stood up and held her arms out to show she held no weapon. Within moments the room was silent, a hushed breath against a blade.

Vortigern walked in, an archer at his side. "Tethion ... check the rooms and the pasture."

Tethion stepped over Mórganthu, who wanted to pull out his arm and release his gag, but found the scene playing out before him a delicious morsel upon his tongue. He would tell, and quickly, but not instantly. The girls could not get far.

Tethion ran back to the room and shook his head. "No one else is here."

Dybris and Safrowana glanced at each other.

The swordsman with the girls, a bully of a man with his front teeth missing, snarled and shook his blade at them. "I gots 'em, Ivort, I gots the two! Does I's gets a reward?"

Vortigern stepped over and cuffed the man across the face. "Not them ... that's not *them*." He swiveled to face Safrowana. "Where are they — Uther's girls? We're here to ... bring them back to their clan ... protect them."

At these words, the man with the spear upon the monk blinked at Vortigern, confused.

Safrowana said nothing. Her chin was out in defiance, but Mórganthu could see the corners of her eyes twitching.

Vortigern grabbed onto her hair and yanked it back, almost pulling her over. But he held her close, suspended against his chest — neck out and face up. Then he pulled out a short blade and brought the tip near her eyes.

"Tell me now. *Where did the girls go?*"

Mórganthu looked up at Vortigern's blade. Would he kill Safrowana? Mórganthu would dearly like that, and it made his slight delay revealing himself and the truth well worth it ... a small bit of revenge for all his troubles.

Someone banged a loud gong in the central hall, waking Merlin up. It was almost mid-day and the time for the ninth year feast had come, but Merlin wanted to visit Natalenya before the festival meal. She had informed Colvarth that she was not going to attend so that she could rest. Her sickness had taken a turn for the worse during their recent journey.

Her room faced north at the far end of the highest inhabitable level of Atle's hall, and Merlin climbed the stairs up three floors to reach her. As he approached the door, he found it ajar, and peeking in, he saw Loth sitting in a chair near her bed. They were chatting.

Merlin knocked and pushed the door open.

Loth stood to face Merlin. "Ye've come at ane good time," he said. "I hae just brought this beautiful lass a trencher from our feast, and was preparing tae leave." He gave a slight bow to Natalenya and then slipped past Merlin without making eye contact.

"What was that about?" Merlin asked, taking the seat where Loth had sat. It was warm. At a small table nearby lay a pewter mug full of red wine and a tray of sliced meats, cheeses, and bread.

"He's quite nice, you know."

"And handsome."

Natalenya pulled up the blanket and faced the wall. "He looks like you — "

"Without the scars. Yes, I know." He reached up to his face and traced the lines again — the ever-present curses.

She spun back, her face pinched. "Loth is helping me with my sickness. The royal physician has already been up twice to visit me."

"And that's more than I've ever done. You don't need to — "

"What? I don't need to get better? The sickness has wormed its way into my bones now — I can feel it — and unless I get help

I'm going to die. Can't you understand that, Merlin? But you're too trapped in the prison of your own scars."

She threw the mug at him. It missed and thudded into the wall, splashing its blood upon the rotting wood.

Her tears flowed freely now, and her voice was hoarse. "Your eyes can see, but I think you're just as blind as ever."

She might as well have plunged a knife in.

He reached out and took her trembling hand. "I'm sorry," was all he could say, and it was true. He had come expecting her to be happy that their slavery had ended — but she wasn't. Of course not! And he'd been a fool to think it. What did slavery to the Picts matter when her very veins were enslaved by this sickness? He'd reveled in his freedom, his cleanliness, his new clothes, in Arthur's recovery — but none of these things mattered to her.

"I'm sorry for everything. I don't know how to help anymore, and I've failed you."

But it wasn't just him that had failed her. Why hadn't the Sangraal healed her? Had Merlin been a fool to trust God?

Maybe Atle's physician could help.

She pulled her hand away and didn't say anything, and so he picked up the empty mug, set it on her table once again, and left.

Merlin could hear the revelers down below, and he looked over the rail as he descended. The central hearth had been lit and veritable racks of hot meats roasted in its steady blaze — beef, fowl, mutton, venison, and a small boar. And there was seafood too — huge fish, speared, and dripping their rich fat over the fires next to pots of boiling rust-colored crustaceans.

All this wafted upward with the smoke, but his stomach was sour, slowing his descent.

As he walked along the final landing, he could see that the area all around the hearth had been filled with guests — warriors and their wives — seated at tables piled high with cheeses, trenchers of dried apples and berries, baskets filled with steaming flatbreads, and pots of hearty broth. There were also bowls of nuts , toasted and salted, along with platters of orange and white boiled roots, smothered with melted butter.

Stepping onto the main floor, Merlin approached the table where his entire party sat and pulled up a low bench between Bedwir and Garth. The boy had just drained some scalded cream with curds from a bowl and had a white moustache draped across his upper lip.

"We told him to wait until Atle officially starts the feast," Peredur said, leaning over and crunching on some nuts. "But he just *wouldn't* wait."

Atle stood, shakily, and declared to the crowd, "Velcome, family, friends, and distant kin. We haf gathered, upon de day o' de great departure o' de glorious ninth year — and ve are ready, yes, ve are ready — danks to our guest o' honor."

And here he pointed to Arthur, smartly dressed in a red tunic and sitting upon a little raised throne beside Atle's. Before him lay a platter of succulent venison, bread smeared with raspberry preserves, and fresh honeyed apples. The boy had a finger in his mouth, and seemed both pleased and confused at the cheers that arose from the crowd.

"Life! Tonight ve celebrate life! Given by the good Woden to all who valk upon de earth andd sail upon de deep."

The king talked on and on like this and Merlin ignored his speech, as well as the barking dog that ran around the room eating scraps the warriors threw him. Instead, he turned his attention to the two barrels in the center of their table — one of ale, and another of spiced cider that Garth kept glugging down. Merlin set his mug below the ale spigot and pulled the plug.

Today, he needed to forget.

Mórganthu held his breath as Vortigern moved the knife closer to Safrowana's face.

She spoke. "My husband took them on a trip. He'll be back next month." She grabbed onto Vortigern's tunic to keep from falling.

Vortigern brought the blade closer and let it hover over her eyes. "A trip? Is that right? And why would he take Uther's girls and not these, *eh*?"

"That's my daughter. She … she's my helper with the … loom."

"And the other?" Vortigern said. He was baiting her and trying to get her talking, Mórganthu thought, for the man knew the answer to this question.

"She's not one of Uther's daughters, I promise … We were given charge of her."

"By who?"

"Merlin." She reached into a small bag hanging from her belt and slipped out a pewter ring with a white stone in it. "Merlin gave us … some money to care for her … and this ring to prove the authority. It was her father's. Please, I'm telling the truth."

Mórganthu had never seen this trinket before, and it meant nothing to him — but it must have meant something to his granddaughter. Upon hearing Merlin's name and seeing the ring, Ganieda shrieked and yelled. She splashed a dye vat onto her guard's feet, poked him in the ribs with her soup spoon, and slipped around his drooping blade.

Screaming, she ran out the open front door and was gone.

Merlin drank until his stomach loosened and he was able to eat. The food satisfied him in a way he'd thought impossible over the last six months. Slabs of bumpy white cheese. Salted roast boar and a savory mutton leg. Slices of saffroned fish as thick as any steak, yet it would flake apart at the slightest touch. Ale. Bread, warm and soft upon his tongue. Fruit. Crab appendages, sucked sweet from their shells. Ale, and more ale, until he felt so full he could hold no more. Everyone else joined in with relish. Even Colvarth ate more than expected. But Garth topped them all — the boy ate four full trenchers of food and by the end looked so sleepy that Merlin could have pushed him over by squishing the cheese curd stuck to his cheek.

Then one of Atle's bards got up and sang a lingering, slow ballad about a battle from times of yore. It seemed to be about the warriors from Dinpelder repelling an attack from the Picts, but the details became a bit fuzzy to Merlin. Somehow the Romans were involved. Or were they? Merlin was confused.

Throughout the song, Peredur's face leaned closer and then faded backward. Why couldn't the man sit still, his jaw flapping as he ate, fergoodnesssakes?

On and on the bard droned, and the sunlight streaming into the hall seemed to become very bright as the ale cask emptied. Merlin laid his head down and closed his eyes against the glare. Thankfully, the grating voice of the bard faded and Merlin soon found himself in a tapestry of darknesses where uncounted days and nights passed, yet, strangely, the sun never rose to snuff out the stars that spun their winking heads. Below him the drifts of snow shone with thousands of gems, each laughing at Merlin's frozen hands and wind-bitten face.

He trudged on through the snow, neither leaving footprints behind, nor finding any ahead. Over an endless plain he trudged until he came to a glade of trees. Upon one of the branches swayed a cloth — red and ragged. He pulled it off, smelled it, and held it to his frozen cheek, but could not remember where he had seen it before. It had an opening, smallish like, and he put his hand in as if it were a bag — thinking only to warm himself — and found three holes at the other end. It was a tunic. A small tunic with an opening for a young head. Two sleeves, finely stitched.

Arthur?

Merlin had last seen it on Arthur! Why was it here? He looked at it again, hoping to find some clue as to the mystery of its presence, but the red cloth broke into a cloud of fluttering moths, each bursting into droplets of blood that fell to the snow. The drops sprouted into lithe birch saplings, pushing upward like snakes. Thicker they grew until, twisting and coiling, a square table was formed with four benches.

And then, over the hill appeared an oxen, and upon it, a rider — a woman. Lissom she was, and her fair skin was wrapped in a thick fox skin fur of rusty orange. No sooner had she appeared than two more women followed behind. The first rode a black boar, and her tresses matched it for color, laying softly upon her leathern wrap. The third journeyed upon a massive ram, horned and fierce. Her dress was a magnificent white fleece, richly woven, well-waulked, brushed, and shorn. And the three were a marvel, for their faces were all alike, and a light shone from them, bright and warm as his hearth at home during the darkest days of winter.

"Who are you?" Merlin asked, but felt they would surely shame him for such an impertinent question.

"Are you worthy of me?" all of them said in unison, "Are you ready now to see?"

The three reached out their hands, and a thorny hedge grew up around the perimeter of the glade, enclosing them, the table, and Merlin within — thick and impassable. He could not leave, but neither could anyone else invade and take him away.

"For you know who we are," they said in a soothing voice, "for we perceive you see far."

They dismounted and approached the table, each one claiming a seat on three of the open benches. Merlin felt tired, and found himself resting upon his own bench, looking in wonder at the bowls and trenchers that had magically appeared. They were filled with fluffy creams, delicate cakes, honey crystal confections, and the most succulent fruits he had ever imagined.

"Take, gentle son, and eat," they said, "for these shall surely taste sweet."

A great desire to devour the luxuries washed over him. All his life he had been denied such things: the opulence of the rich; the extravagance of those who ruled all, owned all, and yet worked not. All day long they sat on their couches of gold being fed such things and growing fat off the hard work of others.

And Merlin's six months of deprivation made his desires all the stronger. It was maddening to wait even a moment more, so he lifted up his hand and stole a cake, dipped it in the cream, and brought it to his lips. He sighed as its creamy sweetness and crunchy essence coated his tongue, filled his cheeks, and sunk softly down his throat.

Somewhere in the heavens, thunder rolled. Merlin did not even glance up as he pilfered one of the fruits by its stem and brought it to his lips. Plump it was, and its syrupy bouquet filled his nostrils even as its scarlet juice ran down his shaven chin and stained his tunic.

The three women all looked at him approvingly, and each of them took one of the fruits and bit, their actions of one mind.

The thunder rolled closer above him, but he ignored it again, for now his appetite could not be sated — the more he ate, the hungrier he became. He stuffed his cheeks with the cream, ate as many cakes as he could, and all the time the three joined him, nodding their approval and feasting upon the never-ending supply of the sumptuous fare.

And just as Merlin reached for one more cake, the middle of the table flashed so brightly that it blinded him for a moment. Fingers of lightning curled outward and singed the table and food. Merlin's hands were burned, the thunder exploding around him, enveloping him, shaking his bones, and rattling his teeth.

When he opened his eyes again, the scene before him had changed. The three women — those whose smooth faces had been filled with such merriment — had become ugly, ugly beyond imagining. Scabs covered their skin. Patches of infections leaked out filthy, green liquids. Their hair was disheveled, torn from their scalps and matted. Their noses had warts upon warts, and their shaking, bony fingers ended in nails long and sharp.

And their teeth, broken and hideously soiled, crunched upon worms, which they devoured with delight. Merlin looked at the food in his own hand and found the sumptuious foods before him were now transformed into maggoty, revolting dishes beyond his worst nightmares.

He retched.

"O mortal, what have you done?" the witches said with their forked, green-scaled tongues. "You've broke the web Brigit spun!"

A fierce wind blew in, scattering the hideous remains of the feast, and blowing the three witches backward. They cried out as the sharp thorns of the bushes pierced their flesh.

Merlin's legs flew backward as well and he seized the edge of the table. Rain pelted his face, then ice, and finally hail. The branches of the table began to crack, and just when the last one broke, the wind died. He fell to the snow, and a glorious light filled the grove, shining from above. A man, an angel, descended within the radiance, and stood upon the remains of the table. His palms burned with a luminous fire, more pure than the sun, and the heat melted the snow and set the table and benches ablaze.

Merlin fell to his knees.

"Arise, O wayward son — for the Lord, whom you have failed to trust in, is the Holy One who has been with you in your sufferings, and is with you now. Open your eyes and see!"

Merlin looked up and saw played out before him all the scenes of their slavery, but now angels aided them. They had been invisible to his mortal eyes before, yet now he saw them revealed in their glory: sustaining, protecting, and guiding.

But then an image of Atle flashed in front of him, and he saw him for what he was … a man dry as a husk and ready to blow away in the wind. But there was malevolence in his eyes as he looked down upon the old, bent woman who cowered at the base of his throne.

Her gaudy purple hat lay twisted in her hands, and she moaned, "But he … he ess de son … of Theneva … Theneva Gweviana! He ess nott to be left out o' de ninth year!"

The king kicked her. "Down to de dungeon vit ye, Kensa! Away from me sight! Dis pompous grandson o' mine shall neither hear yerr prattling nor partake o' me undying strength. I vil nott let him judge de truth o' yerr tales."

Nearby warriors took a key from the king and dragged her toward an iron plate in the floor — one that Merlin had not noticed before. One of them lit a torch while another inserted the key into the center of the plate, slid it to the side, and raised it up. They dragged her, whimpering, down the steep stairs and into the darkness.

The scene vanished. The angel bent over and rested his hand upon Merlin's head.

A burning, painful lightness filled him — a searing away that bit deeply into his soul.

"The snake has snuck into your nest and you have let him escape. The time has now come to perform the task that has been set before you."

Merlin shook his head. He'd been given a task? Had he forgotten? His mother had said something to him, long ago, it seemed. "What am I to do?" he said, feeling foolish to even ask.

"Leave behind those who cannot. Bring all those who dare. Freedom for those in darkness is hidden in the throne. Judge by neither skin nor bones. Follow the light that you have been given — but you must AWAKE!"

The flames and the grove faded. Deep sleep fell upon Merlin, and he closed his eyes.

But someone kept shoving his shoulder. A voice called to him, distantly. He wanted to sleep, but the words strengthened until it became a scream. "Merlin!"

It was Natalenya's voice. What was she doing here? He mumbled that he needed more sleep. That she should go away. Leave him alone.

She called again, more insistently.

This time someone slapped him in the face.

He opened his eyes, and his bleary vision cleared. A pewter mug lay on its side right in front of him, and its contents lay spilled upon the table.

Natalenya came into view. Her mouth was drawn tight, tears covered her cheeks, and her lips trembled as she spoke.

"They've taken Arthur! Atle's taken Arthur and they're gone!"

PART THREE
FOOL'S FAITH

Dark as the dirge, the sharks swimming;
Swift as the swan, the circle shining;
Loud as the lash, the pagans praying;
Gall as the grave, the slayer slaying;
For ancient youth, and innocent's demise.

CHAPTER 28

THAT WHICH IS LOST

Merlin sat up, and Natalenya wept on his shoulder. He wanted to say something, but his tongue felt like wood and his head like ten fish swam in it. What had happened? Where was he?

"Arthur — they've taken Arthur!"

"I need water ..." he croaked. Reaching out carefully, he wrapped his fingers around the spilled mug and peeked inside. It still had a little ale in it — good. The room spun for a moment, and then righted itself. Just as he brought it to his lips, Natalenya knocked it out of his hand, and it crashed to the floor. The echo felt like a hammer blow to his head, and he covered his ears.

"It's poisoned," she said. I've been trying to wake you — *all of you* — since I found they had left."

"Huh?" He looked around. Colvarth lay sleeping on the table with his beard bent sideways. Curled on the floor next to Merlin rested Garth with a loaf of bread for a pillow. Caygek's face lay in his arms, but his hand still cradled his mug of ale. Bedwir snored, a slight smile on his lips. Peredur … well, Peredur lay with his forehead in a tipped pot of stew. And everyone else in the hall had left; only their own group remained.

In front of Merlin sat a trencher full of vomit. His clothes were stained as well.

"You heaved right before you woke up," she explained. "I tried to clean it up."

Every word she said echoed in his head like it was hollow. "I wish I hadn't woken."

"But Arthur …"

"He can sleep too." Merlin covered his eyes. The light still filled the upper reaches of the hall and was just too bright.

"Atle's taken him!"

The little dog pranced next to her and began barking.

"That's fine. We'll see him in the morning. Help me get to my bed." He tried to stand, but the floor wobbled underneath and he fell back to his seat.

"You're not listening. They're *gone!*" Natalenya slapped him in the face again.

His left cheek was already numb, and now his jaw hurt. "Gone?"

"Everyone's gone — except for guards outside. They wouldn't let me pass, and they won't tell me where Arthur's been taken."

Merlin shook his head. Why did it hurt so bad? But Natalenya's words finally began to sink in. Arthur was missing. Stolen from them while Merlin sat here sleeping … and retching. Taken while he sat stuffing his face. Taken while he tried to forget his misery. Taken while he drank too much. While he drank ale mixed with some foul concoction. All his prayers, all his hopes, all his work, all his awful, god-forsaken choices had been intended to protect Arthur. And then, on the very edge of their freedom, Merlin had lost him.

Anger filled his chest, thumping with a burning fury, and from it a measure of strength flowed to his arms. He stood, shaky at first, and took a deep breath, steadying himself on Natalenya. Faithful

Natalenya who had never given up on him, despite all his failures. His sins. His self-pity. His doubts.

"You can find him, Merlin. I know you can. Let's wake the others."

They dashed the faces of their companions with water from a cistern in the deserted kitchens — slowly waking them. Garth took the most splashes before he woke up, and even then he ignored their words until the dog started licking the slops of food on his chin. He told them he dreamed he'd been sailing. Bedwir groaned louder than any of the others, but also rose to action the fastest.

When all the company was up, Merlin explained to them all that Arthur had been taken.

"Taken by Atle?" Caygek asked. "We all know what that might mean ..."

Colvarth looked darkly at the druid. "Let us hope, to the Almighty God, that your conjecture is false."

Merlin sent them out to survey what could be discovered of their situation. Garth and Peredur went to investigate the upper floors, Bedwir to verify Natalenya's reports about the guards, and Caygek to check on the state of provisions in the larder.

Merlin and Colvarth helped the breathless Natalenya create a place to rest on the main floor by pulling off some husk-stuffed cushions from the benches. In her condition, it was amazing she had found the strength to rouse Merlin and to help rouse the others.

Bedwir reported back first. "It seems we are still considered guests here, but guests that cannot leave, or so Digon, the guard, says. Atle instructed him to post thirty warriors around the building day and night, and that we had better not try to escape — upon penalty of death. I asked him how long this was for, and he said we were free to enjoy the hospitality of the hall until at least ten days have passed."

Next, Caygek detailed the state of their provisions. "We've got enough to get through for a bit, including water, smoked meat, and grain — but little else. It seems they've taken the best with them."

Garth jumped down the steps three at a time, and gave his and Peredur's report. "Atle's quarters are locked, and the rest's been abandoned," he said. "We looked out in all directions, and the outer wall is all manned by warriors, includin' the two gates. Even if we broke out o' here, Peredur doesn't think we could escape the fortress."

"Certainly not all of us," Colvarth said, shaking his head. "So what shall we do?"

Merlin weighed their options. "Whatever Atle is up to, it can't be good or he wouldn't have snuck off after putting us all to sleep."

Bedwir suggested they try a weak point of the wall and scale down, but Merlin made it clear that Natalenya could not attempt such a thing.

Peredur suggested they bribe the guards, but Colvarth scoffed at the idea. "We have nothing to give except what Atle already owns, and when he returns he'll punish them for it. No, I do not think they will take a bribe from us."

A great debate ensued until Caygek raised his hands to silence everyone. "I have an idea that will get us out of here. But we all have to be willing to risk it."

Merlin urged him on.

"I say we break up the tables and light them on fire right by the eastern door, then sneak out the west doors and escape through the gate while the warriors are trying to put it out."

Everyone looked to Merlin to see what he thought. What *did* he think, besides the fact that his head still hurt from the tainted ale? He rummaged his brain for a better idea, but none came to him, and he had to admit that Caygek's idea made sense. Atle had honored the age-old custom of not ill-treating guests under one's roof — yet had still betrayed them, and deeply.

If their escape meant some charred wood or worse, then so be it. But just as Merlin verbally agreed to the plan, he heard a moan. Quiet it was, yet it echoed through the hall as if a ghost had passed through their midst.

Mórganthu jerked as two of Vortigern's brutes made moves to follow and catch Ganieda.

"Let her go," Vortigern shouted, calling them back. "I'm not here for *her*."

To make sure she remained safe, Mórganthu made his grand appearance. He pulled his stump of an arm out from the cords, popping off the sand and stick-filled glove. With his good hand free, he tugged the gag off and sat up. "It is I, yes, it is I — Mórganthu, whom you know. The weaver has fled only moments ago — and he has taken the daughters of Uther with him." He pointed toward the back door of the house. "They've escaped under the wall through the kiln."

Vortigern flung Safrowana backward, and she fell roughly against the loom. "Fest and Enison, tie 'em all up, then follow our trail ... we may need your help."

The one with the spear grabbed some cords. "What's about the druid? Haha, should I's tie him back up too?"

"Yes ... if the girls get away, I want him to suffer," Vortigern tapped the other two, one being the archer, and they ran out the back door of the house.

The two brutes left behind began tying up the monk and Safrowana.

While they were distracted, Mórganthu discreetly untied his legs. Then he kept a watchful eye while slowly sliding toward the back door. They didn't turn until he was out of their reach. Mórganthu jumped up and ran into the back bedroom, where the fang lay.

"Hey, stop'n, you!" the toothless brute shouted, tromping after him.

Mórganthu crossed the floor, rounded a table, and made for the window.

The man was right behind.

He reached behind the loom shuttle. It was still there! He grabbed the fang just as the attacker laid hands upon him. Mórganthu held it tightly, and a thrill surged up his arm as he thrust backward, jabbing the fang into the man's gut. He called on Belornos for the man's death.

The brute yelped, dropped his sword, and let go of Mórganthu's tunic. Staggering back, he grabbed on to the doorframe as smoke and blood poured from the hole where he'd been struck.

At the same time, a shock of pain ripped through Mórganthu, dizzying him. The room tilted, and he grabbed the sill.

The brute scratched at his wound, yelling.

Mórganthu's own pain eased enough for him to take his chance. He snapped open the shutters and climbed through the window as the room behind him filled with a fretful scream. The gate — and his freedom — lay only steps away.

Why hadn't she taken her cloak, Ganieda wondered? Gone back and grabbed the fang? Did her grandfather have the orb? But these things didn't matter, anymore, did they? She had lost something far more valuable than such things — she had lost love.

All these months she'd believed that these people really loved her. Cared for her. But it was a lie. A black, infected lie. Infected by her brother. Infected by his coins. The weavers hadn't loved her at all. They had loved the money that Merlin had given them. They had conspired against her. To keep her there. To trick her. To fill her head with their deceits.

But she would have it no more. No more false love from a brother who had killed their father. Who had burned her home and set her adrift in the world. Who had killed her mother.

Her mother.

Had Ganieda forgotten? She tried to remember her mother's face, but the visage of Safrowana, that liar, kept coming to mind instead. False love. False tenderness. False hugs. False instruction. False kisses. False games. False food. False everything. She yelled her curses to the wind, snowflakes flying into her hair and eyelashes. She ran.

Where *was* her mother? Did she still rest in the vale where Ganieda had left her? Was she lonely for Ganieda? A powerful longing overcame her — to be held once more by her mother. Her *real* mother. To gaze up into her mother's tender eyes. To feel the strength in her mother's hard-working arms. To have her mother comb her hair again. To talk in their secret tongue, which Safrowana and all the others in the village did not, could not, understand. It had been so long.

She ran down the village track and off into the woods. It wasn't impossibly far. Just beyond the Keskinpry marsh, past a little-used road, and in a vale where a stream ran.

Her mother would be waiting for her.

Ganieda was sure of it.

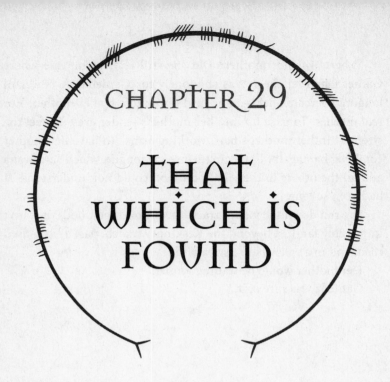

Chapter 29

That Which is Found

Merlin caught his breath as the ghostly moaning faded away. Everyone's eyes scanned the room. Garth jumped to the center of the group and peeked out from behind Bedwir. Even Natalenya, while petting the dog, sat up on her makeshift pallet to listen.

"Just some wind through the upper windows," Peredur said. "I heard the same thing before the feast."

But the sound filled the hall again, this time louder, and the clinking of chains could be distinctly heard.

"Theh ... aye ... ney ... vah ..." called the disembodied voice. And a banging sound echoed — metal upon metal, jangling chain upon solid bar, followed by a muffled wail that sent shivers from the base of Merlin's skull down to his feet.

It was the woman Atle had put in the hall's dungeon! God had showed it to him in his vision, and Merlin had forgotten all about her. He ran beyond the throne to where a low table stood — covered in dirty trenchers, half-consumed bowls of food, bones, and other rubbish. He heaved the table over, revealing a roughly smithed iron plate embedded in the stone floor. About four feet by three feet, it had a hole in the center that looked suspiciously like the simple keyholes his father made back in the blacksmith shop. But where was the key? The group had followed him by now, and he knelt down and banged on the iron plate. The sound that echoed back was hollow.

In answer, they heard the moaning from below, rising to a muffled cry. "Kehn ... sah ... kehn ... shah ..."

Caygek knelt down and put his ear to the iron. "Is someone down there?"

"Yes," Merlin said. "It's the old woman who served Atle food when we first arrived. He's locked her there for some reason."

"Her? The misshapen one? Who cares about her? Let's light the building on fire and let her die in it, I say. She's one of them, and worth nothing compared to our freedom."

"Yes ... your well-loved freedom," Merlin said, remembering their previous altercation after Merlin had decided to give themselves up as slaves. "I love freedom too, but I'm not going to leave her in prison while we run off and possibly burn the hall down above her."

"She'll survive — she's got an iron plate and a stone foundation to protect her."

"And if she doesn't? I won't have her innocent blood on my hands while I try and save Arthur."

"Arthur? Do I care for Arthur? I only care about my own blood."

Merlin looked to the others. "Who's with me?" he asked. "Who will help me free her before we leave?"

Everyone nodded ... everyone except Caygek. The druid's nostrils flared, and he jumped at Merlin, snarling.

Merlin hadn't expected this and so reacted late by trying to jump away.

One of Caygek's hands grabbed his tunic, and the other smashed into his jaw. The next thing he knew, he was on the ground, grappling with the druid, who raised his fist to punch Merlin again.

Bedwir and Peredur arrived, pulling Caygek's arms back and yanking him off of Merlin.

"Peace, young Caygek," Colvarth said. "We accomplish nothing by fighting among ourselves. We either all work together — "

"Or we die!" Caygek said, struggling. "And I'd kill you both if I still had my sword."

Garth stepped over and stood in between Merlin and Caygek. "Even if she survives the fire, she'll still die down there with no food or water. Imagine it. Didn't you learn anythin' about compassion while we were slaves o' the Picts?"

Caygek took a deep breath, and then nodded. "Yes ... I did. Especially from you. But I don't have to like it. I don't want to be trapped here any longer than I have to."

Colvarth held his hands out. "None of us do. Let's work to free this unfortunate soul."

"Fine. Fine. I'll cooperate."

Bedwir and Peredur loosened their grip, and Caygek shook himself free. He grabbed a thick iron spoon from the clutter around the fallen table and started to pry at the edge of the iron plate. "Isn't anyone here going to help?"

The others all found something to pry with: Colvarth and Peredur with more serving spoons, Garth pulled out an iron rod from a tapestry, and Bedwir used the edge of a decorative shield he'd yanked from a well. Merlin found a broad bread knife, dull but tough.

But try as they might, the iron plate would not budge. While others kept trying, Merlin stepped back. What had the angel in his vision said? The words echoed in his mind.

"... *freedom for those in darkness is hidden in the throne* ..."

The throne! Merlin walked around and began to study it. The back was made of an aged oak, inlaid with a lighter wood in the pattern of ocean waves. Dusty-blue gems had been set into these waves in the outline of a boat. But it wasn't only the gems that looked like a ship ... the seat and arms themselves had been shaped like of the hull of a boat. And so there was space where something could be hidden below deck, but Merlin's inspections didn't reveal any hatch.

"Garth," he called after his search proved futile, "Come and help."

The boy looked up from his prying, confused, but dropped his iron rod and walked over.

"The key is hidden in the throne. If you had a boat ... where would you hide a key?"

"Boat's don't have keys ... but they do have *keels*." Garth bent down and knocked hard on the bottom hull of the seat. A clink could be heard inside. "I don't see ... hang on a bit."

Merlin knelt to see what Garth was doing. The bottom of the boat seat did indeed have a keel at the bottom, a small board protruding down. Garth looked closely at it, and finally rotated it sideways on some hidden pin.

Click.

A board at the top of the seat popped up.

"You did it!" Merlin lifted the board more and saw that it had been attached to a cleverly hidden hinge and lock. The inside had two carved slots — a round one for a ring of keys, and a long one shaped like a large dagger. The ring of keys lay in its slot, but the dagger was missing. What looked like dried blood coated the place where the blade would have been.

Garth pointed to the empty slot. "What do you supposed that's for?"

"I'm not sure I want to know." Merlin grabbed the ring of keys and ran over to the iron plate. Everyone backed away as he tried the first, which was too large for the long, thin slit that was the keyhole. The second key fit, however, and he slipped it in on the right side where the iron was scratched. Fiddling with the position of the key, it finally clicked in place and pushed the tumblers out of the way. Merlin smiled as he slid the bar to the left. The plate came loose, allowing them to pry it up. The iron was heavy, however, and they had to heave it to the side, revealing a shaft that was abysmally dark. Stone steps began about two feet down — narrow and steep.

A slight breeze of cool air rose from the depths, bringing with it a pungent smell that reminded Merlin of a cider vinegar jar he'd found at home that'd became infested with dead, putrid flies.

Bedwir took two rush lamps from their sconces and lit them on a coal from the hearth.

"Her name is Kensa," Merlin said as Bedwir handed him one of the lamps. "I hope she's not hurt." With one hand on the edge, Merlin led the way, slowly descending the steps. He was glad his head felt better, for the steps had been cut so narrow that he had to be careful not to lose his balance. At about the ninth step he had to sit to avoid hitting his skull. Soon the steps widened and the ceiling raised so he was able to stand. Behind him came Bedwir, Caygek, Peredur, and last of all, Garth, who'd tucked a dull bread knife into his belt.

Merlin descended in a straight line for about a thirty feet, hesitating when the steps ended in a level passage. Here the walls were rough with cracks, and someone had charcoaled them with ferocious sea serpents who coiled among the waves. Some were crushing charcoal-drawn ships. But a strange thing — a trick to his eyes, perhaps — was that the walls seemed to be moving — no, wiggling — just beyond the rushlight. But as he walked cautiously forward, the walls appeared normal. He stopped to examine the cracks, but finding nothing, he shook his head and kept on.

Farther down the passage — perhaps midway, for it went beyond Merlin's ability to see the end — a door of iron bars had been set into the side, with chains securing it, and the party gathered around. Merlin held up his lamp to illuminate the interior. "Kensa?"

Black hands seized the iron bars and rattled them so hard Merlin was afraid the ancient door would shatter.

Merlin leapt back and accidentally slammed into Peredur's shoulder. He lifted the light with a shaky hand to see an enraged visage emerge from the shadow.

Troslam ran, his spear in his left hand and his other pulling the two girls along. Eilyne kept pace, but the younger, Myrgwen, had bloodied her knee so badly that now tears covered her face. But their lives depended on speed, and she'd have to keep up. They ran west along a path through the village, staying as close as they could to the stone walls. Where the wall's height wasn't sufficient to hide their presence, they ducked, praying Vortigern and his men didn't see them.

Where were they going? Safrowana and he had talked about this eventuality, but had thought they'd have time to prepare. He and the girls had no provisions, and their clothing of boots and cloaks would hardly keep them warm. The best place was his brother's farm in the village of Risrud, but that was twelve leagues west, and it would take four days to get there, what with the girls so young. Maybe they could stop at the abbey in Guronstow for rest and help.

As they ran, Troslam realized his mistake. He'd missed the last turn leading down the mountain, and now the path headed upward. Double back? He didn't dare. All he could do now was look for a place to cut through. Up ahead lay the barrel maker's land, and his ramshackle stone wall.

He helped Myrgwen climb over, then Eilyne, and finally he leapt over. They ran past the barrel maker's crennig, over his other wall, and to a path leading downward.

A shout rang out. Troslam turned and spied three, one who was pointing, another with a bow. The third was Vortigern. They were a thousand feet away and running toward them. It was over. Or was it? The marsh! If a fisherman had left his boat at the docks, he and the girls could —

But there was no time to think. He yanked on Myrgwen's hand and pointed with his spear for Eilyne to see. "To the docks — hurry!"

But Vortigern had two men with him. Troslam could kill one, maybe two, but never three. And not an archer, who'd stand back, away from Troslam's reach. And he'd never taken on trained warriors. He was but a simple weaver. He knew more about selecting the right wool, boiling down dyes, and weaving patterns than he did about war. Sure he had a spear, but it might've been a twig for all it mattered.

The ground began to slope down, and the village's three docks appeared. Neither the center nor the left had any boats, but the right held three. The dock swayed as they sprinted onto it, their feet banging out a cadence upon the old boards. Troslam led them to the end and set the girls in a long but narrow boat with oars, the bottom of which was filled with an old net and some dead fish. But before he jumped in, he went back to sink the other two vessels. The first was a leather-hulled coracle. He jabbed his spear and sliced it through. The boat began to take on water.

He ran over to the second, a wooden tub meant for bringing in the larger nets. He thrust his spear at the bottom, but the thick wood resisted his efforts. Again he stabbed it, but no luck.

He heard a shout and looked up.

Vortigern and his men were rushing down the hill toward them.

Ganieda walked south. The sun would set soon, but she didn't worry, because she was almost there. Her mother would have a fire going, and Ganieda imagined how wonderful the hot oats would taste. Maybe she'd add a little goat milk to her bowl, and she would eat it with her favorite spoon.

And here was the stream. Just a little farther up the valley, and she'd find Mammu. This was the path they'd taken that night, for she'd led her mother here all by herself. Her mother'd been wailing, and Ganieda had held her hand, the fingers so hot. Had her mother's arm been infected? But the infection had healed, hadn't it? And her mother was well again. She would be so happy to see Ganieda. It had been too long.

Ganieda's shoes pinched her toes, but only a short distance remained. She rounded the funny oak with its huge, outspread arms and climbed down into the secret glen — near the spring that bubbled out from the rocks — where no one else had ever come except Ganieda and her mother.

But there was no cheery blaze waiting for her. The sunlight still shone through the trees, but there wasn't much of it left. Ganieda dashed forward to see if her mother had fallen asleep waiting. Yes, perhaps she'd grown tired. She'd likely built a small crennig in the last few months and was inside.

But no such building existed. The ferns swayed in the wind. A jay ridiculed her from a nearby pine as Ganieda ran to the spot where her mother had been. She fell to her knees and parted the cold, stiff ferns. And screamed.

Bones lay upon the ground. Scattered. Picked clean by animals, for teeth marks had been cut into them. And they'd been broken, and the clothing shredded. Her mother's skull was missing, yet a lock of her hair lay upon what was left of her mother's shift.

Ganieda picked up the strand of hair and poured all her tears upon it, weeping there in the dusk. The sun gave up his life, touching her in a final, warm embrace, but Ganieda turned her back and let him sink beyond her reach.

"Are you finished, dear one?" the voice of a low-timbred man asked from behind her.

Ganieda slowly turned, wiping tears from her eyes with her sleeve.

A man in a shadowy cloak stood just a few feet from her.

CHAPTER 30

THE GIVING OF SECRETS

Merlin felt the color drain from his cheeks as the bars rattled again, and in rage the prisoner screamed out, "Ken-sa! Ken-tha! Ken-NA-sa!"

Merlin swallowed. It was indeed Kensa, dirty almost beyond recognition, and angry.

He stepped forward and held the light so she could see him. "We've come to free you." He held up the keys.

The features of her face softened beneath the purple hat, and she blinked at him. "Son of ... Theneva?"

"Yes."

"De son ... of Theneva Gweviana has come ... see old Kensa?" She withdrew her hands from the bars and brought one of her fingers to her pouting lower lip.

Merlin handed his lamp to Peredur. Then he inserted the smallest key into the lock holding the chains, slid it, unthreaded the chains, and pulled the door open. The rusty hinges groaned and echoed through the tunnel.

Kensa stepped timidly into the light of the rush lamps and looked at each one of them. Then she opened her arms and gave Merlin a warm embrace. She was so short, and her spine so permanently bent over that she barely made it to his chest. "Och, och, och," she said as she looked up into his eyes. "I nurse Gweviana when she a liddle bairn. Her muther dust, yes. Liddle bairn grown upp, gone long time. You come … save me. Gweviana send ye!"

Merlin's face turned red. "Yes, Kensa, I've come to save you. Why … why are you so dirty?" He brushed off a layer of soil from her gray hair, and patted her head.

"Kensa vas diggin', yes! Kensa tried dig to light, but many stanes hurt Kensa's old fangers."

With her face so sullied, Merlin wondered if she was digging with her nose as well.

Bedwir stepped in and got her attention by waving his hand. "Kensa … we need your help. The baby, Arthur … where did your king take him?"

"Take de bairn? Atle gonn with bairn? Ah, den old Kensa vil be dust fer sure."

"Where, Kensa? Where did Atle take the child?"

Kensa looked down as if she were ashamed. "To de dark north."

"To the Picts — ?"

"No, no, no," she said, pushing her hat up off one eye, "nott to Pictland. De child haf been taken over de sea."

Merlin took hold of Kensa's hand. "Across the sea? To where?"

"Beyond de land o' de Lochlaners — to de land o' de dead." She stamped her foot and looked at them like they should have known such an obvious thing.

The words thrust into Merlin's heart like a spear, deadly and true. Fearsome tales were told of this mythical land in the far north where the light never shone and the dead walked. And Atle had taken Arthur there? Surely not —

"Dis a ninth year … Efery ninth, King Atle and us — his whole house — return home … to de land o' de dead, andd bring a liddle bairn whose father ess no more. Whose muther ess no more."

"Why, Kensa? Why did he take Arthur?"

"Tay sacrifice the liddle bairn — don'cha know dis? Ever-man know et on Dinpelder."

Merlin's mouth went dry.

Bedwir's face turned ashen, as did Garth's. Peredur's eyes went wide, but Caygek leaned against the wall and studied the embroidered hem of his sleeve.

Merlin forced his tongue to move, even though it felt like lead. He had to know. "Kensa, when will Atle sacrifice Arthur?"

"Och, ye ask a turrible lotsa questions. The babe ess sacrificed when de moon is dark … on de darkest nicht … in de darkest land."

A slight grin of triumph formed on Caygek's face as he looked at Merlin. "The winter solstice? That would mean I was corr — "

"Nott, nott," she said, and she tapped him on the chest. "Yerr a druid, and ye know nothin' o' Lochlan rites. I said whenn de moon is dark."

Merlin tried to think when last he'd seen the moon. It had been a few days ago on their journey, before the clouds had hid its face. It had been waxing, and now it must be half full. That would give them twenty days before Arthur died. And how far would they have to travel to catch Atle? He wanted to ask this, but Kensa began to cry.

Her tears mixed with the dirt on her face, and she grabbed Merlin's blue tunic and smeared them off. "Andd Kensa displease her king and he haf forgotten me. Me own king … he nott taken me vith, and so I ess dust … even as me father ess dust."

"Merlin hasn't forgotten you. None of us have." And he turned and pointed to the others. "We want to help, Kensa."

She smiled then, her crooked teeth showing proudly, and reached out to each one in turn, taking their hand and squeezing it. When she got to Garth, she smiled, compared their heights with her gnarled hand, and then gave a little tug on his red hair.

Merlin addressed them all. "So we know what to do. We have to get to the village below the hill — the one on the seacoast — procure a ship, and follow Atle north. We have less than twenty days."

"But how do we know where to go?" Bedwir asked. "Atle will be far ahead of us. We'll never find him. Not without a guide."

Garth jumped, his eyes bright. "I can sail, sir!"

Merlin nodded. "But where do we go? Kensa, does Atle have any maps to this place?"

Kensa squinted her eyes and scratched her head. "Aye, he do haf lotsa parchments ... efen a codex or two from them suffer-makin' Romans — "

"Merlin," Bedwir interrupted, "we better get back up before the lamps go out."

Bedwir's was burning low, and Peredur's was even worse.

Up they went, Merlin helping Kensa on the steep steps.

Upon emerging to the fresh air in the hall, Merlin gave Garth and Peredur the key ring and sent them up to Atle's quarters. Then he explained to Colvarth and Natalenya what they'd learned of Arthur. Natalenya covered her eyes at the news, and Colvarth's shoulder's drooped.

Kensa went straight to the kitchen, came back with what looked like a bone-shaped root, and began munching on it. Merlin bent over and sniffed, and the aroma stung his nose. He could hardly believe it: She was eating a raw horseradish root — stripping off the moist fibers and mashing them between her teeth.

"The sea radish is to helpp me tumm after dem bugs."

"Bugs?"

She looked at him like he was daft. "Och, they all crawls upp de tunnel — an's I catched 'em and ett 'em, I did. I been put there afore, an if ye gets hungry, that's all der ess to eat."

Something about this pricked Merlin's awareness. "They get in the tunnel from where?"

She took a big bite and chewed thoughtfully.

"Kensa ... *how do the bugs get in the tunnel?*"

She swallowed. "From below ... Dey bugs climb en when its cold uttside. De tunnel goes down to de secret door. It be de king's escape route, but shush, I'm nott supposed to tell."

Colvarth, who'd been listening, stepped closer. "Kensa ... you mean all of us can take the tunnel down to the ground? There are no guards?"

"Och, sure, lad. There're no guards because et ess a secret." She patted him on the head, took another bite, and smiled.

Peredur bounded down from the upper levels, a bunch of parchments under his arms. Behind him came Garth carrying a sword.

Merlin sucked in his breath. It was *his* blade. The one his father had made.

Garth bowed as he handed it over, and Merlin was speechless.

"I found it locked in Atle's room. He seemed to have forgotten to take it. I also found other blades, but they're nothin' special compared to yours." He handed them to Bedwir, Peredur, and Caygek, keeping a short sword for himself.

Merlin's hands fairly shook to hold his father's old sword once again. It had suffered some rust during its stay with Necton, but not badly. A little rubbing, a little oil, and it would be good as new. "How can I thank you?"

"You returned me father's bagpipe once upon a time, and I've got the priv'lege o' giving you back yer father's sword. Consider us even, captain."

Merlin clasped Garth in a bear hug.

Meanwhile, Bedwir and Caygek had cleared a table for Peredur, who laid out his parchments. Kensa stepped over, and, in between bites of horseradish, pointed to a very old one among the pile.

Peredur untied its ribbon and unrolled it upon the table. It was a crudely drawn map, but a map nonetheless. Colvarth studied it, bringing his aged eyes within a hand's breadth of the ink. After a short while, he pointed to a mark on the coast of Britain. "Here is where King Atleuthun's fortress lies." And then he slid his finger northward, across the sea ... and to the coast of some strange land

Merlin had never before seen on a map. "And here is, to the best of my knowledge and understanding of this map, the place Atle is sailing for. It is not close ... No, for the runes indicate three hundred leagues."

So far in only twenty days. Merlin didn't know if they could do it. "Are you sure?" he asked, hoping Colvarth was wrong.

"I have studied Lochlan runes before, and that is my best deduction. Our current location says 'The fortress belonging to Atle,' and far northward, here, in the land of the dead, the runes say 'Atle's Temple.' I cannot be sure, but with what you told me of your conversation with Kensa, and what very little I know of their rites, it seems likely. Why he would go to such a remote place, however, I cannot fathom."

Merlin looked to Kensa, and she nodded with pursed lips. "Och, dat be de place."

"Have you been there before?"

"I vas born der, but since ... since ... I been twenty times, I suppose. Double me fangers. Nort ve always sail for many a day. Rough seas too, dis time o' year. Et's always a cold trip."

Merlin tried to do the math, but the numbers he calculated didn't make sense so he turned to a new problem. "Kensa, are there ships in the village?"

"Aye," she said as she bit off another strip of horseradish.

"So who'll help rescue Arthur?" Merlin asked, turning to the men for the second time.

Bedwir was the first to step forward. "Like you, I've sworn my oath."

Garth jumped next to him, a smile on his face. "If it involves savin' Arth' and sailin' then I'm yer man!"

Caygek shook his head and said nothing.

Peredur started to speak, blinked, and then swallowed. "I owe my freedom to you, Merlin, and though I don't want to go anywhere but home, I'll help ... if you'll have a horse trader's simple son."

Merlin shook his hands and thanked him.

It didn't take long to gather everything needed, including food, for their journey — salted meat, stale bread, and some grain. As Garth retrieved his bagpipe from upstairs, Merlin knelt to help Natalenya stand up. She lay facing the wall, apparently asleep, with the dog resting under her hand.

"It's time to go," he said, tenderly tapping her on the shoulder.

She didn't answer, but only shook her head.

"Natalenya..."

"I'm not coming."

Merlin thought about Loth and Natalenya having hushed conversation in her room. Perhaps Loth had been wooing her, and she wanted to stay. Perhaps he could heal her when he came back. Marry her. Maybe he wasn't like Atle. Maybe he was like Merlin's mother. "I understand. Loth ... and his physician."

Colvarth, who'd been sitting on a nearby bench fingering his harp, spoke up. "That is not why, foolish Merlin. Neither of us think we can survive such a journey. We are agreed in this."

Natalenya turned around then and faced him. "I've gotten worse — even in the last few hours. I don't know what's going to happen to me."

"You don't look any sicker," he said, but it wasn't true. Her breathing was more shallow than he had ever seen. Dear God, what was he to do?

"I feel it ... I know it."

"We will stay," Colvarth said, "and distract the guards so they will not suspect you have left. Perhaps in a few days we will make our own way down through the tunnel and find a place in the village. If the guards catch us, at least they will not be able to stop your mission."

Merlin shook his head. This wasn't how it was supposed to end. What if she died while he was gone? He would never see her again. Maybe he should let Bedwir lead Arthur's rescue. How could he ever face Natalenya's mother and tell her he'd left her to die? How could he ever face himself again? He had failed her, and now what was he to do?

Natalenya sat up, and the pain could be seen in the creased lines on her face. She took hold of his elbow and pulled him close. "Merlin mab Owain — do you love me?"

He wanted to tell her he loved her, but couldn't. He did love her; more than he had realized. And the feeling welled up in him like an overpowering wave that he couldn't suppress.

He swallowed, and then nodded.

She looked at him, as if confused while trying to read his expression. "Merlin, do you love me?"

He tried to look away from her, but her gaze was so strong, so searching, that he couldn't.

"Yes," he said. How had he ever stuffed the feeling down?

"Then go," she whispered. "Go and rescue Arthur if it's the last thing you do. They need you. Arthur needs you. I'll be all right. Colvarth will take care of me. God will take care of me. No matter what happens."

He embraced her, blinking to keep the tears at bay and holding his breath. "We'll come back," he choked out. "I — I — "

"No promises. Now go."

He hugged her. A slow hug, longer than any he'd ever given her.

God, help her to know that I love her. May she hold on to hope and ... and ...

But he couldn't think these thoughts. He had to go. He had to go now — before he cried.

Thankfully, Colvarth broke the tension. "There is one thing more," the bard said, but he sniffled along with his words.

"What's bothering you?" Merlin asked. "Tell me."

"I only regret that I have not yet taught you to be a bard. Who will take up the Harp of Britain after me?"

"Colvarth — I'm coming back."

"I am *Colvarth*, yes, a criminal bard outlawed by the druidow. But I am more than that. I am Bledri, adopted son of the previous Chief Bard of the Mighty, Cadfan. I am a man with a heart and soul, and I have sworn my harp only to whom God chooses. I have sought all my years since deciding to follow the Christ, and now that I have found you, I am loathe to let you go."

"But —"

"I know. Go, thou son of this old, decrepit toadstool, and put your hope in God even as I do the same. Save Arthur and come back quickly, for you have much to learn."

Merlin stood, awkwardly, and found Colvarth holding out the bag with the Sangraal.

"Take this," he said. "I can neither see this holy thing nor touch it. Maybe God —"

"I don't want it," Merlin said as he threw his cloak over his shoulders. After everything Colvarth had said, Merlin didn't want to dissappoint him, but his hand refused to obey.

"But!"

He didn't want it. The Sangraal was useless to him. He'd trusted it once to heal Natalenya, but it had failed.

"Please, take it," Colvarth said, and he set the bag in Merlin's hands.

Merlin took it with a sigh and tied it to his belt. Then he gave a slight bow out of respect for Colvarth.

He grabbed his leather sack of provisions, which included the small bag of coins from Atle. Then he gathered the others and began his descent down the shaft. The last thing he saw was Natalenya laying on her pallet, with Colvarth standing nearby.

Merlin looked down, as he didn't want to slip. Bedwir had given him a light, and he knew the way now. He descended to the tunnel, passed the cell where Kensa had been imprisoned, and then stopped cold, halting the others.

The hallway *was* moving ahead — writhing just beyond the reaches of the light and his vision. He squinted. It couldn't be, and yet he knew the truth: Something was crawling on the walls, in and out of the cracks. He stepped forward and held up the light.

Roaches.

Thousands and thousands of them.

CHAPTER 31

THE STEALING OF SOULS

The spear in Troslam's hands quaked as the three men ran down the hill toward them. There was no time for him to stave in this last boat and get the girls far enough away from the archer. So he sliced its thin tie rope and pushed the boat away from the dock. He ran back to the girls, jumped in, and shoved off as hard as he could to give them some momentum.

Then he rowed — as fast as he could. Every stroke had to count. Every dip had to be perfect. Every pull had to propel the boat as far away from Vortigern as he could get. There was barely enough time.

The girls peeked over his shoulders.

"Get down!" he yelled, but that threw off his rhythm, and his left oar flailed uselessly. He swore. Any delay could mean their death, and so he quickly regained his balance and rowed strong and accurate once again.

"Is there anything I can do?" Eilyne asked.

"Pray."

Myrgwen started to cry, and Eilyne comforted her, leading them both:

Father, Son, and Spirit of Holiness,
From earth we beseech you in your Threeness.
From dust we call to you in your Oneness.
Enliven us, Breath of the zealous wind;
Establish us, Shield of the fortress'd hill;
Purify us, Lord of the rolling waves.
Dear God Almighty, yes, here in our midst,
Protect your children, the ones whom you love.
Guard us and guide us, to you do we pray.

Vortigern had made the docks, and he pointed toward Troslam and the girls. One of the warriors took an anchor and tossed it, still holding on to the rope, into the boat Troslam had pushed away. The other slid an arrow from his quiver, aimed carefully, and shot.

The arrow went wide, zipping into the marsh about a foot from the boat.

Troslam rowed harder and turned the boat past some thick marsh reeds just as another arrow whizzed by. His only hope was to lose them in the maze of rushes. Why hadn't Troslam planned better? Why hadn't he moved the girls to a safe location long ago? What a dupe he'd been to think that Uther's girls would be safe in Bosventor.

He rowed desperately, following the channel in front of him — hoping beyond hope that he didn't come to a dead end and have to turn around.

At one point he had to use his oar to push a huge moss-covered log out of his way to pass by. A moment later — while the wind waved the marsh grasses to the side — he caught a glimpse of Vortigern and his men shoving off from shore and rowing toward them.

Unfortunately for Troslam, the other boat had two sets of oars — so row as he might, he couldn't keep Vortigern and his men from gaining. Worse, while Vortigern and the other warrior rowed, the archer sat up in the prow looking for a good shot.

The reeds rustled together in the cold wind even as Troslam's oars creaked and groaned in their sockets. He rowed harder, trying to keep low, when an arrow struck the side of the boat. The channel broadened before him, and eventually split.

He had just turned the boat down the left fork, heading south, when a rib-cracking pressure hit the right side of his back. Stabbing pain shot through his body and down his right arm. He lost control of his grip and the oar dropped away. He fell over, and the world spun white and hot. The very life breath was yanked from his screaming lungs like an unraveled cord.

Eilyne shouted and tried to help him sit up. She put the oar once again in his hand, and he felt a tugging at his back. But then she, too, cried out — a long, withering scream, soon matched by another beside her. Troslam fought against the whirlpool of agony that was sucking him down into darkness — and for a moment saw Myrgwen, shrieking and struggling, vainly trying to pull out an arrow lodged in her left eye as blood rushed from the wound. Eilyne had taken one in her side, and lay in the front of the boat, a silent scream on her trembling lips.

Vortigern shouted in triumph as he witnessed the third arrow strike true and the youngest of Uther's brats fall into the bottom of the boat. When the weaver had been hit, the girls foolishly tried to help him, making them easy targets for Tethion's arrows.

Now the only thing left was to row over and dump their bodies into the marsh, where the water would finish what he'd started.

He slipped his oars into the water once again, a broad smile on his face, and began rowing. Soon they came to an old trunk of a tree that had somehow floated in their way. Mosses clung to its surface and, strangely, it appeared the center of it had been burnt and hollowed out, maybe by lightning. He lifted his oar from its socket and gave the closest end a shove.

As it floated away, some bubbles rose from the dark water,

popped into the air, and then there was a strange noise, like a weasel or rat had begun to chew upon their boat. Vortigern looked into the water, but couldn't see anything.

Putting his oar back in its slot, he began to row once more — but then stopped. The chunking noise grew louder, and suddenly, between his very feet, a green trickle of water began to leak into the bottom of the boat. He tried to staunch it with his boot, when out from the small hole burst an orange-colored tongue, which began breaking and splintering the old wood of the boat. Then it disappeared only to appear again, this time longer.

Vortigern shouted, and again tried to beat the thing with his foot — only to realize too late that it was metal and he'd sliced his boot open. What he had thought was the tongue of some foul marsh beast was in fact a rusty sword blade. The cold water fountained into the boat, and he cried out to the others to turn back to shore. Vortigern swore, for he didn't know how to swim, and they had nothing to bail with.

They turned the boat awkwardly, and double rowed in double time back to the docks as the water poured in. But the blade was gone now, and Vortigern dared to plug the hole with his boot as best as he could, but could not stop the water entirely.

They made it back to the dock just as the boat's sides submerged into the icy water. Vortigern pulled himself up next to Tethion, dripping, cursing, and shivering. Rewan climbed out next, and they all stood and looked out into the marsh.

The weaver's boat was too far away to see.

And what of the brats? There were no other boats for him to take and finish the job. But did he need to? They'd each been struck deeply and accurately by Tethion's arrows. He'd seen it. They would die, if they weren't dead already. So what if he didn't throw 'em into the marsh? The ravens would finish his job, and soon there'd be nothing left in the boat besides mute bones.

And maybe whatever spirit of the marsh had attacked them would sink the girls' boat with its rusty blade too. Vortigern laughed as he squeezed the water from his tunic. He'd done his task, and he could go to Tregeagle's, change his clothes, and be on his horse headed east before nightfall.

Sure it'd be nice to sit at the man's fire, sip some of his excellent *Mulsum* wine, sleep the night under his roof, and head out again in the morning — but no. He couldn't risk being recognized here. It had been risky enough to come at all.

It would be a long way home, but after the journey, he could truly rest in his newly rebuilt feasting hall. His throne and the throne of his son had been secured at last — for revenge had been visited upon the enemies of his house.

Vortigern quickly changed his clothes in the side chamber of Tregeagle's house. And what a house it had become. The servants were all gone, the tapestries had been stolen or sold, and half of the fine furniture broken up to feed the hearthfire, which wasn't hot enough to keep his breath from icing up. The quicker he got out of here, the better.

And crazy ramblings had been charcoaled upon the walls.

What of the Stone?

Where's my eldest?

Gold — where can I get gold?

Traitors!

Why'd Dyslan go to serve Gorlas?

Burn the whole village!

Whip the smith?

Natalenya will die!

How to remove the sword?

Thankfully, Tregeagle had stepped out briefly so Vortigern could gape at them with the proper sneer. And one was in blood. Thick, dried blood, written in oversized letters.

Kill Merlin!

Merlin? He was a slave now, and probably dead already.

It was evident someone had tried to scrub away the ramblings and clean the house — perhaps Tregeagle's wife, Trevenna — but they'd been written over again just as many times.

Rewan had already finished changing, and Tethion came back with Fest, who snuffled a little like he had a cold.

"Where's Enison?" Vortigern whispered.

Tethion took a swig from his waterskin. "He's ah … not coming."

Fest let out a groan.

Vortigern pulled his dry breeches on. "Taking his time, eh? Havin' a little — "

"He's dead."

"Ehh. Stupid donkey."

"Nah, the druid killed him. Fire came out of Enison's gut, and that was it."

Vortigern snorted. There was only one way for him to fight the druid — with some power of his own. The problem was that Vortigern didn't have any. But what if he could make the Stone work … for himself? Merlin had pierced it with Uther's sword — could someone else pull it out?

And Tregeagle's mad scribblings had reminded Vortigern that the Stone could make gold. Six months ago he had more important things to think about. But he was the High King now, and he required plenty of gold. Perhaps it was worth a stop before riding out of the village.

Tregeagle came holding out an empty bag. "Gold … how much gold will you pay me?"

"How many coins will make you happy?" He hoped it wasn't more than two. He could afford one or two to keep the man quiet.

"Eight! Eight gold coins … four coins for each of Uth — "

Vortigern slammed his hand over Tregeagle's mouth. The man wanted eight coins? Was he mad? Didn't he know Vortigern needed gold to fight the Saxenow? But maybe there was a way out of this. "Let's go down to the Stone. I have something to show you."

Tregeagle nodded, and his eyes brightened.

Vortigern slopped his wet clothes into a bag and then led everyone out, keeping his head down as he passed Trevenna and shuffling his feet a little. Mounting their horses, they rode down to the village green, where the villagers had moved the Stone.

And there it was upon the Rock of Judgment, which was a flat granite slab where Uther had sat before the people of Bosventor six months ago. But now *Vortigern* had the torc of a High King, his grandfather's torc — and that scheming Uther would lay dead in his cairn until the world ended.

Rewan slapped Vortigern in the back, breaking his reverie. "So what're we here for?"

"The Stone"was all Vortigern could say, for as he looked at its black surface, he felt his heart bend. Just a little. Feelings came back to him. Of glory. Of him riding in a chariot of victory rolling over the trampled bodies of his enemies. Of thousands upon thousands of warriors proclaiming, *"Vortigern! Vortigern! Vortigern! Ard-Righ! Ard-Righ! Vortigern—!"*

He stepped forward and knelt before the Stone, caressing its dark, pock-marked surface. Here and there, a metallic hue shone through, dazzling his eyes in the fading sunset.

And the sword. Vortigern had ignored it six months ago. What had it been to him? A paltry thing given to Uther from a traitor who had sunk to be a blacksmith on a forsaken moor. It had been Uther's blade for those brief hours. At least until it had fallen into his own hands for the ... the ... He didn't want to linger on what he had done. And then somehow Merlin had gotten the weapon.

But even now the metal of the sword fairly gleamed before him. Oddly, no rust had marred its surface, and Vortigern touched the edge — deadly sharp. Its hilt had four inlays of red glass that glowed like blood. Uther's blood. Vortigern had shed it. Yes, he could say it. And why not? But the blade accused him of his act of ... fury. Hadn't Mórganthu murdered Vortigern's sister? Didn't he have a right to kill Uther, whose own father had murdered Vortigern's grandfather?

The memory flashed before his eyes. Uther lay upon this very stone, tied up. Vortigern ran at him in rage, this very blade shaking in his fist. Uther had looked up at him ... not with ire, but with pity. A pleading sort of pity as death from a friend approached and snuffed his life out.

Rot. The man deserved it.

Vortigern wanted to throw the sword away. Melt it down. Bend it as an offering to the god of some bog. In a rage he stood over it, grasped its handle, and pulled with all his strength. Anger fueled the fire of his grip as he sought to dislodge it. But no matter how hard he pulled, his boot upon the Stone; no matter how he tried to twist it or bend it, the blade wouldn't budge.

Foul! Foul curse that it was! Vortigern could not dislodge it.

Tethion and Fest simply stared.

Rewan shook his head. "Look at that."

From the fissure where the sword entered the Stone, black liquid trickled down. Vortigern touched his finger to it, and it smelled like fetid eggs. Despite remembering his glimmer of glory, the Stone seemed dead on all accounts. At least he didn't have hope of getting any gold out of it himself.

Tregeagle looked at him with wide eyes. His empty bag still open before him. "They say only the High King can pull it out ..."

"Who says?"

"The villagers. It's the High King's sword. Aren't you the High King?"

"Me? Of course I am."

"Then ..."

"Ehh? Then they're wrong about the sword." But this wasn't why he'd come. He'd lost control of himself. it was time for action. He took a deep breath, opened his money bag, felt carefully with his hands, and withdrew a large copper coin and a smaller gold coin — the gold coin carefully hidden underneath the copper.

"Here," he said, regaining his composure. "I haven't pulled the sword ... but the Stone spoke to me," he lied. "It told me it'll turn twenty copper coins into gold ... for you, Tregeagle, as payment for helping me."

Vortigern bent down and set the stack of two coins onto the Stone with the copper one hiding the gold. He waved his hands, chanted druidish, jumbled words, and then clapped loudly and pointed behind Tregeagle, saying, "Lightning!"

Then, while Tregeagle jerked his head to study the silent clouds, Vortigern slipped the copper coin off and popped it into his wet boot.

"Look!" he said, pointing to the gold coin.

Tregeagle jumped and snatched it up! "Gold! Real gold!"

Vortigern walked off toward his horses, signaling with his head for the others to join him.

"But there's only one!" Tregeagle said. "Where are the others?"

"Go get nineteen copper," Vortigern said, mounting his horse, "bring them back, and the Stone will turn them *all* to gold."

Tregeagle nodded, a silly grin on his face, and ran toward home.

Vortigern kicked his horse and sped off on the road eastward, his men behind him. When he was out of Tregeagle's earshot, he laughed and laughed, finally ending in a snort. For all he cared, the man could throw coins on the Stone till the moonlight froze. Time for home, his warm, delightful bed, and his feasting fire.

Ganieda fingered the length of her mother's hair while she looked up at the heavy-cloaked man — the Voice. He stood over her and she had to lean back to look at him, making her tongue catch in her throat. She scooted away. "W-what do you want?"

"I've been waiting for you to come," the man said, his low voice mingling with the flowing water in such a way that Ganieda could hardly tell them apart.

"You could have come to me." She didn't want to gaze into the dark pits of his eyes, and found herself looking anyway.

"I could not. I was ... unwelcome in the house of your sojourn. I suffered terribly to speak to you once — yet you turned away. Do not do so again, O daughter whom I desperately need."

"Go to Grandfather. He will serve you." She took a few more steps back, expecting he wouldn't seem so tall. But he towered over even more, his fingernails clicking as the wind rose.

"Your grandfather is already my servant, yet he is old, and has failed. The glorious new tasks I require may take many years. Life. Power. Adoration. I will give these things."

He held out his hands, and between them a vision sparkled outward. An image of herself, grown up, with her arms draped around the neck of a handsome, dark-haired man in black armor, and between them stood a boy, a son. The vision changed, and she saw herself leading a great host of warriors — who worshiped even the dust on her shoes, feared her every glance, and charged through the land slaying her enemies. Enraptured victory. The bodies of all who opposed her upon great, reeking piles. Flesh-greedy crows circling overhead. The peace of the druidow enveloping the land. The peace of all who served the Voice.

He clapped his hands and the vision folded up into nothing. "Yet you have not given your heart to me fully. Will you give it, in exchange for all that I offer?"

"I want my mother."

"Ah, but she waits for you, dear one. Be assured that you will go to her and forever share the reward intended for all who faithfully serve me."

"I want her *now!*"

"Then take this from me, and all your desires will be fulfilled. At great expense I have shaped it for you these last many months when we could not visit each other."

He held out to her a torc. Black it was, with the colorful heads of twin dragons fashioned upon the ends — one red with eyes of amethyst, and the other white with eyes of emerald.

Ganieda held her breath. It was so beautiful ... the most intricately crafted thing she had ever seen, far surpassing the smithwork of her father. Far surpassing even Merlin's vaunted torc.

"Will it allow me to see my mother again?"

"Yes."

She snatched it from his hands, flexed it, and placed it eagerly upon her neck. She turned around to see her mother — and was disappointed she wasn't there. Not anywhere. But the torc felt suddenly warm, then hot. Her skin hurt, and then began to burn. She struggled to flex the torc and rip it from her neck, but it was now rigid as iron and could not be removed no matter how furiously she pulled. Pain seared deeply into her skin, and soon she knew nothing else but the blazing torc whose heat jabbed and sliced into her neck.

She lost her balance and fell, screaming at the Voice, "You lied to me! *You lied!*"

"O, child, but you are wrong, for I *never* lie. Because you have taken this great gift from me, you will indeed see your mother again. But not now." He laughed, a hollow, bone-rattling laugh, and then faded away into the gusting wind and was gone.

And with his disappearance, the pain at her neck was gone. Like that. But the clouds had suddenly grown heavy, brooding some mischief. Had time passed so quickly? Had the voice spoken to her so long? Had she slept? Had she dreamt it all?

But it was not so. The torc still lay tightly upon her neck.

Ganieda sat up and tried again to remove the iron — but could not. She tugged, pressed, twisted, and grunted, but it would not come off. Her neck now bled from rubbing the spiraled horns of the dragons across her skin, and she had to stop.

She wept then, caressing the length of hair that had once been her mother's. It was all she truly had left. Even the Voice had tricked her. A few flakes of snow blew past her face, and she shivered. There was nothing for her here anymore. She needed to find her way back to Grandfather. To the warmth of his fire. To his oatcakes and bright, inquiring eyes. Even if he didn't love her, at least he'd take care of her.

She tucked the hair into her bag, wiped her nose, and set out again, this time into the blowing wind.

CHAPTER 32

RIPPLES OF THE STORM

Merlin's stomach flopped as he watched the wriggling roaches crawl across the ceiling and walls. The roaches on the floor were different, however — smaller, white, and they crawled between dark piles scattered along the hallway.

"What is it?" he asked.

"Bat dung," a voice called from behind.

Merlin whirled around. Kensa had spoken from the back. She wore a scarlet traveling cloak, and had a bag tied to her belt.

"What are *you* doing here?"

She smiled. "Telling ya aboot de bat dung. Dem bugs likes it fer supper."

"I mean, why are you following us? Go back."

Kensa's face puckered up and the outside corners of her eyebrow's drooped. "You nott wants me to … do yer? I's got to come, I just haf to come. Else … else …"

Bedwir sidled up to Merlin. "Maybe she can help. She's been there. What if we get lost?"

Merlin blinked. He hadn't considered that. "Okay, you can come, but—"

Kensa pushed her way to him and gave a crushing hug around his stomach. He stopped speaking and held his breath until she let go. She was far stronger than she looked.

"—how do we get past these bugs?" he squeaked out.

"We etts em. Like dis." And she pulled one from the wall and popped it into her mouth.

Merlin looked away while she ... well, he didn't want to think about it.

"Dey don't efen complain, de liddle buggers. Och, but I forgot me sea radish. Maybe I shouldn't ett any more."

Garth nodded. His face was white.

"An here's de way past," she said, holding up a small shovel. "Et was leanin' again' de wall ofer der, an we shovel de bat dung away. Oderwise, dem stairs are mighty slippery. I've bonked me bones afore, ye see."

She proceeded to shovel the center of their walkway, and soon had a path cleared to the next set of stairs. Tireless, she was too, for Merlin offered many times to take over this chore on their way down, but she wouldn't hear of it. Despite her best efforts, though, they had to be careful not to slip on the steps—or to disturb the uncountable number of bats sleeping on the ceiling among the crawling roaches.

The worst was when the roaches dropped onto Merlin's shoulder or into his hair.

The absolute worst was when they fell down his tunic or crawled across his face.

He wanted to scream but held it in lest he dislodge the whole waggling mass of them onto his head, bats included. And so the group's descent was filled with curses, prayers, exclamations, and surprising oaths of every kind.

By the time Merlin got to the bottom he had sixty roaches contentedly attached to his legs, and twelve on his tunic. He had crunched so many under his boots that he thought he would have nightmares — tormented without end by the hissing, popping, and squishing of the bugs.

Just beyond the bottom of the final stair appeared a narrow crack wide enough for a man, cleverly hidden behind another rock that blended into the cliff. An iron gate had once been locked in place here, but it had rusted away ages ago and only the hinges were left now.

He shook and flicked the final bugs off — his companions doing likewise — and then breathed in the cold, sweet air. "I don't want to see another roach as long as I live."

They all nodded, except Kensa, who just smiled.

Their north-facing path was a gently sloping hillside covered in rocks, shale, and gravel, and Merlin led the way down. But soon he felt something funny in his left boot. He sat down and, with a muffled yell, took it off, shaking out a dozen roaches. The other boot had even more.

All the others emptied their boots as well, and then they set off once more. Thick clouds covered the sky, and in this gloom they took a brisk half league walk along a stream to the outskirts of the village. It was nestled at the edge of a small bay, whose water lay silver under a slate-blue sky. In the distance he spied two vessels floating at the short pier.

Only two? What if neither were available? What if they didn't have enough money to borrow or buy one? He turned to discuss how they should proceed — and realized that Caygek was still with them.

Merlin looked the druid in the eye. "There's no need to stay with us anymore," he said, making his words firm. "You know where we're going — "

"Sure," Caygek said, "off to save the High King. Very sacrificial of you."

Merlin grabbed his sleeve. "Look. He's not the High King yet, and I don't know if he ever will be. But I know this — he doesn't deserve death, and I've given my word to protect him."

"But would you do it if he were Necton's *true* son? Would you do it for a Pict?"

Merlin paused, a spark in his heart, deeply embedded. "Yes. I hope I would."

Caygek's stare burned into Merlin, but he didn't flinch because it was the truth. No one innocent deserved to die.

Caygek looked away.

"So," Merlin said, "off with you."

"I'm just coming to the village to buy a better blade, or even a spear. No offense, Garth, but the tang of the one you gave me is nearly rusted through."

"Fine."

Past an outlying farm, the village had over sixty crennigs clustered near the bay. Two men sawing a log looked curiously at Merlin and his scars as they passed down toward the water. A broad pier stretched out into the ocean a short way, and the tide was just letting out, lifting and bobbing the two boats.

One was a fifty-foot wooden-hulled vessel with a stout mast and sail.

The other was … ah, it wasn't much, only a thirty foot long curragh with a leather hide for its hull, having four oars, and two small sails. Not seaworthy at all.

Merlin's eyes wandered back to the big one. What a boat. With that under command, they could chase after Atle and catch him in no time.

But did he have enough coins for it? He opened the leather sack tied at his belt and dug down through the grain and smoked meat until he found the small bag of coins. Pulling the string loose, he poured the coins into his hand. Thirteen … all silver.

Caygek stood nearby, and Merlin gave him two. The druid patted Garth on the shoulder, announced he was off to find a smith and then would be on his way south to Kembry. He bowed, turned his back on them, and walked away.

Merlin was glad to see him go — the man had been nothing but trouble since he joined their party. But his departure left only eleven silver coins in Merlin's hand. They would need to buy a few barrels of water and victuals. By then, they might only end up with ... But buying the great wooden boat seemed unlikely. Maybe they could just borrow it.

A portly man ducked out from the closest crennig to the dock. He wore a green cloak over a dirty yellow shirt. His trousers were held up by flaxen ropes tied over his shoulders and an orange hat covered his balding head, with a long goose feather in it. "Yah, yah," he said, "you're here to buy some of Aulaf's famous herring. I have ten barrels at the end of the pier. I just got 'em smoked, salted and coopered up, yah, very fresh — "

"Actually, I'm interested in — "

"My herring, yah, I know. You heard of famous Aulaf all the way from, from — ?"

"Kernow."

"Kernow, yes." Then his jaw dropped. "Kernow! You come all the way from Kernow?"

"It's a long story."

"Yah, I am now more famous than I thought, and I will sell them to you — just for folks from Kernow — at two coynalls each." The man had a blond beard ending in an upturned point, and his blue eyes reflected the darkness off of the waves. He smelled like a smoked fish himself.

"We want to hire your boat ... the big one. How much?"

"My boat, yah?" he said, a big grin on his face. "Where to? Not back to Kernow?"

"We're ... ahh ... late for King Atle's ... voyage."

"Ahhh ..." he said, nodding his head knowingly.

"Yes."

He shook his head. "Uhhh, that's a long way. My boat might not come back."

"We can pay. I have . . . oh, eleven silver."

"So few?"

Merlin shrugged.

"Coyntallow, or screpallow?"

"Screpall." Each was worth three Contyallow. Merlin held up one and showed that both sides had been struck.

Aulaf swiped the coin from Merlin and turned it over in the light. "These are Atle's coins, yah. Mints them himself. I didn't believe your story — Atle doesn't allow people from Kernow, only his household and warrior-kin, yah? But you have the king's coins, so perhaps you tell the truth." He gave it back. "But it's too little. The seas are rough this time of year, yah? You're just as likely to feed the herring as eat the herring. And my boat would go down."

Merlin pulled out his blade.

Aulaf backed away, his hands up and his belly wiggling.

Merlin realized his mistake, and sheepishly flipped it around and held the handle out to Aulaf. "Here . . . how much is this worth? You could keep it, or sell it if we don't come back."

Garth grabbed Merlin by the arm. "You can't do that! I just gave it to you — "

Merlin shushed him. If it was in his power he would give everything he possessed to save Arthur. Even if he had to sell his boots and cloak — and freeze — he would do it.

Aulaf took the hilt in his hand and let out a long whistle. "Yah, they don't make swords like this around here. Our smith can't hammer straight. This must be worth a couple denarius."

"Is it a deal? We'd also need some water . . . and a barrel of herring."

Aulaf smiled. Merlin gave him the money, and they shook hands.

Kensa joined in and shook Aulaf's hands too, joy spreading across her old face. Garth had already climbed aboard the big wooden boat and began inspecting the rigging.

Merlin ran over and climbed up, but Aulaf shouted after him.

"No, no. You don't understand. That's not my boat. My boat is that one, yah?" And he pointed farther down the pier to the leather-hulled craft, bobbing like a cork in the waves. "This one's owned by the village headmaster — and not only that, but its rudder broke in a storm, yah?"

Merlin walked over to the stern of the ship and inspected the rudder — and sure enough, it had been shorn clean off. He turned and looked at the other — the leather-hulled boat — and his stomach gurgled and a sour burp burned his throat. "Garth," he whispered, "we can't take that skin and bones across the ocean. What'll we do?"

Garth shrugged his shoulders. "Hmm ... sure it's small, but with a little care an' a little prayer, those kinds o' boats go all over. Me father used to own one when he first started fishin'."

Merlin crossed his arms, unconvinced. "What happened to it?"

Garth dodged away, and Merlin grabbed his arm.

"Okay, so it sunk ... but it sailed eight years. Anyway, let me take a gander at Aulaf's."

"Sure, but, don't say yes just because it's our only option. I mean ... I mean ... well, see what can be done with it."

Garth scampered over and everyone else followed, including Aulaf.

"It's really a sturdy little boat, yah? Most don't come wid' such fine oars. An to have two sails on such a lightweight craft makes 'er fly like a bird right o'er the waves."

Merlin's opinion wasn't so glowing. First of all, the boat just smelled bad — like a dirty, wet sheep who'd been eating fish. Sure, it was long enough to hold them all, including Kensa, and it did have two small leather tents for sleeping in — but how fast could it really sail? Was the leather hull up to such a journey? How old were the wooden ribs? Unlike Garth, Merlin hadn't grown up on the shore, and so the thought of sailing in such a boat frightened him.

A commotion on land caught Merlin's eye. Someone jumped onto the pier and was dashing toward them.

Oh my — no — not him. It was Caygek. Chased by a mob of men with axes.

"Get in the boat," Merlin yelled. *"Now!"*

Mórganthu rose from his pallet, rekindled the fire to take the chill from his tent, and warmed up some gelled barley soup that had sat too long in its pot. Ah, but his head felt like the soup as well, for he'd lain too long upon his bed, and the dusk would soon approach He had much to do, yes, much!

After gulping the soup down, he wrapped his cloak once more upon his frame and sat upon his druid's throne with the fang upon his lap. He took out the orb. Its shiny surface always fascinated him, but the mystery of its depths were beyond imagining. He held the sphere up and looked deeply into it, his lip twitching in anticipation as the purple flames swirled, yes, swirled inside — revealing the face of Merlin.

Finally, after all these months of waiting, Mórganthu could do more than just *look* at the villain. Mórganthu could hurt him.

The scene spread out and he saw that Merlin and Garth were inspecting a wooden boat.

Ah, then they were going to sea! But what for? Perhaps to sail back to Kernow and give Mórganthu trouble? But he, the illustrious arch druid, wouldn't have that. No, no. Merlin must drown on the way, and what more perfect method to accomplish such than to call forth a storm!

But what if Merlin sailed back to shore? Mórganthu would have to make him lost first ... and then the storm could blow him into the watery depths. Mórganthu needed to blot out the sun and the heavens and the moon. Fog upon the ocean. Everything to confuse that scarred fool!

The fang sat upon his lap, and he pressed it with his stump. He spoke out loud so that the spirits of the earth and sky could join with him in his plee:

Dark power of the fang, orb, and of sky,
Hurl my enemy upon the waters!
Surround him in mist, vapor, fog, and murk,
Confuse and confound, perplex, and baffle!

A zing shot up Mórganthu's limb, and his whole body felt weightless, tired, and drained of strength. The wind began to blow outside his tent, clanking the ceiling-hung bones into each other. Vapors began to swim at Mórganthu's feet, undulate, and cover the ground inside his tent.

Here? Fog was here? He rose, unsteady on his feet from the effort, went to the flap and looked out ... and all over the moor the fog rose, covering the land in a thick whiteness. What was the fog doing here? The orb still blazed before him, and he looked deeply into it once more — and the same thing was happening to Merlin — the clouds churned in the far-distant sky, and a fog began to leach its way across the sea. So he had called it forth in both places.

Mórganthu coughed gleefully. The power of the fang had worked!

Ganieda sneezed and pulled her cloak tighter. The gray clouds had only thickened since setting out, and now they seemed to press upon her, mirroring the sadness choking her heart.

The strange thing was that each step seemed to bring forth wisps of fog from the ground, as if she were puncturing the earth and causing it to bleed white blood into the air.

She passed by a marsh on the right, and not only did its rich stink fill the air, but claws of fog coursed from it too — spilling over onto the land and reaching out to her. Walking over the next hill, she halted. The entire valley before her was filled with fog. She spun around, and it was the same everywhere. No matter where she turned, the mist crawled up the hill.

And which way had she been heading? She made her best guess

and set off down the hill. It wasn't more than a score of steps, and the fog covered her head. She could hardly see, and had to make sure not to trip. And the fog deepened the chill, so that she sneezed again. How long would it take her to find Grandfather's tent? Behind her, she heard a great snuffing sound. Scratching noises. Distant laughter. The grunts of strange beasts. All chasing her.

She ran, hardly daring to look behind and seeing nothing in front save the whiteness, which she tried to swipe away. But it was never ending, and the great breathing sounds at her back set her heart to racing even faster than her feet could carry her.

CHAPTER 33

POWER OF THE STORM

The onrushing men made the pier tremble underneath Merlin's feet. "Get in!" he shouted.

Caygek pounded down toward them — the mob of axe-bearing warriors close behind.

Garth was already in the boat inspecting its steerboard, and Peredur jumped in next to him, awkwardly helping Kensa down. Bedwir stood beside Merlin and drew his blade.

"There are too many," Merlin yelled. "Get in!"

Bedwir hesitated.

Aulaf saw the commotion and hid behind his stack of herring barrels, giving Merlin an idea. The barrels measured about two feet long and half that in diameter. He grabbed one and rolled it as fast as he could down the pier. He picked up another as Bedwir rolled one down, and soon they had three barrels hurtling toward the men.

Caygek, running singly on the pier, jumped over the first and dodged the next two.

When the barrels rolled toward the warriors, however, the men tripped and ran into each other trying to avoid them. The entire front line went down.

Caygek made it into the boat as Merlin and Bedwir each rolled another barrel down. But one of Atle's warriors vaulted over the cask and was rushing down the pier.

"Get in!" Merlin called, pulling Bedwir's blade from his belt.

Bedwir obeyed while Caygek hacked at the rope tying them to the pier.

The axe-wielding warrior jumped to a fighting position in front of Merlin, who jabbed with his sword.

The warrior caught the tip of the blade from underneath using the haft of his axe, lifted it up, and slammed Merlin in the chest with his head.

Merlin fell, and the boards of the dock groaned and shuddered under the impact.

The warrior stood above him, stepped on Merlin's sword arm, and raised his axe to strike.

Merlin shifted and rammed his knee into the man's calf.

The warrior stumbled as he swung, and the axe blade came down on the dock, cutting into the bottom of the bag that held the Sangraal.

Merlin yelled, grabbed the warrior's leg and pulled him down, dumping him off the pier.

As Merlin scrambled to his feet and jumped into the boat, the Sangraal slipped out of the hole in the bag and fell.

Merlin grabbed for it and missed. It hit the water on its side, and the bowl sank.

He lunged half over the rail and stuck his arm in the water, but the Sangraal slipped through his fingers and was gone.

More warriros were running toward them, and Merlin fell back into the boat, defeated. Colvarth had given the Sangraal to him, and now he had lost it. Ah, but the thing would only be a worthless burden to carry around. He hadn't wanted it in the first place, and so good riddance.

Garth had already raised the mainsail halfway when Aulaf shouted at them, "Hey, take these … water and herring." And he rolled four barrels clunking into the boat.

The warriors were almost upon them.

Peredur raised the anchor and Garth lifted the sail. The wind took it full, and they pulled away smartly from the dock.

The warriors shouted from the edge for a moment, and then ran back to the large sailboat.

Merlin gave the sword back to Bedwir.

"They'll catch us!" Caygek shouted.

Merlin wanted to knock him down, but held his hand. "And if they do, it's your fault. You nearly got us all killed!"

"How was I to know some of the guards were in the village? Digon saw me and gave the hue and cry."

"And so you had to lead them to us, huh? Thankfully, their boat has a broken rudder."

Caygek snorted. "I couldn't outrun 'em … so just drop me off down the coast."

"We're headed for the open sea. North."

"But —"

"You want to be dropped off in Pictland? If Arthur's life weren't in danger, I'd sail south to let you off — believe me, I would."

The druid's hand made a move for his sword, but Garth stepped over. "Whether you like it or not, you're one o' us again. Now help raise the headsail, or they'll catch us, rudder or no." Garth pointed. The warriors on the pier had raised their own sail and had set out after them.

Caygek and Merlin both helped to raise the sail on the front mast, tying the ropes down, and this increased their speed. But the other ship raised its headsail too, and the warriors gained on them. Merlin was glad none of them were archers.

The bay before them widened, and Garth steered the boat, strangely, toward a small island of rocks that showed its gray and scrubby head above the water.

"What're you doing?" Merlin asked. "Don't strand us!"

Garth didn't answer, but kept his eyes swiveling back and forth from the island to the boat behind. The warriors had sailed directly behind them now, and the big boat overshadowed the stern of the curragh.

Merlin panicked, wishing he hadn't given his blade to Aulaf.

The enemy warriors prepared to jump.

Kensa handed a long oar to Merlin. "Kop dem in de luggers!" she shouted, her hat balanced precariously on her hair.

Grabbing the oar, he lifted it and knocked a jumping warrior into the drink. Garth turned the boat then, just in time to avoid the island, and the next jumping warrior missed and sunk, flailing out his hands as he splashed cold water across Merlin's chest.

The big boat, unable to steer, ran its bow, onto the rocks, cracking the wood. The boat tilted and began taking on water.

The warriors yelled, but there was nothing they could do.

"Landy softs," Garth was heard to say. "Should not ha' come sailin' without a rudder. They don't know a clam's shell what they're doin'."

Merlin patted Garth on the shoulder.

They sailed onward until a hazy dusk fell over the water, much earlier than Merlin had expected. The sun never set this early in Kernow.

Only then did Merlin get a chance to really study the boat. It was different from the wooden-hulled fishing boat they'd crossed the Kembry Sea with six months earlier. When the waves hit that boat you heard them loud and clear — but this boat was quiet, the oxhide skin first stretching, the wooden ribs then compressing, with only a bit of creaking and complaining. In fact, the boat almost undulated in the water like a stiff snake — for its ribs were, after all, only held to each other, to the spine of the ship, and to the rail by tough leather straps.

And the leather hull was only three times the thickness of his boots.

How could a boat like this survive in the open ocean? Had he been daft to have them jump on board? Maybe facing the axe-laden warriors would have been safer. They could have pled for mercy and gone quietly back to Atle's hall. Sure, they probably would have all been shut up in Kensa's prison cell, but at least they'd be alive.

As it was, Merlin worried that he'd doomed them all to a swift, watery grave.

So he tried not to think about the boat, and looked up at the stars, which Garth was using to guide them on their journey. At first the clouds were thin enough to let a few cheery points cast their light — but soon a gray mass rolled in and thickened. No stars could be seen at all.

Then a fog arose upon the water. All had seemed clear when Merlin bent down to help secure the barrels with the other ballast of stowed rocks. When he stood again, their ship was nearly suffocated in a thick bank of whiteness.

He immediately loosened the ropes holding the sail to let it slacken.

Garth left the helm and grabbed his arm. "Why'd you do that?"

"I don't want us getting lost," Merlin said. "If we can't tell which way is north, we can't steer, and this fog makes it even worse."

Garth pulled the rope from Merlin's hands. "The wind's from the west — "

"But — ?"

"I know, you thought we were headed north. But the waves are goin' the wrong way. We'll have to go north-wester-like till the current pleases."

"Won't we get lost without the stars?"

"The wind's light, but seems to be holdin' steady," Garth said. "If it keeps like that, we can still make progress, even in the fog, and if we get a little lost, we'll have to leave Arthur in God's hands. Our only other option is to just sit here until the fog clears."

"How long could that take?"

"Who knows. Maybe days. I've seen fog-frettin' last weeks."

Merlin shook his head. Days? Weeks? Merlin helped raise the sail again, and the boat kept up its speed. The fog drifted by in ragged splotches, and ahead of them all was white. At first Merlin was glad they were moving, but soon a fearful knot tightened in his stomach: the fear of not knowing what lay ahead of them. "What about rocks?" he finally asked. "We could crash."

Garth put his face right up to Merlin's, dew dripping off his hood and nose. "Do you want me to wait till the fog clears, or what? Just say it."

"Keep going," Merlin said — but it was hard not to tell him to roll up the sails and float the anchor. He'd trusted so completely in himself and his own ability to fix their problems during the last six months that it was difficult to put himself so entirely into God's hands — or anyone else's. He wanted to pray for Arthur. Pray for their own safety. Desperately, he did. The angel had said that Merlin was wayward, and it was true. His soul felt dry, beaten, and lonely.

He fell down upon the wooden ribs of the boat, hugged his knees, and whispered out to God, "Don't let me go, Father. Hold me in your mighty hand and help me to hold on to you. Please, Father ..."

Mórganthu cursed as he looked into the orb, for the fog hadn't slowed Merlin down. If anything, they moved confidently forward, skimming over the waves, with that insufferable Garth at the helm: unseeing and uncaring what awaited them.

Ah, but Mórganthu knew what was coming, for he'd planned it. A storm! A storm to drown them all to the grimy ocean bottom! He could picture their bones picked clean by fish.

With his stump upon the fang, he called forth yet again:

Shadowed might of the fang, orb, and the sea,
Drown my enemies within the waters!
Make their way be storm, surge, and potent gale,
May they never again see land or cove!

And even as Mórganthu strength waned from the effort, he saw within the orb the winds pick up, and the mast of their little ship bend. "Aha!" he gloated — until his own tent began to shake as a powerful gust of wind blew past. Then it began to rain.

"What! Not here as well. Not again!" he said, as the whole tent tilted to the side and strained against its moorings.

Merlin held on as the boat was tossed like a rag caught in the wind, the power of which had risen so suddenly that his heart nearly leapt into his lungs.

"Lower it," Garth shouted at the sail, "or the mast'll break!"

Merlin crawled toward the rope that held the mainsail's crossyard in place, but a giant wave caught the ship, and he fell over onto his side. The boat tilted. He grabbed the leather straps that held the ribs of the boat together and narrowly avoided being thrown into the water.

The wave lifted them high into the air. Garth worked the steerboard frantically, and turned them toward the rush of the water. The boat now lay upon the very top, and then, slipping to the edge, pointed downward. Merlin yelled at God for getting them into this, yet he didn't know if he could even be heard over the crash of water. The boat sped into the valley. He closed his eyes as cold water splashed him across the face.

"The sail!" Garth yelled. "Drop it!" He angled the boat once more to face the next oncoming wave.

Merlin sat up, pulled himself forward, and untied the rigging. The wind was so fierce that the line almost ripped out of his hand. But Caygek was there, and helped grab on. Together, they let it out as slowly as possible, dropping the mainsail's crossyard about three feet, until the mast ceased to bend before the wind. While Caygek held it in place, Merlin tied it down again.

Bedwir did the same for the headsail, and then it was time for another wave. The boat rose, slowly at first, but then higher and higher, water crashing over the bow until they reached the crest. The boat shuddered, hesitated, and then dropped down with maddening force.

Merlin's stomach lurched.

At the bottom of the valley, Garth called to the front of the boat. "We need a sea anchor! Do we have an extra sail?"

Peredur dug into the leather-covered bow of the boat. "Here's a ripped one," he called back. Garth nodded, and they passed it to him.

"What's a sea anchor?" Merlin asked as Garth frantically tied the old sail to a rope, tied the rope to the boat, and threw it out the back. But there was no time to answer, for the boat rose upward yet again. At the top, the gusts whipped Merlin's hood back, and the rain blinded him for a moment. The boat hung precariously over the edge of the wave, wobbled, and then plummeted once more. This time the sea anchor slowed their descent, allowing Garth to keep better control.

But the crashing waves and pouring rain came with their own price. The boat had begun to fill with water.

"We need to bail," Caygek called, fruitlessly trying to find something to use.

Merlin helped search for something to bail with — at the sides of the hull and in the stern — but found nothing. If they didn't do something soon, the boat would sink.

Garth tapped him on the shoulder. "Your sack is leather ... dump your food in my bag and use your sack!"

And the boy was right. He untied the bag, opened it up ... and fell backward in shock.

The Sangraal.

The boat rose again on the next wave, and Merlin had to hold on for the descent. When the boat steadied, he looked again — and it was true. The Sangraal sat in his food bag, half submerged with the grain. But he had dropped it in the water! It couldn't be there, but there it sat, its dark wood staring at him, daring him, and searing his mind with its utter uselessness.

Natalenya lay dying back in Briton.

His anger flared. Why had this useless thing come back to him? He picked up the bowl, cocked his arm back ... and threw it far into the waves. It hit the water, floated for a moment, tilted — and sunk.

"Hey!" Caygek yelled at him. "We needed that bowl for bailing!"

Merlin turned to him in shock. "You saw it?"

Caygek scowled at Merlin as he bailed with his hands. "Why wouldn't I see a bowl flung from the hands of a fool!"

"Merlin!" Garth called. "Use your bag to bail, or we're sunk."

Merlin turned to face Garth. "Did *you* see the bowl?"

"What? Dump your grain into mine, and bail!"

Merlin did as he was told, and his leather sack worked excellently for scooping up the water and throwing it out. Kensa had found some wooden cups in front, and she, Bedwir, and Peredur bailed from there. That, and with Garth steering true, the storm finally seemed survivable, even if it frightened him when each wave sent them plummeting downward.

But Merlin didn't understand. How had the Sangraal gotten into his bag?

And how had Caygek seen it?

Mórganthu shook the orb when he saw Merlin and the others survive — even overcome — his best efforts to drown them. Mórganthu's own tent had nearly been knocked over in the first blast of wind, and even now the rain poured through the moth-eaten holes in the roof. Only a few moments before he'd had to retie the doorflap, for the wind had blown it open, and it was cold enough as it was.

So what next? How could he stop Merlin if his fog and even his storm had failed? Maybe he needed to dispirit them all. Freeze them in their boat until they begged for death. But how would that affect Bosventor? The ice would come here too, and fall upon his own tent.

Ah, but he had to try it. He checked the knots on his doorflap once again and threw more wood upon his fire until it blazed. Finally, he wrapped himself in a blanket, and then, and only then, did he pull out the orb and fang once more. And looking at it reminded him of how tired it made him to give the fang such a command. Did he have the strength? He felt weak from the two previous attempts. Maybe just one more. And so his voice called forth:

> *Cloaked voice of the fang, orb, and bitter wind,*
> *Freeze my enemies within their curragh!*
> *May they die from blizzards and shattered bones,*
> *Ripped sail, broken bow, a smashed, sinking boat!*

His vision blurred, and he almost passed out. The sound of the rain changed. Small pellets began to assault his tent. Mórganthu fell to his knees, took a breath, and crawled to the door to look out. Within less time than it took his fire to need another log, all the land was covered in ice, from the smallest leaf to the thickest trunk. And his tent began to hang low as its roof and sides froze solid. Then the snow began to blow — great swathes of it furiously swirling around. Mórganthu broke the ice from the flaps and tied them tight. Then he sat and warmed himself by the fire to nurse his strength while he watched Merlin and his companions suffer.

Ganieda tripped and fell down upon a rock. She'd been running recklessly and hadn't seen the stone until too late. She cried out, for the sniffing beast was almost upon her. She could hear him. Slavering behind her in the fog. A shadow approached. Monstrously tall.

She forced herself up and ran.

The beast loped behind her. A deep growl. Chasing her.

She ran behind a pine. If only she had the fang, she could kill it. She peeked through the branches. Two gleaming eyes stared at her from twelve feet off of the ground. The monster was huge!

It stepped forward, and its foul breath blew the fog away from its face.

It was a black wolf. Not Tellyk. Ganieda had never been threatened by a wolf before, but this one's teeth were so long. So sharp. She ran, screaming.

It was behind her again, yet somehow always just beyond her fog-shrouded sight. It could easily catch her and kill her in one swift bite.

Then it began to rain. The trees bent, pushed by a gale that sucked the breath from Ganieda's mouth. She ran on, propelled by the wind, covering her eyes to keep the lashing rain from blinding her.

Up and down hills. Through a stream. Under the dark and thick canopy of a forest, which kept most of the rain out. To a spring. Only then did she realize the monstrous wolf was gone. She had lost it in the fog. Falling down, she drank from the earthy burbles of water, and laid upon her side. A great drowsiness crept over her. Nevertheless, before she gave in to its forgetful call, she tried once more to pull the iron torc from her neck, but could not remove it.

She gave up and fell asleep.

When she awoke, something kept stinging and pestering her face and hands. Ice was falling from the black god of the sky, nipping at her flesh.

She wanted to sleep again where it had been warm. Her dream had been so warm. But she forced herself to climb stiffly to her feet. If she stayed, she would freeze and the monster of a wolf would find her and eat her.

She set off once more. Her feet felt like ice, but she had to find her grandfather.

CHAPTER 34

LAND OF THE DEAD

The murky sun whirled above Troslam, slowly dipping down-ward, and finally — along with the distant screams and cries — fell beyond his remembrance. Shadows. Rocking. Creaking. Cold. Darkness. Shivering. The sound of water splashing. Of his own breath. Fading. Fading.

He awoke within a boat.

Where was he?

It was night. The stars shone in the sky like brilliant candles out of his reach, each one lit by the hand of an angel and held there just for him. He had been so cold, he remembered, but here the warmth soaked into his skin and filled his bones with strength. Reeds floated by. Frogs chirruped, announcing that all was right in the world.

He sat upon a broad bench with two young girls, one on each side. The left wore a white gown, luminous as the moon, and her hair lay as a flower of gold intertwined with strands of silver. The girl on his right was smaller than the other, and her gown shone like the blue of the most radiant sky, with dark tresses as fine as the feathers of a black swan, smooth and pure.

The boat moved through the marsh seemingly of its own accord. Neither rower nor tower could be seen, and none pushed from behind. Yet they moved steadily and slowly through the mazes of rushes, reeds, and water channels. Hours passed. Maybe days. The sun rose and set. Stars twinkled again. Abruptly, the boat came to rest upon the bank of a broad island jacketed in green grass with tufts of fragrant daisies. Here and there stood outcroppings of rocks where wild roses grew. And everywhere stood ancient apple trees. Gleaming fruit hung from every branch, sweet-scented and beckoning.

The peace of the island settled over Troslam, and he departed from the boat with the girls just behind. Walking there amongst the trees, he reached out and touched a branch, and felt it pulsing — with life and beauty, deeper than what he had ever experienced. He cradled one of the fruit in his hands and just held it, looking intently as a heavenly light shown from its flesh.

"Here! Come here!" It was Eilyne's voice. Yes, it was her, Uther's daughter, the one in the moon-lit dress. How had he forgotten who she was? She waved to him and pointed to where a fortress stood upon a little hill with a single tower. Its stones were a rich, milky white, and their radiance fairly blinded him.

"It's Father's hall!" she declared with a smile. "Come and see!" She grabbed Myrgwen by the hand, and they raced to the open gate and leapt inside.

Troslam was right on their heels and stepped through the door. Wonders met his gaze. Hundreds of warriors and their spouses and children reclined at tables filled with steaming salmons, spiced grains, soups, and overladen with yeasty breads. Hearty drinks were passed around, and with a cheer all the people raised their bowls to their lord and lady, who sat upon twin thrones raised above the feast. The lord, like a prince of old, wore a coat of purple threaded richly with argent knotwork. Next to him sat his wife graced in a gown so blue it rivaled the brightest ocean.

The queen smiled, looking out upon her subjects — and then spotted Troslam and the girls, who had quietly stopped in front of him. The queen stood, and a hush fell upon the room. "Who are these that enter this hall unbidden?"

Troslam felt foolish. They didn't belong here and had come without welcome. Yet, like a dog at the door, he wished with all his heart to join the feast. He stepped forward to the aisle leading to the thrones and fell to a knee. "It is I, Troslam, a poor weaver, and one unworthy to enter this great house ..."

The king stepped down from his throne, walked to Troslam, took him by the hand, and lifted him up. "Arise, fellow son of the Britons, for all are welcome who come in through the gate, bidden or not."

At that point the king observed the two girls. Their eyes shown as wide as dumplings, and their mouths formed hesitant smiles.

"Sir," Myrgwen said, "do you know us?"

"Know you?" the king said, a strange look upon his face.

The queen stepped down and rested a loving hand upon the heads of each of the girls. "Only one of you is supposed to be here, although all shall be welcome at this table in time. Yet for the others, the full weaving of your lives is not ready to be unrolled from God's loom. Go back," she said. "Go back."

"But, Mammu!" little Myrgwen said, and she rushed into the queen's arms. "Surely you wish me to stay. I never want to leave you. Don't make me go."

"You have been brave before, little one, and I ask you to be brave once again. It is your elder sister who is to stay."

Myrgwen burst into tears and hugged tighter to the queen.

It was all Troslam could do not to cry with her.

"But you must go back. There are tasks left for you to accomplish. You are privileged to be the Lord's handmaid to aid your brother in his mighty tasks."

The king hugged Eilyne. "And you, dear one, will stay here, even while your sister and companion return."

His soothing tone brought peace even to Troslam, whose heart was troubled. But he was still unsure of how to proceed. "I don't know the way back," he said, "for I do not know how I have come."

Then the king went to the high table that stood before his throne, and there he retrieved a wooden bowl. Simple in design it was, yet apparently ancient — even to Troslam's untrained eyes.

"The Sangraal will be your guide," the king said, "for Merlin has given it back to us." As he lifted it up, the bowl shown with a holy light so pure and lovely that it appeared to Troslam as a doorway to the throne of heaven itself.

The Sangraal began to float above the king's hands, illuminating the whole feasting hall. Then it rose through the ceiling, and the island outside the doorway became bathed in majestic brilliance. A longing filled Troslam's heart to behold this light again, and he and Myrgwen, holding hands, left the hall.

And now the Sangraal had become much more than a bowl, for it was a veritable star above them, lighting their path and leading them back to the boat whence they had come. And there, on the very edge of the island, Myrgwen paused.

A voice floated from behind. "Dearest ..."

It was the queen, caressing a luscious apple that still hung from one of the trees. "This, my dearest daughter, has been granted as a boon from the most High God to be yours and yours alone. Take it now."

Myrgwen reached forth and wrapped her small hands upon the fruit.

She plucked, she ate.

Unlike any apple Troslam had ever seen, red juice flowed from it, but there was no stain left upon her lips or cheek — only a happy smile.

"This gift will be sweet upon your tongue," the queen said, "and then for a little while it will be bitter to your soul, for with it will come knowledge both dire and puzzling, yes, but such that will be needed in the deadly time that is coming upon the world."

With that costly gift in hand, Myrgwen joined Troslam, and together they returned to their positions in the boat. And just as before, the boat moved off under no apparent oarsman, although this time it followed the light of the Sangraal that lit the way through the marsh and led them onward into the night.

The king stood upon the distant shore and waved good-bye to them, and next to him stood the queen, and a shining Eilyne, all in bright array. A deep sleep fell over Troslam, and soon he lost all track of time and place and only knew two things: the rocking and creaking of the boat upon the water — and that an old man was with them. His combed hair was long and gray, and he wore clothes both clean and bright.

"Stay still," the man said, "and poor Musca will take good care of you."

Merlin felt the tightness leave his shoulders as the storm eased. The waves had raged all night, and Merlin's eyes stung with salt and lack of sleep. His limbs ached as well, and his clothes were completely soaked. He longed to crawl into one of the little tents, sleep, and forget the horror that was the sea.

Thankfully, the sun had finally risen, even if Merlin couldn't tell from what direction. The clouds and rain were that thick, making it a dim, pale light. At least the seas had finally calmed to the point that Merlin wasn't worried about drowning for awhile.

"So where are we?" he asked.

Garth stretched, yawned, and shook water from his hair. "I don't really know. Navigatin's near impossible with these clouds, and the wind's prob'ly changed a lot since we set out."

Small ice pellets began assaulting Merlin's face — softly at first, but then more solidly. Soon they stung. If he thought the rain was bad, this was worse. The wooden ribs of the boat began to slicken, and soon ice had covered most of the surface.

Merlin had been shivering before, but now it grew worse. And poor Peredur; he had left his cloak on shore, and couldn't keep his teeth from chattering. Merlin had offered him his, but it was so wet that Peredur didn't think it would help.

Bedwir filled the bailing bowls with fresh water and passed them around, followed by a helping of smoked herring for everyone.

Merlin could hardly taste his herring, for even his tongue was numb with cold. But it filled the barrenness in his stomach, and brought a measure of warmth back to his limbs.

Then it began to snow, and soon it blinded them to the point that Merlin could hardly see the mainsail in front of him. And it collected inside the boat, making movement dangerous.

"We can't see!" Merlin said. "We need to furl the sail and drop anchor!"

"No!" Garth said. "Let's keep sailing."

"But you don't know where we're going — "

"God knows the way."

And with Garth's proclamation, a light appeared in the distance — to the left. Caygek saw it too, and he shouted for everyone to look. Just below the clouds, like a star, yet brighter than any Merlin had ever seen, its beams penetrating the thickest blast of snow.

And it seemed to be moving away from them.

"Have you ever seen anything like it?" Merlin asked.

Garth shrugged. "What? I don't see anything."

"There's a star, lighting up the sky ... can't you see it?"

But no one could except Merlin and Caygek.

"Could God be showing us the way?" Garth asked.

"I suppose it's possible."

"Then set the sail toward the steerboard side. You tell me where, and I'll guide us toward it." In no time they had the boat sailing toward the light, and it led them through the snow as sure as any guide.

Garth began to sing a hymn. His voice quavered, and even squeaked here and there, but it was sincere and humbled Merlin for his lack of faith.

Thanks be to you, Jesu Christ who brought us up from the night
To the glad light of this day to have life for our poor souls
Through your blood, shed for our sin!
For your good gifts given us, our fishing, nets, and boating;
For your favor blessing our hands, our work, and our health.
Praise you, O God, forever!
May the Spirit claim us, protect us on wave and wind
Lead us on from shoal to shoal, to the peace of your City,
Your Everlasting City!

"You remember all that?" Merlin asked. "I didn't think you paid attention to the monks."

"Ahh, I learned that from me father. Them monks only sang about plantin', harvestin', and scribblin'. That sort o' thing. What we needed was a right sailin' sorta thanks."

A bird landed on one of the oarlocks, a strange kind of gull, and it stayed through the rest of their watch. "It must be exhausted," Peredur remarked, and he held out a herring to it, but the bird turned its beak away.

By morning it was dead.

Mórganthu smashed the sharp edge of his sword again and again into the blazing logs of his fire, sending sparks and ashes high into the air. He wanted to cut Merlin and slice him. Kill him. For the orb had shown him how they sailed on even through the worst of his snow and ice.

Ah, but the fang could kill them! He set his useless blade down and lifted the fang up toward the orb, which sat upon his throne, burning and crackling in purple flame around Merlin's upturned face. Mórganthu raised his voice, calling for Merlin's death, the shattering of their boat, the piercing of their hull, and the shredding of their sail.

But nothing happened. He felt no power in the fang.

He tried again, but … there was nothing.

Inside the orb, Merlin kept on adjusting the ropes for the sail. Garth kept at his steering. The boat sailed incessantly on. Mórganthu cursed the fang. He understood it a little, but evidently not enough to use it rightly. If only Ganieda were present, then she could teach him its inestimable secrets.

But where were Merlin and his ragged crew sailing? Mórganthu had always assumed southward to Kernow for the purpose of troubling him further. But really, he didn't know. He set the fang down and touched the top of the orb. "Where, O master of all visions, does Merlin go? To what end shall he come?"

The inside of the orb flashed, shifted, and churned. The image changed.

Mórganthu studied the images for a long time, fascinated. Their destination was not Kernow. Rather they traveled *northward*. To darkness. And death.

He laughed then — a hearty, gut-heaving guffaw that tickled his being in devious places he hardly knew existed. How could he have been wrong all this time? He had only been slowing the inevitable, for Merlin and his fellows would surely die, and swiftly at that.

Ganieda was horribly lost. And behind her, the wolf's massive claws clicked upon the frozen ground. She ran as fast as she could through the blowing snow, but kept slipping, banging her knees bloody. Over the hills, through icy streams, and around rocks and boulders — she ran. Soon she found a road, but ignored it and ran to the cover of the pines, hoping the wolf couldn't fit underneath its low branches. The scented needles brushed against her face, both pricking her and wiping away her tears.

The hill steepened, and sometimes she had to pull herself up by the branches to keep from slipping on the icy mud. Sticky wax clung to her fingers and covered her arms and dress before she found herself on flatter ground.

But the wolf was right behind, its ice-covered fur shining through the snowfall as it pushed its way past the trees, snapping branches and cracking the trunks.

It howled at her. So close behind.

A massive pit appeared before her running feet. She twisted to avoid falling in and slammed into the ground, crying out as her legs slipped down into its mouth. Her fingers scrabbled at the soil trying to seize onto something.

The wolf's head appeared, its fangs snapping at her hands.

She fell. And hit, squishing her legs downward into the some-thing. Yielding mixed with hard and sharp. Cold liquid on her legs. She turned, and through the snow and ice saw a skull. Empty eyes. Slack jaw. Frozen flesh. Beyond it, another skull. And another. She could hardly breathe — they were everywhere. She had fallen into the pit that the druidow had dug and thrown their dead comrades into. The body pit. The more she struggled, the deeper she sank into the mass of corpses.

She screamed.

Notwithstanding the strange light that guided their boat, the unend-ing waves and continually thick cloud cover left Merlin morose. Was Arthur still alive? Had the moon gone dark yet? How many days did they have left? How far from their course had they strayed during the storm?

And most upsetting was that every day appeared shorter than the last. Every night longer. And now, on what he calculated to be their tenth day of sailing — the sun didn't come up at all. The night wore on, oppressive, cold, and endless. For they'd finally entered the sea of darkness, and the fables of his youth gnawed at his mind. Tales of coiling sea monsters. Reports of floating islands where the souls of the dead crawled around in the shape of long-fanged demons.

And most maddening of all was that the wind ceaselessly whispered, "… Arrthur … Arrr — thhhhur …" He had to cover his ears at times just to shut it out.

What helped was the routine. They had developed a system of alternating shifts of three working together, with the others on call in case of an emergency. This allowed for what little rest and warmth the small tents could afford them. Peredur, Merlin, and Garth took one shift, followed by Bedwir, Caygek, and Kensa. Each group worked as long as strength allowed, and then called the others to take their place. It was important for Merlin and Caygek to be on different shifts, for they alone could see the strange light that guided their craft.

And just when would they make landfall? And how would they know if they'd found the right place? Perhaps Kensa knew, but she said little, and what she did say had more to do with the salted herring and the dwindling water supply than their ultimate destination.

Merlin was near the end of his strength and ready to trade places with the others when he spotted something on the horizon. No more than a small light at first, it seemed to move closer to them, or maybe they to it. As it drew near, Merlin could see that the light came from individual lamps, and by them he made out the black outline of a ship, for the lights were attached to the rails. But something was wrong, for even though its huge sail reached toward the thundering clouds, the boat lay low in the sea as if it had taken on water or was overloaded.

Peredur ran up to Merlin. "Turn the sail!"

"What?"

"We're going to hit!"

Merlin panicked. The black hulled ship was bearing down on them. But couldn't Garth steer them to the side? Merlin turned. The boy had fallen asleep!

His face lay sideways, and a quiet snore flowed from his open mouth. A little ice had gathered on his nose, and his hand had fallen from the steerboard, which thumped quietly against the hull.

"Garth! Wake up!" Merlin lunged at the boy, grabbed the steerboard, and fought against the waves to turn the ship to the side.

A wave lifted the black ship and sent it sliding down toward them.

Peredur let out a rope and shifted the sail.

Garth woke, glimpsed the ship, and yelped. All the others had awakened as well and stood on deck, mute and wide-eyed.

The curragh turned at the last moment, and the black ship sailed past on their port side. Merlin held his breath, for it was so close he could have reached out and touched its barnacled hull. The oil lamps were made of glass set in the iron mouths of fell beasts, each decapitated head swinging from a chain hung between iron poles. These cast ghostly light upon the deck of the black-hulled boat, revealing piles of bodies, their faces frozen in the agony of death.

A lone man stood upon a high platform near the back of the boat. He wore a black robe, with a cowl covering his face, and his whitened hand lay upon the rudder.

That quickly, the boat passed ... and was soon lost from sight.

Peredur shouldered up to Merlin. "What was it?"

"It's going to the land of the dead."

CHAPTER 35

SHADOW OF THE DEAD

Safrowana held Imelys on her lap, and they hugged until their mutual tears dried once more. Ten days had passed since Troslam had fled, taking Uther's daughters into hiding. Nine days since Kyallna, her neighbor, had found and untied her, Imelys, and Dybris from their ropes.

Troslam had not returned.

Dybris had looked for them, but the good monk's limp made his progress slow. And Allun the miller — the only other person she could trust in the village — had been sent to see if he could find Troslam in Guronstow, and if needed, further on in Risrud.

So far, nothing.

And she could no longer push down the thoughts that stole her breath and froze her hands at the loom — that he and the girls had been caught and killed.

A heavy knock came at the door.

More wary than ever, and not expecting Dybris, she peeked out a high window in the front of their roundhouse. An old man with long hair stood on the other side of the hedge. He was rocking on his heels as he looked around nervously.

It was Mórganthu.

She ducked down and motioned for Imelys to be absolutely quiet. She wanted to pretend she wasn't home and have him just go away, yet fury rose in her like a storm cloud, and she grabbed an old weaving rod. She would open the door and clout him, yes. He was just an old man with one hand. She could handle him, couldn't she?

She also pulled a small axe from the woodbox and handed it to Imelys.

"Stay behind me," she whispered, "but swing at his legs if you have to."

The knocking sounded again, this time more insistent.

She crept to the door.

Lifting the bar silently, she set it down on a pile of shorn wool.

Then she flung the door wide and charged out with the weaver's rod swinging. "Get away from here, you devil of a druid!"

But no one was there.

A head popped up from behind the hedge. "Hello!"

She screamed and swung at him.

He ducked, and then popped back up again. "Don't hit poor Musca!"

She started to swing again, but stopped. Musca? Was this Muscarvel?

She'd never seen the ancient man of the marsh, and had wondered if he was just a legend. She looked closer, and sure, it wasn't Mórganthu at all. This man was older, with patches of long hair growing from his scalp. His eyebrows had been burned away. And he had marshweeds slimed into his hair.

"I have news," he said, ducking down. "If thou wilt stop sporting at my pate. Thy husband sent poor Musca for help. Bandages. I am to bring bandages!"

Safrowana dropped the weaving rod and fell back against the doorframe. "My husband?"

He jumped up and down. "Yes!"

Imelys stepped out of the door. "Take us there!"

He nodded, stepped out, and then bowed before them, his shirt hanging in tatters. "Poor Musca at your service!"

One of the endless nights passed fitfully for Merlin in the tent, for another storm had arisen, and every twenty winks he'd get splashed either in the legs or the face, the tent flaps notwithstanding. And he became seasick and lay there next to Garth and Peredur on their stinky, wet sheepskins. Not that those two got any better sleep than he did.

As it was, Merlin felt awful and exhausted when their watch came again. Fourteen days at sea had taxed him beyond what he thought possible — but he got up nonetheless and left the tent. To his surprise, a huge white *something* floated past on the lee side, a stone's throw away.

"It's ice," Bedwir told him before retiring. "Keep a sharp watch."

The hours passed and the storm continued, with ice floes occasionally drifting past. The waves lifted the boat up and down. Ever and on. Merlin's eyes glazed over, and he had to pinch his own leg to stay awake, trying with all his strength to focus on the light that guided them. Each time the boat was blown off course, he had to point out the light to Garth and then follow commands for adjusting the mainsail. Oh, when would the darkness end? When would this nightmare of a journey bring them to shore?

During a calm stretch, Garth gave the steerboard to Peredur and played his bagpipe to keep their spirits up, and this helped some. But he soon tired, took his place once more, and set his bagpipe next to him.

Peredur assumed the management of the sail, and so Merlin sat down next to Garth and leaned against the small leather tarp at the back of the boat. Maybe he could just close his eyes for a moment. Garth was such a reliable navigator ... if the boy just kept his course steady, they'd be fine. Only a short rest.

Merlin dozed.

He woke to shouts.

The deck of the boat was a frenzy of panic. Bedwir raised the mainsail to its highest peak, causing the mast to bend in the quickening wind. Peredur turned it to face the port side, but the wind blew it backward.

Caygek and Kensa tried to adjust the headsail, but had no better results.

"What's going on?" Merlin yelled.

Garth was shouting instructions, his face purple. "Turn the sails, turn the sails!"

Merlin grabbed Garth's cloak. "Why?"

"We fell asleep. Look at the rocks!"

Just a short distance away loomed the dark outline of a steep headland with piles of surf-sprayed rocks at its base, whose sharp teeth could rip their little boat to shreds. And the wind and tide had conspired together to send them to a certain death.

Bedwir and Peredur untied the mainsail's ropes in an attempt to swing her about, but Bedwir's rope caught and cut furiously into the spar rope, which snapped. The spar fell with a crash, spinning in the wind. Bedwir and Peredur were both knocked into the water.

Merlin lunged toward the nearest edge, where Peredur had gone down, but couldn't find him. The next thing he knew, a massive wave lifted the boat high and smashed it against the cliff. The wood cracked, the seams of the leather ripped, and the boat broke in two.

Merlin hung on to a rope, but it was torn from his grasp. The world turned upside down. He plunged into the icy water, which shocked his head and paralyzed his chest like a vise. He felt himself lifted up—or was it down? His arm hit something hard. Smooth. He grabbed at it, but it slipped away. He gasped for air, and received a mouthful of freezing water.

Upward the waves roared once more, and this time he was thrown upon the rocks and clung there, coughing and wheezing. He wiped the water from his eyes and looked out. Kensa and her purple hat had somehow found their way onto a rock lower down. He reached to her and pulled her up just before the next wave hit. She screamed, grabbing on to him as the water washed over them. It lifted them upward yet again. Merlin lost his grip, and they were tossed backward against another rock.

"Are you hurt?" Merlin asked when the water fell back.

"Nott, nott. Me auld bones are tough," Kensa said.

The next wave didn't reach as high, and Merlin helped Kensa up onto the next level of rocks, and then climbed up himself. Coughing to clear his lungs, he looked around and was relieved to see Bedwir and Peredur had climbed up about ten paces away. Below him, the boat had been shattered into five pieces, and one began sinking.

Nowhere could he see either Garth or Caygek.

Merlin's lungs had recovered from the shock of the water, and he yelled, "*Garth!*"

There was no answer but the water breaking on the rocks.

Merlin started pacing on the small ledge ... and shivering.

Away to his right, he saw a hand reach up from the waves. Bedwir laid down, stuck out his arm, and pulled a wet Caygek from the water; the man's lips were blue and his limbs stiff.

Where was Garth?

Surely the boy knew how to swim?

"*Garth!*"

As Bedwir helped Caygek find his feet, Peredur made his way over to Merlin. "We've got to get up ... find some shelter. We'll die here."

Merlin shook his head. No, he couldn't leave without Garth.

"We've got to go ... Kensa's found a path ... see?"

But Merlin didn't want to see. He wanted to plunge into the waves and find Garth. But it was hopeless, and he knew it. There was no way he could survive in that water. Peredur took his arm, but

Merlin shook him off. And while they all climbed upward, toward the top of the cliff, Merlin stayed by the dark ocean that had claimed his friend.

At first Ganieda tried to pull herself from the corpses and their cracking, flaking, ghastly fingers, but could not. She had screamed, but no sound came. Emptiness engulfed her and she felt herself sinking down and down into the depths of the pit. But no bottom for her feet could be found, and she sunk farther and farther until she felt herself falling, head over heels.

It felt as if she had been tumbling forever.

She heard howling. She looked down as the wind whipped past her face, and there below her stood the black wolf, aglow in some ethereal light. The beast stood ten times his previous size. He opened his massive jaws and she fell onto his drooling, slime-coated tongue. The teeth snapped shut and she cried. The tongue convulsed below her, pushing her backward. She tried to grab on, but could not, and she slipped down to darkness.

The Voice appeared before her, his black cloak hiding a rich, blazing blue robe. She knelt upon a floor of granite, and long chains bound her wrists. Torches flickered with a bluish light and gave off a smoke that seeped onto the floor.

Behind the Voice stood a stone pillar, draped with a blue cloth decorated with intricately woven spirals and symbols. Something lay upon the table, but she could not see it, and her legs refused to let her stand. The desire grew stronger so that she called out to the Voice, "Will you help me?"

"Rise and see!" he said, and as he lifted his hand her legs raised her from the ground to behold four drinking horns, which had been placed at the corners of the pillar. Each one had been made from the long curving horn of a ram that spiraled inward and downward until coming to rest in an iron stand with the finger-like talons of some great lizard. The first horn was red as sweet cherries, the second of gold, the third a beautiful white, and the fourth a shining silver.

"Once I offered these drinks to Merlin," the Voice said. "Did you know that? He was foolish enough to refuse me, and soon he will die at the hands of Atle, my faithful servant. But you aren't so daft as Merlin, are you?"

The torc tingled at her throat, and she looked at the Voice's face and the scar that ran upward to his temple. "No," she said, shaking her head. She was smarter than her blind brother. She always had been.

"Everyone in the world drinks from my table, whether they know it or not. Ah, but most of them drink only a little. If they drink too much, they die, for my enemy has snuck a poison into my broths. But you are being given a special gift, for you have received the iron torc from my hand, and have become my special servant forever. Thus you may drink to the dregs and I will protect you from the poison. Won't you trust me? Good. Take and drink."

Ganieda approached and leaned forward to peek inside the red horn. It was filled with the freshest-smelling water — upon which flickered images of scary things she didn't understand. She tried to look away, but couldn't find the will. The pictures kept changing, nearly blinding her, and to get rid of them she took up the horn and drank until it stared back at her, empty.

Her throat still felt thirsty, and she stepped over to the second, the golden horn. A brown, frothy cream filled it, and it made a bubbling sound. Entrancing words slipped from the horn, telling of the sweetness of herself above all others, and her need to protect her freedom by any means possible. Others mattered nothing, it said. She brought the horn to her lips. The liquid coated her tongue and fled down her throat until it was all gone, and still she wanted more.

The third horn lay before her, white like alabaster, and she desired to drink it before she even looked within, for it smelled sweet and luscious, like the essence of a thousand wild plum trees. Ganieda saw her life, then, stretching out before her. Men and women adored her. Fell prostrate before her majestic glory. Praised her and served her every whim. And she protected them all though they feared her … Mórgana, Druid Queen of the Britons. Yes, she was the fulfillment of all her grandfather's dreams.

The white horn was in her hands in an instant and she sucked down its jade-colored soup. Sweet, yes, but there was so much to drink! It never seemed to end, and Ganieda began to feel full — almost ready to burst.

The Voice reached out and pulled the horn from her grasp. "There is more, here, than you can now hold. But you will come back, and one day finish it to the very bottom." He directed her to the last horn of all, the silver one, which shone like the brightest, most beautiful jewelry Ganieda had ever seen.

Did she really have room to drink more?

And the final horn was huge, made only for a great monarch …

The voice lifted the horn from the table and held its thick, black liquid before her. And though her stomach felt so full, her throat underneath the iron torc still longed for more and more. She reached out and grabbed the horn from his cold hands.

A vision overtook her of a great battle. Warriors, dark and grim, fought for her against Merlin and those with him, and pools of blood had been spilled for the delight of the circling birds. A young man stood at her side wearing lustrous armor. Long and golden lay his hair, and his black sword had been smeared with the filth of their enemies.

Yet a kingly warrior opposed them with rank upon rank of men at his side. His hair was dark. his eyes shone with the fierceness of death, and he held a beautiful sword in his hands.

Ganieda blinked.

That sword had been smithed by her father. It was the same blade that Merlin had driven into the Stone. Why was it in this strange man's gauntleted hand? And what had become of the Stone?

But the Voice covered her eyes and said, "This vision is not for you to see!"

"But why?" Ganieda asked, wishing she could view the sword again and glimpse the end of the battle. His hand was tight across her face and chilled her eyes.

"Drink now, and be filled!"

She heard the dark liquid glop toward her lips, and some of it splashed her cheek. It burned, and she flinched away.

The Voice let go of her eyes, seized her hair tightly in one hand, the horn in the other, and forced it to her lips. She wanted to scream as he decanted the black stuff into her mouth, for it burned her tongue like embers, smoking the roof of her mouth and setting her gums, teeth, and throat on fire.

All of it went down. Burning. Filling her insides with a fire that could not be doused. Then the Voice threw her to the ground, and she wept as flames poured from her mouth.

"Bow and worship, my servant, for this blaze shall keep your body alive in the coldness of the world, and it will burn in your soul too, until all you desire is my will."

She yelled as her clothing began to smoke. The last thing she remembered was his laughter echoing through the room.

Merlin fell to his knees, wiping the tears from his stinging eyes. He had stayed so long looking for his friend that he knew the boy couldn't have survived. Garth was dead. And if Merlin didn't go and join the others soon, he'd be dead too, for the arctic wind had picked up and his arms and legs had begun to go numb despite the uncontrollable shaking that wracked his body. But he didn't want to go. He felt like a traitor.

If only Garth's body would wash up on shore, he could at least say good-bye — but the waves had cheated him of that. If only he could see Garth's smile once more. If only he could hear the boy's bagpipe once more. If only —

A sound, distant yet distinct, floated upon the wind.

A bagpipe.

Merlin jumped up and listened. It seemed to come from the cliff top. He picked his way upward using the path the others had found. About halfway, he had to scale a four-foot cliff, and he scraped his shins raw trying to get up.

At the top stood Bedwir, Peredur, Caygek, and Kensa. And situated in the middle was a wet and bedraggled bagpipe player with a wet and bedraggled bagpipe, pumping his arms and making the most beautiful, warbling music.

Merlin ran, picked Garth up in a hug, squeaking the bagpipe. "How'd you survive?"

Garth slipped from the embrace, righted the single drone upon his shoulder, and stood up perfectly straight. "A bagpiper can always survive a dunkin'. You just twist yer pipes tight, fill up yer bag with air — and float."

"But where were you?"

"I never went under, and the waves washed me farther over where walkin' up was easy. I saw you all made it, and went scoutin' for help. There's a farmstead over the next hill." His teeth were chattering.

Without any more words, he led them toward it, and Merlin's feet nearly became blocks of ice by the time they arrived. The farmhouse had been built using a different construction than Merlin had ever seen. Its shape formed a two-story triangle, with the thatch roof starting from the ground on each side and rising up to a sharp point.

Nearby lay a tightly built barn of similar construction, surrounded by rock walls that meandered around the land apparently to keep animals in — but none were present.

Kensa knocked on the broad door.

No one answered, and no light could be seen inside.

Bedwir stepped up and banged it. "Open up! We need help ..."

After a long time, and more banging, a man's voice called from above in a language Merlin didn't understand. There was a little triangular window at the very top, and whoever it was looked down upon them from there. Kensa answered back, and the two argued for awhile. Finally, the man climbed from his perch, and they could hear him approaching the door.

"De name o' Sveinrod Kjaringoy, and he haf a family who try to sleep," she said. "I's tellin' him about de vreck, I's did, so he knows it."

The man opened the door, eyed them all suspiciously, and grudgingly let them in. He wore a rough woolen tunic with the stitched images of pines, hunters with spears, and an odd type of deer. He stoked the hearthfire and handed around cups of a strange drink that stung Merlin's nose, but otherwise warmed him. It was good to be out of the cold, and even better to sit next to Garth. He took off his boots and stretched his feet toward the fire. It felt so good that it hurt.

Kensa asked the man for something to eat and gave him a few coins, which the man studied curiously. He found some old bread and passed it around. The crust hurt Merlin's teeth, but he devoured it voraciously. Anything was better than herring day after day.

The man sat up with them for an hour while they continued to eat, dried their clothes as best they could, and drank more of his warming liquid. And he asked Kensa lots of questions, often giving dark glances at the group, especially Merlin. But time wore on, and the man finally stood and motioned them toward the door.

"Ve's to sleep in de barn," Kensa told them while she put on her hat once again.

So what if the barn wasn't clean? At least it was warmer than Merlin had expected, what with all the shaggy cows and sheep to warm the place up. Either way, he felt the blessing of just being out of the cold air, having a full stomach, and having the stinging eased in his feet. He covered himself in hay and slept.

Before he knew it, Sveinrod and his wife came to them with warm, roasted eggs and a thin milk that tasted like cheese. Like before, it was always dark outside, but for some reason they seemed to think it was day. What an awful thing to live in such a land without the sun.

Thankfully, Kensa still had a good supply of coins left from which to pay them, for Merlin had given all of his to Aulaf for the boat. During their meal, Merlin asked questions of their hosts, using Kensa as an interpreter.

"We are looking for a temple. The temple of Atleuthun. Do you know it?"

Sveinrod pursed his lips before answering. Kensa translated the man's strange language. "No, ve don't know it."

"It should be near here. Surely there is a temple you know about?"

Sveinrod looked to his wife, who glared at him. "No, ve don't know of a temple."

His wife slapped him lightly and then spoke herself. "I am Berghild Egilsdatter. Ve an' our children live in peace here in Kjaringoy, andd vish de spirits nott to trouble us, nor our stock, nor our liddle parcel o' grain. I vant to ask — why do ye seek dis temple?"

"A child has been taken from us. Taken there by this Atleuthun, a king. We've come to take the child back with us to safety."

When they heard this news, the woman and her husband spoke at length, the husband getting more and more agitated. Finally, he turned to Merlin and said, "Ve don't know o' a temple. Leave us andd do nott trouble us more."

But the wife spoke up again, her nostrils flared. Kensa gladly translated. "Do nott listen to dis liar. He does nott vant to say it, but der is a temple. On der island, vay up de *hoven* — a sacred mountain to some — which we call de *mara-hoven*. Long ago der was a great city at etts base, but de vaves rose and vashed it up. De winds shattered de temple too, an' der are only ruins now. Ett es a dark place, with savage people living about who gather victims efery ninth year. None come back, ett es said. Do nott go der or ye will die."

"But we must. Do you know the way?"

"Ett es nott close. Ten leagues ett es, ofer land andd sea, andd our family's boat es a liddle thing, nott big enough for de lot o' you. De nearest farm with a bigg boat vould be a day's march by yer feet, andd den anither part o' a day at sea after dat. But ya must hurry, for de men der will go back to der farms very soon."

Almost two days to get there? That far? And they would need at least a day to gather their strength before setting out. If only they hadn't fallen asleep on the boat and sunk. He looked around, and all of them had been weakened by their voyage and capsize, especially Peredur, who'd had no cloak, and Caygek, who'd been the longest in the water.

Merlin went to the barn door and opened it a crack, hoping the clouds had cleared enough to see the moon. And it was there, laying on its white side with a thin, mocking sneer. Not much of it could still be seen, so at most they had two, maybe three days before Atle sacrificed Arthur.

Time was running out.

CHAPTER 36

THE RAVEN GROVE

Merlin and the others rested that day, attempting to recover for the journey ahead. If his own strength had allowed it, Merlin would have set out right away, but it was not to be. Sveinrod allowed them back into the house during that time, and the fire did wonders to revive them.

All, that is, except for Caygek, for he sat glumly at the corner of the hearth and did little more than nod when food or drink was passed to him. For his own part, Merlin left him alone, letting the man sit and think — for something was clearly bothering him.

Merlin himself spent the time sharpening a short blade Garth had tucked in his belt before their boat capsized. A smooth rock was all he had to do it with, but the scraping motion — back and forth, smoothing and sharpening — comforted him as he prepared his mind for action. He would kill Atle if he could, and he imagined skewering the old man with every stroke of the rock.

Sveinrod and his wife fed them well, for Kensa's coins helped loosen the door of their larder. Creamy cheeses, white and rich. Flatbreads rolled out and baked before their eyes. Ground meats, intestine-cased and broiled. Pickled apples, tart and joyous on the tongue. It was a heartening feast for all of them, especially Garth, who received extra portions from Kensa — along with a few tugs to his ruddy hair.

That night in the barn, Merlin could hardly sleep despite his tiredness — for while they had all fattened up, the moon had gotten thinner.

When he could stand waiting no longer, he woke the others up.

"But it's still night," Garth protested.

"It's always night. Get up!"

"Lemme sleep."

Merlin didn't, and soon they were all shaking the hay from their cloaks and putting on their boots. And kindly Kensa had purchased a cloak for Peredur... Oh, what would they have done without her help? Merlin, all of them, would have been complete beggars in this strange, dark land, and probably would have ended up as slaves under masters worse than the Picts.

Caygek had bought a spear from Sveinrod, for he still had his money from before. Bedwir also had his blade, so that made three of them with weapons. Against how many? Merlin would have to wait to find out.

For their journey, they had bought some smoked venison from Berghild, enough to last two days. They had only three waterskins, but she assured them they could eat the snow.

Merlin rolled up the leather map Sveinrod had drawn with a burning stick and stuffed it in his bag. They were to follow a ridge of pines until they came to a road where they would turn left. The road would take them to the great farm of Ulfsvag, where men had gathered for a short fishing season and were smoking the fish before returning to their own scattered farms. Hopefully, they could hire someone to boat them across the bay to the island where the temple stood.

Their hoods up and their cloaks pulled tightly about them, they set off across the snowy landscape. What Merlin would have done for a little sunshine to warm his back! But then the words of Abbot Prontwon — whom Merlin had known in Kernow, and who had battled against the Stone as well — came back to him. The man had been teaching Merlin to trust in God despite his blindness, and Merlin recalled the scripture he quoted from one of the prophets:

Who among your clan fears the power of the Lord?
And who will swear fealty to be a servant of the Lord?
For the warrior who marches in the darkness and cannot see —
He must trust in God, the Lord who keeps your foot from slipping.

But he found no comfort in the distant memory, and the darkness oppressed him, his thoughts turning gloomy as the endless night trudged onward. Even finding the road heading north didn't raise his spirits. What was happening to Arthur? How could Merlin have let him be taken? What kind of a fool was he? The lowest of fools. For Arthur was so little. Defenseless. What would Uther and Igerna have thought of his stewardship? Of his oath to protect their son?

And what was King Atle up to? Something far stronger than just his religious beliefs must have goaded the man to sail this far with Arthur.

They kept plodding, and it was hard going, for the land was filled with mountains, and the snow was deep. Twice they lost the road altogether and had to double back to find where they had gone astray. When the lighted windows of the farm finally appeared in the distance, Merlin wanted to run to it, but his feet were so numb he could hardly pick them up to walk.

At last they arrived at the farm, which was the equivalent of a very small village, with six buildings and three barns. Kensa knocked on the door of the nearest and spoke with a fair-haired woman wrapped in a broad, black fur. At first she was suspicious of them, but when she heard that Sveinrod and Berghilde had sent them, she welcomed them hesitantly.

Merlin slapped as much snow and ice as he could from his cloak, breeches, and boots before entering. Sitting before the woman's hearth was welcome indeed, and she passed them all cups of hot, soothing milk mixed with a local pungent spice that Merlin didn't recognize.

"Torsten, me husband, ess out chopping vood fer de fish smoking," Kensa translated for her, "andd he'll be back in a stitch. Now Which o' Odin's raven's has flown ye here from such a far land? Andd vat do ye vant?"

He paused, not wanting to scare her. "We want to hire men to take us across the bay."

She backed up against the brick wall and grabbed a poker. "Are ye one of dem Marachlans? If so, I'll — "

"Who?"

"De *Mara-Hoven* people — "

"No — "

"Den what ferr?" she said, letting her poker down.

"We need to go there, but we're not one of them."

She looked at him darkly, and her eyes traced the scars that crossed his face. "Och, andd what ferr? I von't ask again, so tell me straight if ye vant our help. Ve're nott a people fer trifling."

Merlin swallowed. "We need to get to the temple. They've taken a child from us, a very special one, and we need to rescue him."

Kensa looked a little peculiar before she translated this.

"I was afraid o' such," the woman said, shaking her poker at him to warn him away. "Ye'll haf to exchange vits w' Jarl Lhudvig about ett. He's de owner o' de whole farm."

Torsten came back soon. A broad man with thick arms, he was as wary of strangers as his hanging, braided moustache was long. His wife explained the situation to him, and then told Kensa that Torsten would take them to the Jarl.

Torsten found his spear and then escorted them through the farm.

Merlin became concerned, however, when Torsten knocked on

every door — and gathered a man or two to join them, each of which brought along a sword or spear. Finally, with eight men surrounding their party, Torsten led them to the biggest house of the farm, set on a hillock of snow and stones. Torsten knocked.

When the Jarl answered, Merlin had to take a second look. He hadn't seen anyone as big and strong as the Jarl since he'd fought a giant in the smithy. A full head taller than Merlin, he had a brown beard that hung down in great hairy curls to his chest.

He eyed them all suspiciously, and Merlin most of all. He took a step forward, slammed his fist on the doorframe, and interrogated Torsten before allowing them in.

The dwelling was much like Torsten's but larger. The hearthfire needed a new log, and the dim light barely illuminated the room. Merlin squinted his eyes to orient himself as everyone shuffled in. A table appeared before him, full of fishbones, and Torsten shoved Merlin down onto a bench. Kensa slid next to him, her drooping, purple hat looking sad in the faint light.

On the left wall hung the skulls of bears, various horned deer, and huge, fanged cats. One of the creatures had the broadest antlers he'd ever seen ... five feet of sharp points with the ends shaped like clawed paddles.

But the right wall took Merlin's breath away. Upon it hung the jawless skulls of fifteen men, some with cracks and holes bashed into their craniums. That was when Merlin noticed that the Jarl had a large war hammer leaning against the wall behind him.

The big man took a seat across from them, the bench complaining under his weight. Torsten sat next to him. The exit behind was blocked by the men. The Jarl spoke first, and Kensa translated for everyone. "So. I am telled o' yer rudeness. Ye vish us to row ye to *Mara-Hoven* Isle across de bay. Es dis de truth?"

Merlin nodded.

The Jarl laughed. "En dis weather?"

Merlin nodded again.

The Jarl stopped laughing, and a furious discussion broke out amongst the men. Some of them yelled. A few put their hands to the hilts of their blades. Finally, the Jarl smoothed out his beard and raised his hands, and when he spoke, the room thankfully quieted so Merlin could catch Kensa's translation. "Ve vill nott do dis for ye. Ett es nott worth de risk. Ve already risk much to live so close, and vill nott risk anything more. Be on yer way, den."

The Jarl stood.

Kensa jumped up and, to see the Jarl properly, cocked her head back on the end of her hunched-over spine. Swifter than Merlin expected, she brought forth a knife.

The Jarl and Torsten stepped back, knocking over their bench.

She raised the knife up ... and stuck it into her hat, lifting it from her head. She slipped the sharp tip into a seam and began ripping. A gold coin fell out. Then another. This continued until her gaudy purple hat lay in shreds, and fifteen gold coins lay on the table.

The funny thing was that although the gold coins had been molded with flat, featureless sides, the shape of a large cockroach had been scratched into the surface of each one.

Kensa smiled in triumph despite the strange expression on the Jarl's face. His lip twitched as he leaned forward and grabbed not the coins but Merlin's head on both sides. His massive fingers, smelling of sweat and fish, pressed against Merlin's skull. Merlin braced himself. The man could break his neck in one quick twist.

The Jarl kissed Merlin on the forehead. Then he kissed Kensa the same way, and taking up the coins, passed one to each of the men, leaving seven for himself.

"Ye see?" Kensa said. "I does more dan just ettin' bugs. I catch dem andd hides dem in me hat!"

"Can you ask them for swords? Can that be included? We need three."

Kensa negotiated with the Jarl, and he agreed. But when the blades were brought, they appeared to be cast-offs. Peredur's blade was bent. Garth's, though serviceable, wasn't quite long enough to be called a sword. And Merlin's handle was loose and the blade badly notched. He hoped it could hold up in a fight and that he wouldn't have to rely on his knife.

Then, just as silently as the village's men had come, they slipped away and disappeared back to their houses. Within a short while each one showed up with thicker cloaks tightened about their necks and warm fur hats. The Jarl led them down to the harbor, where boats of various sizes lay upside down for the winter on wooden blocks. In no time they had the biggest boat flipped and brought down to the water, and promptly outfitted the craft with oars and a small sail.

Kensa led Merlin and the others to the boat. She was practically skipping. What would he have done without her? Arthur would shortly be dead without her help, for the newly risen moon had only the slightest sliver of white left in it. They were nearly out of time.

The voyage across the inlet took many hours, despite a good wind and the aid of the oars. Thankfully, the hired men did the hard work, letting Merlin and the others rest.

Upon entering the immense bay between some islands, the men furled the sail, took it down, and stowed it.

"Won't we go faster with the sail?" Merlin asked through Kensa.

"Ya, but de sail might be seen. Stealth ess better."

But Merlin didn't care about stealth. It was so dark. Who would see them? And the moon was nearly black — they needed to hurry. He tried to explain this to the Jarl, but the man just kept rowing along with his men down the long bay.

They passed three tall ridges on their right, each one like a colossal finger reaching out into the ocean to grab their tiny ship and crush it. Ahead of them lay a lone island with a snow-capped mountain upon it, and the Jarl pointed to it. This was their destination.

They approached slowly, the white mountain rearing up above them and blotting out the low stars. The Jarl directed them to the left and followed a channel a little way in. There, they brought the boat up on the strand, and the Jarl told Merlin and the others to get out.

"So this is the mountain?" Merlin asked.

The Jarl shook his head. "No ... yerr *hoven* is de far one." And he pointed farther down the island — past the immediate mountain, across a flat plain of snow-covered rocks and trees — to a smaller mountain. Specks of lights glinted from its far summit as if men roamed there with torches.

"Der is yerr place," the Jarl said.

"This is too far away. Row us closer. We've paid you good coinage."

He shook his head and twisted his long beard. "Ve go no farther."

"But why?" Merlin asked.

No one answered Kensa's translated question. The faces of the men were tense, and their glances anxious. Every one of them had their hand on their blades as if a giant slept on that very beach, ready to rise up and smash their heads together. Sweat dripped down their cheeks and onto their beards. The nearest rower's hands flexed nervously.

Fear. Merlin could sense it. Something about the island made these men quake. And there must be a reason behind it, for they lived nearby. Merlin had hoped to persuade them all to join in rescuing Arthur. Nine stout warriors would have greatly helped. Hadn't Kensa paid them enough for such service? Back in Kernow a poor man might sell himself into slavery for a year for such a sum.

But it was not to be, for the Jarl pointed at the shore and gnashed his teeth.

Merlin directed everyone off the ship and helped Kensa out last of all.

The men heaved the boat away from the shore and rowed off. Merlin watched them until they were lost in the darkness and waves.

He and his companions were alone now. Abandoned. And the moon had risen farther into the sky with only the thinnest sliver of white to tease them. Touching the hilt of his knife once more, he envisioned it lodged in Atle's gut.

Following the beach, they found a way to climb to the snowy plain that led to the distant mountain. On top, Merlin could see the lights even better. There must be many men up there.

"Come on!" he called. "There's no time to lose."

Setting off at a jog, he ran through the snow as quickly as he could. A league or more he ran, the others trailing behind and sometimes running ahead. To his left lay a broad bay whose dark waves roared and lapped against the shoreline. Around the bay he ran, turning toward the mountain. The heads of large rocks stood in the snow, and here and there a wind-mangled tree had fought its way up toward the dark sky.

Merlin's strength waned. His lungs began to hurt. And then his cold and numb legs tripped over a sharp rock hidden in the powder. He fell.

Bedwir, his breath an icy swirl in the wind, helped him up, and then ran on ahead.

Merlin's shin was bleeding, and his ice-crusted trouser was torn. He stumbled on, and now everyone passed him — even Kensa with her wobbling, bent-over gait. He looked down, being more careful of his steps, and kept plodding in the tracks of the others, forcing each foot to lift and carry him forward yet one more painful step.

The time passed achingly slow, and even if he didn't look up through his slogging, he was thankful that each stride and ragged breath brought him closer to the mountain and Arthur.

Then he heard cries. Birds. Ravens. There must be hundreds, by the sound of it.

Merlin looked around. He had descended onto a shallow, frozen lakebed at the foot of the mountain ... and trapped in the iced-over lake stood the devastated remains of an old city. Broken pillars and smashed walls reached out of the ice, all part of once opulent buildings. He tried to pick up a broken stone with a masterfully carved fish on it, but it was frozen in place.

And the city must have fallen to ruin long ago, for great trees had grown up and taken over so that the place now looked like a grove — a dead grove. For the ice had killed the trees and cracked the trunks, and their dead limbs clawed skyward in mocking sneers at the heavens. Had the land sunken since the trees had grown? How many generations had passed?

And this is where the ravens had gathered.

Bedwir faced him, mouth agape, and Peredur beside him. Garth and Kensa suffered the sight from the left side. Caygek, alone on his knees, had vomited.

For before them — in the trees — hung forty or more corpses. Not old, rotting corpses, but fresh ones. With their red blood frozen to their limbs. Each one had been impaled upon a great branch, and the ravens greedily devoured their flesh.

After endless dreams of fire smoldering within the marrow of her bones, Ganieda awoke. The world was dark, wherever she was, and it clutched at her with a viselike grip, cold and breathless. She screamed for air and clawed upward. Buried; someone had buried her. She fought, lifting her tired knees and kicking down, ever downward, until her head rose up to freedom. She sucked it in and found it to be salty and sick, but at least it was air.

A dead face leaned toward her. She screamed, for she knew where she was now — the druid pit. Pushing away from the dead man and his thin, ruddy beard, she found the wall of the pit and grabbed upward. Anything. Anything.

She kicked herself sideways, and there her hand found a root. She pulled herself up, but halfway out, it snapped. She fell back. There were more roots. She grabbed one, and pulled, then another, and tugged upward. She lifted a leg onto the freezing ground, grabbed the trunk of the tree, and slid her whole body to the top. Her shoes had been lost in the muck, but she didn't care.

She sat up, and the stink from the pit and from her own clothes stung her nose. Taking handfuls of snow, she rubbed her clothes with it to wipe off the grime.

Then she remembered the giant wolf. She whipped her head around but didn't see it. Where had it gone? The beast might come back, and then what would she do? Ganieda stood on shaky legs and ran off into the snowstorm that swirled and pulled at her cloak and hair.

The thin trees ended and she came out onto an open hillside. Where was her grandfather? And then she stumbled. Weariness had pulled her down, but she forced herself up and kept moving. Her legs felt so weak, she needed to rest somewhere out of the wind.

Trees ... just ahead. A thick grove. She ducked under the leafless branches and picked her way forward. Before her — at the edge of a clearing — loomed up a massive stone. She trudged to it, leaned against it, and found its shelter kept the snow from blowing in her face. She slumped down, determined to rest for awhile.

She laid her head down, and covered herself with her cloak. She would get up soon, she told herself. Darkness and sleep embraced her, and she embraced them back.

CHAPTER 37

THE TEMPLE OF ATLEUTHUN

erlin turned away from the dead bodies — not wanting to gag and not wanting to see them any longer. But mainly, he didn't want to see if Arthur was there. Were they too late?

"Is … is he there?" he choked out without turning to look. "We need to make sure."

Merlin sat down on his haunches while the others searched the grove. He prayed for the first time since the storm at sea.

Someone crunched across the ice and snow and came to stand next to him. He looked at the boots and saw the person's big toe sticking out of a hole. It was Garth. "Art's not here, but we scared off two wolves before we found this … hangin' on a branch." He passed a red cloth to Merlin, torn but not bloody. It was a small tunic — the one Arthur had last worn at the feast, and the same one Merlin had seen in his vision.

Maybe there was still time.

Merlin looked up at the moon, now nearing its apex in the southern sky. The thin white line that had been there during their journey across the plain had become nothing more than a glow around the rim.

Merlin stood, and a new strength filled his legs.

They had to get up the mountain.

Now.

But what if they were captured before they could rescue Arthur? Then their weapons would be taken, including his sword and knife. Arthur might die because of the noise of one footfall. The glint off a sword in the wrong direction.

But what if Merlin could keep his knife? That might allow him a second chance. He pulled the short blade out from his belt and compared its length to the rolled-up leather map still in his bag. It would fit. And so, lacking any better place to hide it, he opened the bag, slipped the knife into the roll of leather, and tied the bag once more to his belt. No, the knife wouldn't be immediately available to him, but he still had his sword. And besides, with all the torches swarming the upper mountain, their best chance was stealth.

Meanwhile, the others had all been talking about how best to approach the top.

"Can't we climb?" Bedwir asked. "They won't expect us to do that."

"No, no," Kensa said. "Ett's too steep, so take de path up. But den nott all o' ye are wanted. Ah, but we'll make de best o' ett."

"Won't they see us coming?" Peredur asked.

"Dey're busy," she said, "and dey keep no lookout. Straight up and de trees vil hide ya. But we must hurry. *Der's no time!*" Her voice was urgent, and she began to push Merlin forward.

Merlin held her off with a hand so he could look up and see what she was talking about. This hoven was very similar in size to Dinpelder back in Britain, except here the entire mountain was slanted on one side all the way to the plain, making a natural path to the top from the ruined city where they stood. And she was also right about where to hide — a stand of thick trees grew on both sides of the path just near the top.

"Let's try it, and everyone be as quiet as you can. Keep your weapons under your cloak if possible."

Peredur stepped up to Merlin. "May I pray?" he said in his humble, quiet way.

Merlin nodded, and hushed the others to listen. Peredur cleared his throat and prayed:

> *O bright, precious Father, in our thoughts, be present,*
> *In our actions, be near, always in our hearts and souls.*
> *Mighty Spirit, swift and sure, of the fragrance of heaven,*
> *Of the running, happy stream, flow in our hearts and souls.*
> *May your blessed Son, of the line of David,*
> *Of the suffering cross, dwell in our hearts and souls.*

Merlin thanked him, and Peredur blushed.

"It's just a prayer o' me father. He always prayed like that to begin our day training horses. I dunno if it's appropriate for sech a task as this, but I s'pose it's better than naught."

Merlin led the way through the rest of the ruins and trees, trying not look at the corpses. The path up the mountain was harder than he had expected — relentlessly it rose, higher and higher, and Merlin's tired lungs could hardly suck in the cold air.

Bedwir walked to his left, his blade hidden, but his eyes sharp, and Garth, wary, walked to his right. Caygek and Peredur followed behind, with Kensa bringing up the rear. Two things aided them — the darkness, which the enemy had desired for their own purposes, and carelessness, for no guard appeared to accost them as they climbed toward Atle's temple.

When they reached the trees, Merlin gathered everyone together and instructed them all to be as quiet as they could and to watch their step. Thankfully, the woods were mostly filled with pines, and the thick layer of soft, wet needles muffled their steps.

Merlin hiked upward very slowly, picking his way. He tried

to keep them together, but it was so dark under the canopy, and the trees so thick that they spread out farther than he'd intended. Merlin could barely see anything at all.

When he finally reached the edge of the trees, he crouched down into the brush. What he saw took his breath away. Just a few feet away chanted and danced an assembly of over five hundred people — men, women, and children of all ages. Each of them held daggers in one hand and a small torch in the other. And their feet, as well as the snow, were stained red with the blood of their many victims.

The temple itself was in ruins. Ancient stone columns made a wide circle upon the crest of the hill, and the closest was no more than eight paces from where Merlin hid. The stone roof, which had once formed a dome over the columns, had somehow been knocked down, for a great pile of mason-cut rubble lay heaped up on the right side, and part of the dome was still intact. Many of the fluted columns themselves had either been shorn off or toppled.

Atle stood in the center of the circle, and Arthur was with him — standing stiffly on a low, stone altar with his hands tied by a thin rope held in Atle's hand. He was bare chested, and fear covered his little face.

Then Merlin saw Kensa.

She stood beside Atle, holding her shredded purple hat and talking to him. He was nodding. Merlin looked behind him to where he had thought she would be, but only Bedwir, Peredur, Garth, and Caygek were with him. Merlin wondered if she had even entered the woods when they had left the road. She had probably set off straight to Atle.

Then he heard — back in the trees — the cracking of branches and the padding of many feet. *She had betrayed them!* Atle's warriors jumped forward with axes. Caygek leapt up and gutted one with his spear, but two more appeared right behind. Bedwir barely had time to draw his sword before they were upon them. Peredur and Garth ducked.

Anger flared up in Merlin's veins, and he took up his sword and swung it at the nearest warrior, slicing him through the ribs. Whirling, he slammed the pommel into the next one's head, and the man crumpled with a scream. One of the warriors was swinging an axe at Garth, and Merlin slammed his shoulder into the man and knocked him down.

Within moments another warrior stepped up and swung a heavy hammer. Merlin spun to get away, but not quickly enough. The hammer slammed him in the left arm just above the elbow. Something cracked, and Merlin fell to the ground in agonizing pain.

Bedwir had just killed a warrior when the man with the hammer slipped behind him.

Merlin yelled to warn him.

Bedwir ducked, but he hammer still gave him a glancing blow, and he collapsed.

Merlin tried to use his left arm, but something had broken in the elbow, and the intense pain shot to his shoulder and down his ribs. Where had his sword gone? He realized he had lost it in the dark. The muscles in his left hand began to cramp up, so he used his right to reach for the bag where his knife was hidden.

Ten more warriors jumped into the fray. Two of them disarmed Caygek. Garth and Peredur lay on their knees with their hands on the backs of their heads. Loth appeared out of the darkness, a sneering scowl on his face, and put the tip of his sword to Merlin's throat.

Merlin let go of the bag's knot. He would have to trust to his ruse now. There was no other hope.

The cold fled away, for the darkness was deliciously warm for Ganieda. It enfolded her. Held her. And its blackness was like the locks of her mother's hair. Her family's hearth appeared, and her mother was there, taking a loaf of honeyed bread from the fire. It smelled so delectably fresh, and the warm, soft bread slid down her throat to fill the emptiness.

Ganieda smiled at her mother. She was so beautiful. Even the druid scars that laced her arms and hands like spiderwebs added to her attraction. Most of the druid wives didn't undergo the scarring process, but her mother had. As the daughter of the arch druid, this was her right, and she had taken it.

Ganieda touched one of the blue lines and traced it upward toward her mother's sleeve until it swirled and knotted with another line. Ganieda became lost in the knot, and followed the line upward until she was lifted into the sky, and still the line plunged onward. Stars whirled above her, forming a shape. A wolf.

She heard a howl all around her. Deafening. Something breathed heavily nearby. Wetness dripped upon her cheek. More howls. She covered her ears.

The beast had returned.

She glanced upward, and its yellow fangs hung right above her, the horrid, black lips sagging over its blood-covered gums.

She screamed and closed her eyes. It was about to eat her, and she couldn't move. Couldn't breathe. Couldn't get away. Her running was over.

The wolf licked her. Again.

She opened her eyes and realized this wolf had a white muzzle. It was her wolf, Tellyk. He'd found her, after all this time.

He whimpered and nudged her again.

She sat up, and with her last ounce of strength pulled herself onto his back. Tellyk loped forward effortlessly. The snow stung her face, but she gripped his warm fur as they passed through the pines, through the trees, and to a tent where the light of a small fire shone upon the fabric walls. An old, cracked stump sat outside that she recognized. *This is Grandfather's tent!*

Tellyk barked as Ganieda slipped off.

"Grandfather ..." she called, falling on the ground before the door.

"My daughter's daughter, is that you?" He untied the flap, and soon he had it all the way open, displaying a face full of surprise. He helped her up, and she stepped in.

Tellyk made a move to follow her.

"I won't have that wolf in here. Out! Out!" he yelled. He tried to kick Tellyk, and the wolf backed up with a slight growl. Grandfather hastily tied the flaps again. "I've ... I've been worried. You've been missing so long, I had almost given up hope."

Ganieda wished Tellyk could come in and feel the warmth of the fire, but she didn't have the strength to protest. And besides, she saw the wolf lay down and lean his body against the door, leaving an impression on the tent wall. She could always reach her hand out and pet him if she wanted to show appreciation for her friend. Tellyk had helped her so much.

Grandfather threw on a few logs and warmed up some oatmeal for her.

"So ... so where did you get that torc?" he asked as he stirred the little pot. "I have not seen its like before in Britain, or in all of my travels." He touched the heads of the dragons; first the red one, then the white one. "Is this ... is this ..."

"A gift for me — from the Voice," she said, and her words sounded cold in her own ears. It was strange — her heart wanted to weep because of the torc, and the emotions welled up within her. But somehow that part of her had turned mute. No tears would come.

"From ... from the Voice?" her grandfather asked. "You have *seen* the Voice?"

"I've been with him an eternity. I see him all the time. He appears, and I speak with him. He is powerful and beautiful in my eyes, Grandpa." Her mind could still see the Voice. He was her father now, and he had always loved her. Oddly, she loved him and would do whatever he wanted of her. Had she felt that way before? She couldn't remember.

The wind blew against the tent then, and the bones hanging from the ceiling clinked into each other. Grandpa handed her the pot of oatmeal.

She wanted to eat it right away but instead took a moment to fill her lungs with its goodness before digging in her spoon. Oh, how the oatmeal gave her strength, and how the fire warmed her life and limbs. She laid her head down on the oxhide and slept for awhile, finally waking to see her grandfather sitting on his carved chair.

"You have slept long, my daughter's daughter, while our enemies await their doom!" His lone hand held the orb engulfed in a violence of purple fire. The fang was not in sight.

Ganieda leapt up to see the images flashing in the orb, and Merlin was there. A hatred for him, pure and delightful, burned deeply in her. He was being forced to bow before an old man upon a windswept mountain that she had never seen before. And someone held a sword at Merlin's throat, a man who looked much like Merlin did, with his long black hair and handsome nose, but without the scars. The man scowled at Merlin, and this pleased her. Perhaps he could be useful to her. Useful to the Voice.

"He is Loth," her grandfather said. "I have heard his name spoken in another vision the orb gave to me. He is — "

"Most helpful!" Ganieda finished. The man was young and strong, and there was a certain spirit about him, opposite of Merlin's, that thrilled her.

And there stood little Arthur. The child whom her grandfather hated. Whom the Voice hated. Whom she now hated most deeply. His hands were bound, and he stood upon an altar covered in clotted blood. The old man held the rope in one hand, and a long knife in the other.

Grandfather laughed. "See ... see! Both Merlin and Arthur will soon be no more!"

CHAPTER 38

THE SCARS OF FAILURE

Merlin gagged, for a horrible smell wafted up from the blood-soaked ground where he knelt.

Atle stood before him, his legs wrapped in furs, and if Loth hadn't had a sword at the back of Merlin's neck, he would jump up and...

Merlin sighed. His sword was gone, and his bag had been snatched from him and thrown in a heap with the rest of their things about ten feet away — his hidden knife within it.

And even if Merlin did get away from Loth and attack Atle, it would be more likely that Atle would kill Merlin first, for Merlin's left elbow was indeed broken. The joint sent waves of cramping pain so intense that he couldn't do anything with it except let it hang limp. And the old man was stronger than he looked. Merlin had learned that when they'd sparred over the candlestick in the king's private chamber.

The king cleared his throat. "Look up to me, O Merlin. For Kensa has, beyond my amazement, arrived at de last moment to preserve her own life ... andd dat of yers as well."

"Preserve my life? You mean she betrayed me."

"Betrayed you? No, dat is not my mother's intent, for she loves you more dan you know. You are de son of my daughter, Theneva Gweviana, as Kensa most ardently reminds me, andd therefore ye have de right to participate by blood in de rite that is about to be performed."

"I don't care—"

Atle kicked Merlin hard in the mouth. "Listen, O Fool! I hadd chosen to withhold dis from you because of your mother's disobedience, but now dat you are here, I will give ett, at Kensa's behest, if you are nott impudent andd presuming."

"Give what?" Merlin slurred, spitting out the blood that had begun to gather.

"I offer you nothing less dan undying strength, eternal youth, andd joy. I offer ye a place en me family for eternity."

"I only want Arthur free," Merlin said.

"Ah, but ye don't understand *properly*. Lett me help ye before yerr choice es no longer possible." He held the rope so Arthur's hands were lifted upward, and he cut a thin line down Arthur's chest with his knife. The child cried out, squirmed, and tried to get away, but Atle held him fast. He let the blood to trickle downward and caught some on the tip of his knife.

"Here, feel and desire de gift I offer you, for ett es amazement." With these words, he let Arthur's blood drip into an old pool of gore at his feet. Then he grabbed onto Merlin's hair and hauled him forward until Merlin stared into the liquid. In the murky mirror, a vision appeared.

Merlin saw himself rising upward, strong and hale. In the vision the years passed, and he began to age a little, until another ninth year approached when he needed to renew the blood sacrifice to make himself young again. For an eon the cycle raged, and each time Merlin matured more quickly until he, too, grew old by the ninth year — like Atle. But Merlin could still live, couldn't he? Yes, it was true. For as long as the sacrifices were renewed.

Something else caught his attention. In the vision, his scars had vanished completely from his face. Utterly gone.

Natalenya could love him. His heart could trust her. Trust that she wouldn't abandon him when she tired of looking at his ugly visage. Trust that she wouldn't regret her marriage to him.

Did Atle really offer him what God had denied him? Could it be true? And all he had to do was say yes. He could look like Loth. They could be brothers. Two alike, friends, and handsome forever. Every part of him longed to say the word. Every part of him screamed at God for the injustice of his disfigurement. Why hadn't God taken his scars away? Protected them during their journeys? Why?

"Vat is your answer?" the king asked. "Vill ye partake in de blood of de little one?"

Merlin looked once more at Arthur. His dark hair was disheveled, and his wrists raw from the rope. But he was just a child. Not even capable of real speech. Wasn't the world filled with uncountable children? Did it really matter if one was slain so that Merlin could be free of his scars? No one would even miss Arthur's passing. The boy's parents were dead. Perhaps it was best for Arthur. This way, he would never know the anguish of loneliness. The world was cruel, was it not? His suffering would end, and in that end he would also relieve Merlin's suffering.

Atle gave a wheezing chuckle. "I see your thoughts, andd ye are right. A little suffering ferr everlasting profit. Perhaps one day everyone in de world can benefit from de blood of de little ones. You vill join me, yes?"

Merlin wanted to agree. To nod his head. To whimper out the word. But then he beheld Arthur's eyes, and saw fear, confusion, pain, suffering. All these emotions and more, accusing Merlin. But an accusation only had weight before a judge. Was God a judge? Would God judge Merlin?

Yes. For it was God who had formed Arthur in Igerna's womb.

God who had fashioned the boy in mystery and fear. God who had planned his days before any of them came to pass. And God would hold Merlin accountable for his blood.

Do not murder, the Scriptures said, and so Merlin spit into the pool of blood and sent the horrible vision rippling away. He would stay the same. Merlin the scarred. Merlin the unloved. Merlin the despised. Merlin the dead — yes — but better dead in God's righteous hands than alive and hale in the devil's filthy ones. So be it.

"No," he said. "Take your bloody knife and kill me as well. Get it over with."

"Dat I shall. Each o' you will be sacrificed after de child dies. Too bad you don't appreciate me hard bargain: yerr freedom for Arthur. Now ye lose both." And he plunged the knife deep into Arthur's gut. A scream ripped forth from the child, his face turned red, and he began to thrash in agony. Arthur's blood poured down onto the altar, and Atle smiled in triumph.

Ganieda rubbed her hands together as she watched Merlin through the orb. He was considering his fate, bowed with his gaze intent upon the strange vision in the pool of blood.

And when he finally spoke his answer, and Atle plunged the knife into Arthur, she clapped. Yes — their family's vengeance was nearly complete! When the Stone still had its power, Uther had killed her grandfather's son — Ganieda's uncle — and now Uther's son was dead. Merlin's death would soon follow.

Mórganthu got up from his chair and began to dance around the tent, the orb a streak of purple light as he giddily jumped about.

Ganieda joined him, holding on to his waist.

Around and around they twirled in celebration, until a sound echoed from the orb. A man's scream. It sounded like Merlin's voice.

Mórganthu knelt on one knee, and together they looked once more.

CHAPTER 39

BLOOD AND DARKNESS

Merlin struggled to rise, yelling. If he had two good arms, he could —

Loth viscously kicked him in the small of his back. "Stay down, dog head. Ye'll have no part in this."

As Merlin fell flat on his stomach, he lifted his head to keep it from dropping into the bloody snow, and so the tip of Loth's sword cut into the nape of his neck. The pain tore a yell from his throat — yet he kept his eyes fixed on Arthur, who was in the throes of death.

Like sparks from a fire, a crackling darkness burst out from Atle's knife where it had sunk into Arthur. A stain upon the air, it climbed Atle's arm and engulfed his whole being. Kensa grabbed his belt. All around Merlin, the people of Atle's household stepped up and held hands, making a direct connection to the king. Then others — natives of these islands — joined as well.

And the darkness spread.

The sword slipped away from Merlin's neck, and Loth's boot

eased its pressure. Merlin spun savagely around and lifted himself into a crouch. Pain surged from his broken elbow, and he had to prop it on his thigh as best he could.

All around him, a black undulating web covered the people — everyone but his friends, who were cowering down in shock. The torches took on an eerie, red glow in the hands of the people, frozen in position.

Atle himself began to change. Taller he grew, and less stooped. The deep lines of his face smoothed. His arms and legs solidified with muscle. His hair lengthened, thickened, and the gray disappeared.

Merlin panicked. He had only a few moments. Atle's youth would soon be complete and Merlin would be overpowered. He leapt at the pile of their belongings, but the weapons weren't there. They had been left in the woods, no doubt. With no time to look for them, he dug, found his bag, and opened it with one hand. There was the map! He pulled the rolled-up leather out and dumped the knife to the ground.

He froze before taking the knife. A strangely familiar lump lay in the bottom of the bag. He opened it wide. It was the Sangraal. The very bowl he had flung into the ocean. The bowl he'd rejected. How did it — ? Why — ?

He looked from the knife ... to the bowl ... and back to the knife. He had to choose.

Black smoke swirled inside the orb, and then lit up with a soft purple radiance. Soon the image cleared and Ganieda spied Arthur crying out in pain and kicking his legs. She felt like a happy pig, wallowing in his death.

And Merlin, her poor, poor brother — hah! — did that little slice to the neck hurt? Soon Loth would thrust the blade right through his heart, and Ganieda wouldn't even shed a tear.

A black, bubbling web began to cover Atle, and all the people with him. The king began to get younger, and Loth as well — yet in the midst of the changes happening to his body, he forgot to keep Merlin pinned down.

"Stop him!" she cried out, but Loth couldn't hear.

Her brother escaped and dove to his bag, his left arm hanging like a broken branch. He dropped a roll of leather from it and shook a knife from the center. Then he opened the bag wider to reveal a wooden bowl.

Strange. Why would he care about a bowl at such a time?

But the bowl grew larger and larger inside the orb, its grain and edges beginning to glow. Soon the bowl became a white blaze, which stung Ganieda's eyes. She continued to look, but the light became so bright that she fell backward, squinting until she could stand it no longer.

The orb began to burn in Grandfather's hand and he dropped it, yelling.

The light faded and the orb cooled, and he tried once more to see Merlin, but the only image to appear was of the sky and the bright sun shining down from the heavens. It refused to show Merlin or anyone else with him.

She grabbed onto her grandfather's arm. "What's happening? What's wrong with it?"

He shook his head. "Perhaps the orb is wounded. Perhaps afraid."

"But I need to see. I want to see Arthur die. *I need to see Merlin die!*" She screamed at him and stamped her foot.

"Perhaps, my daughter's daughter, you can travel there and see for yourself. Then come back and tell me."

She glimpsed fear on his countenance, and she pondered this for a moment. Had she ever seen real fear in him before?

"Why do you wait?" he said, holding out the orb. "Remember ... remember when you visited Vortigern on the boat? And the Pictish chieftain in the valley? Do it again!"

He handed it to her, and a delight buzzed up her arm as its warm, soft flesh filled her palm. She called upon the orb to take her to Merlin.

Once again it began to grow heavy in her hand until it rolled to the floor. Soon it was beyond her height, and still it grew, changing shape now into the head of a phantasmal lizard. Like a dragon it was; red, gigantic, and powerful, with great curled horns like that of a ram's. Its mouth opened and a flickering light could be seen down its throat. This time she did not scream. She did not flinch. She lunged within, and the ghostlike creature swallowed her whole. The great tongue pushed her down the greasy, palpating throat, the world darkened, and she floated down. The air chilled and her feet rested upon a slushy, bloody hilltop not three paces from Merlin.

Merlin had to decide between the knife and the Sangraal, for his left arm throbbed uselessly at his side.

Without more than a moment's hesitation, he grabbed the knife.

But after two steps, he realized he was holding the Sangraal. He turned back angrily and saw the knife laying on the ground. He dropped the bowl, grabbed the knife, and again the same thing happened. The bowl, with its gritty wooden rim, was pinched between the fingers of his right hand. He fell to his knees, set the bowl down, and picked up the knife.

Why would the Sangraal be here? Now? And why couldn't he get rid of it? The fool thing hadn't worked. Yet a voice from his vision filled his head. It was the fisherman turned king, singing in joy as his great and painful wound had been healed:

Trust not in guile, or in a hoard —
trust in the power of Christ, your Lord.
Not in the wood, or in a sword —
here lays the blood of Christ, yes, poured.
Let death break forth, and blade's bright rust —
at the judgment they turn to dust.
And when you fail, in thick disgust —
there, in the Christ of heaven, do trust.

No greed for life, or soul who's dead —
can steal you from the Son, who bled.
And for your sin, and feeble dread —
Christ brought his blood to earth, to shed.
When fools must choose, and black the night —
when all is wrong and wrong seems right —
Then take the cup, your faith in Christ,
and wage the war, with His great might.

The words echoed in Merlin's ears, and for the first time he really listened to them. Like the gentian tea his mother had made him drink when he was young, the words were bitter yet cleansing. He'd been wrong. So wrong. Wrong to trust in the Sangraal rather than the *God* of the Sangraal. Wrong to trust in his own abilities apart from the God who had made him. Wrong to lose faith in God.

He cried out then, and tears began to blur his eyes. But there was no time for that — for Arthur's dying screams filled the air.

A spark of hope — and of faith — filled Merlin's heart. Faith in the God who had led him during each painful step of his life: his childhood, his blindness, his battle with the Stone — even during this journey of suffering over the last half of a year. Faith in the One who had, up until now, protected them all. Protected them in the midst of Natalenya's sickness. She hadn't died, had she? At least not yet as far as Merlin knew. Could he trust God even for that?

But what if she did die? What if Merlin died — all of them? The worst thing that would happen was God would enfold them in His arms and lead them on high to a feasting hall so great and mighty that the richest kings of the world would be as beggars at the door.

Begging to see God.

God.

The true reward.

Merlin had been such a fool.

He dropped the knife and picked up the bowl — such a simple bowl, really, blackened with antiquity. There in the bottom lay a single drop of blood. And this wasn't at all like the blood shed by Atle — who lusted after the life of others — but rather it *must* be, somehow, the blood of Christ, who had given it willingly for his children. The smell of a flower radiated from the bowl more fragrant than if all the bursting, tender rose petals of Kernow had been gathered togethe.

Merlin ran, then, in faith. Not at Atle for revenge — but to the pagan altar next to Atle where Arthur jerked against the impaled knife.

And there she stood. Little Ganieda. His sister. Once more she had appeared to him, and now stood in his way. A torc with the heads of dragons lay curled around her throat, and an icy hatred gleamed from her eyes. She put up a hand to stop him.

"Dear brother ... where are you going with that?"

He edged sideways, but she turned to block him.

"What are you holding? Let me look."

So he held it out to her.

She backed away.

He pushed it closer.

"Don't touch me with it!" she hissed.

Another step, and he held it right under her nose. "Please, this is for you as well. Take it."

She screamed, dodged past Loth — and disappeared among the black pulses of the web.

Merlin spun around. Where had she gone?

Arthur cried again — hardly more than a whimper.

The boy had fallen onto his blood-soaked knees. The crackling darkness engulfed him and he fell prone. His body grew, as in a vision: his legs and arms lengthened until soon Arthur lay there on the altar as a mighty man with a glorious torc upon his throat — the torc of a king! Light shown from his flesh and Merlin started to cover his eyes. But then the blobs of shadow grew upon his chest into two, huge ravens, black and fell, and they clawed at his wound and ripped at his flesh with their beaks. Arthur's light began to fade.

Merlin shouted at the birds and tried to scare them away, but they turned on him and the right one scratched his shoulder with its talon, cutting deeply.

Merlin yelled in pain and backed up. Then, holding the Sangraal before him, he shoved it at the birds.

They screeched, the smell of death issuing from their throats.

Merlin stepped closer, holding his breath, and the birds flapped off into the air and burst like rain clouds, pouring their blackness down to the ground in great, sizzling drops.

Arthur was now little again, the kingly vision having faded.

Yet the freakish smile covering Atle's face was no vision, and his transformation was almost complete. His arms had become three times as strong. His hair had darkened, and lay upon his shoulders in long and wavy tendrils. His torso and legs were muscled, and even his clothes had been renewed. But the king's eyes were dead, with only a lust for more blood written around the pupils.

Well, Merlin would give him one drop more. He poured out the solitary trickle upon the altar between Arthur's little knees, trusting Christ that no matter what came, all would be well.

And nothing happened.

Arthur fell down in a heap.

The black web had left Atle now, and he released the rope and withdrew the knife. The man looked with pleasure upon his hands and arms.

Poor Arthur rolled onto his back, his lifeless eyes looking up to the dark sky.

Clutching the Sangraal, Merlin lifted the boy up and held him close.

Atle turned and saw Merlin. He clenched his teeth and raised the knife to strike.

Merlin kissed Arthur on his cold cheek and bowed his head before Atle. He wanted to die with the boy, and tensed himself.

But the stroke didn't fall.

Atle stepped back even as water began to trickle down the altar.

There was something strange about this water, however — it was bright with a crystal shine unlike anything Merlin had ever seen. It bubbled up from where he had poured the drop from the Sangraal, and the previous gore fizzled away. Even the altar itself began to disappear — like a chunk of snow thrown into a stream.

At first the water poured past Merlin's boots. Then it made waves over his ankles. The altar broke apart and sunk so that the water burst from the ground itself, as if a well had opened up in the earth. The mountain shook, and a roaring sound echoed from its depths.

Atle and the others of his household stepped away, but fissures opened all around them.

A youthful Kensa screamed as geysers of glowing water poured from the ground, charring her beautiful purple gown and flawless skin. The old columns of the temple crashed down, crushing many. Atle shouted as he was knocked into the swirling cataclysm of water, his body burning and smoking until nothing more could be seen of it.

Merlin slipped and fell — the deluge washing him away. The trees cracked off around him, the mountainside shook, and the roar of the water washed downward. He gasped for air, holding tightly to Arthur's body, and trying to keep his head up.

Down the mountain he rolled, first on his side, then on his back. The bright water gushed over his face and he coughed. Arthur's body began to escape his grip, but he scooped him closer. His knee hit a rock, and a tree limb slammed into his back. Kicking with his legs, he broke to the air and struggled for breath. Down the mountainside, faster and faster he spun until the first walls of the ruined city passed by, and still the water poured from the top of the mountain.

He reached out to a wide ledge of rock, grabbed on, and pulled himself up with help from his legs. Only at that time did he realize his left arm didn't hurt. A winter breeze picked up across the island, tousling his hair, but his skin had been strangely warmed by the water, and he didn't feel cold. He sat up wearily and laid Arthur's body on his knees.

All around him the old, dead trees caught fire, snapped, and fell into the water. The bodies of the sacrificed fell with them and disappeared beneath the flood. Above him, the night sky lit up with undulating swirls of blue, green, purple, and red. The strange lights illuminated the devastation flowing by: broken trees, brush, and vegetation were mixed with the smoking bodies of Atle's household.

Arthur sneezed.

Merlin saw, then, that the dreadful wound in the boy's stomach had been healed, though a great scar remained. Merlin picked him up again just as Arthur opened his eyes. The boy reached out, clasped Merlin's wet hair — and sighed.

Only then did Merlin weep.

Ganieda panicked. Merlin was pushing the bowl closer and closer, and it smelled more foul than anything she had ever encountered. She started to gag.

And then the bowl began to glow, just as it had when she'd seen it in the orb. She could feel its white-hot heat on her neck. "Don't touch me with it!" she said, backing away.

But Merlin came closer and pressed the horrible thing to her nose as if to brand her. Yes, he wanted to scar *her* face just as his had been. Vile revenge! His mouth spoke some words, but they were lost in her own screaming.

She whirled to the side, slipped behind Loth's black, pulsing body, and watched.

Merlin looked confused for a moment, searching for her. Then he brought the gleaming bowl to the king's altar — and poured forth a liquid brighter than the sun itself. It burned her vision and she hid her eyes.

A deep sense of doom gripped her heart. They would die, yes, all of them, unless she ... But what could she do? Her grandfather had foolishly not remembered to give her the fang. *If only he'd given her the fang!*

Then the Voice whispered in her ear — giving her a new task. Yes, she would do it — for this man before her was attractive and his soul would serve the Voice's cause well.

Ganieda reached forward, grabbed on to Loth's belt, and pulled him backward until his grip broke with those around him.

When he realized what had happened, he turned angrily upon her.

She embraced him, calling upon the orb to take her back. Her vision blurred and they lifted from the mountaintop. Far away, as if through a tunnel, she saw water pour forth from the altar. King Atle perished in a puff of smoke, as did the others. The vision fled away from her sight, and through darkness and wind she tumbled, gripping Loth tightly, until her vision cleared.

Once again she stood in Grandfather's tent — this time with Loth beside her. The orb rested in her hand once again, but where was the fang? She needed it to kill Merlin. Her grandfather had it, had kept it from her ... and his surprised face at their arrival told her that now was the time to take what was by rights hers alone.

"Give it to me," Ganieda demanded.

He shook his head, confused. "What, what? You come back so soon? And with Loth? But why ... What has happened?"

"Merlin isn't dead, and I know nothing of Arthur." She narrowed her eyes. "*Give me the fang!*"

"I will not. You have trifled with it for too long, and I found it at the risk of my life. You are a foolish child, and I will not give it."

"Where am I?" Loth demanded. "What happened to my father ... the others?"

"All will be answered," Ganieda said, glancing at his youthful strength. Yes, he would be *very* helpful to the Voice. But she would need more. A very army of loyal servants.

She turned back to her grandfather — for he had to submit as well. The Voice had told her so. "Give it to me," Ganieda said once more, this time with more vehemence. The orb in her hand began to burn purple before her, and sparks flew from its center. She advanced on her grandfather.

He backed up, fumbling in his bag with his one hand.

Ganieda would need help here. If only Loth were trained ... but no, he was not yet useful. He would not understand. She whistled, and the tent ripped behind her. Within moments, Tellyk stood at her side, growling at her grandfather.

"Give me the fang!"

"I will not!" He had it out now, threatening her. Jumping to the side to put Ganieda between himself and the wolf, he lunged at her and jabbed the fang into her shoulder.

She didn't recoil, for it didn't hurt. The Voice had said that the fang was *hers* and it could not harm her. Strength emanated from the bloodless wound, and Ganieda grew. Taller. Stronger.

Grandfather staggered back, gasping. He shrunk down before her.

No longer Ganieda the little, she would now and always be Gana the great ... *Mórgana*. A fear to all Britons who followed the Christ. High servant of the Voice. True master of the Stone, the Fang, and the Orb. A worthy wife for Loth. Yes, *she* would return the rule of Britain to the Voice, and no one — not even Merlin — would stop her.

Tellyk lunged at Grandfather and knocked him down. Ganieda — no, *Mórgana* — stepped over and wrenched the green glowing fang from his quivering grasp.

The deadly power of the fang writhed in her hand, bringing even more strength. Lifting high the orb, she commanded it to take her to Merlin. Its flame rekindled, and it grew within her palm. But then the orb paused ... and then shrunk back to its normal size.

"Take me to Merlin!" she screamed, but it refused. She yelled in rage. Lightning split the heavens and a thunderous wind buffeted the tent. Loth fell to his knees before her rage; even Tellyk crouched and whined.

Then a whisper tickled her ear, and her temper receded. The answer, the Voice said, lay not with the orb or fang, but within the Stone — and she must go and speak with it. Truly it had been injured by Merlin's blade, and even though Grandfather was too old to hear its weakened voice, she could.

To the Stone, then ... To the Stone!

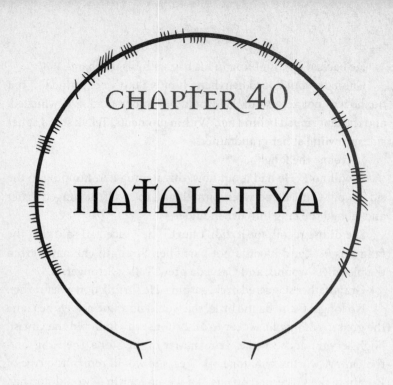

CHAPTER 40

ΠΑΤΑΛΕΠΥΑ

Merlin knelt in a silent prayer of thanksgiving once their boat set sail.

Everyone was accounted for and on board — everyone that is except Kensa, who had died with Atle and the others whose lives relied on the pagan ritual. Merlin had fished Bedwir from the water as he floated by. Peredur had found his way to a pillar and held on until the flood passed. Garth had pulled two small logs together and climbed on top. And Caygek, poor Caygek; he'd grabbed on to a shattered tree stump at the top of the hill and had nearly been drowned by the onrush.

And each one of them rejoiced in Arthur's return — not only to health, but also to their safekeeping. Before they left, Peredur found a needle used to repair sails and stitched up a tunic and small cloak for the boy, and soon he was running around on the deck of the ship as if nothing had happened to him.

The ship itself was provided by Atle, for his death left many boats abandoned in a small harbor on the other side of the mountain. Garth picked the biggest — provisioned, seaworthy, and ready to sail.

As Merlin prayed, there at the prow of the ship he heard and felt the old boards creak under his knees as someone knelt next to him. Not wanting to disturb the other, he kept his eyes closed and kept praying. His companion was praying too, for Merlin caught a few of his whispered words. The two of them stayed there for a good while, and only then did Merlin sit up and open his eyes.

And blinked. Caygek, praying? When he finished, he laid his arm over the rail and eyed Merlin with a solemn face.

"Were you ...?" Merlin asked.

"What of it? You've seen it before."

"Not you."

"I've offered up prayers all my life. Is there a problem?"

"But I heard you ... you were praying ... to Jesu Christus."

"Let's just say that I've never seen anything like what happened up there. The others saw it too. Bedwir says it was the Sangraal you held, the bowl that caught the blood of Christ at his death."

But Merlin guessed there was something more, and had been suspecting it for a long time. "Is that the only thing that brought you to believe?"

Caygek looked away toward the west. "No. It was your love for Arthur. Your willingness to sacrifice yourself for him. You ... and everyone else."

Merlin felt very humble. Where Caygek had seen faith, all Merlin had felt was doubt and failure. If God could use such an imperfect servant, then God was great indeed.

Caygek reached out and touched Merlin on the shoulder. "I've been a man of principle all my life," he said, "and I have rarely found it in others. And so I was ashamed that you all — even Peredur — were willing to risk everything when all I wanted to do was run away like a hunted buck."

"We were all afraid," Merlin said. "Most of all me." He held Caygek's shoulder in return. "I'm glad you came."

"Not that I had much choice with those warriors chasing me down the dock. I guess God had other ideas."

"For me as well. Where will you go from here?"

Caygek shrugged. "I want you to know, I've learned that those who are humbled the most have their eyes opened widest. I was hoping ... hoping you'd have me as one of Arthur's protectors."

"But, Caygek — "

"Bedwir's already sworn himself, and Peredur too."

"But — "

"He'll need more than two, won't he?"

A smile crept slowly over Merlin's face. "He'll need an entire warband, yes."

"Then you'll have me?"

Merlin nodded, and they embraced.

The voyage back to Britain was, to say the least, uneventful considering the travails of their journey north. A solid, wooden hull helped with that, and they even had a sturdy cabin below deck to retreat to, warm themselves up, and sleep in. Garth sailed them on a different route, however, because the winds and waves forced them a long way westward before they could turn south.

Yet as the days passed, the ocean rolled on, and the winds blew them toward Dinpelder, Merlin's worry grew. Was Natalenya still alive? Dread roiled his gut like a rancid meal he couldn't get rid of. Each night he fell asleep holding on to the Sangraal, yet putting his trust in the God of the Sangraal as much as he could rather than the bowl itself. But it was hard, for when he tried to pray, his old doubts throttled him, and he had to beat them back with his newly strengthened faith. God was in control. God was sovereign and ruling from his throne.

When they sailed within sight of the Pictish coast, Garth kept them a safe distance away, and they followed this route down until they neared the northern lands of Atle's kingdom. When the morning of their arrival came, Merlin was awakened by a shout from Garth, who stood on deck above the hold.

"Merlin, we're here! Come quick!"

He rubbed his eyes, and in the dim light gathered his few things. Then he wrapped his cloak about himself, pulled himself up onto the deck, and stepped out into the morbid light of a thinly veiled sun, the wind running from the steerboard side. From the prow he spied the land of northern Britain, the little harbor village, and the great hill of Dinpelder beyond.

Smoke billowed upward from the fortress.

"What is it?" he asked Garth, who stood beside him.

"I was hopin' you'd tell me."

They sailed into the harbor and found the town in chaos, with villagers gathering things and many of them fleeing. Letting down the sail, Garth steered them near to the dock, and Merlin tied the ship to a post.

The smoke from Atle's fortress thickened.

Merlin jumped out and spied Aulaf with some men loading barrels into one of the many small rowboats. No other large vessels could be seen in the harbor.

"Aulaf!" Merlin called. "What's happening?"

The man looked up in surprise to see Merlin. He rushed over. "We are attacked, yah? We must leave!"

"We have friends at the hof!"

"It's gone. Collapsed days ago. Very strange, yah? And even if you tried, you won't make it. The Picti are burning the fortress, yah? Thousands of them!"

So Necton had raised an army and come back for revenge. Merlin shuddered to think of it. Atle had controlled most of the northern kingdom. Would Necton take it all? Would this increase the slave raids to the south? If that Pict knew Merlin and the others were here, he'd want Arthur back as his son.

"They're coming!" Aulaf said. "And since you lost my little ship, all I have is a few rowboats."

Merlin smiled at him. "I'm giving you this one, Aulaf. King Atle and his house will never need it again. But I need to find my friends — an old man and a girl who are strangers here."

Aulaf gave Merlin a worried glance. "No girl, but an old man, yah. Named Colly-bar."

"Colvarth … his name is Colvarth. You've seen him?"

"Sure, he was walking through the village less than an hour ago. Looked very sad. Asked if I had a shovel. He said he had to bury something. I told him there was no time, yah?"

Merlin gulped.

"Hey … you give me a bigger boat, you get your sword back. You may need it. I don't know how to use it, anyway. I just catch fish and pickle 'em, yah? Swords are no good for that." He unstrapped a new leather scabbard from his waist and handed it and the blade to Merlin.

Merlin took hold of it, hardly caring. "W-Where's Colvarth now?"

"Down the shore, I think, a brown house, yah?"

Aulaf yelled for his men to start loading the cargo onto Merlin's ship. Before Aulaf could go and help them, Merlin grabbed his arm and turned him around.

"Don't sail away without us."

"Wait here, yah?"

"Yes." Merlin turned and called to Bedwir, instructing him and the others to stay on the boat. Then he ran down the dock to the shore.

But he was quickly frustrated. A brown house? They were all built from a type of brown rock, every last one of them. The first house was deserted, with the door hanging open. The second one had the door closed, and Merlin knocked loudly.

"Colvarth! It's Merlin," he yelled, but no one answered. The next house was the same, and the one after that. At the fourth house, a man opened the door, brandishing a spear. Merlin backed away, telling him he wasn't a Pict.

At the end of the row, he finally arrived at a ramshackle roundhouse with a rotting roof. What had been the door now lay in decayed chunks and splinters on the ground. He caught his breath when he heard the faint sounds of a harp. Stepping closer, he spied Colvarth sitting near a small fire with his eyes closed, playing a sad and mournful tune. Next to him lay a pallet lumped with moth-eaten woolen blankets.

Merlin's words caught in his throat, so he purposefully scuffed his boot.

Colvarth saw him and his fingers froze on the harp strings. He stood stiffly, bowed, and shuffled over to him, his head down. "I saw the ship coming, and I'd hoped it was you. But I was afraid to — "

"It-It's all right," Merlin said, his throat closing up.

"That is best, for she needs the rest, and I didn't want to wake her."

"Wake her? You mean — "

"She sleeps, yes."

Merlin blinked. "Aulaf, the man at the dock, he told me you needed to bury — "

"The dog, yes. Yapping thing! It choked on a bone and I could not save it, not that I was sure I wanted to, for it ate too much food. But it comforted Natalenya, so I tried."

An arm raised up from the wool blankets, and Natalenya rolled to face them. The boils now covered her face, and she blinked at him.

"Colvarth, is someone here?"

The bard leaned close to Merlin. "She cannot see anymore, it is that bad."

Merlin went to her, dropped to his knees, and gently lifted her into his arms.

"Who is this?" she said. "Colvarth, who is this?" She pushed him to arms length, sniffed the air, and then reached her hand out ...

and touched his nose gently, hesitantly. Her fingers found one of his scars and traced it down to his left cheek, wet with a newly shed tear. Then she pulled him close and they hugged in earnest.

"Merlin, you've come back to me. Is Arthur — ?"

"He's safe, and we have him with us. God gave us the victory, and Atle is dead, along with his household."

But there was other news he didn't know how to say.

"Loth died too."

"I don't care about him. I only want you. I only ever wanted you."

He pulled back a little and turned his face to the side. "Not with the scars."

She touched his chin and turned him to face her. Then she kissed him on the thickest scar that cut across his right cheekbone. "Always with the scars. Never without. You wouldn't be you without each and every one. I need them. I'm safe with them and them only."

Merlin cried, his mouth open and his breath catching in his throat. Did she really love him that way? He had been wrong to doubt her. To doubt himself. Could he fully trust his heart to her? He would only know if he asked.

"Natalenya ... will you ... will you still marry me?"

She pulled away from him.

"Natalenya, I — "

"You can't marry me. I'm untouchable ... I'm ..."

Now this was a switch. He'd worried about her ability to love him, while she couldn't believe that he could love her. But he *could*, boils and all, and if he could love her unconditionally, couldn't she do the same?

He stroked the hair on top of her head. "I don't care about the sickness. I need you. No matter what happens, we'll face it together, to the very end ... Will you marry me?"

"Oh, yes," she said, and turned back and embraced him again, sobbing onto his cloak, and he onto the blanket that lay across her shoulder, and he wanted their hug to never end.

Except — but he had to try. In trust this time, not in the Sangraal but in God himself. He knew that God meant good, and if he chose to heal her now, then fine. And if not, then God would do so in heaven.

He pulled back, wiped his eyes, and untied his bag. His hands shook as he slipped the Sangraal out and placed it in her hands. He didn't even look inside, but rather trusted.

"Drink this," he said.

"What is it?"

"Love and trust the Lord your God with all your heart, with all your soul, and with all your strength ... come what may."

She drank from it, her blind eyes staring into nothingness. And then she blinked.

"Merlin!"

"Yes?"

"I see you. I can see you!"

And the black boils upon her face began to shrink away and melt into her skin. The oozing sores dried up and disappeared. A rosy flush returned to her cheeks.

She sat up, feeling the skin on her forearms, and pulled up her sleeves to look for any boils that remained — yet there were none. She smiled, then, brighter and happier than Merlin had ever seen. She stood on two hale feet and walked into his arms.

Colvarth coughed at the door, looking embarrassed. "Sorry, my Merlin, to interrupt, but we must leave. I fear it may already be too late."

Outside, screams could be heard.

"The Picts are raiding the village. We must go, or become slaves again."

Merlin led the way, holding Natalenya's hand, and she helping Colvarth. He had them crouch down at each house as they made their way back along the shore to the dock. Some of the houses in the distance had been put to flame, and villagers ran past them, their arms full of blankets, pots, and weapons.

Merlin drew his father's sword. It felt good to have it just now.

They barely made it to the dock in time, and when they reached the boat, Caygek threw them a rope ladder. Natalenya climbed up first, followed by Colvarth

Merlin grabbed on to the ladder and pulled himself upward. Caygek smiled and helped him onto the deck.eredur and Aulaf raised the sail, and Garth steered them away from the harbor.

That night they all gathered and ate roasted fish over an iron pot of embers. Natalenya sat next to Merlin with little Arthur eating from a bowl next to her. Taking her hand, Merlin squeezed it and asked, "Where shall we put ashore?"

She looked once more at him with her beautiful green eyes and leaned her head upon his shoulder. "Does it matter?"

He sighed. No, it didn't matter. It really didn't matter anymore. *Natalenya.*

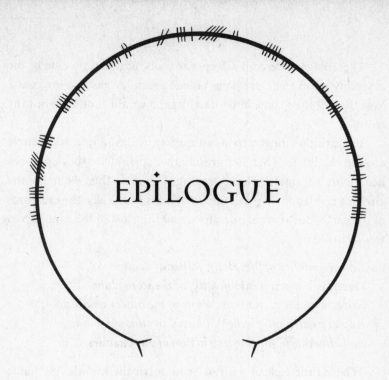

EPILOGUE

It was the time of *Hanternos*, and Mórgana had goaded the remaining four druidow to attend her at the Stone, including her impudent grandfather. Loth supported her with his ready blade in this task, but the druidow didn't need much coaxing — they were, after all, hoping that some sign of life might come from the Stone.

And aiding her cause was their astonishment at her transformation from a girl to a grown woman. Mórgana reveled in her newfound strength.

And Loth was more than eager to see the Stone, all his questions about how he came to Kernow having been answered to his satisfaction. Indeed, though he mourned the death of his father, his father's household, and the destruction of the temple that made their long life possible, he found a deep satisfaction in his association with Mórgana. The man longed to heap bloody revenge upon the heads of Merlin and Arthur, and in this they found their common ground.

The villagers were all asleep, the fools, and had no clue of the assembly upon their precious village green. A pasture for goats? Was that all they considered it? Mórgana would soon find out the truth.

The druidow began to chant quietly, walking in a wide circle around the Stone. Then her grandfather sprinkled ashes upon her head with a trembling hand, saying, "Thus ... thus we make the circle of revelation. We call upon the stars in the sky, the creatures of the earth, our revered ancestors, and this dust of the nine sacred woods to aid us:

Rowan, mother of life; Holly, father of death;
Hazel, of darkest wisdom; Oak, of the stout club;
Birch, with the secret roots; Pine, of the otherworldly door;
Apple, feeding our flesh; Willow, of the unseen wind;
and Hawthorn, for the destruction of our enemies.

"These nine I plead with to bring forth the knowledge that is hidden."

Mórgana knelt down amongst some abandoned copper coins and touched the craggy surface of the Stone — avoiding the offending blade that stuck out from it.

Mórgana must make the Stone speak once more. In the past, her grandfather had spoken to the Voice himself by touching the Stone, but there was a deeper secret here, for there were *other voices* hiding within the Stone.

Did Grandfather even know this secret? Mórgana doubted it. The Voice had told her, and her alone. To Grandfather, the purpose of the Stone was simply to enchant the stupid Britons so that they would follow him. How quaint. How boring. He knew nothing. *Nothing.* The orb and the fang should have been his clue, but did he even take a moment to ponder their origin? Why had she found them in the bottom of her father's forge underneath the hole made by the sword?

But the faintest hint of a hum interrupted her thoughts — emanating from the surface of the Stone. She pressed her palms more firmly, bending her soul to the very center of the Stone, listening, because voices stirred within. Breathing. Sighing. Hungering. Speaking.

"I hear you," Mórgana answered, "and I sense your power."

Yet the Stone screamed at her. It was suffering at the intrusion of the blade.

"Then we must remove it. But how?" she asked.

An image of Merlin arose. Her brother hammering in the blade.

"We hate him," Mórgana told the Stone, "for he will never remove it."

A snarl of rage coursed through the Stone. A faint blue light flickered within, and then an image of High King Uther appeared.

Yet *he* could not remove the sword. "He was sacrificed upon you and is dead."

Groans, rumblings, and cries echoed from deep within the Stone, and an image of Arthur, the heir of Uther, appeared.

Mórgana lifted her head and opened her eyes in wonder — Arthur? "He may be dead."

The stone rumbled, sighed, and shook. An image came to her of Arthur, and he was alive.

Mórgana seethed, for Atle had failed to kill the boy. And so now Arthur was the only one who could pull the sword out besides Merlin?

"But he is still young, and it will take many years. A great trap must be thought up to deceive him, and this will be an immense effort. Why should I do this? What do you offer me in return for my service?"

Smoke and blue fire rose from the Stone. Her hands began to burn. The sound of snapping jaws could be heard, and the Stone shook. Images began to swirl around her of all the Britons cowering in fear at her, and those who would not lying dead and torn before her.

Mórgana nodded. "I will do it."

If the Voice and the Stone could wait, then Mórgana could also wait. In patience she would set her trap for Merlin and Arthur — and when the time was ripe she would have her vengeance.

PRONUNCIATION GUIDE

The following helps are for British names, places, and terms and do not apply to Latin. If you find an easy way to pronounce a name, however, feel free to ignore the following. Your first goal is to enjoy the novel, not to become an expert in ancient languages.

Vowels

a	short as in *far*, long as in *late*, but sometimes as in *cat*
e	short as in *bet*, long as in *pay*, but sometimes as in *key*
i / y	short as in *tin*, long as in *bead*, but sometimes as in *pie*
o	short as in *got*, long as in *foam*
u	short as in *fun*, long as in *loom*

Consonants — the same as English with a few exceptions:

c / k	hard, as in *crank*, not like *city*
ch	hard, as in Scottish *loch*, or *sack*, not like *chat*
f	*f* as in *fall*, sometimes *v* as in *vine*
ff	*f* as in *offer*
g	hard as in *get*, not like *George*
gh	soft as in *sigh*
r	lightly trilled when found between two vowels
rh	pronounced as *hr*, strong on the *h* sound
s	as in *sat*, not with a *z* sound

GLOSSARY

Pronunciation Note: The goal is for you to enjoy reading the Merlin Spiral series, and so, where possible, easier spellings have been chosen for many ancient words. For instance, the word *gorseth* would more properly be spelled *gorsedd*, with the "dd" pronounced similar to our "th". This is also true of the decision, in some words, to use "k" instead of "c". The goal is readability. A pronunciation suggestion has been provided for each word. Again, please don't worry about how you say the names. If you find an easy way to pronounce something, that is fine. If you are a language purist, then indulge the author, knowing he is well aware of the depth, history, and complexities of the Brythonic and Goidelic languages represented here.

Also, since this spiral of Arthurian stories begin and end in Cornwall, Cornish has been chosen as a basis for many of the names and places. Though Welsh, Irish, or Scots Gaelic could have each served for this purpose, Cornwall is the nexus of the storyline.

Historical Note: Although many of the following explanations are based on history and legend, they are given to aid your understanding of *Merlin's Shadow*, and thus are fictional. You are encouraged to research the Roman, Celtic, and Arthurian literature for a deeper appreciation of how they've been uniquely woven into the entire Merlin Spiral series. An asterisk has been placed next to words that will yield a wealth of information.

Ailill Molt* — (EYE-leel MOLT) The Christian king of Erin whom Mórganthu hates.

Allun — (AL-lun) The miller of the village of Bosventor.

Anviv — (ON-veev) The son of Mórganthu, Mônda's brother; he was killed by Uther in book 1.

Ard-Dre — (ARD-dray) A title some call Mórganthu, meaning "arch druid."

Arthur* — (AR-thur) The orphaned son of Igerna and Uther, and heir to the High Kingship. His sisters are Eilyne and Myrgwen. He is one and one-half years old.

Atle / Atleuthun — (AT-lee / at-lee-OOH-thun) The king of Guotodin in the far north; when Owain visited there, his fortress was at Dinpelder. He is Gwevian's father and Merlin's grandfather. In legend he is known as King Lleuddun*.

Aulaf — (OW-loff) A fisherman who lives near Dinpelder.

Aurelianus* — (ow-rell-ee-AH-noos) the former High King, Uther's father, and Arthur's grandfather. He slew Vitalinus Gloui to revenge his father's murder.

Baegower — (bay-GOW-er) A village perched upon a cliff on the southern coast of Kembry. This is placed on the modern-day Gower* peninsula.

Bedwir* — (BED-weer) A chieftain under Vortigern.

Belornos — (bel-OAR-noss) An ancient god of the Celts, personal god of Mórganthu, and god of the underworld. In *Merlin's Blade*, he is represented by the moon in the night sky. Normally spelled Belenos*, here his name is embedded with *lor*, which means "moon," and *nos*, which means "night."

Beltayne* — The druid rite performed near the beginning of May each year. Also known as Bel's High Day of Fire, it is dedicated to Belornos.

Benignus — (ben-IG-noos) The leader of the Irish church after Pádraig died. He is more fully known as Benignus of Armagh*.

Berghild — (BERG-hild) A farmer's wife who lives in Kjaringoy, Lochlan. Married to Sveinrod.

Bosvenna Abbey — (bos-VENN-ah) An abbey of the Celtic church, which was created by the missionary efforts of early Christians in Britain, Ireland, and Scotland — Pádraig (St. Patrick) being one of the first. *Bosvenna** (or *Bos-menegh)* means "the abiding place of monks." There is another, older abbey to the west established by Guron. Bosvenna Abbey was destroyed by fire in book 1.

Bosvenna Moor — (bos-VENN-ah) The highland area in central Kernow, covered with forests and marshes. Before the monks came, it was known as *Tir Gwygoen*, "land of the woodland moor". Today it is called Bodmin Moor* and is cleared for grazing.

Bosventor — (bos-VEN-tore) The village and fortress built upon the slopes of the Meneth Gellik mountain, it was established six years after the abbey. South of modern-day Bolventor*, Cornwall, an actual iron-age village and fortress existed at this exact location.

Brihem — (BRIH-hem) The order of judges within the wider order of the druidow. There are five regular Brihemow, and one arch brihem, making a total of six who vote. The arch druid and arch fili also vote. In olden times, the chief bard and high king were included in the vote, if present, but these offices have been abandoned by the druidow due to them falling into the hands of the Christians. Normally spelled brithem* or brehon*.

Brinnoc — (BRINN-ock) Trevenna's uncle, who lives in Oswistor.

Britain — (BRIH-ten) The land occupied by the people who speak various forms of the ancient Brythonic* language south of the River Forth*.

Brithanvy — (brith-AHN-vee) Modern-day Brittany*, France.

Bysall — (BY-sall) A small coin, usually a ring of brass or iron. Bysallow is the plural.

Caygek — (KAY-gek) A fili who opposed Mórganthu in book 1. He is named Cai* in the Arthurian legends.

Colvarth — (COAL-varth) This is the name taken by the chief bard of Britain, who served High King Uther and now seeks to protect Arthur. Colvarth, which means "criminal bard," was originally meant as an epithet against him by the druidow after he converted to Christianity. He took the name as his own, however, to remind himself of his culpability before God. His given name is Bledri mab Cadfan, and he is known as Bleheris* in Arthurian literature.

Connek — (CON-neck) A young thief from book 1 who tried to kill Merlin.

Coynall — (COIN-all) A single-sided coin made of silver. It is worth eight bysallow, and it takes three coyntallow to make one screpall.

Crennig — (CREN-nigg) A fifth-century roundhouse. They are normally made of wooden timbers staked into the ground to form a circle, but sometimes they are made of stone if it is readily available. The roof is conical and typically woven from thatch. On occasion they are built out in a lake for easier defense. *Cren* means "circlular," or "round". Spelled Crannog* outside of the Merlin Spiral.

Crothak — (CRO-thak) A sea fisherman between Kembry and Kernow. A friend of Inktor and Henktor.

Demetae* — (de-MEH-tay) A kingdom in the southwest corner of Kembry, along the coast.

Digon — (DIG-uhn) One of Atle's guards at Dinpelder.

Dinpelder — (din-PELL-dehr) The abode ruled by King Atle when Owain visited there. This is east of Dineidean (Edinburgh*) in modern-day Scotland, and is known today as Traprain Law*. Dinpelder means "fortress on a steep hill."

Dintaga — (din-TA-guh) The fortress of Gorlas, King of Kernow. Dintaga means "the strangled fortress," and is modern-day Tintagel*. It is on an island separated from the land by a narrow, or "strangled"causeway that is inundated with water when the tide comes in.

Dosmurtanlin Lake — (doss-mur-TAN-lin) A lake north of Bosventor, on the other side of the Meneth Gellik mountain. Legend says that when a portion of the Dragon Star fell, it gouged out the earth, and the water filled it in, forming the lake. Dosmurtanlin means "the lake where a great fire came." It is the same as modern-day Dozmary Pool*. Merlin's mother, who was changed by the Stone into a water creature, is confined to this lake.

Dragon Star — The comet that Muscarvel saw in the night sky seventy years before the beginning of book 1.

Druid* — (DREW-id) The order of priests within the wider order of the druidow. They also carry out the laws as set forth by the Brihem judges.

Druidow — (DREW-i-dow) The plural form of druid, this term can sometimes refer to the wider order of all the druidow, filidow, and Brihemow combined.

Dybris / Dybricius* — (DIE-bris / die-BRIK-ee-oos) A monk who recently joined Bosvenna Abbey. He brought Garth, the orphan, with him from Porthloc, a small village on the northern coast of Difnonia. He is known in modern-times as St. Dubricius*.

Dyslan — (DIE-slan) Natalenya's younger brother.

Ealtain — (EEL-tain) A chieftain of the Picts who invades Kembry.

Eilyne — (EYE-line-uh) The oldest, orphaned daughter of Uther and Igerna, and sister to Myrgwen and Arthur. She is thirteen. In the legends, she is Elaine of Garlot*.

Enison — (en-IH-son) One of Vortigern's selected warriors. Brother to Fest.

Erbin — (ERR-bin) Tregeagle's lictor and servant, he protects the Magister as well as executes his judgments.

Erin — (ERR-in) The island of Ireland west of Britain.

Ewenna — (ee-WHEN-ah) Gorlas's consort at Dintaga.

Fest — (FEST) One of Vortigern's selected warriors. Brother to Enison.

Fili* — (FILL-ee) The order of sages and poets within the wider order of the druidow. Filidow is the plural, and they are led by the arch fili.

Gana / Ganieda* — (GAH-nuh / gah-NYE-dah) Merlin's half-sister, who is nine years old. She is the daughter of Mônda and granddaughter to Mórganthu.

Garth / Garthwys* — (GARTH / GARTH-wiss) An orphan who used to live at the abbey with Dybris. His father, Gorgyr, was a fisherman at Porthloc in Difnonia, and so Garth was raised on the sea. Red-haired and slightly chubby, he is always hungry.

Gaul* — (GALL) Modern-day France, which was ruled by Rome for six hundred years.

Gentian* — (JENT-shin) A bitter-tasting plant that produces blue flowers in spring. It has been used medicinally to treat stomach ailments since ancient times.

Gladius* — (GLA-dee-oos) A stout Roman-style sword, generally of medium length.

Glevum* — (GLEH-vuhm) The Roman fortress of Glevum, and the seat of Vitalinus's kingdom. This is where Vortigern and Igerna grew up. Modern-day Gloucester*.

Gorlas* — (GORE-lass) King of Kernow, whose fortress is Dintaga. He and Uther were rival suitors for Igerna's love, and this rivalry colors their relationship to this day.

Gorse* — (GORSE) A thorny evergreen shrub that is highly flammable.

Gorseth Cawmen — (GORE-seth CAW-men) The stone circle northeast from the village of Bosventor. Literally means "The meeting place of giant stones." On modern maps it is shown as the Goodaver Stone Circle*, though *Merlin's Blade* describes it as having larger stones.

Guotodin* — (goo-OH-toe-din) The most-northern Brythonic kingdom. It was ruled by Atle when Owain visited, and it lies between the two walls built by the Romans, just south of the land of the Prithager. Its principal cities are Dineidean (modern-day Edinburgh*), and the fortress of Dinpelder.

Guronstow — (goo-RUHN-stow) The village on the moor where the abbey established by St. Guron* is located. Now known as the city of Bodmin*.

Gwevian — (GWEV-ee-ahn) Merlin's mother, the daughter of King Atle. She supposedly drowned in Lake Dosmurtanlin when Merlin was young, and her body was never found. Merlin discovered her alive at the end of book 1, changed by the Stone into a water creature to serve it when the Stone was in the lake. She is now the Lady of the Lake*, and a merging of the legends of Vivian* and St. Theneva*.

Hanternos — (han-TEHR-nos) The Brythonic word for Midnight.

Harp of Britain — The harp that has been passed down through the ages from one chief bard to the next, now possessed by Colvarth. The druidow desire to take it back, but must wait for Colvarth's natural death, according to their laws, and hope that he doesn't pass it on to someone else.

Hengist* — (HEN-gist) The leader of the Saxenow army that has invaded Britain.

Henktor — (HENK-tore) A sea fisherman between Kembry and Kernow. The son of Ynktor, and a friend of Crothak.

Igerna* — (ee-GERR-nah) The deceased wife of Uther, she is Vortigern's sister, and therefore descended from Vitalinus Gloui, a former High King of Britain. Her children are Eilyne, Myrgwen, and Arthur. Gorlas vied with Uther for her hand in marriage.

Imelys — (ee-MEL-iss) Troslam and Safrowana's daughter.

Inis Avallow — (IN-iss AV-all-ow) The largest island in the marsh. It has an old tower and broken-down fortress surrounded by an ancient apple orchard. Legend says this was built by a pilgrim and tin merchant known only as the Pergiryn. Its name means "Island of Apples," and is known in legend as Avalon*.

Inis Môn* — (IN-iss MOAN) The sacred island of the druidow. Gaius Suetonius Paulinus broke the power of the druidow and destroyed the shrines and sacred groves on the isle of Inis Môn in 61 A.D.

Inktor — (INK-tore) A sea fisherman between Kembry and Kernow. The father of Henktor, and a friend of Crothak.

Ivor — (EYE-vor) A false name that Vortigern uses for himself.

Jarl Lhudvig — (YARL LUD-vig) A chieftain of a region in northern Lochlan. He owns Ulfsvag farm.

Jesu Christus* — (HEY-soo KRIS-toos) Latin for Jesus Christ.

Kallicia* — (kal-ih-SEE-ah) Literally, "the forest people," from what is now known as Galicia* in northwest Spain. Many scholars think they are of Celtic origin. You can still hear bagpipes played there today.

Kembry — (KEM-bree) The land stretching from the Kembry Sea in the south to the isle of Inis Môn in the northwest. It is made up of multiple kingdoms. Modern-day Wales*.

Kensa — (KEN-sah) An old, hunched-over woman who wears a funny purple hat and serves King Atle*.

Kernow* — (KER-now) The kingdom that lay on the peninsula of land in southwest Britain, between Lyhonesse and Difnonia. Ruled by Gorlas from his fortress, Dintaga, which is on an island on the northern coast. Kernewek is their local dialect of Brythonic. Modern-day Cornwall*.

Keskinpry Marsh — (kes-KIN-pry) A marsh south of Bosventor.

Kjaringoy — (kjar-ING-oy) A farm in northwest Lochlan.

Kyallna — (kee-ALL-nah) An elderly widow who lives near Safrowana and Troslam. She always liked Garth and would pinch his cheek.

Lictor* — (LIK-tor) A Roman guardian of a magistrate, and one who executes his judgments. Thus, Erbin is Tregeagle's lictor and servant.

Lochlan* — (LOCK-lan) A people group inhabiting Britain who came from what is now known as Norway.

Londinium* — (LUN-din-ee-um) A city taken by the Romans in 43 A.D. and named Lundnisow by the Britons. Because of its river and harbor, they made it the capital of their provinces in Britain. Modern-day London*.

Loth — (LOTH) The son of King Atle, and Merlin's uncle.

Magister* — (ma-JEE-stare) Literally "master," which is the title Tregeagle has as the appointed official over the tin mining region around Bosventor. A holdover from the Roman empire.

Marachlans — (marr-OCK-lanns) The Lochlan epithet given to Atle, his people, and his people that remained behind after he moved to Britain. In *Merlin's Shadow*, this epithet is meant to mean the "nightmare people."

Mara-Hoven — (MAR-ah HO-ven) A mountain with a temple on an island just beyond the arctic circle in northwestern Norway, which is known as the land of the Lochlans. Mara-Hoven means "nightmare temple."

McEwan — (mik-YOU-ahn) A huge eirish warrior who served Mórganthu in book 1.

Meneth Gellik Mountain — (MEN-eth GELL-ick) The mountain upon whose southern side the village of Bosventor is built. Halfway up on a plateau sits a fortress and beacon, which is familiarly known to the villagers as the "Tor." The mountain is over 1100 feet above sea level, its tallest point is 100 feet above the marsh, and it is the third highest in Kernow. Today it is known as Brown Gelly*. Literally, "The Brown Mountain." Lake Dosmurtanlin is situated just to the north.

Merlin* — (MER-lin) The son of the village blacksmith/sword-smith. His face was badly scratched by wolves at the age of eleven when he tried to protect his younger sister, Gana. This also scarred his eyes, half blinding him. His eyesight was healed at the end of book 1, but his scars remain. The Latin form of his name is Merlinus.

Mônda / Môndargana — (MOAN-dah / moan-DAR-gone-ah) Owain's wife, she is the daughter of Mórganthu, the arch druid and mother to Gana. She is Merlin's stepmother, but she despises his Christianity. Her full name of Môndargana means "Prophetess of Inis Môn."

Mórganthu — (more-GAN-thoo) The arch druid, and son of Mórfryn. He is father to Môndargana and Anviv, and grandfather to Ganieda. His name is a merging of the name *Mórgant* with *huder*, which means "magician."

Mulsum* — (MUL-sum) A rich cinnamon, thyme, and peppery wine imported into Britain, and a favorite of Tregeagle.

Muscarvel — (musk-AR-vel) A seventy-year-old man who lived deep in the marsh to the west of Bosventor. He has not been seen since he tried to free Uther from his Eirish captors.

Myrgwen — (MEER-gwen) The orphaned, youngest daughter of Uther and Igerna, and sister to Eilyne and Arthur. She is nine years old. In legend, she is called Morgause*.

Natalenya — (nah-tah-LEAN-yah) Tregeagle and Trevenna's daughter who plays the harp and sings. She has agreed to marry Merlin and goes with him to save Arthur.

Necton mac Erip* — (NECK-ton MACK ERR-ip) A cruel pict who raids Kembry with Ealtain. He is the son of Erip, whom Ealtain slew many years ago.

Ogmios* — (og-ME-os) The Celtic god of wind and eloquence, he is represented by Mercury in the night sky.

Oswistor — (os-WEE-store) A strong hillfort in Pengwern*, Kembry, a minor kingdom of the greater kingdom of Powys. Natalenya's mother, Trevenna, has relatives here. Modern-day Oswestry*.

Owain* — (O-wayne) Merlin's father, he grew up in Rheged, north of Kembry, as the son of a chieftain. Owain's first wife, Gwevian, drowned while they were boating on Lake Dosmurtanlin. His second wife, Mônda, is the mother of Gana, Merlin's half sister. Owain was the smith in the village of Bosventor prior to his death, and so was given the title of *An Gof*, which means "the smith."

Pace — The unit of measurement of a grown man's stride from the time the heel leaves the ground until the same heel touches the ground again. Typically five feet.

Pádraig* — (PAH-dreeg) St. Patrick, a Briton who first brought Christianity to the Eirish, and then sent missionaries back to Briton.

Penkoref — (pen-CORE-eff) One of Vortigern's warriors, who doesn't like sailing.

Pergiryn's Tower — (per-GIH-rin) All that is left of the fortress built by the Pergiryn on the island of Inis Avallow. Some say a light can sometimes be seen from its top-most window. The Pergiryn was an unknown tin merchant who, legend says, built the fortress and planted the apple orchard. Pergiryn means "pilgrim."

Porthloc — (PORTH-lock) The seaside village in Difnonia where Garth grew up and met Dybris. Modern-day Porlock*.

Prithager / Picti* — (prih-THAY-girr / PIC-tie) The people who live in the wild lands of the north. They often raid the southern realms now that Hadrian's Wall has been abandoned by the Romans, and even more so now that the Saxenow are weakening what is left of the British army. They call themselves the Chrithane.

Prontwon — (PRON-twon) The deceased abbot of Bosvenna Abbey, who taught Merlin.

Rewan — (REH-wan) A chieftain under Vortigern.

Rheged* — (HREE-ged) A Brythonic kingdom in the north, it is situated northeast of Kembry and south of Guotodin. This is the land Owain is from.

Rhitherch — (RITH-erk) The king in Rheged when Colvarth was younger. More commonly spelled as Rhydderch*.

Risrud — (RIS-rude) Modern-day Redruth*, Cornwall.

Romans* — The sprawling empire that conquered Britain and ruled it for 360 years. They never conquered the northern area controlled by the Picts, nor Erin, the island of the Eirish. In 407, Constantine III (Uther's great-grandfather) took the majority of the Roman army that had been stationed in Britain over to Gaul in a failed bid to become the Roman Emperor, and they never returned.

Rondroc — (RON-drock) Natalenya's older brother.

Safrowana — (saf-ROW-ah-nah) Mother to Imelys and wife of Troslam. They are weavers.

Sangraal* — An ancient wooden bowl found by Colvarth after Uther's kidnapping in book 1. At the Last Supper it held the wine, and the Pergiryn used it to catch Christ's blood when he lay dying upon the cross. It is also called the Sancte Gradale, and is more commonly called the Holy Grail*.

Saxenow* — (SACKS-eh-now) An invading people group from what is now known as Germany, they are landing on the southeastern shore of Britain. Today know as the Saxons*.

Scafta — (SCAFE-tah) The witch doctor/shaman of the Picti who raid Kembry.

Scoti* — (SCOT-eye) A sea-faring tribe of the Irish that have settled in what is now western Scotland.

Screpall — (SCREH-pall) A double-sided silver coin worth three Coyntallow.

Sveinrod — (SVINE-rod) A farmer who lives in Kjaringoy, Lochlan. Married to Berghild.

Tara* — (TEAR-ah) The hill that is considered the pagan spiritual center of Erin, and also the seat of their kings until the sixth century.

Taranis* — (tah-RAN-iss) The Celtic god of clouds and thunder; he is traditionally depicted as carrying a pot which he beats with a hammer.

Tasgwyn — (TASS-gwin) Literally, "grandfather" in the language of Kernow.

Tauchen-Twilloch — (TAU-ken TWILL-ock) A Pictish village on the southwest shore of the lake known in modern times as Loch Lomond*. The bay there is now called Auchentullich Bay*.

Tellyk — (TELL-ick) A wolf that has befriended Ganieda.

Tethion — (teth-EE-on) An archer employed by Vortigern.

The Stone — A strange stone that was found by Mórganthu at the edge of Lake Dosmurtanlin. Everyone who sees it is enchanted by it, and so Merlin drove Uther's sword into it at the end of book 1 in an attempt to destroy it.

The Tor — The fortress situated part way up the side of the Meneth Gellik mountain. It has a timber-built tower with a beacon on top. Its formal name is Dinas Bosventor.

The Voice — A shadowy figure that appears to Ganieda and instructs her.

Thrail — The Pictish way of saying *thrall*, or *slave*.

Thrall — Another word for *slave*.

Torc* — (TORK) A sign of authority, social status, and nobility in ancient Brythonic society. Made in the shape of a ring with an opening, it is worn upon the neck. They are usually twisted from wires of gold, bronze, silver, iron, or other metals, and have finely sculpted ornaments at the ends.

Torsten — (TOR-sten) A farmer staying temporarily at Uflsvag Farm to help with the fishing.

Tregeagle* — (treh-GAY-gull) He is the Magister of Bosventor and the surrounding tin mining region. He is the village judge and he collects taxes. He is also responsible for maintaining the fortress (the 'Tor") built on the Meneth Gellik mountain, which includes a timber-built tower and beacon. His wife is Trevenna, and his children are Natalenya, Rondroc, and Dyslan. He was enchanted by the Stone in book 1.

Trevenna — (treh-VENN-nah) Tregeagle's wife, and mother to Natalenya, Rondroc, and Dyslan.

Troslam — (TROS-lum) The village weaver. Safrowana is his wife, and Imelys is his daughter.

Twilloch-Scwane — (TWILL-ock SKWAYNE) In the Merlin Spiral, the hill where a coronation stone was kept by the Picts, near Perth*, Scotland. In history, this would be equivalent to the Stone of Scone*.

Ulfsvag Farm — (ULF-svagg) A farm in northwest Lochlan.

Uther* — (UTH-er) The deceased High King of the Britons, he was descended from a long line of Roman governors and kings. His father was Aurelianus, his wife was Igerna. He has two daughters, Eilyne and Myrgwen, as well as his son, Arthur. His name in Latin is Uthrelius.

Vallum Aelium* — (VALL-um AY-lie) Hadrian's Wall*, 73 miles long, built beginning in AD 122 by Roman Emperor Hadrian. It was officially abandoned by the main Roman force in 410, but continued to be guarded using conscripted British warriors for many years afterward.

Vallum Antoninus* — (VALL-um on-to-KNEE-nus) The Antonine Wall*, 39 miles long, built beginning in AD 142 by the Roman Emperor Antoninus Pius. It was abandoned after only twenty years.

Vitalinus — (vi-TAL-ee-noos) Usurper High King who slew Uther's grandfather Constans. His grandson is Vortigern, and his granddaughter is Igerna, Uther's wife. He was slain in battle by Aurelianus. In history he is known as Vitalinus Gloui*.

Vortigern* — (vor-TUH-gern) The grandson of the former High King, Vitalinus Gloui, who killed Uther in book 1 due to his enchantment by the Stone.

Vortipor* — (vor-TUH-poor) Vortigern's son.

Woad* — (WODE) A blue body paint made from the woad plant. It was not used for tattoos.

Check out this exclusive excerpt
from book three in the Merlin Spiral series,

MERLiN'S
NiGHTMARE

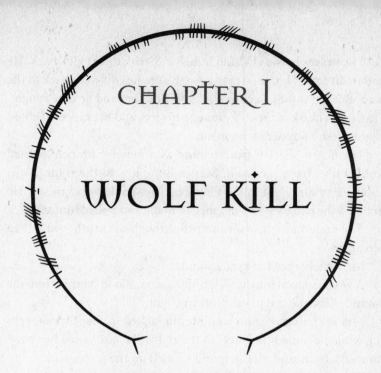

CHAPTER I

WOLF KILL

En route to the village of Dinas Crag,
Rheged, in northern Britain,
Spring, in the year of our Lord 493

Merlin should have heeded the wild cawing of the crows, but it was too late: a dozen wolves looked up from their fallen prey as his horse reared up in terror. A massive buck, slain and gutted, lay in their midst, and all around the greedy, black-feathered sentinels looked on in anticipation.

Merlin's mission had just gone from urgent to life-or-death.

He wheeled his horse to the left and kicked her onward, off the path and between two trees. The mask that Merlin wore to cover his scars shifted upward on his face momentarily, obscuring his vision. He righted it just in time to see a thin branch before it lashed him across the face, nearly cutting his lip through the black cloth.

The wolves howled behind him, but Merlin didn't look back. He had to direct his horse farther down before he could cut back to the path. But the woods were too thick to ride fast, and he'd be caught. Fear, like a cloak of thistles, clung to his legs and back. A wolf could rip his flesh away at any moment.

The beasts snarled from behind as a massive branch loomed toward him from the front. Merlin hung low to the right, but it still banged him hard in the shoulder. The saddle began to slip. He grabbed the horse's sweat-dampened mane and pulled himself back up. The mare snorted as she jumped through the brush — and then screamed.

Merlin whipped his gaze around.

A wolf had torn into her left hindquarter. Blood poured from the wound, slick and red in the morning light.

The wolf lunged again, and Merlin kicked its black snout, yelling while he pulled the horse to the right. She quickened her pace, jumped a bush, and Merlin found himself on the path again.

Three wolves leapt just behind.

Faster now, Merlin leaned forward, easing his weight off the horse's injured haunch and urging her to run for both their lives. Having hardly seen a wolf in the sixteen years since leaving Bosventor, he'd become careless, and now he'd interrupted an entire pack at their meal. Panic sank into his stomach like rotten meat, churning his innards. He had to get away, he had to!

But the wolves were faster, and the mare began to wheeze from the effort. Merlin had been anxious to get back to Dinas Crag with the news he carried and had ridden her hard for hours. Her strength was almost gone.

Another wolf snapped at her right side, ripping a leg open. The horse kicked, screaming in terror, and then staggered forward again.

Merlin panicked. He wouldn't get away. His horse was going to die. He was going to die. He could kill one wolf with his sword, maybe two, but never a whole pack. An image of his body, mangled and gutted like the buck, flashed before his eyes.

A wolf latched onto his boot, its teeth like small daggers, slicing into his foot. He tried to draw his sword, but the horse reared up, forcing the wolf to drop off. The hackles of the wolf's neck twitched, and its yellow eyes lusted for Merlin's blood as it prepared to leap.

A wolf on his left gashed the mare's belly.

Merlin turned to face the beast, but a large branch filled his vision. He reached, clamped his hands onto the smooth bark, pulled free from his horse, and wrapped his legs around the branch.

The horse, relieved of his weight, shot forward into the brush, all three wolves slashing her with their bloody jaws. The end came quickly, with the wolves pulling her down about fifty paces away.

Merlin climbed up and listened painfully his mount's last screams.

When the horse's silence came, and only the wolves' gory feast could be heard, he took in some deep breaths and tried to discern his position on the path. He'd been traveling south from Luguvalium, the capital of Rheged, and was on his way back home to Dinas Crag. There awaited his wife Natalenya and their two children: Tingada, their little daughter, and Taliesin, their growing boy. And then there was their adopted Arthur, now eighteen winters old.

Surely he had passed the long lake already . . . or had he?

Ahead of him he could hear a stream burbling in the dark, so the path must have swung closer to it again. But was this in fact *the* stream, the Derwent, as he had thought? If so, then he was close to home, and there must be a crossroad just beyond.

A faint splash. Maybe a fish. Then another. Full splashing now. Then clopping. A rider, coming his way, heading toward the wolves.

Merlin had to warn him. "Who's there?" he called. "Take care! Wolves just killed my horse, and more are just beyond."

The rider cantered forward, slowing just below Merlin. A man with a broad face and a gray beard looked up at him.

"And what am I to do about such a dilemma? I must get through."

"They'll scatter if you give them enough time —"

"No. I've an urgent and vital message that must get through."

Howling sounded far down the path. The three who had just killed the horse answered, and soon the howling echoed from all around.

"Maybe it would be best to turn back for now. Is there a village nearby?"

"Dinas Crag. I'll take you there."

"Not on my horse. You'll walk, you will."

Another howl split the air, and the man wheeled his horse around, cursing. Merlin swung down and dropped onto its back, just behind the man.

"Get off!"

"Go!" Merlin drove his heels into the horse's flanks, sending it flying down the path and splashing through the stream, thinned by the long spring drought.

When they were a good distance away and no pursuit could be heard, the man yanked his horse to a stop. He turned, spittle spraying across Merlin's mask as he said, "Get off."

"I saved your life."

Moving faster than Merlin thought possible for one so pompous, the man shoved him in the chest so he fell off the back of the horse.

But Merlin landed on his feet, dashed around to the left, lifted the man's boot and threw him from the horse.

The man scrambled to his feet, spitting dry grass, and glared at Merlin from the other side of the saddle. His face was red. "Take off your mask!"

"No."

"Who are you?"

"Ambrosious."

The man waited a beat, as if expecting more. Then his lips twisted in a sneer. "Your parentage, dishonorable knucklebone, and your purpose in these woods."

"What's *your* name, *your* parentage, and *your* mission?"

The man wrinkled up his nose and scowled back.

A howling split the air, so close that Merlin jerked.

Both men leapt onto the horse, Merlin clutching the back of the ornate saddle as the beast hopped a few steps and took off away from the wolves.

"Which way?" the man asked.

"Can I trust you?"

"On my honor."

"Before who?"

"Before God. What, do I look like a druid?"

The wolves howled again. Merlin pointed. "Go straight when you come to the crossroads and follow the path along the stream."

"Hardly wide enough for a one-legged deer."

"Trust me."

They raced along the path until they encountered the northern shore of a large lake, from which the overflow of the stream ran. The path curved to follow its western shore for half a league, where the lake ended, and the stream, which now fed the lake, began again.

Mountains had arisen on each side, and their tops could be seen through the trees. The sky now brightened with the rising sun, and the thick woods changed from oak to pine as the path climbed slowly, and the mountains squeezed closer and closer, their sides ever steeper.

When the valley finally tightened to the jaws of a narrow gorge, the stream drew closer to the path, which strangely ended before a vertical pile of rocks, about twelve feet tall, with dry grasses covering the center of the pile. The stream itself poured from a spring on the left side.

The man pulled his horse to a stop. "What's this? If you plan to rob me — "

Merlin cupped his hands. "Porter! Open the door, Ambrosious has come."

Nothing stirred except a rustle of brush behind them. The horse trembled.

Merlin called again. "Porter! Open — "

A jaw clamped on his arm, the full weight of a mature wolf slamming into his leg from the side and ripping at his captured arm. The stockade spun away. Merlin's legs hung in the air and then his knees slammed downward. Neighing. Cursing. The sound of steel sliding. Where was his sword? Growling in his ear. Pungent, bloody fur against his face. Ragged claws on his chest. It was going for his throat.

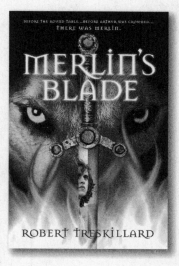